Desirea's Escape

Book Two in the Destiny Series

By

L.A. Hilden

Print ISBN: 978-0-9829897-6-0
eBook ISBN: 978-0-9829897-7-7

Also available in ebook formats

CHAPTER ONE

June 26, 2011
London, England

This has to be some kind of joke. Desirea Leighton crossed her arms over her chest. She was furious about the photo-shoot in London, which had taken her manager months to set up. She vowed that her agent would find himself short one client when she finished with him. She stood in the middle of a tavern called the Back Room, surrounded by photography equipment set up in front of the pile of beach sand in the tavern's main room. *Ridiculous!* When they brought the extra model out from the back, Desirea did not even try to hide her contempt.

"Unfrikkenbelievable!" the young blond hollered. "You expect me to pose with a model in a string bikini while I wear this silly Regency dress. You must be out of your ever-loving mind. Where's my agent? I want to speak to him now!"

The owner of the tavern tried to interrupt her tirade. "Desirea, if you'd just give me a moment..."

"Give you a moment?" Desirea screeched. "I won't be outshined in my own frikken photo-shoot." Did these people not understand how hard she worked to keep her twenty year-old body looking this good, she wondered? Not that anyone would notice with all the layers of clothing she was wearing. "And *why t*he hell am I dressed like this in a bar with sand on the floor anyway? This entire theme is beyond ridiculous. I've had enough! I'm going outside for some air. When I return, have her dressed in something more appropriate or have her gone!"

Desirea turned on her heel and left the building by the front door, immediately hitting the text message button on her phone as she entered the sunlight. Cars zoomed by, engine noise monopolizing the atmosphere. Two men on rollerblades nearly mowed her down because she wasn't looking where she was going but at her phone, and she screeched, jumping out of the way. *This is going to be a bitch session my agent won't soon forget.* She, a celebrity who deserved five-star treatment, had traveled all the way to England for these pictures. She earned her place at the top through years of hard work on the Disney channel, where she had her own show, and then years after, as a singer of opera *and* pop. How dare her agent link her image with some starved runway model?

She sat on a fairly high stoop on the side of the building, well out of the way of the business people walking along the busy road, and continued to punch furiously on her Blackberry. The dark-haired woman Desirea had seen standing with the owner of the Back Room approached her, but she was in no mood for conversation.

"Miss Leighton, my name is London Burton. I thought perhaps I could be of assistance." She could tell by the woman's speech that she was a fellow American, likely another irritating fan. She often wished she had never become a celebrity. "Do you have a *Cat in the Hat* super-vacuum that will suck up five hundred pounds of sand and my manager? If not, I'm afraid you can't help." She looked up to give the attractive woman a haughty look of dismissal, but then she caught sight of Marvin disappearing around the building. Her hands began to shake uncontrollably when she saw the crazed fan who had broken into her Malibu home countless times, once nearly raping her. *Marvin is here? In England?* Her mind refused to believe what she saw.

"What is it?" the brunette asked, concern lacing her voice.

Desirea dropped her phone to the ground as panic and fear took over her body. "It's him," was all she could manage to say.

"Him who?" The lady spun around to look at all the people walking down the sidewalk.

"Marvin Travers, my stalker."

"Is he dangerous?" the lady asked. A car drove by through a puddle and just missed splashing them, but Desirea barely noticed.

"Shhh or he'll hear you. I don't think he saw me. He's behind the building now." Desirea looked around frantically at her surroundings. She felt like a sitting duck out in the open. "Oh my god. You have to hide me," she begged the woman.

"Hide you? Really? Is that necessary? I mean, he's a fan, right?"

"A crazed fan." Desirea stood and grabbed the woman's arm. There was no time to waste. She needed to disappear, and quickly. "Please," she pleaded. Her hands were clammy.

The woman obviously noticed the very real fear taking over Desirea for she said, "Okay, okay. Let me think." Thankfully, after only a few more seconds, the woman took her arm and led her back into the tavern. Desirea was having a hard time putting one foot in front of the other.

After they entered the front door, they veered off to a room in the back and to a far wall. She watched the lady press her hand against the wall and a door opened toward them. Desirea looked into the hidden hidey-hole, thinking it clever.

"Hurry. In here," the lady ordered.

If this lady thought she was going to get inside the closet alone in the dark, she was wrong. Desirea didn't like dark closed spaces. "Wait," she exclaimed as she stepped inside. "It's too dark. You have to come too." She didn't care if she sounded like a child. Her fear was real and she wasn't hiding in there alone. "Come on. Before he sees me."

"There's not enough room in there for the two of us," the woman said in protest.

"The hell there isn't." Desirea yanked her closer.

"Don't be silly," the woman said in a placating voice, as if she was indeed dealing with a child. "I'll get rid of him and then let you know when it's safe to come out."

"I'm not hiding in here by myself," Desirea said sternly, not letting go of the woman's arm.

"Well, I'm afraid you are just going to have to…"

Stubborn woman. Desirea yanked with all her might and the lady fell into the closet right on top of her, causing Desirea's head to hit the back closet wall, which in turn triggered some hidden tunnel to open up before their eyes. "A hidden passage," Desirea said, awed by the sight as she rubbed the back of her head. *How cool.* Desirea got to her feet. When she moved, the door to the closet slammed shut.

"Look what you've done!" the woman hollered at her. "There's no latch on this side. We're stuck."

Well, how was I supposed to know that would happen? She hadn't intentionally trapped them in the closet. The space was so dark and smelled of rotting wood so strongly that Desirea fought the urge to retch.

"Hello," a male voice called from the other side of the door, and Desirea's heart leaped into her throat. *Marvin.*

"We're…" Desirea quickly clamped her hand over the woman's mouth.

"Shut up! It's Marvin," Desirea hissed in her ear. *Didn't this lady understand the danger?* Desirea began to shake uncontrollably. Images of the night when Marvin had crawled into her bed and held her down suddenly filled her head, the way he thrust himself at her with that look of dementia on his face. She remembered her frantic attempts to free herself as she clawed at his deranged eyes. Thank God for her car keys on her nightstand, for when she hit her car alarm, it spooked Marvin and he fled back out the window.

"Desirea. It's Marvin. Now where are ya hiding, my pretty? Bet you didn't expect to see me on this side of the Atlantic." It was Desirea's fervent wish to have never seen him again. "Come on out now, so we can talk. It wasn't nice of you to sic the cops on me. You didn't think a restraining order and a stint in prison would keep me away, did you?" he bellowed in anger, and the lady with Desirea was now shaking too. "No one will stop your most devoted fan from paying you proper homage."

"Come on," the lady whispered, taking Desirea's hand and leading her into the tunnel. They'd cross to the other side of the tunnel and be free of Marvin, Desirea thought with some relief, a perfect plan. *Yikes, the walls are close.* But at least it wasn't completely dark. A weird glow surrounded them. Desirea shut her eyes for a second as they inched sideways through the narrow corridor. She imagined the tight space was probably like being in one of those CAT scan machine's her father had complained about years ago.

Suddenly, the beams overhead began to moan and creak as if the corridor was about to collapse and bury them alive. Desirea tried to hurry behind the woman, bumping into her, when a scary buzzing noise grew so loud that her ears ached. She didn't dare cover them and give up her new friend's hand. Smoke followed the sound, stealing the oxygen and causing Desirea to hack. "What's happening?" she asked the lady. The lady had to be a good ten years older than Desirea, and Desirea hoped that perhaps the woman had experienced something like this before.

"I don't know," shouted the woman, the moaning, creaking, and smoke all increasing. The smoke was now heavy and tasted of chemicals. Then a rush of air whistled through the space, removing the smoke and stealing their breaths with its intensity. The wind pulled and tugged at them. Desirea cursed the stupid Regency dress she wore because it hindered her mobility. She turned to the woman to see her head dip sideways. "The smoke's making me ill," she yelled.

"Me too," the woman choked.

Both women screamed as they pushed against the wind, but then the current changed and suddenly they were propelled forward amongst dirt and dust, which stung their eyes. Then it all stopped: the wind, the smoke, and even the creaking. The air was now fresh. The scent of coffee and tobacco filled the passageway. They hurried to the door.

"What happened?" Desirea asked.

"How should I know?" the lady replied, obviously frustrated by what they just experienced.

"This must be our stop." Desirea tried to tease the lady into a smile. After all, whether this lady knew it or not, she had saved her from Marvin. Desirea was her friend for life.

Silently, they both looked at the door, which was identical to the one they left behind them. They could hear men laughing on the other side. "Is there a latch?" Desirea asked, not seeing one.

"No." The woman began to move her fingers around the edges of the door. Desirea had no patience for this.

"Well then, give it a shove, girlfriend. I want the hell out of here." When the woman didn't move, Desirea huffed, "Oh, come on, already! Get out of the way." Moving around the speechless lady, Desirea turned sideways and, taking a few steps back, ran at the door with her shoulder. She flew out the door, tripping over the doorjamb, and fell to the floor, her Regency dress fluttering around her. She went to look back at the lady only to see the woman's eyes gloss over.

"Holy hell," her rescuer exclaimed before fainting right on top of Desirea. Her weight knocked the air out of Desirea's lungs and stunned her momentarily. The door to the closet slammed shut, closing off the passageway through which they came.

Desirea looked up from beneath the woman to find three very attractive and very angry men glaring at her, all dressed in Regency attire.

CHAPTER TWO

London, England 1817

"I thought this was to be a serious discussion of the Back Room's future, Declan. Not once have you hinted at having two lovely ladies encased in the wall. Good show, my friend. I applaud your originality," a sandy blond-haired man said to the man among them glaring most angrily at Desirea.

"I daresay the dark-haired dame has swooned on top of her ever-so-lovely companion. How long have you kept them holed in the wall, Declan?"

Nice of these gentlemen to discuss her as if she wasn't in the room, Desirea thought. She hated that. You would think one of them would at least offer some assistance and help her up. The man they called Declan merely continued to frown at her. "I assure you, gentlemen, I had nothing to do with this."

"Next you'll be telling us ladies just fall out of the woodwork when you're near. Do the gods rain sovereigns upon you too?"

"Enough jabbering, Logan. I'm telling you that I don't know where the bloody hell these ladies came from. But..." Declan said, his green gaze now meeting with Desirea's. "I *will* find out."

Desirea blinked up at the man towering over her, his supposed anger first irritating her and then making her quite angry. She swore, and she continued swearing until she got out from under the dark-haired woman who had saved her from Marvin.

She finally gained her footing, no thanks to the men in the room, and placed her hands on her hips.

"A gift from the deity, do you think?" the man named Logan asked with a chuckle.

Declan moved toward her. "I'm the ninth Earl of Nankin, Declan Devinn, and you are?"

"Desirea Leighton." She watched him closely. She never knew how people were going to react when meeting a celebrity of her caliber. Men tended to salivate in her vicinity, but she was quite used to it. This man just continued to stare at her, probably struck speechless by her beauty. She shrugged and went to revive the lady with her. She grabbed the woman by the shoulders and began to shake her. "Wake up!"

"I don't believe her revival will come until she is ready to wake," exclaimed Logan.

"What's your friend's name?" Declan asked.

Desirea looked down at the woman who had led her through the tunnel. "I uh…don't know." Truly, she hadn't paid attention when the woman introduced herself. *What a trying day this is turning out to be.*

"You've been stuck in a closet with this woman for God knows how long, and you don't even know her name?" the big man with shoulder length auburn hair, who'd yet to speak, asked her. His tone suggested he didn't believe she spoke the truth. He bent over to tap on her companion's face.

"It's not a closet," Desirea said heatedly, getting back to her feet. *What the hell is wrong with these men?* Something seemed off with this entire scene.

"Not a closet?" asked Logan. He looked to be the youngest man in their group. Desirea watched him move closer to the closed corridor's door. "Then what is it, if not a closet?"

"A secret corridor," said Desirea with a shudder. No way was she ever going to step into that tunnel again.

"Are you bamming me?" the man asked. She had no idea what he was saying.

"Bamming? What the hell is bamming?" She looked toward Declan. "Dude, is he knackered or pissed, or whatever it is you English say when someone is drunk?"

The man named Declan stared at her as if confused. "No, the Earl of Isles is not in his cups," he answered.

Logan had made it to the closet and pushed on the door. Desirea took a few steps back as the panel sprang forward with a loud screech and Logan stepped inside. Desirea waited for him to scream as he was sucked down the tunnel. She closed her eyes.

"As I expected. Nothing but a hidey-hole. Definitely lacking the corridor you describe, Miss."

Her eyes sprang open. "What are you talking about, sir?" She moved forward. "It's right…" She swung the door open further and peered inside. Stunned by what she saw, she stepped inside and began to bang on the walls, cursing and screaming, trying to get the corridor to reopen. Logan leapt away from her, but Desirea continued to throw a tantrum in the closet. *What happened to the corridor? It was here a few minutes ago.* She turned back to the men to find them all staring at her with matching looks of astonishment. She was feeling very dizzy. "It seems the corridor has disappeared," she said before crumpling to the floor in a dead faint.

***

"Desirea. Desirea, talk to me."

"You seem very familiar with a woman who claims not to know your name," replied one of the men, and Desirea opened her eyes and sat up. She looked around the room and realized that, although this seemed like the same building where the photo-shoot was being held, this one was much nicer.

"Where are we?" Desirea asked, taking her new friend's hand. She was unsure about what happened and did not know why she was lying on the couch.

"Sir?" said her companion in an effort to ask the men for a moment alone. At least Desirea thought that was what she was doing. The lady looked very concerned about something. She was dressed in jeans and a green shirt, but her brown hair had the windblown effect. Her outfit looked quite clean considering what they had been through.

Desirea's dress, of course, was very glamorous and had tons of silver sequins so she'd shimmer on her album cover. It had been a pristine shade of white, but it was somewhat tinged gray now. She hated the dress but had to admit that her boobs looked awesome. A silver sash cinched right beneath them, where her skirts waterfalled to the floor.

"It's Lord Nankin, or my lord," Declan corrected, as if Desirea's companion had broken some law by not addressing him the correct way.

"Lord Nankin," said the woman she was with, and Desirea wanted to applaud the sarcastic way she said it.

"I like this room," said Desirea. "No sand. Don't you think we should have the photo-shoot in here?" Desirea gestured toward their opulent surroundings. The room was lovely, with gold velvet curtains and ornate wooden side tables. Her gaze returned to the lady in front of her. "What's your name?"

"London. London Burton," she said, her shaking hands holding one of Desirea's. The lady still looked green around the gills.

Desirea returned her smile. "Where are we?" she asked again, and both women looked toward Declan.

"You are in the back parlor of the Back Room Gentlemen's Club," the man named Declan answered, studying them with a look of puzzlement on his handsome face. Desirea noticed how Declan's gaze lingered on London in that predatory male way that said he wanted to have his way with her. The man was definitely into Desirea's new friend.

"Trust me, dude. This isn't the Back Room Tavern," Desirea pointed out. "Everything's so new and clean. Smell the air. It smells of coffee, not beer and human stench." Desirea rubbed her eyes, doubting the sight before her.

"This isn't a tavern," the big one named Gabriel responded, and his tone indicated he had been completely offended by Desirea's comparison. *The man needs to chilax.* He seemed far too uptight. "How did you ladies come to learn of our

Gentlemen's Club?" he asked, moving closer to them, a hint of menace in his tone. "Did you learn all you needed to while hiding in the cupboard? Our conversation was not meant to be overheard, ladies." He paused, rubbing his chin in thought. "Now, what do you propose my friend and I do about this?"

What were they going to do about this? Was this man serious with these silly-ass threats? "Don't look now, London, but I think we angered a bear," Desirea said to her new friend with a laugh.

"Who's paying you?" shouted Gabriel.

When she saw London's cheeks redden in embarrassment, Desirea's anger came to the surface. She stood up and marched over to the big bear of a man, glaring up at him with her hands on her hips. "Excuse me!" she huffed. "This may surprise you, dude. But I don't give a flying fuck about you or your fucking establishment. This has been the worst day imaginable. And trust me, I've had many unimaginable days. I'm physically and mentally exhausted. And yet you stand there trying to accuse us of listening to some lame-ass conversation about things I am sure we have no interest in knowing about. Surely you do not believe the entire universe revolves around you, do you, big guy?" She turned back to her new friend. "London, could you tell someone who understands that I'm no longer interested in doing this photo-shoot. I no longer care how realistic they can make the damn scene. Besides…" she said with a wave toward the two men, the other having disappeared while she was unconscious. "These guys look ridiculous."

"Translation, Declan?" asked Gabriel. "Guys? Some kind of shoot?"

"Hell if I know," said Declan, causing Desirea to huff in irritation. She threw herself back on the sofa and turned to London.

"London, you said you would assist me. Then assist. Please have these two buffoons removed from my sight. I'll call my agent to take care of the rest." Desirea closed her eyes to block the bothersome men from view.

"If you men will excuse us please," she heard London say, and then she heard the men shuffling out of the room.

The moment they were gone, Desirea opened her eyes. "Where's my phone?"

London shrugged. The lady seemed absorbed at staring at the old-fashioned room.

"This is unfuckenbelievable. I lost my damn phone. London, give me yours."

"Desirea, please calm yourself," said London. "I don't have my phone."

Desirea began to rant, cursing everything she could think of.

"I believe you left your phone on the ground outside," replied London after Desirea let her last F-bomb fly.

Son of a bitch! Her phone was likely gone by now, and without it, she had no contact numbers. She needed her phone. "I'll get it," she said, moving out the door to find the two men standing there. They had clearly been listening to their conversation. "Sirs," she said, and they frowned at her. "I mean, lords." She cocked her head sideways at them. "You know you really are carrying this Regency theme a bit too far."

When neither of them responded but only continued to look at her like two morons, she waved her hand at their silliness. "Whatever. Have at it then, but I need to ask a favor. I left my phone outside, and although its likely stolen by now, I need one of you to help me find it." They both stood there mute, shaking their heads in what she assumed was confusion, which was odd. "Right," she said with a huff. Slowly, so they could understand, she said, "Will one of you escort me outside while *I* look for it then?" They still said nothing. "You," she said, her patience now gone. She pointed at the big man named Gabriel. "You're big enough to scare off Marvin." She looked around, suddenly noticing the spectacular remodeling of the entryway. "I do like what you've done to the place though. It's dope!"

"Dope?" questioned Declan as if he'd never heard the phrase.

Ah, the English.

"Who's Marvin?" Gabriel asked with a raised brow.

"I have no idea." Declan tried to intimidate her by coming closer.

"Like I said," Desirea replied with a loud exhale. She rubbed her temples, feeling a headache coming on. "Enough role playing. I need one of you strong, capable men to walk me outside to scare off my stalker."

"Your what?" Gabriel smacked his hand off his forehead.

"What is the matter with you two? Ah, hell," she said, grabbing Gabriel's arm and towing him toward the door. *Enough games.* She turned to the hulking man she was holding onto. "Marvin is a crazed fan. He scares me to death. He has broken into my Malibu home many times. I had a judge issue a restraining order to keep him at a distance. A whole hell of a lot of good that did me." She threw open the door and tugged on Gabriel's arm. "Come on, big guy. I'm not going out there alone."

Gabriel looked back at Declan as if to say, "Help me."

Declan shrugged, saying, "You heard the lady, Gabe. Take your tough hide outside and retrieve this item she seeks so avidly."

"Right, the phone," said Gabriel, and Desirea looked at him oddly. Something was not right with these men, but she couldn't quite put her finger on what that was.

She stepped outside to see carriages littering the roadway. *Holy mother of God, what happened?* With each step she took toward the corner, her temper spiked. *Is this a joke? There have to be hidden cameras somewhere. Am I on MTV's* Boiling Point *or something?* She looked around at the horses pulling carriages of various types, and then at the people dressed in old clothing, Regency clothing, much like the dress she wore. She let go of Gabriel's arm, staring at a pile of horseshit in the road. Where were all the cars? If this was a hoax, it was a very good one. Was her manager a part of this? He knew her temper. He knew she had a serious problem with cursing. *Why would he do this to me?*

She reached the corner, and of course, as expected, her phone was gone, but so was the jewelry store that was there an hour ago. It was now a store for antiquities, according to the sign and the displays in the window. *Oh my God!*

"My manager has gone completely overboard with this Regency shoot. I'm going to kill him."

A newspaper boy came by shouting out the top story. "Sympathy continues to be debated for exiled Napoleon."

"All right, enough," she said, and Gabriel just stared at her. "I said, cut the shit! I don't have time for this fucking game you seem to be playing." She marched toward a carriage driver stopped on the side of the road. "You! Get those horses out of here!"

"You appear a bit distressed," said Gabriel, stepping up beside her.

Distressed? Yes, she was distressed. The entire atmosphere had changed. Her world had shifted and he thought she was a *bit* distressed. Walking toward him, she kicked him in the shin three times in rapid succession, and then smiled as he hopped around on one leg. "Who the hell paid for this scene?" she asked heatedly, ready to kick him again. *Let them get this on camera.*

"I don't know what the bleeding hell you're talking about, woman. Are you mad? Stop yelling at the horses! You can't go about town yelling at horses and kicking people."

"Oh, really?" She turned and began to holler curses at everyone who passed, many hurrying quickly away from her tantrum. She looked around, frantic as her anger gave way to something close to panic. Nothing looked the same. There wasn't a car or a traffic sign anywhere. She couldn't even find one normally dressed person. The wind picked up and she shivered. She fell silent as fear gripped her. She realized no one could pull off a stunt like this. Even the trees in Hyde Park looked smaller. She turned to Gabriel, who was nearly growling at her. "What year is it?" she asked, her hands shaking.

"Are you unhinged, Miss Leighton? It's the year of our lord 1817." His head cocked sideways, and she knew he was wondering about her sanity. He'd probably have her locked up for mental illness, she thought. Seeing a clear path through the crowd, Desirea lifted her skirts and ran for all she was worth. She heard Gabriel yell after her, but she refused to stop. She continued to run until her side cramped and the breath wheezed from her chest. When she was no longer able to trudge another step, she ducked into an alley and crouched in a doorway to think.

What the hell am I doing in 1817?

CHAPTER THREE

Desirea sat in the alleyway out of sight, peeking around the strands of her blond hair to watch people pass back and forth. She shivered in fear for all the changes she saw before her. *Perhaps I shouldn't have run from that Gabriel dude, but he had looked at me so strangely.* The only thing she could think to do was run. And now, she was lost in a world she knew nothing about. She didn't understand how this happened, but she had traveled through time. Either that or someone slipped some kind of strong hallucinogen in her drinking glass earlier. Those were the only explanations she could come up with for finding herself in 1817.

She closed her eyes to block out the images and focused in listening. She only heard people's voices, the creaking of carriage wheels, and occasionally a horse whinnying. The people spoke and shouted about the things they were selling on the streets in strong British accents. There were no car horns or loud engines.

On top of these daunting thoughts of change, it was starting to get dark. She really didn't like the idea of being alone in the dark. She heard voices behind her and stood from the stoop on which she sat. Someone was moving toward the door behind her. Desirea moved out of sight, hiding behind a pile of garbage, breathing through her mouth as the stench of decay hit her. She looked down at the ground as her foot went sideways on something. She saw a used condom and choked on her response to find them littering the ground around her. *Oh, gross! How unsanitary can you be?* The little skins had stings at the top, certainly a condom like none she'd ever seen. Someone was having a lot of sex. She was more careful with her footing. The door opened and her eyes followed.

"If I ever hear of this happening with someone in my household again, I will be sure to go to the authorities and see you put out of business," a man's deep voice said in a threatening manner.

"I'm terribly sorry, Your Grace. Terribly sorry," another man said, his voice trembling as if the man was crying while he spoke. Curious, Desirea peeked around some of the refuse to find a short bald-headed man inside the door, cradling his arm as tears and sweat poured down his face.

"Anne, go on home now. Your family is worried about you," said the man, who had his broad back to Desirea. He was clearly the hero in this drama playing out before her eyes. She moved closer to see a young girl hurry out of the alley and into an awaiting maid's arms. Desirea looked back toward the men when she heard grunts and scuffling to find that the solidly built man, who had likely saved that girl, looked much like her talented fellow performer and all-time hottie Paul Wesley, but as a blond. "Oh my!" she said aloud. Paul Wesley was a gorgeous specimen of man she had often dreamt about doing some passionate love scene with, but such dreams never came to be. Of course, she liked Paul before he became the lead vampire in the *Vampire Diaries*, back when he got his start on *Guiding Light*. But unlike Wesley, the handsome devil before her wore his hair just above his shoulders and slicked back from his face with gel or some similar product. She'd always been partial to blonds, and this one was so unbelievably hot that Desirea let out some kind of dreamy sigh and then gasped, throwing a hand over her mouth when she realized it was audible. *Shit, shit, shit!*

This caused the beautiful one to release the chokehold he had on the bald man. He shoved the man back into the building, slammed the door closed, and spun around on the balls of his feet in a matter of seconds. Desirea thought it quite impressive. The bald man wisely remained behind the closed door and Desirea wisely moved back to her hiding place. But she knew hottie's attention was now fixed on her, well not on her exactly, since he had yet to see her, but he had certainly heard the sigh she made.

"Come out," he ordered, menace filling his voice.

Whether he was hot or not was irrelevant. Was he *kind* became the important question. She tried to remain calm by reminding herself of what she just witnessed. He had sent the young girl home to her family, a good thing, but Desirea remained hidden. Her body began to shake even more and she fought off the urge to cry, but she knew caving into her fear would not benefit her right now. As he moved closer, the crunch of his shoes on the littered ground traveled to her ears only to be drowned out by the loud and rapid beat of her heart. She thought to dart around him and make a run for it, but the alley was too narrow. He'd catch her. Or even worse, she'd slip and fall on top of the disgusting condoms.

"Who's there? Come out from behind the trash."

"I don't want to," she replied, realizing there was no escape.

"A female? Now, I'm surprised." His voice lost its menacing tone and changed to a more cordial sound. "Has Tarnin hurt you? Are you well?"

"I'm fine," she said, wanting him to go away and leave her in her confusion.

"I'd like to judge that for myself. Come out, please."

Desirea really had no choice. She walked away from the garbage and turned to stand before him. *Damn, he is perfect.* He smiled and the air rushed out of her lungs in a whoosh as two deep dimples formed in his cheeks. When his green eyes met hers, the pull of attraction she felt was stronger than anything she had ever experienced. He bowed and introduced himself, and she was charmed, her fear vanquished by his smile.

"I am Ellis Pemble, the Duke of Lancaster. May I be of assistance to you, Miss…?"

"Miss Desirea Leighton. You know," she said as she put her hands up to her own blond locks and pulled them back into a pony behind her head, "*Mindy's Adventures,* from Disney?" She let her hair fall back. Most people recognized her from her show when she did that, but he stared at her as if she were crazy. *Oh well. It was worth a shot.* She felt a blush fill her face. Of course, this man didn't know she had a hit television show for many years. *Many years. Now that's a laugh.* Her life took place 194 years into the future. The thought numbed her mind. No one in this time knew anything about television let alone about her. But she had to at least try one last time to prove to herself she had definitely left the world she had once known.

Of course, this meant she had no fans here. *Huh!* Such a thing was hard to imagine. She'd been a star since the age of seven. Although she had retired the Disney show, she had gone on to become a pop star and had even performed opera in some of New York's finest theaters, and yet no one here knew any of this. The people in this time didn't have any ill-conceived notions about her. They didn't care where she went or with whom she kept company.

Desirea smiled at the handsome man before her. Perhaps this could be her new start, a new world in which to reinvent herself. This time she'd be sure to make some true friends, she told herself. She had found it difficult to make any lasting friendships in the world she seemed to have left behind. People tended to like being in her company for the attention it garnered them with the paparazzi, but most women didn't like competing with her for male attention, nor were they satisfied with her leavings. It wasn't Desirea's fault that her beauty seemed to garner as much attention as her fame. This feeling of always being used had caused Desirea to avoid people in general for the last few years. Lord knew she was lonely, but perhaps with the twenty-first century behind her, she could find all the things she lacked in her life to this point. Friendship and love would be her top priorities. She smiled at this thought.

She planned to begin with the intriguing man standing in front of her. He was definitely someone she was determined to get to know, definitely some part of the something she lacked in her life. She could see in his light green eyes that he appreciated the fine form she presented as he looked her over. She tried not to preen under his alluring gaze. Truthfully, she thought she looked silly in this white Regency gown with lacy sleeves and deep v-necked bodice, dingy gray and likely stained from the hell she'd been put through. Although the neckline did show her breasts at their best, thanks to her corset that pushed them up for his viewing, but she still knew she didn't look as fabulous as she could.

He was dressed in severe black, from his boots to his coat collar. Even his cravat was black. He had lean cheekbones and a chiseled jaw, complete with an adorable cleft in his chin, a sign of wealth according to an old wives tale she once heard. When Ellis Pemble smiled, deep dimples formed on his lean cheeks, and she felt her stomach lift with butterflies of attraction. Feeling inclined to return his unspoken compliment, she took her time admiring him with her eyes. She held back a sigh this time, but barely.

"You seem none the worse for wear," he said.

His words disappointed her. She had really thought he was checking her out because he was attracted to her, not because he was looking for injuries. *Damn the man.* She suddenly wished he *was* a fan and felt compelled to compliment her beauty and talent profusely. Men usually acted like fools around her, but the duke appeared extremely composed. *How odd.* But you're tired of false flattery and fake friends, she reminded herself. And so what if he's the only male she ever met who wasn't immediately taken aback by her beauty. In fact, this spoke well of him. At least he wouldn't spout any nonsense about love from the get-go. *Damn.* Now she was even more intrigued by him. "I told you. I am fine," she huffed, angry he wasn't feeling the shimmer of desire between them as she did.

"Indeed." He crossed his arms over his chest, his posture indicating a haughtiness she was not sure she cared for.

"What?" she asked.

"Why are you hiding back here?"

Desirea decided she did not like his tone at all. "That's none of your business."

"And if I wish to make it my business?"

She shrugged and rolled her eyes at his domineering manner. "And what are you going to do?" She probably shouldn't have dared him in such a way, but she found she wasn't scared of him. His manner was too relaxed and carefree for him to be contemplating harming her. At least she hoped this was the case.

"Help you, I think," he said with an adorable tilt of his head and that mind-numbing smile, which had Desirea shaking her head to stay focused. She was suddenly physically and mentally exhausted. She could really use this man's help.

"Listen, dude… I mean, Ellis." She knew she needed to speak more like these people or no one would ever understand her. She smiled at this, finding this suddenly funny in its own special way. She basically spoke another language now. Although she sang Italian opera, she usually had no idea what she was singing when she did so.

"It's Your Grace. I told you. I'm the Duke of Lancaster."

"Yes, well, I'm an American, which means I'm not easily impressed with titles, since we don't have any. A duke, that's pretty high up there though, isn't it?"

"A mere step beneath royalty," he said in a puffed-up manner, which made her want to laugh, since she had perfected her haughtiness to an art form in order to keep fans away. Oddly enough, however, she found his words charming. "From where in America do you hail?" he asked.

Not wanting to tell this man about her crazy life right now, she said, "The west coast."

"Indeed," he said, looking at her as if that explained a great deal to him, and likely it did, she realized. The American West, at this point in time, was probably wild and as unsettled as her nerves right now. *Unreal.* She really was having a hard time believing this was happening.

"Are you staying in the city? Perhaps I could drive you somewhere. My carriage is out front."

Yes, he was kind and attractive, and he had a powerful manner, as if he was well aware of his importance. But then, so was she. "I have nowhere to stay," she admitted, hoping he'd decide to take her home and into his bed. *May as well start this new life off the right way.* At the moment, she could think of no better way than sweating up the sheets with Ellis Pemble, the duke, a man who, like her, was used to attention because of who he was. Besides, she'd love to see how someone as important as the Duke of Lancaster lived in this era. She was now curious how someone as calm and cool as he appeared to be handled his fawning fans. She also found herself wanting to know, most desperately, just how well this gorgeous man performed under the covers. Shameful, she told herself, but then, she always went after what she wanted. Right now, she wanted Ellis Pemble. She was definitely looking forward to the challenge of capturing the duke.

It was strange really. She had avoided intimacy even more than friendship in the last two years. Bizarre how this man's heady stare had her thinking lustful thoughts. *Perhaps that is why I am here, to find my one true love. A romantic notion, but what other reason could there be? How about some freaky cosmic accident?* The last came from a little voice in her head she decided must be what was left of her reason.

"Do you work here?" he asked.

"Uh, no. I guess you could say I'm unemployed at the moment, between jobs." She laughed, finding this suddenly amusing. Why would he ask if she worked here anyway? It seemed an odd question considering his dislike of the place. She took a second to consider her occupation. She certainly had the ability to get a job if she wished, after she had been here longer than two seconds, but she found she didn't wish to return to singing or the stage. At home, she had been busy writing her next album. The photo-shoot at the Back Room

Tavern was to provide the cover of her album, which she was calling *Into the Here and Now.*

"Come home with me," he invited, pulling Desirea from her thoughts on her employability and into her steamy visions of sexual fulfillment with him. Truthfully, she was disappointed to find him so easily captured. She had thought he would prove to be a bit more of a challenge, since he was such a handsome and important duke and all. She smiled, trying not to let his invite spoil her mood, since in essence, she did wish to go home with him. But still, he could have built up the moment some, played the game for longer than five minutes instead of taking the thrill from the hunt. She had heard this same invitation countless times and had never taken the men up on their offer, but tonight was a night like no other. And at least the duke wasn't inviting her home because of her fame. He was unaware how in demand she was in her time. Her heart filled with giddiness. She recognized the fact that she was, at least at this moment, a victim to her impulses. Since this was usually not the case, she decided to go with the flow. Besides, for all she knew this might be her one and only night in this time period. She was going to enjoy it. And what better way than in this hottie's company. She might find herself zapped back to the twenty-first century by morning and then she'd be mad at herself for passing up such a glorious opportunity. Although she did have a few modern day toys stuffed in her nightstand, she hadn't had real sex in a year. It was past time. "I'd love to," she said. When he held out an arm to her, she immediately linked hers with his, allowing him to take her away. She found herself sinking into the warm comfort of a powerful man.

It was growing darker by the minute as he assisted her into his carriage, and she was grateful to be out of the darkness and sitting in a plush-backed seat. She couldn't help running her hands over the softness. She thought of London Burton and wondered how she was doing. She had seen the way the lady had handled herself, and Desirea was quite confident

London was fine. The woman was older than she and so must have more wherewithal than Desirea could lay claim to, and besides, the way Lord Nankin stared at London told Desirea the lady would be kept safe. Surely London was making this change in time work to her advantage too. Desirea certainly planned to live this night like it was her last, especially when the duke invited her to his bed.

"So, who was the young girl you helped back there?" she asked when the vehicle got underway. She swayed in her seat and the lantern hanging inside seemed to follow her moves, throwing shadows around the plush compartment.

"Anne happens to be the granddaughter of my housekeeper, Mimi. She went missing this morning on her way to market."

"And you thought to look for her with that man? Why? Did he kidnap her or something?"

His light green eyes looked at her intently, as if he hadn't understood her question. She couldn't help but wonder if she phrased her words wrong. "The man's name is Tarnin. He is not a good man. Do you know him?"

"No, of course not. Why would I? What does he do?"

"He runs a brothel. Did you not know what building you were near?"

"No, I didn't. I told you, I'm lost." *And obviously in a Red Light district.*

"You said nothing of the sort." His eyes widened and he pushed his fingers through his hair.

He was right. She only said she had no place to stay. She was lucky he got her out of the alley. God knows what would have happened to her if one of those bad men had nabbed her. So he had saved that young girl from a terrible fate. And he had saved her too. He was a hero. *And so utterly appealing.* "I'm sorry," she apologized for not telling him she was lost. "It must have slipped my mind. It's been a trying day."

"Why? Are you in trouble?"

"Uh, no. Not with the law or anything. But the truth is, you wouldn't believe me if I told you. Hell, I don't even believe this fucking shit is happening. I certainly can't expect you to."

"Excuse me?" He stared at her as if she had grown two more heads. She realized she really needed to stop cursing so much. Doubtless, ladies probably didn't swear at all in this time. *Ah, hell! This is going to be tougher than I thought!* She was fortunate enough to have spent many hours with her father and his friends while growing up, but unfortunately, she had picked up their flare for cursing as well.

"I apologize, my lord… I mean, Your Grace, for my French."

"You weren't speaking French, Miss Leighton. You were cursing more fluently than I have ever heard before, at least from a woman."

She could feel a blush fill her cheeks, embarrassed by her outburst. "I'm terribly sorry, Ellis."

"Miss Leighton, it would be best if you only refer to me as Your Grace. We wouldn't want people to hear you speak to me in such a familiar manner and think something untoward."

Now here's where our opinions differ, she thought. *I could give two shits what people think of me here.* She was in fact tired of caring about such things in her own time too. But of course caring how others viewed her really couldn't be helped, could it? She didn't like people thinking badly of her. It seemed the duke suffered from the same issue. Nevertheless, he needed to learn what had taken her years to learn: no matter how well one behaved, reporters will print their own spin about you. It was not her fault if people believed all the BS printed about her. And it was pointless to pitch a fit about every lie in thousands of tabloids, when the next day there'd be another set of untruths to dispute. "Right. Sorry again, Your Grace." The man was certainly being formal, considering the fact that he had invited her home with him. "So you're bothered if people talk negatively about you?"

"It depends on what society is saying, but I tend to strive to keep my name off of their lips." For Desirea that had proved an impossible task.

He suddenly fell silent, as if he was turning inward, thinking of something from his past perhaps. Desirea wasn't sure, but he seemed saddened by his thoughts as a frown formed on his face. His hand went to his coat front and he fisted the pocket. Desirea thought she heard the sound of paper crinkling. She'd bet whatever was in his pocket was the cause for his sudden troubled look.

"Is your house much further?" she asked, trying to pull him from his thoughts.

"Actually, it's right here," he said, and the vehicle stopped in front of a large domicile lit with gas lanterns affixed to the mammoth stone entryway. *Holy shit, his house is huge.* And she'd seen her fair share of mansions. Her own home was 10,000 square feet, far too much room for her and a few servants, but she did love the space. She wanted to applaud when a dozen servants dressed in red with gold accents came down the steps and the driver pulled open the vehicle door. The servants lined up on both sides of the walkway, and two others stood at the door awaiting their approach. She got out of the vehicle with Ellis's assistance, wondering if trumpets would begin to play and a red carpet would roll out to welcome the duke home. She had taken many turns on the Red Carpet, but it seemed the servants' line-up was welcome enough. She was quite impressed.

The duke escorted her into his home, and the butler hurried to take his employer's coat and gloves. But for the most part, the servants remained in their positions, their heads down in a show of complete obedience.

"Temple, I'd like a word with you in the parlor in ten minutes," said the duke.

"Of course, Your Grace," replied his servant dutifully before he went off to get rid of the duke's coat, backing his way in the opposite direction. Desirea realized that the staff was not allowed to present the duke their backs. It was fascinating to watch. His staff treated him like royalty.

"Miss Leighton," said Ellis, leading her into a beautifully decorated parlor complete with comfy sofas and a center table with a tea service set up with ivory porcelain. "Please make yourself at home. I will return shortly."

"Okay," said Desirea, looking about the walls at the various hunting pictures. The room was growing darker by the second and so the duke lit a few candles before he left, shaking his head at her as if confused.

Desirea would kill for a pair of sweats and a t-shirt right now, but she knew her old clothing could be lost to her forever. She was having a hard time believing everything around her was real, that she was stuck in 1817, but an especially hard time believing Mr. All-Too-Handsome Duke was real. She pinched herself hard for the circumstances seemed to call for such an action, but it left a nasty mark on her arm and tears in her eyes and so she stopped. Well, she certainly felt pain in 1817. She found a mirror behind the door and began to pull her fingers through her blond hair in an effort to tame it. Her hair was pretty knotted after the day she had and the windstorm she had survived getting to the nineteenth century. She was pinching her cheeks for color, realizing she had no make-up and how much that sucked, when the door smacked into the back of her head. "Ow, shit!" She backed away from behind the door rubbing her head.

"Oh, goodness me. Are you hurt, dear?" A short older lady with blue eyes and graying brown hair smiled to her. Her uniform told Desirea that she was part of the duke's staff.

"No, I'm fine. I shouldn't have been standing behind the door."

"Silly place for a mirror, if you ask me," said the woman. "But men tend to overlook such things. My master certainly has need of a new wife; that he does. A lady would never place a mirror in such an awkward place. But I don't blame His Grace for not finding one, a wife that is, not a mirror; but once you lose a spouse, it takes the fun out of finding another."

Desirea didn't know what to say to this. The duke was a widower? This made sense, and it certainly explained the air of melancholy she saw in his eyes earlier. "I would imagine," said Desirea. Losing her father had been sheer torture, and she still suffered for his loss.

"So now, Miss Leighton," the duke said, walking into the room and smiling at his servant. "Ah, Mimi. I assume your granddaughter has returned to you."

"Yes, Your Grace, and I can't tell you how grateful I am for your assistance." She approached the duke. Desirea watched when she picked up his hand and placed a kiss on the man's ring. "Thank you," she said.

"In truth, dear woman, I enjoyed it. It would probably not serve me well if people knew this, but those scoundrels needed to be taught a lesson."

"And I'm sure you doled out a just punishment to them, Your Grace."

"Yes, well, tell Miss Anne she's to be accompanied by a footman on future trips to the market."

"Thank you, Your Grace." Mimi bowed again before backing away and disappearing out of the room.

"She's very grateful, Your Grace. You did a wonderful thing."

"Have a seat, Miss Leighton," he said abruptly, moving to stand near the fireplace. "Tell me about your family."

What is this? Doesn't this man realize it is now dark and my time here could be limited? Of course, he didn't know this, she told herself, but you'd think he'd skip this small talk and show her to his room. Admittedly, this thought made her feel like some kind of slut, but she might only have hours, maybe only minutes—even seconds. He had to kiss her now, before she was zapped back to her own time. But how to make that happen when he wanted to talk about her family? And what kind of man brought you home for a booty call and then brought up your family? She was starting to second-guess her first impression of Ellis Pemble. The duke was acting too weird.

"I was raised by my father," she said, hoping to make this conversation short and sweet. "He died three years ago. My mother ran off when I was too young to even remember. My grandfather, my dad's dad, was a producer, and he was the one who jump started my career."

"And what is your vocation?"

"Say what?" she said, not recognizing the word.

Now he stared at her, his brow scrunched in total confusion. *Damn.* This man would never understand her acting on television. What was the matter with her for sharing such things? For now, she needed to keep her talents to herself. Who knew how they might come in handy in this age? She might even have to act herself out of this house.

"Are you educated, Miss Leighton?"

"Are you serious?" she asked. What was this, a frikken interview? "I was homeschooled," she replied when he remained silent. Truthfully, she had been tutored in her trailer on the set of *Mindy's Adventure,* but she was sure he wouldn't understand that.

"I see," he said. "Do you have family in London?"

"No, but what's with the twenty-one questions? I don't remember agreeing to an interview." She purposely tried to confuse him, because in truth he confused her. He was sending her different signals, and they were not the "welcome to my bed" kind she had expected.

"You wished to see me, Your Grace," the butler said from the doorway.

"Yes, Temple, do come in. I'd like you to meet Miss Desirea Leighton."

Desirea was totally confused about why he was introducing her to his staff, but she stood with a smile. "It's nice to meet you, sir," she said.

"Likewise, Miss." They both now turned to the duke, and Desirea wondered again what this handsome man was about.

The Duke of Lancaster smiled his handsome smile, dropping his arm down from where it rested on the mantel before saying, "Please find Miss Leighton a uniform that fits. She's in need of employment and shelter. And I am in need of another maid."

"Now wait one goddamn minute!" Desirea crossed her hands over her chest and glared heatedly at Ellis.

He wants to hire me as his maid? Is he out of his frikken mind?

Some part of her wanted to laugh, but she was way too pissed off. Mr. High and Mighty was in for a battle now. How dare he try to belittle her in such a way. She was a star. She was idolized and emulated.

Desirea Leighton was NOT a servant!

CHAPTER FOUR

"Temple, please excuse us," ordered Ellis at the end of her screech of outrage. *What the bloody hell is wrong with this woman?* He'd certainly stepped in it this time. He might have been far better off not trying to help this one.

She was pretty though, with the lightest blond hair he'd yet to see, and blue eyes that sparkled like the ocean, especially when angered. "You take issue with being under my employ?"

Her skin was flawless perfection, like an angel's from heaven. *Or a furious goddess, probably a more apt description, and a disheveled goddess at that, considering her untamed hair and filthy, but very flattering, white sequined dress.* Her breasts were glorious and he had a hard time focusing on her face with so much of her chest on display. Women's fashions boggled his mind.

She huffed and began to march about the room, throwing her arms in the air and glaring at him as she hollered her words. Her honey colored complexion certainly reddened when she was angry.

"Dude, seriously. I'm finding everything about you troubling. This is madness! Here I thought you were taking me home to, well, you know, tap this." Her hand smacked off her buttocks and he felt his eyes nearly cross at the obscene gesture. "And yet you sit there with that doe-eyed look upon your far too handsome face as you offer me a job! What the hell is the matter with you?"

He blinked in surprise. Never had a woman made her feelings more known to him, or indeed, made them known to him in such a manner. He found her shocking and now worried about the trouble she may bring him. "I apologize if I have offended you in any way, Miss Leighton."

"And stop calling me that! My name is Desirea. I find your formality insulting!"

Ah hell, I should have never tried to help this one. She appeared to be disturbed in the head. He would not apologize for being a gentleman. He had seen a lady in obvious distress and decided to help. He was already on a humanitarian mission so it had seemed appropriate. "I am a duke. I always speak formally. I was not raised in London's East End tenements."

"Are you insulting me?" she shouted, and he shook his head at her in amazement. He'd never seen a woman more animated nor heard one more loud.

Of course he was insulting her, and yet, he normally never do so; but she was acting so unusual. He couldn't help it if his response to her was abnormal. He looked over her soiled attire. "I was trying to employ you, but perhaps I was presumptuous in assuming you needed money and a roof over your head," he said a bit testily. After all, he was being extremely generous. He needed to trudge through much reading before Parliament convened tomorrow and did not have time for this.

"As your maid?" she said with hands on her hips and a haughty look of disproval on her pretty face that he couldn't for the life of him understand. She couldn't have possibly believed he would bed some woman he pulled from behind a refuse pile, could she? The idea was ludicrous, to say the least. *I am the Duke of Lancaster, for heaven's sake, and this woman must be mad to believe I'd bed her.*

"As my maid," he said in an exhausted tone. He was tired of this game. His friend Remy was meeting him at White's for a drink, and at the rate he was going with this woman, he was sure to be late and then he'd never get to his reading.

"I see," she said, suddenly calmer. She sat on the sofa and he watched as she shakily poured herself a spot of tea.

"I can send for some hot tea." He couldn't help feeling sorry for her. She seemed so alone.

"No thanks. I prefer it cold."

He thought that odd but didn't say so. "Would you like the job? You'd have every Thursday off." He thought it must be the fact that he felt sorry for her that he was still offering her the position. She was actually lucky he hadn't shown her to the door.

"Um, yes. Yes, I think I shall," she said with a firm nod and a dazzling smile that caught him a little off guard. He made a mental note to be sure to keep any of his male visitors away from this lovely maid. He was amazed that she, in fact, tempted him. Her allure was powerful.

"Good," he said, crossing the parlor to the door to have Temple show the woman to her attic room. Thankfully, Temple was waiting nearby and entered at once. "Please show Miss Leighton to her room and have Mimi decide where she's needed most. I'm going out for the evening. No need to wait up. And tell Mimi that she is welcome. I told her I'd fix the staffing problem."

Before he left, he nodded toward his new servant. "Welcome to my home, Miss Leighton." Then he thanked another maid for retrieving his coat in the foyer and headed out of the house with a sigh of relief, and not just because he wanted to be on his way so that he could get back to his reading. The maid had gotten under his skin and he was having a difficult time pushing her from his mind. He assumed she must have stolen the pretty ensemble she was wearing and had somehow ended up in an area she should not have been. She was an original, which surely was the reason he felt drawn to her, or so he rationalized. And he was attracted to her to a very strong degree. The lady had not read those signals wrong.

A short while later, he sat at his favorite table in White's next to the Earl of Gatlin, Remy, and one of his close friends. It was a loud smoke-filled atmosphere at this time of the evening, but he and Remy held a table in the nook where they could speak with normal voices. "You won't believe what happened today," said Ellis.

"Why? What happened?" asked Remy, pouring more bourbon into their glasses while nodding at a group of gentlemen passing them on their way to the card tables.

"I actually found myself drawn to a woman." Ellis looked at his friend sideways. He could have told him about Anne, Mimi's granddaughter, but he knew his friend would find his renewed interest in a female a more startling revelation than the fact he had broken some thug's arm. And the disappointing letter in his pocket could surely wait.

"Really?" Remy asked with complete skepticism.

"Yes. Why would I mention it otherwise?"

"Just to bam me, I suppose." Remy shrugged, leaning a bit closer. "It wasn't Colonel Stuart's new wife, was it? She's a looker, that one. I caught her giving me those come-have-me eyes a few times."

"No, it's not the colonel's wife. I never even noticed her. Is she handsome?"

"Stunning," replied Remy.

It was Ellis's turn to shrug. Since his wife passed away five years ago, Ellis had pretty much ignored women in general, the thought of finding a new wife somehow beyond his ability. He spent his time hunting and visiting his sister when parliament wasn't in session. It had been years since he felt the stir of his passions, which was the reason his attraction to the maid was such great news. Perhaps his desires weren't dead, which had been his concern on more than one occasion.

"Well, I'm happy for you. What is this goddess' name?"

"Her name is Miss Desirea Leighton. She's my new maid."

"Your what?" shouted Remy, and Ellis merely shook his head at him when gentlemen turned their way.

"Calm yourself. This is a breakthrough, and certainly no cause for alarm."

"No cause for alarm?" Remy stammered. "You sound as crazy as a loon. After five long years, you have finally found yourself attracted to another woman, and you decide to hire her and make her your maid? Why not your mistress? What is wrong with you, Ellis? You can't have your mistress under your roof. Think of what people will say."

"She's not my mistress. Nor will she be. I told you. She's my maid."

Remy guffawed and bent over in laughter. Ellis felt his temper spike at his friend's mirth. "This is not a laughing matter."

"Oh, I beg to differ, my friend. You just put a woman you are attracted to under your very own roof after five long years of abstinence…"

Ellis was offended. "I have had sex over the last five years, Remy."

"Certainly not often enough to give you the strength to withstand these circumstances," countered Remy. "How can you not find this amusing? You cannot tell me you didn't take into consideration how difficult it will be to have a woman you desire living with you, especially knowing she is forbidden fruit."

"You act as if I'm a rutting animal. I assure you I can control my baser instincts. Unlike you, my friend, I take pride in proving my restraint."

"Restraint, bah! You'll be trying to move in with me before long, just you wait and see."

"Now you're being preposterous. I have many estates to which I could disappear." Ellis laughed at his friend's false look of hurt. "It won't be a problem, Remy, because I won't allow it. It's not as if I spend time with my servants. Let us talk of something else."

"You're the one who brought it up. Now I can't help but wonder how pretty this maid is. What color is her hair? I assume, knowing your preference for brunettes, that she has dark hair."

"Actually, she's blond with pretty blue eyes and a body that puts Venus to shame. Her lips are perfect, but her vocabulary and manner are a bit eccentric. Not that any of this matters because…"

"Yes. I know. She's your maid. It will serve you well not to forget it. As a matter of fact, I suggest you remind yourself of that fact every morning and every evening while you lie in your bed thinking about her."

"You're annoying, you know," exclaimed Ellis. Both men fell silently into their own thoughts for a moment. "I received a letter from my sister today."

"And I assume from the downcast tone of your voice that she gave birth to another girl?"

"She did." Ellis shrugged. Both men knew what this meant to him.

"Ah, well, the Regent wouldn't have likely agreed with passing your title to your sister's child regardless. Besides, it's not as if you are dying. This news only means you have to marry again. It's not like you didn't already know this."

"Yes, I know. I had hoped, though, if she had a boy, some of the pressure would be taken off me to find another wife and produce an heir, that's all. But you are right. I probably wouldn't have been able to petition the courts to pass my title to my sister's son anyway."

"Since you're feeling more up to the game that we real men like to play with females, and since you are now wife hunting, perhaps you'd like to join me at the Peppering gala. It's sure to be a crush."

"Is the colonel's pretty wife attending?" asked Ellis.

"That's the only reason I'm attending," said Remy, waggling his eyebrows as if he said something funny. While women flocked to Ellis because of his title, though he liked to think his handsome looks also played a part, women flocked to Remy because of his unfailing charm and his dark, menacing looks.

"You know, one day your transgressions will catch up to you, Remy. You may find yourself running naked before the barrel of a loaded gun. No man likes to be cuckolded, no matter the lack of feeling between the married couple."

"I do not foresee such a thing ever occurring," Remy said resolutely. "I am most discreet. But if such a thing does come to pass, I will hide myself away with you at one of your estates."

"I'll have no reason to go into hiding, Remy. But you, my friend, surely will if you continue to chase married women."

"Unhappy married women," Remy corrected.

"No matter. It's not a good place to put yourself."

"That statement just proves that you haven't had a woman's legs wrapped around you in far too long."

"I'm going home." Ellis stood and threw some money on the table.

"Ah, don't leave. You know I didn't mean to goad you."

"I know you meant me no insult, but I have an early morning. I'll see you tomorrow."

"Damn right. I'll be coming by to meet your new maid."

Ellis laughed and walked out the door.

***

Desirea Leighton spun around in front of the cracked looking glass, glaring at her uniform, which was not easy to do in a round fifteen-inch mirror. Her uniform was gray, a dull, ugly gray, with a stiff collar and tiny black buttons all the way to her throat. *Bummer I don't have my pink scarf.* She wished Ellis had made her a footman. She'd look awesome in the burgundy ensemble with the gold accents that she noticed the male servants in this household sporting.

"A maid," Desirea said to herself in the mirror. She didn't doubt she could play this part. She could play any part. But she did wonder how this could help her capture the Duke of Lancaster's heart. She'd never had to seduce a man, and the task invigorated her. Finally, she had found a man to challenge her, a man not smitten with a simple smile from her. She had no idea how she was going to gain his devotion, but she hoped a plan would come to her by morning. That was, if she was still here in the morning and had not been whisked back to her own time. She had a feeling she would be here, however, and this thrilled her. She removed her new uniform and crawled into bed. The duke had made his stand clear. She would not be sleeping in his bed. *At least, not tonight.* She smiled, anxious to begin the fun task before her. She never had to do the chasing in the game of love. This was sure to be entertaining.

***

Desirea was thrilled to find herself still in 1817 when she woke, which meant she had an opportunity to make the duke fall in love with her. But she was soon disappointed to learn that the duke had gone out for the day. She had hoped they could have spent some time together. Her body practically vibrated with pleasure when she was near him, which felt wonderful. *His absence sucks.* For now, she was going to have to actually clean something.

She looked around at her spartanly furnished room located in the attic section of the monstrous house. It was certainly nothing to write home about, but then, she had no one to write home to anyway. She was in the wrong century. There was a small bed, a wooden nightstand with a pitcher and bowl for water, and of course the cracked oval mirror affixed to the wall by a dangling wire over a metal hook.

There was only the tiniest of windows, and it didn't even open, plus it was wavy glass so you couldn't even see through it. In other words, the window was pointless. Desirea was used to five-star hotels with concierge treatment and panoramic views that made your breath catch. Her every whim was always fulfilled. This living in the attic in a tiny room thing was going to take some getting used to. One thing was certain, she was not about to play the role of maid forever, but she also knew that this was the easiest way to keep a roof over her head and food in her mouth. Speaking of which, she was absolutely starving.

She walked down the many flights of stairs to the main floor, looking at the intricately coved ceilings, the artwork along the walls, and even some statuary tucked in various ornate niches. Instead of curtains, many of the rooms had huge wooden shutters, which were folded back to let in the light. This was a grand home, even if it didn't have electricity and proper plumbing. She walked into the parlor and called out for Mimi. She continued to walk through the house, checking the rooms for the housekeeper, when she was drawn to the voices coming down the hall. She pushed open the dark wood door to find herself in a spacious kitchen.

"Oh good," said Mimi, rushing toward her. "Your uniform fits and you're ready to work. Now I need you to go down to the larder."

"What's a larder?"

Mimi had shoved her gently toward a green door, returning to chopping carrots on her work counter, but she turned at Desirea's question. A young maid laughed at Desirea's ignorance, but when Desirea glared at her, the stupid girl shut up, hustling out of the room with two other female servants and the butler she met earlier. *Temple, what a silly name for a butler. He needs a new name.* Desirea thought Jeeves a far more fitting name for a butler. She'd be sure to tell him this the next chance she got.

"A larder is a buttery or a cellar where food is stored in a colder temperature." Mimi had that look one got when you had to explain something to a simpleton.

"Got ya. So where's this refrigerator, and what am I fetching? You know, chicken sounds good. Perhaps with a mushroom cream sauce and some whipped potatoes."

"Oh dear me," Mimi put her hands to her head and then pulled out a stool on which to sit. "Where are you from, dear girl? I've never heard anyone talk quite like you."

"America," Desirea said with a sigh. This talking different thing was becoming tedious. "I can assure you that where I'm from everyone talks like me, or at least close to it. It's just the way we talk, ya dig?" Desirea couldn't help adding that last bit. She loved watching confusion fill the woman's face as she tried to decipher her meaning.

"Yes, well," said Mimi, still staring at her oddly as she got up from the stool. "We are not having chicken. The servants will be having some soup I prepared from yesterday's dinner."

"Oooh, yummy," said Desirea sarcastically. *No way in hell am I eating the duke's leavings.* She hated leftovers of any kind.

The woman continued to stare at her, and so Desirea asked, "What am I fetching from the larder?" She left out the "r" just like the modern Brits tended to do, but with an overdone accent.

Mimi shook her head. "I need the ham hock. It's on the shelf. But be careful of the meat on the hook above. It's dripping blood something awful."

Desirea fought off the urge to hurl. Bloody meat hanging from a hook was gross. She opened the larder door to find five steps and another door. Of course, the larder would be underground to keep the food cold, but how cold was the question. She was sure a larder was nowhere near as efficient in keeping food from spoiling as her sub-zero refrigerator. She couldn't help wondering if these people suffered from food poisoning often. She got food poisoning once after eating some bad Chinese food, not an experience she wished to relive.

In the tiled larder, she shivered from the cold and smiled. The coldness relieved her in a way; perhaps she wouldn't die from the food. She flinched when she looked at the far end where a carcass of some unrecognizable animal hung on a meat hook from the ceiling. The room smelled of what she assumed must be blood, which was pooled on the floor. She preferred her steaks in nicely wrapped packages, thank you very much. Better yet, cooked and served on a platter with some A1 and mushroom caps sounded wonderful right now.

She perused the shelves, then grabbed the ham and a chunk of yellow cheese. A cheese sandwich would tide her over for now. With food in hand, she closed the door with her shoulder and marched back up the steps to close the other door behind her with her foot. She set the ham bone on the counter next to Mimi's chopping board, washed her hands at the water pump, and then looked about for some bread to make her sandwich. She was sure there wasn't any mayonnaise or Miracle Whip, but there had to be bread somewhere.

"Do you have some bread? I wish to make a sandwich?" Desirea asked Mimi, who was staring at her again with a look of amazement.

"Oh dear, what are you about, girl?"

"I'm starving," said Desirea. She grabbed a knife, settled herself at the long wood table, and cut herself a hunk of the cheese.

"Here," said Mimi, setting a couple of chunks of bread in front of her. "This should fill you up until the soup is ready for dinner. But after you eat, I need you to wash the dishes."

Desirea looked over at a large sink piled high with filthy pots and pans. "Oh, let's not and say we did. I can't do dishes, Mimi. I mean, my nails can't take much more abuse." Mimi glared at her and Desirea smiled. "Just saying." She couldn't remember the last time she had washed a dish. She'd rinsed some, of course, but washing, no. Such things were left to her staff, or at the very least, the high efficiency dishwasher beneath her granite counter.

"Your fingernails don't concern me, Miss Leighton."

"I don't expect them to be your concern since they belong to me, but I already chipped one and…"

"Mimi, how are things with…" The Duke of Lancaster walked into the kitchen, and Desirea had trouble swallowing the piece of bread she was busily chewing. "Oh, good. The uniform fits and you're under Mimi's care. I'll leave you to your duties then." He smiled at Desirea and she smiled back.

He is such a handsome devil. She knew he likely realized his appearance had her tongue-tied, but then, she was used to having the same effect on men. *So what is wrong with this one?* Nervous butterflies filled her again as his green eyes held hers in a heated stare.

"Mimi," he said, breaking his gaze with a physical jerk, which she thought was adorably telling. Perhaps he wasn't as immune to her charms as he liked to portray. A fellow actor at heart, she knew the duke had a certain persona he felt necessary to portray at all times.

"Yes, Your Grace?" Mimi dipped into a curtsey.

"I need one of the servants who can alphabetize to straighten out the bookshelves in my study." His eyes returned to Desirea. "Somehow the tomes were moved out of their proper places and I can't seem to find any of the reference books I need."

"Traci knows her alphabet, Your Grace, but I'm afraid she can't read."

Desirea flushed. The duke did not move his eyes to Mimi when she spoke. He was too busy staring at her. *Now this was more like it.* "I can read," said Desirea, realizing this was a wonderful opportunity to duck out on washing dishes. Perhaps organizing his lordship's books would put her in his vicinity, which is where she really wished to be. And aside from survival, the duke was the real reason for her agreeing to play the role of maid in the first place.

"Come along then, Miss Desirea. I'll show you to the study."

Desirea stood, wiping her hands on her ugly white apron complete with frilly ruffle. She frowned when the duke did not offer her his arm as he turned and walked out of the room, clearly expecting her to follow him like a well-trained dog. She didn't like him thinking her beneath him, but obviously, he did.

She snatched up the rest of her sandwich and gobbled it on the way, an idea beginning to form in her mind. Perhaps being his maid was exactly what the duke needed her to be, if only to help him overcome his feeling of superiority. Playing a maid could be the answer to all her prayers. She had always complained about men wanting to date her because of her celebrity status, but as a maid, she had no status; and if she could get the high and mighty duke to fall in love with her, that would mean he truly loved her, Desirea the person, not the star. Oh, yes, being a maid might be just the ticket to finding the love and happiness she had always prayed for. They could even become friends first. If she could find herself a man to love, she'd never be lonely again.

But first she needed to do something with her appearance. The duke was sure to lose the "friends first" battle if she walked around his house looking gorgeous all the time.

"Your Grace, would you mind if I met you in the study in a few minutes? I have to, ah…use the necessary." It would have been nice if she could have come up with an excuse that wasn't a bodily function, but her brain seemed fuzzy when she was around him and she had a hard time not staring at his lips.

"Of course, Miss Desirea. I'll meet you in the study. It's…"

"Oh, I know where it is. I noticed it this morning. You have an impressive collection of books." He frowned at her and she realized people most likely didn't interrupt the duke, especially one of his maids. *Oh, well. Too late to take my words back.* "Go on. I'll see you in a minute," she said, realizing even as she said it that people likely didn't order him about either. As she hurried up the stairs, she noticed out of the corner of her eye that he was watching her and shaking his head in what she assumed was confusion. It seemed no one in this house understood her. *Ugh!*

CHAPTER FIVE

Desirea hurried up two flights of stairs, grabbed a mobcap off the hook in the hall, and closed herself in her tiny room. Not wanting to keep the duke waiting, she made quick use of the chamber pot and moved toward the mirror. She sighed at her reflection, wondering how she could change her appearance enough so the duke could talk to her without their attraction to one another getting in the way. She tied the mobcap on her head and began to shove all her blond hair up underneath the thing. She was looking uglier by the second, she noted with satisfaction. Crossing to the fireplace, she grabbed a bit of soot from the grate and rubbed it on her cheeks, giving herself a gray complexion, which removed the glow from her normally tanned skin. With a firm nod and a promise not to show the duke her winning smile, she hurried back down the steps and into the study.

She entered the room to find the duke sitting at a desk and staring at a picture he held in his hand. Wondering who held him so enthralled, she crossed the room to lean over his shoulder. "She's pretty. Is she your sister," she asked, because that's who she hoped it was, but deep down she knew exactly who's visage he stared at so fondly.

He jumped at the sound of her voice. He seemed to be extremely surprised to find her so close. She pretended not to notice. "This is Evelyn, my wife."

His no-longer-of-this-earth wife, she wanted to remind him, but she held her tongue. Having lost her father, Desirea knew not to make light of his loss. *Death is inevitable but it sucks for the ones left behind.* "How did she die?" she asked. If she wanted to be his friend before his lover, she had to ask the tough questions to get to know him. And this question was tough, because truthfully, she didn't want to hear about how much he loved his wife. She could not compete with a ghost.

"She had a weakness of the lungs," he said, setting the picture of the dark-haired lady back on the desk. The duke's wife had been as lovely as Desirea had assumed she was. They must have made a stunning couple, the duke with his blondness and dimples and his brunette wife with her heart-shaped face. Desirea's face was more of an oval, and there wasn't a single dark hair on her head; but she had felt the earth move when he looked at her. She was sure of it.

"The books are over there." He pointed unnecessarily, ruining their private moment. Intentionally, she was sure. He appeared uncomfortable talking with her. Desirea was not used to being ordered about and glared at the back of his head. Then, with a huff, crossed to the book-shelved wall.

She scanned the rows of leather books, purposely ignoring him and refusing to look his way. At least the books weren't dusty. She hated dirt nearly as much as she hated small dark spaces, like the scary tunnel that brought her here. She pulled her mind away from that terrifying experience.

Reading the titles on the top row, she could tell most of them were in their proper places. But the middle sections of the shelves were completely out of order. She began to pull them out and stack them alphabetically all around her, a stack to represent every letter of the alphabet. In her peripheral vision, she could see the duke studying her, and she wondered if her attempt to make herself less appealing was working. Wisely, she pretended as if his presence didn't matter to her in the least, but her stomach fluttered the entire time. He shook his head as he often did after staring at her, and then he looked back down at some papers on his desk.

Hidden behind her stacks, she peeked over at him. Her soon-to-be-boyfriend — she couldn't help thinking of him as such — was writing with a weird tipped pen. He dipped it in ink and then scribbled on some thick paper. She'd been stacking books for the last forty-five minutes and the man had yet to say another word to her, or even to acknowledge her by glancing in her direction. But then, he likely didn't feel the need to talk to his maid, she thought. Why would he? Perhaps playing his maid wasn't such a stellar idea. He didn't seem game for the whole lord with the French maid thing, but then she wasn't wearing a French maid costume. *And you don't want him to fall for your looks. You want him to go against all his beliefs and fall in love with his lowly maid.* She wanted nothing less of him than to prove his love for her, mind, body and soul; and for once, she wanted a man to profess his love for reasons other than wanting a hot celebrity rich chick on his arm. She had enough of those fools in the 21st century. She'd take nothing less than the best of boyfriend's in the 19th century. She wanted this duke. And if had he lived in the 21st century, she could have made that happen. But then she would have never truly known if it was Desirea Leighton he liked or the limelight.

Yet, as his maid, he didn't seem to notice her much at all. *Oh, but he will. I plan to make sure of it.*

Another forty minutes later, Desirea stood from her position on the floor, her back killing her. She walked to a comfy looking chair, which sat directly across from Ellis's desk, with her hand on her lower back.

He immediately looked up with that adorable puzzled look on his face as she sat. "What are you doing?"

She laughed. "My back is killing me, Ellis." He scowled at her use of his first name, but she ignored it. "I've been sitting on the floor for the last two hours, or haven't you noticed? I could go for a beverage. What do you have around here to drink?"

"I think it would be more fitting if you took yourself into the kitchen to find yourself something to quench your thirst." She couldn't help but be stung by his need to have her away. She hadn't expected his refusal, and being denied was a new experience for her. She found she didn't like it in the least.

She hated this feeling of insignificance, which was how the duke was making her feel. *Who does this man think he is? I'm Desirea Leighton, for crying out loud! And damn it, he will notice me!* She refused to be insignificant to him. She liked him. The portraying-herself-as-frumpy-until-they-became-friends thing was an utterly stupid plan and clearly not working. Of course, Desirea was not known for her patience. In fact, quite the opposite.

It seems seduction is necessary.

Desirea gave the ever-so-proper duke a huge smile. "Right then," she said, getting to her feet. "I'll rest and return shortly." He nodded, not looking up from the paper he was reading. *What an uppity, arrogant man!* Well, he'd notice her when she returned. She planned to make sure of it.

Mimi was in the hall holding a tray containing lemonade, obviously for the duke. Desirea, deciding to pour herself a glass, stopped her. Mimi *tsked* as she tried to pull the tray away, but Desirea was faster and she snatched the glass pitcher and poured some lemonade in her glass. She replaced the pitcher on the tray and Mimi glared at her. "I was thirsty," she said, fleeing up the stairs to her room. *How ridiculous! I've been working my ass off. The least I deserve is something to drink. These people freak out over everything.*

Downing a good portion of the lemonade, she made her way into her room and to her washstand. She immediately went to work scrubbing the gray ash from her face. What a stupid idea to try and ugly herself up, she thought. It was clear that capturing a man like the duke was going to take her entire arsenal. Her cheeks were again red by the time she finished. She then undid the mobcap and flounced her blond hair, a prized asset, about with her fingers until it floated gloriously around her. Satisfied with the result, she looked down at her attire. *A French maid?* Opening the drawer to the washstand, she took out the scissors, which were placed next to some hand towels. Sitting on the edge of the bed, she grabbed the bottom of the dress and began to cut right at the level of her thighs. She was sure Mimi would be furious with the uniform's alterations, but Desirea was sure the uniform could be replaced. A mini skirt just became a necessity.

She stood to check out her handy work. The edge wasn't even, but when she bent over, she could tell the bottom half of her ass cheeks were exposed. She'd worn far less in magazine spreads, and so she wasn't at all uncomfortable with the length. "This ought to get Mr. Almighty's attention." Squaring her shoulders, she marched out of the room. Thankfully, she didn't come across any of the other servants. She reentered the study to find the duke still studying the papers before him so intently that he didn't bother to look up. She smiled, making her way to her stacks of books. Eventually he'd look her way.

But after an hour of no conversation, Desirea gave up and bent over to carry one of the stacks back to its proper place on the shelf. One of the books almost fell, which would have caused her to drop more, and she grunted as she shifted her weight to adjust the stack's balance. Out of the corner of her eye, she noticed her grunt had garnered the duke's attention. She set down the stack. His mouth fell open and stayed that way as he continued to stare. She smiled to herself and reached up to place one of the books on the top shelf where it didn't belong. She'd be sure to move it later, but it did allow him to view a hint of her ass, which was her intent. She had worked too hard on that part of her body to not be proud of it.

She then continued to put the other books on the shelf. According to her peripheral vision, he was still staring. And he was still not speaking either, and she fought back a laugh. He was adorable.

***

What in the bloody hell was this maid about? Where was the rest of her uniform? The Duke of Lancaster was so shocked by Desirea's lovely ass on display that he couldn't speak. He'd never seen anything like this. He fought back not only overwhelming desire but the urge to laugh. He, of course, knew exactly what she was about. She was trying to seduce him, to move him to act on their attraction, but why? It was a wasted effort. Even if she wasn't really a maid, she was not of his caliber and so out of the question as a female companion.

He should have seen this coming, he thought. Desirea Leighton had all but propositioned him when they met. His attraction and his concern for her safety were the blame for her living under his roof in the first place. And as he had predicted, Desirea was turning into quite a handful, a tempting lovely-assed handful. He couldn't help but imagine how wonderful it would be to take her standing up against the bookshelves. He'd always wanted to have sex in his study, but his wife had been far too prudish for such "disgraceful nonsense," as she called it.

By contrast, there didn't seem to be a modest bone in Miss Desirea's perfect body. He felt his cock harden while he continued to imagine many naughty scenarios he would like to play out with Desirea. He couldn't help himself. It felt like a lifetime since he'd felt sexual stirrings this intense.

"Ellis, Temple said you were in the stu..." His friend Remy stood in the doorway and his eyes widened like a boy at his first bordello when he noticed Desirea. "*Merde!* What the hell are you doing, Ellis?"

At the sound of the Earl of Gatlin's voice, Desirea stopped shelving books and turned to Ellis with a look of horrified embarrassment on her face. Her beautiful skin turned a ruddy shade of red, and Ellis felt sympathy for the shame she suffered. But he had immensely enjoyed the show. He knew he had to stop Remy from staring at the lady. Otherwise he was going to come to blows with his friend. "Miss Desirea, please have Mimi find you a new uniform. You can finish the books tomorrow."

"Yes, Your Grace," she said, and he was surprised when she bowed her head slightly in obedience, dropped the two books she was holding, and fled from the room holding her skirt down with both hands. Remy stepped out of her way, shaking his head in amazement.

Ellis exhaled loudly, retaking his seat. "Sit, Remy. What brings you by?" He knew this line of questioning wouldn't work to misdirect his friend's questions, but he didn't want to discuss Desirea's behavior…or his reaction.

"Funny, Ellis." Remy sat down in the chair across from his desk. "What the devil did I walk in on?"

"My seduction. I think."

"Your new maid is trying to seduce you?"

"So it seems." Ellis stared at the bookshelves. He could still picture the perfect roundness of Desirea's bottom as she stretched up on her toes, and… *Ah, hell.* Lusting after his maid could bring heaps of scandal and malicious talk he didn't wish to start. Throughout history, the Dukes of Lancaster had always been viewed as upstanding, honorable men who stayed out of gossip, men who strived for a stellar reputation to pass onto their future generations. This need for a pristine reputation was instilled from birth. Lancaster's were also encouraged to marry young and marry well, which was the reason he had married Evelyn Farris, the daughter of the Duke of Havel, when he was twenty. She was the best stock to be found. Perhaps this wasn't the romantic way to go about choosing one's wife, but it was expected of him, and as a Lancaster, he made it his mission not to disappoint his ancestors. So he married a lady who married him for the same reason, position. And although they hadn't loved each other, they had formed a friendship of a sort, and then she had taken ill and died. He'd not felt the need for another wife, or even female company, since. As a matter of fact, it had been hard for him to drum up even a speck of enthusiasm to have sex, that is until he met Desirea, a woman completely unsuitable for him. She had his groin tightening with a simple smile. *Damn it to hell.* Remy was smiling at him in a gloating I-told-you-so manner.

"So what are you waiting for, my friend? Find your mistress a house and set up shop."

"I don't believe it would be so simple. She's different, Remy. She's not like any woman I've ever met." Ellis was embarrassed to admit how much difficulty he had understanding Desirea. She spoke in the most bizarre manner, using words he never heard of before.

"And how is she different? Her ass looked bloody perfect, if you ask me."

"Well, I didn't ask, and I wish you wouldn't share your thoughts. It irks me."

"Jealous, eh?'

"I have no reason to be," said Ellis, though obviously confused about his feelings for Desirea.

"Of course you do. This is the first time in far too long you've felt desire."

"Perhaps that's part of it. But I know there's something else."

"Yes, well, she's a looker. Even prettier than the colonel's wife." Remy laughed. "Only *you* would come upon such a fair damsel and turn her into your maid."

"You're probably right. Mimi was in here earlier, and she made it abundantly clear that Miss Desirea isn't fit to be a servant of any kind. The minx even confiscated the lemonade Mimi was bringing me. Desirea is trouble, and the truth is, I don't know what to do with her. My first instinct is to throw her back on the streets where I found her."

"But you won't."

"Hell no! The lady's got my mind reeling. You saw the outfit she was wearing. I was near to salivating like a damn dog waiting for a big juicy steak." No, he would not set her out on the street. He wanted her company. He wanted her. *Blast it all!*

"All well and good if you do your drooling far off your premises where your servants aren't discussing it with others.

That could have been Mimi or Temple in the doorway. You're lucky I'm not a gossipmonger."

Ellis grimaced at the thought.

"You work so tirelessly to keep yourself out of the scandal sheets. I'd hate to see all your efforts wasted."

"It hasn't been entirely difficult, since the only dust I stir up is in Parliament, but you're right. I should move Miss Leighton away from the premises, from me. And as an aside, what do you know about the Leighton family surname in America?"

"I've never heard of them, except for Richard Leighton being knighted by King Edward the 11th eons ago. I believe the surname is of Scottish decent. But there aren't any Leightons I know of. Have you asked her about her family?"

"No, I haven't." And the reason he hadn't was because he didn't want to hear anything negative that would force him to send her away. If her past was tainted, she couldn't stay under his roof, and finding her lost in an alley did not tell a story of higher origin. He had felt compelled to help her, and so he had made her a maid to keep her close, but she wasn't a maid. She was far too pernickety and demanding with the other servants. "Mimi wants me to get rid of her."

"But you aren't going to," Remy stated. It wasn't a question.

"I'm afraid I cannot. I can't seem to help it. She needs me. I can sense it."

"And just perhaps you need her too?" asked Remy.

Ellis nodded. "Yes, perhaps."

"What are you going to do?" Remy questioned, crossing one leg over the other as if this was a group decision.

"I'm going to think on it. That's what I'm going to do. I'm not like you, Remy. I can't go off half-cocked and plunge forward without thinking. Risks like that start scandals."

"I like your imagery. Your problem is over-thinking everything. You're impossible. You need to learn to take some risks in life. What's the point to life if you stay sheltered behind safe walls and never take a chance? You need to learn to say yes to opportunities, my friend, because one day you may not have any more opportunities to say no to."

"And my maid is an opportunity?"

"Hell, no!" said Remy aghast. "You made her a servant in your household. She can never be your wife. Bloody hell. Could you imagine the scandal you'd cause if you wed one of your servants?" Remy laughed.

Ellis frowned. "I already admitted I erred in making her a servant. I should have realized immediately that she wasn't the subservient type. My mistake. But why the hell are you linking my new maid with marriage in the first place? I'd never marry her. I told you. I found her in the alley, for Christ's sake. Her manners are atrocious, her behavior defiant, and she knows the power her far-too-lovely body wields. All those things equal a lethal combination. She's a dangerous woman. No. I'd never marry a woman like Desirea Leighton."

"You can stop protesting. I think I understand your position." Remy came to his feet, giving Ellis a sly smile as if he knew something Ellis did not.

"And what do you think you have figured out?" The duke's hands clenched into fists. His friend was being most annoying, again.

"How knee-deep in scandal you'll soon be."

"Go home, Remy. I don't have time for this."

"You have nothing but time, Ellis." When Ellis cocked a questioning brow at him, Remy said, "You leave for your country estate soon. Isn't that what you told me? 'It needs a staff and fixing up,' you said." Remy roared with laughter. "Don't tell me you forgot about your trip out of town, and the reason you needed to hire more servants in the first place? That is the reason you hired Miss Leighton, wasn't it?"

"I didn't forget," Ellis retorted defensively. *Bloody hell!* He definitely forgot about his planned departure. He needed to fix the one and only scandal he had purposely caused: his ducal estate.

"And I hired her for a few reasons. Don't look at me like that." Ellis glowered at his friend. "Her safety and her need for shelter were the initial motivators."

"Yes. And you're also lying. You did forget your trip," replied Remy, his face crinkling around his eyes as he grinned in amusement. "Unbelievable. The look on your face says it all."

Ellis didn't care what his face was saying. He couldn't believe he actually forgot about restoring his estate to its former glory. "What am I going to do with her? I can't leave her here or Mimi will likely quit. She finds Desirea troublesome."

"I know what I would do," said Remy. "But I'm sure you'll find some dull way to deal with Miss Leighton. You will see her placed in a nunnery until your return, perhaps?"

Ellis didn't want to ask, because truthfully he knew the response he'd receive, but a part of him really needed to hear it. "And what would *you* do, Remy the Bold?"

"Why I'd take the lovely damsel with me, of course. Although *I* would have locked that study door the moment she walked in dressed like that." Remy gave another chuckle and turned to go. "Keep me informed of the particulars. I'm most curious to see how this turns out," he said over his shoulder as he walked out the door.

Ellis stared at the empty doorway. He did need to take at least one servant with him north. He'd need someone to organize the hiring of additional staff. And although he knew Desirea wasn't cut out to be a maid, she seemed to have no qualms with issuing orders. She could, in turn, be quite useful to him in putting his country estate to rights. And perhaps, just this once, the Duke of Lancaster would say "yes" to something he should say "no" to.

CHAPTER SIX

Two weeks later, Desirea finally found herself back in the study. She was dressed in a new gray uniform and sorting through the books again. Mimi had been keeping her busy in the kitchen, chopping vegetables and mixing dough for days on end, likely her punishment for taking the scissors to her uniform, she assumed. *My nails are ruined.*

Desirea had portrayed the perfect slacker today, which thankfully got her banned from the kitchen, at least temporarily. She was finishing with the last stack of books when the duke entered followed by three other gentlemen talking all at once. Over the last two weeks, she had only talked to the duke briefly, and that was only because he wished to criticize her work ethic and to remind her exactly why he hired her. It seemed Mimi complained about her often. *The tattletale.* Even though the duke disapproved of her lack of enthusiasm for cleaning, however, he still stared at her like he wanted to gobble her up. She saw his attraction to her as a positive sign.

She listened while she continued working, glad the duke had yet to notice her and send her from the room.

"As one of our leading patrons, Your Grace, we thought to let you decide the course we should take," said one man while doffing his cap and taking a seat.

"The Theatre Royal owes a great deal of its success to you, Your Grace," said a short balding man with, Desirea noticed, an ass-kissing smile, before taking a seat.

Although Desirea knew her moment of fame was at an end when she left her own century, she couldn't help the excitement filling her by their talk. To hear that the duke was part of the theater's success only proved how right she was in choosing this man for her. Andrew Lloyd Webber owned the theater on Drury Lane, Desirea thought excitedly. *At least he did in the twenty-first century.* Surely, if the duke was such a fan of the theater, that would mean he wouldn't judge her harshly or see her as a woman of loose morals when she told him that acting was how she made her living, once upon a time. Desirea knew actresses were seen as prostitutes of some sort in this day and age, which was absurd to say the least, but she willingly would admit that she didn't know much about 1817 actresses and their sexual habits.

Perhaps the duke wasn't as stuffy as he appeared. He saved innocent children and supported the theater. Desirea believed, in fact, that the duke was a wonderful man, inside and out, even if he was uppity. Desirea could be an uppity bitch without even trying, but how to get him to see that she was wonderful too?

"What do you have to say, Mr. Arnold. You're the manager?" asked the duke, moving around his desk to sit.

Mr. Arnold took a seat. "I've spoken with the committee, and they are in agreement in letting you decide. Naturally, I would like to do Shakespeare, since Kean excels when he plays Shylock."

"I agree," said the duke. "Then do *The Merchant of Venice* again. The seats always sell out for that play."

"True, Your Grace, but some say we need to do something new. Something more exciting," exclaimed Mr. Arnold.

"But we still wish to do Shakespeare," said the bald man.

Desirea felt her heart speed up when they started talking about Shakespeare. A Shakespeare montage she saw in New York came to mind and she stood up. There was no way she could remain quiet when the rush of excitement filled her. "I know," she said, walking closer to the men. "Why don't you do a show in three acts."

All the men turned her way, shock evident on their faces. Of course, they would be shocked. She was sure maids' never contributed to these types of conversations, but she was a Shakespearean expert and felt compelled to speak.

"We always do three acts, Miss."

"Miss Desirea Leighton," she said with a smile, although he hadn't really asked her name. "Of course you always have three acts, sir; but have you ever thought to represent a different play in each act?" They all continued to stare at her. She glanced at the duke to see his face redden. He seemed embarrassed to have his maid speaking to these gentlemen. Desirea ignored him. She would not be shushed. Her idea was far too good.

"Desirea, perhaps it's time for a break," Ellis said, frowning his disproval.

"I'm not done yet," she said, glaring back at him. She moved to center herself in front of his desk with her back to him so she could face the other gentlemen. "If I were you, gentlemen, I would do *The Merchant of Venice, As You Like It, and The Two Gentlemen from Verona.*"

"Oh, I see what you're saying, Miss Leighton," said the bald man.

"What a marvelous idea," said Mr. Arnold.

"Yes, the idea does have merit," exclaimed the third man. "Every one of those plays has the heroine dressed as a male for most of the scenes."

"Exactly," said Desirea, no longer able to contain her excitement. "You take the main focal point from each story, and that's the piece you play out on stage."

"It's brilliant, Miss Leighton," said Mr. Arnold, who then tried to look around her to seek approval from the duke. Desirea moved from where she had been blocking Ellis's view.

"Sorry," she said meekly. The duke said nothing, and so she wisely moved back to finish the books.

"Only you would have a maid on your staff who loves the theater, Your Grace. What say you to your maid's idea?"

Desirea tried to pretend like his opinion didn't matter and that she was no longer listening to the conversation, but she froze, awaiting his reply.

"I think," he said, glancing over at her with a look of amazement on his face, or perhaps it was irritation. She could not tell. "It is a splendid idea. I don't know why we never thought of it before."

Desirea fought back the urge to say it was because he never had such a brilliant maid before, but she thought it might be wiser if she didn't interfere further.

With the decision made, all the men stood with smiles and exchanged handshakes. None thanked her for her helpfulness.

"You'll be back for opening night, Your Grace?"

Back? Desirea wondered what they meant. Where was the duke going?

"I wouldn't miss it," replied the duke. The men then happily took their leave.

The room fell silent, and she could practically feel his stare. Her hands shook as she placed the last two books on the shelf. Perhaps she should apologize. "Your books are now alphabetized, Your Grace." He nodded. "Listen, I'm sorry if I spoke out of turn. I tend to get revved up when Shakespeare's mentioned."

"Have a seat, Desirea," he ordered, and she immediately moved to the chair in front of him and sat.

When he remained silent and only continued to stare at her as if puzzled, she said, "All right. Have at it." She tried to ready herself for the lecture he was sure to give her: making sure she knew her proper place and blah, blah, blah!

"You know a great deal about Shakespeare," he said in a snappish tone, like knowing the famous playwright was against the law.

"Yes, I do. I studied Shakespeare for many years."

"Where's your family from?"

Boy, he is certainly curious all of a sudden. "From America. Remember? I told you, the west coast."

"Yes, I recall your words. You come from a very uncivilized area. I find myself surprised by your education. "

"Are you?" she said just to be difficult.

"Impressed, may be a better word."

She beamed under his praise. "If you think that's impressive, you should see me on stage," she mumbled.

"What?"

"Oh, nothing. I thought you were going to go postal or something once everyone left."

"I'm sorry. Did you say 'go postal'? What does that mean? Why do you speak in such a manner? Why do you use words I've never heard before? Just why are you here, Miss Leighton?"

"You hired me as your maid, remember?" His face was reddening again. It seemed his temper was on the rise, which was silly since she did nothing to deserve his hostility.

"Yes, but you are *not* a maid," he said in an accusatory tone as if she was somehow playing him for a fool.

"There's no reason to get your panties in a bunch. So I know a lot about Shakespeare." She shrugged at the insignificance of it. "I know tons of things you don't."

"What did you say to me?" He stood with his hands planted on the desk and glared at her.

Ah, shit. I pissed him off royally now. Time to make her escape.

***

Ellis looked at the pretty lady in front of him. He was angrier than he had been in many years, perhaps angrier than he'd ever been. This lady insulted him and turned his head backward with her words. *"Tons?"* He'd never heard the expression used in such a manner, although he could deduce her meaning. And what the hell were "panties" and how did he have them bunched? He sighed loudly. "You have much explaining to do."

"I do?" she asked innocently.

"Indeed. I know you can read, Miss Leighton. Can you write as well?" *What is it with this woman?* Why did he find himself so impressed with her? Her knowledge of Shakespeare was a great surprise, and her idea for the play nothing short of creative brilliance. Her education was obviously thorough, which only confirmed his suspicions that there was more than met the eye to Miss Leighton, and there was certainly much to meet the eye about her too. She had charmed the pants of the committee members. *Hell, she could charm my pants off, which makes her dangerous.* Remy was right. He should have never made this lady his maid. *An educated maid: whoever heard of such a thing? Bloody hell, she is a complication I do not need.* Although she wouldn't be a complication if he wasn't so taken by her beauty, and now her intelligence too. He was even intrigued by her sharp tongue, which she never feared using in his presence. Ladies never spoke so openly to a duke, at least not to the Duke of Lancaster. He couldn't help being charmed. *This is terrible.*

"Of course I can write. What a dumb question."

He felt his face tighten as he looked at her. He was usually good at categorizing people, but he couldn't fit Desirea into any of the neat categories in his mind. She was unique, of that he was certain, but she had a viper's tongue. He wondered where she found the gall to use it with her betters. Stymied by her obvious insult, he cocked his head sideways. His questions were never frivolous, and yet she implied his question irrelevant. Nothing a duke said was irrelevant. *Why does this lady not know this? Do they teach such disrespect in America?*

"You can take that hurt expression off your face, Your Grace. I certainly didn't mean you were dumb, only your question. Re*lax*, already!" So she knew he found her comment insulting. She amazed him at every turn, amazed him at how attuned she was to his thoughts. But how utterly disrespectful it was for her to tell him to relax!

"That tears it!" He jumped up and slammed his hands down on his desk, and she leaned back from him in her chair. "Since you are so well educated, Miss Leighton. I'd like you to construct an essay."

"An essay? About Shakespeare?" she asked, her pretty face scrunched and her blue eyes searched his as if she was confused by his request.

"No!" he shouted, and she flinched. He took a deep breath, striving to reclaim his sanity, and sat back down. "I want you to write an essay about yourself, starting with your childhood and ending with how you came to be my maid."

"Well you know how that happened."

"Don't interrupt!"

"Yes, Your Grace. Sorry, Your Grace." She smiled but appeared only semi-contrite, which he somehow knew was all he'd get from her.

"I find myself exhausted by this conversation." She had his mind launching questions at him rapidly. He had *too* many questions when it came to her, because he was interested in this maid in a way he shouldn't be. He shook his head, trying to clear his troubled thoughts. "Since Parliament convenes in an hour, thankfully, I must go. You will retire to your room with ink and pen. I'd like a full accounting of your history to be on my desk first thing in the morning. Is this understood, Miss Leighton?"

"Yeah, of course. A report all about me. What fun," she said sarcastically.

"Go!" he shouted, his tolerance for her caustic tone at an end, but he could not help but smile when she stood with a screech and ran out of the room. *That should teach the lady to talk back to her betters.* He began to play back her odd vocabulary. Yeah: slang for yes, obviously. He'd solve the mystery of Miss Desirea Leighton and cure himself of his need to have her all at the same time. This was his hope. He wasn't certain how successful he'd be, however, for he couldn't seem to put the lady from his mind. And although she was attired appropriately, he could still picture her in the short hand-cut uniform that she had constructed just for him.

Her intelligence now merely fueled his ardor. The play she devised was sure to be a smashing success. He could not help but wonder if God was smiling down on him the day he put Desirea in his path or perhaps wanted to torture him by dangling something before him that he couldn't have. *Marry my maid. Ha! I'd be a laughing stock. A scandal of such a magnitude would tarnish the Lancaster name for generations to come. Damn it all, I should have never made her a servant.*

"Yes, but you did," said an irksome voice in his head.

With a heavy sigh, he stood and headed for the door of the house. He went off to parliament to do his civic duty, still unsure whether he should take the outspoken woman with him north.

***

Desirea went to her room as ordered to write an essay about herself, wondering what in the hell she'd write on the paper. If things worked out the way she dreamed they would, then eventually she would tell the duke all about where she came from, but now was not that time. Of course, she could always make up a bunch of stuff. But she didn't wish to fill Ellis's head with untruths about her, nor did she wish to deceive him in such a way.

"Where do you think you are going, Miss Leighton?" Mimi asked, her hands on her hips and a feather duster sticking out of one fist.

Desirea stopped with her foot on the bottom step of the stairway. She turned toward her warden. "To my room to write."

"You will do no such thing when there is work to be done. Now put those things down and hurry yourself into the dining room. There's silver to polish."

Desirea was about to pitch a fit with this woman for bossing her around for she was getting tired of it, but since nothing good could come from it, she didn't. In a huff, Desirea walked up to the lady and shoved the writing implements and vellum into her chest. "Here," she said. When Mimi took the stuff, Desirea twirled around and marched down the hall toward the kitchen instead of the dining room in order to get a drink first.

Walking into the kitchen, Desirea squealed with delight at seeing her friend from the twenty-first century standing in the kitchen with a big smile on her face. Overwhelmed that she had actually made a true friend, one who would seek her out, moved her nearly to tears. She pulled her from-the-future buddy into a tight hug.

"Desirea," London exclaimed happily, hugging her tightly. When they released each other, she said, "It's so good to see you. How are you?" London hugged her again and then took her hands. "I've missed you. Are you well?" Her friend then proceeded to give her uniform the once over as if to say, "What gives?"

"Dude, I seriously thought you'd seek me out sooner. What took you so frikken long?" Desirea teased, knowing finding her had to be difficult. "No, don't answer. I tried to visit the Back Room, but the asshole doorman said women weren't allowed and slammed the door in my face." Of course, it didn't help that she was wearing her maid uniform at the time, but she didn't have any other clothes to wear. The Regency dress for the photo-shoot had been soiled beyond repair by the end of that first night in this century. "Anyway, I heard all about your love affair with the Earl of Nankin." Desirea loved sneaking the paper to her room and reading the society columns, which seemed fitting because she planned to one day be amongst this glamorous set. "You're getting married, aren't you?"

London smiled at her and hugged her again before saying, "Actually, the wedding is off."

Desirea saw tears filling her only friend's eyes and immediately pulled her out of the kitchen, through the parlor, and out a set of French doors. It was a pleasant day, somewhere in the seventies, Desirea assumed, the sun was shining with few clouds in the sky. "Holy shit, girlfriend. Don't tell me the bastard dumped you?" Desirea felt a surge of anger for London's suffering. She led them to a vine-surrounded bench so they could sit. "Of course. That's why you came looking for me. I have to admit living in the nineteenth century is a trip. So do you want to return home now?"

"Do you?" her friend countered.

"Hell, no! I love it here. The men are far more intuitive to a real lady's needs." At least Desirea believed this to be true of her duke.

"But you were once a star, adored and revered by many fans," London told her as if Desirea was unaware of her own fame. Desirea shrugged. Her career no longer mattered in this world because true ladies didn't work and they did not become actresses. She had a new set of goals for this new life, and a career didn't factor into the equation. High society did like to entertain their guests with impromptu plays, however, which sounded ideal to Desirea and she knew she'd find herself on stage again. Likely, the stage would be set up in the duke's parlor, but that only made the vision perfect in her opinion.

"I was growing tired with my celebrity status," she said, thinking of all the crazy fans she had to fend off over her lifetime, especially psycho Marvin. Fame came with a heavy price.

"Oh," replied London, seemingly surprised by Desirea's confession.

"My current employment is part of the master plan," Desirea explained, not wanting her friend to worry about her. "I do have a plan, you know."

"And being a maid for one of the theater district's leading patrons is part of that plan?"

London was clever. Desirea liked that about her. "Yes, that too is part of the plan." Truthfully, the duke's affiliation with the theater was merely an added bonus, but she wanted

London to know she was on a path she had chosen. "I'd still like to be involved with the theater, only without all the hype. You know actresses were frowned upon in the past?" Desirea scowled for a moment and then cast London a sly smile.

"And just what is this *plan?*"

"It all revolves around the pompous, charming, and ever so gorgeous Duke of Lancaster. But that is a story for another time." London needed a friend right now. They could discuss Desirea's ideas for her future another time. "So, tell me. What the hell happened between you and Declan? Do we need to go twenty-first-century-woman on him and kick his ass or what?"

London burst into laughter and Desirea smiled. "It's not Declan's fault we're apart — it's mine."

"Got cold feet?"

"Not exactly. It seems..." London was too choked up to speak. Her eyes filled with tears and she cursed.

"There you go. Let it all out," Desirea coaxed. "Curse the clouds down if you must. Believe me, swearing definitely helps."

London gave her a wobbly smile. "Yes, well, Declan is an asshole. Nevertheless, it's my own fault for believing in a man again and thinking I'm worthy enough to hold his attention for longer than five minutes."

"Unfuckenbelievable! The bastard cheated on you?"

London nodded as tears fell down her cheeks. "I saw him kissing another woman," she all but sobbed and then cursed again.

Shushing her, Desirea pulled her into a hug and patted her back. "Do you want to go home?"

"We can't," replied London, wiping at her tears.

Desirea, though surprised by this news, was not unhappy about this discovery. She really had no desire to return to her old life, no matter how spoiled and adored she had once been. She liked it here. And she really liked the duke. She even liked her new friend. "Well, good then. So we stay. Although I didn't wish to return, I'm saddened such an endeavor isn't at all possible. I guess I always thought the option would be open to us, but most likely it is for the best. We belong here, you and I. I just know it." She wasn't too young to feel her soul belonged with the duke. She was drawn to him like some heroine in a sultry romance novel, trapped by his gaze, chained by his strength, bound by his love, and caged by his desire. She thought it was beyond weird, but she truly felt she belonged here with the Duke of Lancaster in 1817.

"Why do you think so?" London had asked an impossible question. Desirea had no idea why she felt so strongly about being here, but she did.

"Because here is where I found my one, true friend." Desirea squeezed her hand, wanting London to know she wasn't alone, that they were in this together.

"But in our own time you had thousands of adoring fans."

"Well, of course I did. I'm brilliantly talented." Desirea pretended her hair was down and she was flipping it off her shoulder in a haughty manner. London laughed, which had been Desirea's goal for her performance. "Anyway, friends and fans are not at all the same," said Desirea. She inhaled, catching the scent of honeysuckle in the air. She loved this garden with its old statues and hedged shrubs.

London nodded as if she understood. "So what is your plan, Desirea? Do you need anything from me?"

Desirea shrugged. "My plan is to start life anew, just like you. I view my time here as a do-over. This time I plan to make lasting friendships." She squeezed London's hand, letting her know she considered her one of them. "I search for love. It is far too lonely for a person when on top. No, this time I plan to take the man of my dreams with me wherever I go. I want shared dreams for the future. Of course, the man of my dreams isn't aware he's the man of my dreams yet, but he will learn soon enough. I'm needed here far more than I was needed in the twenty-first century. And, yes, I could use a few dresses if you have any to spare."

"Consider it done," said London.

"Miss Leighton," the butler interrupted in a disapproving voice from five feet away.

"Yes, Jeeves. What is it?" Desirea asked in her normal haughty manner, which the staff absolutely hated. She saw London hiding her grin when Jeeves stiffened.

"My name is Temple, Miss Leighton."

"I know, Jeeves. We've been through this already. Like I told you, Jeeves sounds more like a butler's name to me. Trust me, I know. You'll get used to it." She couldn't help teasing the man.

"I don't believe his lordship would approve of your visitors. Thursday is your day off, and Thursday is when you should visit with your friends and family."

Desirea rolled her eyes skyward at his bristling tone. Didn't these people realize she did not take kindly to orders? "I do not see the problem. I have one visitor, not twenty. What is it you need, Jeeves?"

"The Earl of Nankin is in the parlor. He's asked to see you." He looked at her accusingly, like having a member of high society visit her was a problem for him.

"He's most likely here for Miss Burton, but I thank you just the same for bringing me the message." She smiled at Temple because, if everything went according to plan, this man could one day be working for her. It was very difficult to curb her normal speech, which these people didn't seem to understand at all. When she became the duke's live-in guest and his girlfriend, she'd have need of the self-important butler and the rest of the people in this household.

Desirea stood, motioning London back into the house, but when they reached the parlor doors, her friend would move no further. Desirea opened the door to find the Earl of Nankin standing near the fireplace. Her eyes darted back and forth between him and London's odd expression. Then she grabbed

London's arm and pulled her into the room, closing the doors behind them.

"Lord Nankin," Desirea said in greeting.

He bowed. "Miss Desirea Leighton. A pleasure to see you again." Desirea noted how kindly he treated her regardless of her maid status.

"Why, of course it is, my lord. I'd ask you what prompted your sudden visit." She looked to London and back to him before saying, "But I already know. So," she said to London, "tell him."

"No, Desirea. I don't think…"

"Fine, then I will." Desirea stalked toward Declan, growing angrier on her friend's behalf with each step she took. She pointed an accusing finger at him. "You are a dog, Lord Nankin!"

"A dog?" he asked, looking very confused.

Desirea waved a furious hand at him. "Yes, a dog. D-O-G! Also known as a cad or a scoundrel, a betrayer of women, an immoral unto soulless monster! You broke my friend's heart."

Declan turned frantic eyes to her friend. "London," his voice croaked with his concern.

Desirea harrumphed, and then she stormed from the room, leaving them alone for exactly ten minutes before she sailed back into the room to check on her friend. "So how are things progressing?" She had to jump back as Declan made a sudden move toward London. She then stepped to the foyer, out of the way, as Declan stomped out of the room with an angry London thrown over his shoulder. She was going to protest him abusing her friend in such a manner, but the romantic rightness of the gesture left her silent. For the Earl of Nankin to make such a spectacle of himself had to mean he loved her friend a great deal. It was the type of grand gesture she hoped the duke would one day make for her.

"London will visit you after her sojourn in the country, Miss Leighton," Declan said as he brushed past her headed for the front door.

Although London seemed to wiggle in protest, she didn't ask for Desirea's assistance, which was a telling sign. "Enjoy your trip, girlfriend," said Desirea. "I'll see you soon." She waved from the front steps while she considered ways to make the duke fall in love with her.

CHAPTER SEVEN

Desirea, a take-out connoisseur in her own century, stood outside the study listening to Mimi complain about her ineptness in the kitchen. Desirea had no idea how to peel vegetables, only how to chop them. When she refused vegetable duty this morning, Mimi had marched off to tell on her. Desirea had followed a few steps behind her.

"I don't know where you found her, Your Grace, but Miss Leighton doesn't belong here! She's a terribly odd girl, and the worst maid I've ever seen. The staff can't make sense of her words, and I'm not referring to her accent but her vocabulary. I think she purposely goes out of her way to confuse us."

Desirea snickered upon hearing this. She did intentionally confuse them with her slang, but their expressions of utter confusion were priceless and it was hard to not have fun with them.

"I cannot explain Miss Leighton's eccentricities to you, Mimi, but rest assured, I will take care of the matter."

"I have worked for you for two decades, Your Grace, but if she stays…"

"I said, I'll handle it, Mimi. Do not threaten me."

"I'm terribly sorry, Your Grace. I never meant… It's just, this girl. She's most odd."

"So you've said," exclaimed the duke. "Return to your duties now, and send in Miss Leighton."

"Thank you, Your Grace."

Desirea jumped back from the door as Mimi came out with a smile on her face. When she saw Desirea, her smile widened even further. *The meddlesome woman.* "The duke wishes to see you," she said in a gloating manner as she walked off down the hall.

Desirea stared at the door. "Come in, Miss Leighton," intoned the duke. He'd obviously heard Mimi order her inside.

Desirea squared her shoulders, lifted her head, and flounced her hair with her fingers, arranging some over her left shoulder, before she walked in. She refused to wear a mobcap ever again. "You wished to see me, Your Grace," she said, all innocence in tone and expression.

"Close the door," he said. After doing so, Desirea stood before his desk. "Have a seat," he ordered.

With a huff, she sat in the chair across from his desk, fighting off the urge to make some sarcastic remark about his gruff demeanor. *People had better stop bossing me around.*

He sighed, and then he paused as if he didn't know where to begin with this lecture. After all, there had been so many lately, which Desirea was also finding tiring.

"I did not find your essay on my desk," he said, and he paused again. She assumed he was counting the days since his order to write her essay. "Five mornings ago," he finally said.

"I've been very busy, Your Grace. Mimi's a slave driver."

His eyes nearly bugged out of his head at her comment. "I'm told you are the worst maid ever."

"I have no doubt of that, Ellis, since I'm not a maid."

"Do not call me Ellis."

"Whatever. It's your name," she said with a sneer, rolling her eyes at his obstinate manner.

"That tears it!" he shouted, and she couldn't help but roll her eyes again, but when she did, his face turned red. He didn't seem amused by her sarcasm in the least. "I want you to go pack your bags."

"You're firing me?" screeched Desirea. She hadn't expected him to send her away. Her heart sank. Had she only imagined his interest in her? She really hadn't thought her maid duties all that important to him. She thought he returned her feelings and felt the strong pull between them.

"No, I'm not dismissing you. I find I have use of your authoritative nature. You, Miss Leighton, are going north to my estate in Durham County at Seaham. The estate's in disrepair and in dire need of staff. You will hire that staff and instruct them accordingly. Do you think you are up to this task, Miss Leighton?"

Relief filled her until she realized he might not be joining her on this trip. "I have any number of talents, Your Grace. Hiring you a staff will be a piece of cake." Surely this job would be a snap-of-the-finger kind and she'd be able to return to his side in a matter of days. She excelled at bossing people around. Of course, she realized, he could in fact be planning to go with her. Was it possible he was creating a job to get her out in the country with him and away from the city where there were too many prying eyes? "Is Mimi joining *us*. I will so miss her company," she said with a sweet smile, warming inside when she saw the corners of his kissable mouth lift in amusement.

"No. For now, it will only be the two of us," he said, his green gaze meeting hers.

Just the two of us? Her insides melted like butter. *Yes, yes, a thousand times yes.* He was giving her the opportunity to spend time alone with him. With his bedroom eyes focused on her, she felt like she could sing Pavarotti's opera *The Golden Girl of the West.* True, she wasn't a saloon owner and Ellis wasn't a bandit, but she was from the West and Ellis was dangerously handsome. The song would fit the powerful feelings she had for him and her soprano would blow the duke away. Her voice was her gift.

Ellis was like no other man she had ever met. He did not fall all over himself trying to talk to her, and he wasn't spouting nonsense about loving her or staring at her like some lovesick puppy. No, the Duke of Lancaster was above such nonsense, and although she sensed he was attracted to her, he remained cool — and always in complete control. She looked forward to the day when his unerring control snapped. He was perfect for her. Her heart raced and her hands shook as she got to her feet. She didn't want him to see how excited she was at the prospect of this trip. "I'm willing to help you anyway I can, Your Grace. When do we leave?"

"In the morning."

Ah, music to my ears. "Then I'll go pack," she said. Not able to hide her exhilaration, her smile wouldn't go away. He nodded and she went to leave, but she turned back at the door to witness him smiling at her. "Thank you, Your Grace," she said.

"For what?" he asked.

"For taking away my status as a maid. I really wasn't cut out for manual labor."

"Now wait, Miss Leighton…"

She hurriedly left, closing the door before he could finish his statement. She was sure he was going to inform her that she was still a member of his staff. *But I am not about to let that shit happen again.*

Reaching her room, she opened the empty leather trunk that served as a bench at the end of her tiny bed and began to organize all the lovely dresses her friend London had sent her. She laid them across the bed since this room didn't even have a closet. London had also told Desirea not to worry about her. It seemed her friend was able to mend fences with her fiancé, and Desirea was thrilled for her. Holding up a deep teal carriage dress, she smiled. Perhaps her new attire would finally show the duke how un-maid like she really was.

***

Desirea approached the waiting vehicle the next morning, which patiently sat out front of number twelve Parker Street. She looked up briefly at the overcast sky, hoping it would rain. She loved the rain. The door was open on the vehicle, and she was about to step inside when someone grasped her elbow. She moved back off the step to find herself being escorted to the back of the coach by the driver. "What the hell are you doing?" she spat, yanking her arm away from him.

"The tiger's perch is in the back."

"So?" said Desirea. She did not know what a tiger's perch was and did not care to know. She didn't care what animals rode on the back of the vehicle as long as she was tucked inside with Ellis.

"It's where you are to ride," he said with a smile she didn't like.

She followed his line of vision to find a small seat in the back of the vehicle. Desirea looked down at her lovely teal dress with its deeply cut bodice. Her breasts looked perfect. She looked fabulous in her Regency getup and was *not* riding in the tiger's perch. "I am not riding outside this vehicle, and you cannot make me." She knew she sounded childish, but she had taken a lot of time to ready herself for this trip, even going so far as to curl her hair before securing it on her head. This had not been an easy task because she first had to learn how to heat the curling tongs on coals before using them, but she had managed. She even succeeded in securing a small square teal hat with a white feather next to the nest of curls.

The driver sputtered in indignation at her adamant refusal, and she smiled at him sweetly. This caused him to smile back and hold eye contact for too long. The about face he made was so typical she almost laughed. Her voice was a gift, but her looks were her best weapon.

"Is there a problem?" the duke asked as he came down the sidewalk toward them. Desirea felt butterflies fill her stomach as she took in his glorious appearance. He was casually dressed in a loose fitting white shirt and buff colored breeches that were tucked in shiny black boots. He was smoking hot and so unbelievably intoxicating that Desirea had to repeat his question back to her in her mind.

"This idiot expects me to ride in the back!" she said, hoping he too felt outraged by this belittling. She noticed the duke's surprised expression regarding her outfit when he gave her the once over, stopping briefly at her chest before his arresting gaze finally met hers. Obviously he thought the only clothing she had was her uniform. *Hee-hee.*

"Does he?" asked the duke with a dimpled smile.

Could he be any better looking? "Yes, but I refused." She stared at him pointedly, daring him to make her ride on the back. She'd wrestle Ellis to the ground before she let go of her dignity and rode outside. *Ohhh, wrestling with Ellis… What a perfect idea.*

"Quentin, return to your place," ordered the duke.

"Yes, Your Grace," said the driver, backing away before returning to his seat at the front of the vehicle.

Desirea thought the duke would lecture her about her behavior now, but instead he held out his arm to her. "Miss Leighton," he said, and she wrapped her gloved fingers over his forearm and he assisted her into the comfortable carriage. She could smell his manly scent invade the space and inhaled deeply as she took her seat. He was giving in to her demand, but now her nervousness at being so close to him hit her. Great, she'd be a basket case by the time they reached their destination. Once the vehicle began to move through the loud and crowded streets, she asked, "How far to your estate in Seaham?"

"No more than a week's drive at most. If the weather allows and we keep a good clip, we'll make it there in four days."

Desirea began to feel lightheaded. She had thought this would be a few hours' journey, not days cooped up in a vehicle with the man of her dreams. She didn't know how she'd be able to ward off her attraction to him for that long. She didn't know how he'd respond if she jumped his bones on the way. *Perhaps I should have sat in the tiger's perch.*

She saw him smiling at her, and she had a feeling that he knew exactly what she was thinking. "I'm thinking I should have sat outside," she said with a nervous laugh.

"No worries, Desirea. We'll be fine."

When he said her name, her heart lifted with possibilities. "If you say so, Ellis." Perhaps he was finally feeling the unbreakable pull between them.

The feeling of destiny.

***

For the first two days of the trip, they talked about Shakespeare at length, even touching on Lord Byron, who used to write in Seaham and met his wife there. For the two days after that, they spoke of Ellis's family, his sister who lived in Scotland, and the loss of his parents when he was but a boy.

"I was with them when it happened," he said one late rainy afternoon. The rain fell around them in a hush, cocooning them inside the vehicle. It was cozy.

Desirea dipped sideways in her seat as the carriage shifted its way over a bridge. "Oh, my god! How terrible for you, Ellis." The smell of wet earth filled the interior, reminding Desirea of her own father, how they would sit together near the open garage door and watch the rain pound on the pavement. She had always felt soothed by a good storm. "You know, I lost my father when I was seventeen."

"Losing loved ones is never easy," he said, pulling his shirt out of the waistband of his pants.

No, it wasn't. She couldn't help but wonder if he was thinking of his wife, but when he lifted his arms and pulled the shirt over his head to expose his sculpted chest, she forgot her thoughts completely. Desirea stared transfixed.

What is he doing? She felt near to fainting. She could see his light chest hair and his sculpted pecs and... *Is it hot in here?* She was suddenly sweltering. She tried to play it cool, refusing to respond to his undressing.

"I find it wonderful that we both share a love for the theater." She tried to say this calmly, but she could hear the tremor in her voice.

He set his shirt beside him and Desirea fought to keep her mouth closed and not let it fall open like a panting hyena. Ellis had the build of a man who spent many days in the gym, which of course, he likely didn't, but his physique was beautiful. And he had a killer six-pack of abs that wouldn't quit.

"We do have that, I suppose," he said, turning so she could see a wicked scar that slashed across his shoulder blade.

"Was that from the carriage accident?"

"Yes. When we went into the ravine, the vehicle broke apart and I was punctured. By what, I am not sure. I remember my father grabbing my hand, begging me to survive, begging me to carry on the family name with dignity and honor." His eyes clenched shut as if he was warding off understandable tears. *What a tragedy to lose his parents in such a way.* Tears filled her eyes.

"You were lucky to have survived," she said. He jumped when she ran a finger over the puckered scar. When he turned back, he snatched up his shirt and pulled it over his head.

"There were many times I didn't feel lucky. I'm eternally grateful my older sister was staying with our grandmother at the time."

"Oh, you still have a grandparent?"

"Unfortunately, no. Grandma Bess passed on a year after my wife, but I was glad she was alive long enough to see me wed."

Ah, his deceased wife, my least favorite topic. "And your marriage, although a chosen course in your opinion, was it a happy marriage?" She dreaded the answer, but a wise woman would want to know this. She felt terrible that he suffered from losing the person he loved most in the world.

"According to society, we were the perfect couple."

"Huh," she said, fixing her gaze out the window. A "perfect couple" would be a hard act to follow. Not impossible, but a struggle, considering she spoke and acted differently from the people in this time. Not that she was anywhere near ready for marriage with anyone, but she certainly favored the idea of them being a couple.

Ellis tried to steer the conversation toward Desirea's past. He'd done this continually during the trip, but she always redirected the dialogue to something else. For the remainder of the trip, they spoke of his estate in Seaham and all the things needing to be done. By the way the duke spoke, Desirea expected to find a pile of rocks when they finally reached their destination. *Not that I care if we are here to polish a turd.* As long as they were alone, she didn't care if they slept in a cave. *Ooh! What an interesting idea.*

After leaving the last inn on this journey on their way north in the swaying vehicle, Ellis told her it wasn't much further now. Desirea couldn't have been more grateful. Jostled by a carriage for hours at a time became unnerving. and she fought the urge not to fidget obsessively. But she wouldn't have traded this trip for anything. She loved spending time with Ellis when he wasn't acting the powerful duke. And she had learned so much about him on the trip. They had even laughed together numerous times. A boyfriend with a sense of humor was a must in her book.

The bond between them grew stronger with every mile they traveled. They had become friends, which thrilled her to no end. This was why, when he asked her about her past again, she decided to tell him and trust in their new friendship. She assumed the worst thing he would think was that she was crazy. Although she knew her new friend London would validate her story, she thought it would be nice if Ellis took her at her word, no matter how unrealistic the truth sounded. With him, she felt a comfort she had never felt with anyone before. It was marvelous! She felt secure enough to open up to him.

"Well, as I said, I grew up on the west coast of America, in Malibu, California to be precise. My grandfather was a producer in what *we* call movies. Movies are like plays acted out in front of what *we* call a camera, and then movies are sent to televisions around the world. I've been told there are two to five TVs in every household. I guess that's probably accurate, but then, I had TVs in my bathrooms so I had more than the norm." She halted her discussion of TVs, realizing the subject was far too complicated to come up with a better explanation than this. But she knew she hadn't really explained a thing, since cameras and televisions weren't invented yet. He had no idea what she was talking about. She decided to finish her explanation and allow him to ask questions when she finished her recap of her life's story. "Due to my grandfather's connections, and tons of encouragement from my father, I ended up on a hit television show. I was educated on the set and I took some classes in college. When my acting career on the Disney channel came to a close, due to my advancing age, I decided to work on a singing career. I sang opera for a while in New York and then moved on to pop. I have two platinum albums. I was in London doing a photo-shoot for my new album." She stopped at this point, knowing she told him so many things that he likely would never really be able to picture any of this in his mind or even fathom how these things were possible. "Are you still with me?"

"I'm… I don't really know what to say. I'm afraid I didn't even understand much of what you said. Did you say you were an actress?"

"I did." *Of course, that resonated in his mind.* She prayed this wouldn't kill all the feelings she knew he had for her.

"And an opera singer?" he asked.

"Yes, and a pop star, which means I sang modern day songs that generally appeal to teenagers, kids between the ages of thirteen and nineteen."

"And why did you keep referring to 'we' as if Americans are another species?"

"Because *my* America and your America are very different."

"How so?"

"Because in my America… I mean… Ah, damn, this is harder than I thought. Let me ask you this, Ellis." He seemed to be allowing her the use of his name, which in her mind cemented the bond they had formed. "Do you believe in time travel?"

"To be honest, I've never given it any thought. You don't expect me to believe *you* traveled through time?"

Desirea was stuck. Now she didn't know what to say. Would he think her some kind of freak if she said yes? "Perhaps I should tell you what happened."

"I'm listening," he said with an amused smile, which told her that he thought she was making this story up to entertain him. *Great!*

"I arrived in London to do my photo-shoot at the Back Room Tavern."

"You mean the Back Room Gentlemen's Club? The club recently opened its doors."

"Yes. Well, when I was there, it was a tavern."

"But that's not possible, since I distinctly remember it being a coffee house."

"Are you going to let me tell my story?"

He grinned at her. "Yes, of course. Do continue."

"Anyway, I was unhappy with the shoot, so I went outside to call my agent. Except, while I was outside, I saw Marvin Travers, my stalker."

"Your what?"

"He is what *we* call a stalker. He follows me, ambushes me, has broken into my home, and has even tried to rape me, but he was unsuccessful."

"Where the hell is this man now?" he asked with tight fists. She smiled at his anger on her behalf. It was wonderful to feel safe. If only she would have met the powerful duke in the twenty-first century, perhaps Marvin wouldn't have been such a scary individual.

"Why?" she asked, curious to hear his response.

"Because I plan to see him no longer of this world." His taut face and clenched teeth showed his sincerity.

My hero. "I like you, Ellis." She smiled again. "But Marvin is no longer a concern for me, thank God."

"Is he dead, then?"

"No, just not of this time." She shrugged. "Once I saw him, I panicked and asked London Burton, my new friend, to assist me in hiding from my nemesis. She's such a nice woman. She agreed and hurried me back into the Back Room, where we hid ourselves in a closet. At least we thought it was a closet, until another door opened showing us a corridor. With Marvin yelling at me from inside the tavern, London and I decided to take our chances with the corridor and began to move through it. The tunnel was dark, smelly, and scary. While we were moving sideways through the corridor, the beams above began to creak and some kind of poisonous smoke filled the tunnel, nearly choking us to death. Then the wind picked up and began to throw us forward. When it finally calmed, we were at the opposite end of this scary tunnel facing a similar door to the one we originally entered."

"And where did this tunnel lead you?"

"To the Back Room Gentlemen's Club, but not the tavern of 2011. It seems we somehow traveled through time and found ourselves here, in your time."

He began to laugh hysterically, and she smiled at his amusement, but she continued to stare at him stonily. He immediately sobered. "So you are telling me you traveled back in time nearly 200 years?" His tone told her he did not believe this possible.

"Yes, and I'm told, returning isn't possible. It seems I'm stuck here."

"Who told you that you couldn't return? A powerful wizard?"

"Ha-ha, Ellis. No, my friend London. She's engaged to the Earl of Nankin. Do you know him?"

"We've met," he said. He seemed shocked by her story, but then she knew he would be. It still shocked her too.

"And does the earl know his soon-to-be bride is a time traveler?"

Desirea laughed. "Yes, I believe she told him. But we aren't time travelers, Ellis. What happened was a fluke. Time travel isn't possible in my time either. Some scientific people from my time believe it's possible to travel through time, but they haven't figured out how to do it. What happened was a bizarre twist of fate, one I'm happy about."

"You're happy about traveling back in time and away from your family and friends?" He ran a hand over his face as if overwhelmed by her story. She couldn't blame him.

"I didn't have either of those things any longer, and so it wasn't a great hardship. Plus, it got me away from fans like Marvin."

"Fans? I assume you don't mean the hand-painted fans ladies like to dangle from their wrists?"

"No, totally different. See, I was a celebrity, a star of renown. I was a bit like yourself, but my title was pop star, not duke. People followed me everywhere, usually to get my autograph, that's my signature. Or they liked to have their picture taken with me. Young girls often cried in excitement from seeing me. And men… Well, men seem to come apart at the seams by my mere presence."

"And you didn't care for all this adoration?"

She shrugged. "In the beginning, it was fun, but I grew to hate all the attention."

"So you're happy then, in my time?"

"At the moment, I'm extremely happy."

"And why is that?"

"Because I found you and my friend London in my travels," she said, not willing to explain her feelings further. His head fell back against his seat. She asked, "Are you okay?"

"Does 'okay' mean all right?" he asked.

She smiled. "Yes, it does."

"Then you'll have to give me a moment, Desirea. I'm afraid my head is spinning from all you told me."

Desirea nodded and fell silent. She knew it was a lot to absorb. She stared out the window, watching the scenery fly by and listening to the rushing fall of rain as it hit the ground. The English countryside was breathtaking, but she had trouble focusing on anything other than Ellis sitting across from her.

CHAPTER EIGHT

The Duke of Lancaster didn't know what to think. What Desirea told him was so out of the realm of normal thought, like saying that fairies, trolls, and other mythical creatures were real. But from the future? Could this be possible? Was she playing a game of some sort with him? And if so, why? And why involve the Earl of Nankin's future bride. Her story of being educated near America's western edge just didn't add up in his mind, for that land was barely civilized, indeed filled with Indians to his knowledge, whereas Desirea seemed quite cultured, albeit in a very strange way.

Although time travel was not even in the realm of his thinking when he tried to explain Desirea's behavior and vocabulary this past couple of months, the possibility did answer some of the questions that filled his mind.

He would have thought her friendship with the Earl of Nankin's fiancée untrue if it wasn't for the fact that Temple had told him of her lofty visitors. *Whoever heard of a maid receiving a visit from an earl?* He was surprised to find Desirea had such a friend, and then again, he wasn't so surprised for the lady confounded him. So, aside from sex, what was she after, and how would this unbelievable tale help her achieve her ends?

Or was it a tale? The from-the-future story helps to explain Desirea's eccentricities, certainly, but... Oh, bloody hell! There are so many questions.

Ellis had thought to dismiss Desirea after receiving so many complaints from his staff, but for some reason, a reason he didn't wish to examine too closely, he didn't. Instead, his brilliant idea was to bring her north.

Alone.

With him.

Perhaps it wasn't a well-thought out plan, but after his friend Remy accused him of over-thinking things, he thought to do what his heart told him to. But after hearing Desirea's story, he was unsure of the wisdom of this decision. For a man who tried to live the life of a quiet duke, untarnished by society's viciousness and unblemished by scandal, he had a feeling he brought the worst kind of scandal upon him when he befriended the captivating woman across from him. *And she is captivating.* He couldn't look at her without wanting to touch her. But she was a woman from the future, and an actress and a singer. *Good Lord, what kind of trouble have I brought upon myself by taking such a creature into my household?*

"You're very quiet, Ellis," Desirea finally commented. He could see concern on her face.

"Sorry," was all he could think to say.

"That's all right. I understand. It's much to absorb. Indeed, it's hard to fathom."

"And yet you've seem to have adjusted well enough." He admired her resolve and her unfettered nature. She did not seem bothered by her trip through time, and in fact, she appeared happily resigned to her fate.

"Oh, don't let my smooth veneer fool you," she said. "Your reaction has my body shaking. I know how you like to live an orderly no-surprises kind of life. I'm smart enough to realize I represent trouble for you, but I want you to know I wouldn't do anything to cause people to talk negatively about you."

She is intuitive. "Sometimes these things cannot be helped, Desirea. You can't stop people from speaking their minds. Or can you?" He gave her a crooked grin, teasing her.

"I wish I could. But no, I'm afraid I don't have any special powers since I left my magic wand in the twenty-first century." He stared at her, perplexed, and she laughed. "I'm teasing, Ellis. There are no magic wands in my time either."

"But the twenty-first century is very different from the world you now find yourself in?" he asked, crossing his arms over his chest. A slight breeze came through the window, stirring the air and bringing him a whiff of her wonderful flowery scent. Desirea affected him in a way he had never thought possible, filling him with longing, with yearning need; and the thought of her not being in his life filled him with sadness. *What is this madness?*

"Definitely different," she said.

"Tell me about the twenty-first century. What's different?" He noticed her eyes widen at his request and he laughed. "That many changes, eh?"

"So many, it's hard to know where to begin." She laughed. "I certainly understand your curiosity though, because I'm just as curious about your time."

"I'll tell you whatever you wish to know," he promised.

"Then I shall begin by telling you about transportation, about how I traveled to London in an airplane." She adjusted her seat as if she was preparing to amaze him with knowledge from the modern world.

He nodded and smiled his encouragement for her to continue. He was ready to be amazed. He didn't know if what she told him was true, but finding out as much as he could from her may help him with conclusions regarding her sanity. Admittedly, he was very curious about the woman who stirred his ardor back to life. He crossed his arms over his chest and listened to her singsong voice as she described these things called airplanes, which she claimed flew through the sky.

After two hours of dialogue, he no longer doubted her sanity and knew she was being truthful. The things she told him were too spectacular not to be real. Ellis sat back, flummoxed, when she finished telling him about television and radio. Everything she had told him about was a marvel, and he was not only amazed but strangely proud of the human race. She even told him how people landed on the moon and about space stations. *Unbelievable!* He shook his head in awe, focusing his questions to learn more about this unique woman. "So you sing."

"Yes, but my occupation is revered in my time. Women are not looked down upon because of their talents. In my time, women can vote, make their own income, and raise their own families, if they wish. These independent women are not viewed as loose women, but are in fact often emulated by their fans."

She defended her occupation most vehemently, but still, he could not see her view, likely because he didn't share her view. She was an actress and a singer and she probably excelled at both. Although her previous occupation didn't concern him much, it would certainly alter the way people viewed her in this time. Whether she deemed that acceptable or not, didn't really matter. Society *would* view her harshly. Women voting seemed an odd notion, but he could tell she'd defend her rights if he questioned her further about it. So he said, "Sing for me, Desirea." Now that he knew she hid such a talent, he was very eager to hear her sing.

"All right," she said with a heart-stopping smile and her blue eyes sparkling. "Pop or opera?"

"Pop, I think, since I've never heard it before." This lovely woman was teaching him things he couldn't even imagine. He was going to ask her some questions regarding world history and other matters of great importance, but he found he wanted to hear her sing more than he wanted to learn about the future of his country. She claimed she traveled to London, England, and so, obviously, his country was still a profitable, thriving nation in the twenty-first century.

And then she began to sing a song she titled "Come Fly with Me," and it was moving, uplifting, and sad. But she sang the song with true feeling, as if the words poured from her soul, her voice hypnotic, mesmerizing. And he stared, not able to help himself. She had the voice of an angel. He'd never heard a prettier sound in his life. Like a siren's call, his body stirred to life, but hopefully this particular siren wouldn't lead to his destruction. She finished the song with tears in her eyes.

She swiped a tear from her cheek. "That's a number one hit. I get emotional when I sing it because I wrote it after I lost my father to cancer, a disease that kills many."

"It was exceptional, Desirea. You sing like an angel." Her smile lit up so big at his compliment that he fought the urge to lean over and… *The hell with it. Enough thinking.* Ellis leaned over and placed a soft kiss on her lovely pink lips.

When he leaned back, she looked at him with her head at an angle and a questioning look on her face. "What was that for?"

"It was a token of my admiration. You are a gift to the world, Desirea."

She blushed. "I do believe that is the nicest compliment I've ever received."

"You do not only yourself but the world a disservice if you take yourself from the stage," he said, and he meant every word. Although there couldn't be anything between them aside, from friendship, and he knew that there was no place for her by his side, her calling was obviously to entertain. There was no reason she couldn't live like a queen because of her talent.

"I'm not a woman of loose morals, Ellis, and I absolutely refuse to be viewed as one," she huffed, crossing her arms over her chest in a defiant manner.

"Well, you sure as hell can't be a maid."

"I told you I wasn't a maid!"

"Then why did you allow me to make you one?" he asked, aghast.

"Well, at first I didn't believe that was the reason I was going home with you," she pointed out.

He knew well why she agreed to join him that night. Their attraction to each other was palpable; there was no denying it. Nevertheless, he let her believe whatever she wanted because making her his maid had been his objective. *Not your only objective,* said the voice in his head, but he ignored it. This beauty had stirred his dead heart back to life that night he found her, and he wasn't willing to let her go. It was really that simple. "Why don't you explain to me how you saw that night progressing?"

"Ellis, I have explained a great deal to you already. I'm tired and my body hurts from sitting for hours on end."

He realized how difficult it might be for her to be sitting so long when she was likely used to speeding around in those automobiles she described. "I don't wish to see you wasting your time and talent by being my…" She interrupted him before he could say "maid." He thought she did it on purpose. She seemed to find distaste with the title, and now he understood why. She was used to having maids, not being one.

"It's my talent to waste," she said in a haughty tone he'd heard described by Mimi, one he rarely witnessed. She usually dished out defiance to him, but he found her superior manner impressive. A queen could not have done better. Desirea had determination, which was probably another reason for her fame and success.

He knew he had angered her, and so he fell silent until they pulled down the estate's drive. He had a feeling he did not want to see Desirea in a full temper. *Damn, but she is so beautiful. It is no wonder men fell all over themselves for her.* "We're here." He laughed when she stuck nearly half her body out the window to look. Luckily the rain had stopped or she would have soaked herself.

"Holy sheep shit!" she exclaimed.

"The sheep were sold some time ago, Desirea." She had a penchant for swearing that he couldn't help but find amusing.

She laughed at him and threw her arms wide toward his neglected estate. "It's a castle, Ellis. You never said you owned a castle." Awe laced her voice and he chuckled.

"Don't get so excited, future girl. You haven't seen the inside yet."

"Oh, I'm sure it won't disappoint. It's a castle."

"No castles where you're from?" Her excitement was palpable.

"Oh, there are castles, but they are called mansions and don't have turrets like yours, nor do they have a great deal of history. How old is your castle?"

"It dates back to the early 1600s." He tried not to groan at the sight of the landscape. The garden was so weed-choked it would have to be dug up and replanted. He knew things had fallen into a state of disrepair, but he'd been far too busy with political matters after the war to see to matters here. His estate had suffered when he purposely left it vacant for nearly three years. *Kind of like your love life.* He nearly scoffed at his inner voice.

"Wow! Is that the ocean?" Desirea asked, poking her head out the opposite window.

"It's the North Sea," he said, completely amused by her obvious excitement.

"Oh, smell the salty air. It's fabulous. Can you see the water from the turrets?"

"Yes, and from the master's chambers," he added, inhaling the sea air and remembering how much he used to enjoy winter at the castle. Until their arrival, he hadn't realized how much he missed the place.

"It's sweet!" she said.

"Pardon?" He couldn't help but laugh as a blush filled her face.

"This place is beautiful," she said, and he thought how wonderful it was to have this woman all to himself. Perhaps bringing her along wasn't such a mistake after all. He hadn't felt this lighthearted in years. And she was certainly interesting. He'd never tire of listening to her stories. The future fascinated him. She fascinated him. Instead of looking at the estate as a huge chore, he was starting to view this renovation project with great enthusiasm. With Desirea assisting him, he might even find some fun in the work. He decided that he'd merely try to view her as another sister, which seemed simple enough. As long as he kept his hands to himself and his wicked thoughts in his head, all would be well.

When the vehicle stopped, Quentin opened the door and Ellis assisted Desirea to the ground and up the walkway leading to the solid wood entry. Her head nearly spun in circles on her neck as she looked around, amazement written on her lovely face. Resisting her was going to take much control on his part.

The wooden door creaked on its exposed black triangle hinges when it swung open, and the smell of vacancy and mold smacked them in the face. Desirea's nose wrinkled in distaste and Ellis wanted to laugh. "I told you there was much work to be done."

"Airing out the place should be our first priority," said Desirea as she stepped into the large stone entryway.

"Yes, well, we need a staff first," he said, and she turned to look at him.

"You're kidding, right? I'm sure we can handle opening a few doors and windows, Ellis."

"All right," he said, feeling some shame at his need for servants. As a duke, he'd never spent much time alone. There was always a servant nearby to cater to him. It suddenly seemed sad to say that he'd never opened a window in his life, never done any menial chores, but he was willing to do so if it made Desirea happy. He felt a need to show her she belonged in this time, even if it wasn't with him. And even if their time together was short… Well, perhaps their time together would not be too short since the neglected castle needed plenty of work. *Months of work, actually.* He smiled at this thought.

He watched her turn in circles when she reached the great room, and then he laughed as she dashed across the room to stand in the stone fireplace.

"Wow. I can fit my entire body inside your fireplace, Ellis."

He smiled at her obvious joy. "So it seems. I can't say I've ever stood in there."

"Not even as a child?" she asked in surprise.

He was reminded of how quickly he had tried to grow up and become the man his sister and grandmother needed him to be. "Future dukes do not behave in such a manner," he said with a smile, reminded of the common phrase he heard throughout his childhood.

"So you weren't allowed to act like a child even when you were one?"

He was astonished by how in-tune she seemed to be with him. "It wasn't a great hardship," he said with a smile, but he could tell she was saddened by his words.

"I grew up a bit quickly myself," she admitted. She exited the fireplace knocking spider webs off her navy blue carriage dress. She was completely unalarmed by the webs. He should have known a woman like Desirea wouldn't fear a silly spider. His sister would have been screaming hysterically. "What are we doing first?"

"I thought we should find us both a clean, semi-decent bedchamber and ready them first. We will need a place to sleep."

"And you don't wish to sleep together?" she asked with a coy smile that had him clenching his hands. Her invitation went straight to his cock. Did she not realize what such words did to him? He studied her and couldn't help but smile. *She taunts me on purpose, the minx!*

"I'm teasing, Ellis. You are not at all ready for me."

Now she is challenging me? Just what will they teach women in the twenty-first century? He said nothing to her comment, since he didn't know how to respond. If asked right this moment to take her, he had no idea if he could say anything but "yes." Desirea walked to the sofa that was draped with a Holland cover.

"May I?" she asked, her hands gripping the linen sheet.

"By all means," he said, and she yanked the cloth, revealing the dark sofa.

"Oh, comfy," she said, throwing herself on the sofa. "This is the biggest great room I've ever seen."

"It used to serve as the main dining hall, complete with long trestle tables and rushes on the floor."

"How cool."

"Pardon?"

She smiled and said, "Interesting."

"Ah, I concur."

"You've owned this place a long time?" She took her gloves off and set them on the sofa arm above her head. She seemed utterly carefree and relaxed in his company, which he found both disconcerting and disarming. He wasn't used to it, aside from when with his sister. People usually remained either stuffy or quiet around him. Most people feared bringing his displeasure, which was silly since he strived to be pleasant to everyone. But from the moment their conversation began in the carriage, they really never stopped talking. Although he did notice that even silences felt comfortable between them. He genuinely liked her. He never had a woman as a friend before. It was nice.

"Since my birth," he replied.

"How old are you, Ellis?"

"Twenty-five. And you?"

"Twenty and a half."

"And a half?" He laughed.

She laughed with him. "Yes, I turn twenty-one in six months, which is where the half comes in. I'll be the legal drinking age soon, so watch out."

"Drinking age?" he asked.

"Oh, you probably don't have that here. How disappointing." She scrunched her face. "It's a monumental birthday in my time, just like sixteen and eighteen."

He moved closer to her and she pulled her legs up beneath her so he could sit. "Care to explain," he asked, sitting next to her.

"Sure." She kicked her legs up and placed her calves across his lap in a relaxed manner. "When you turn sixteen, you get a driver's license and you're allowed to drive those cars I told you about. When you turn eighteen, you can vote and you're considered an adult. And when you turn twenty-one, you are allowed to legally drink alcoholic beverages."

"So they are milestones."

"Yes, I guess they are."

"Are there other monumental birthdays?" he asked, his curiosity piqued yet once again.

"Nope, that's it. Just the three. Unless you count when you become a teen at the age of thirteen, but no special privileges come with that age."

"Fascinating," he said, and she shrugged.

She was staring at a collection of dusty medieval weapons hung from hooks along one wall. "Those look wicked."

"Yes," he agreed, looking at a spiked mace and a battered ax. "What kinds of weapons do they have in your time?"

"We still have guns, but they are more modern than that old pistol on the wall. They can shoot many bullets in a row without reloading. We have bombs, tanks, fighter jets, and nuclear weapons, which are capable of blowing countries off the map. Weaponry has come a long way."

Blowing countries off the map? Unbelievable! He was shocked the modern world was capable of such destruction.

"You're speechless?" she teased.

"Astounded is a better world. It's hard to imagine this time you are from. Is it safe?"

"It's not safe in all countries, but in America and England, the people are relatively safe. We still have our share of psychos. Marvin being my very own. The economy is in the crapper all over the world and people are having difficulty finding work." She blinked as if ridding her mind of such thoughts, since they were no longer relevant.

"I like talking with you, Desirea."

She sat up and patted his hand. "Of course you do, Ellis. Everyone does."

Ellis also liked the sarcastic edge in her personality and found her utterly amusing. "I'm sure they do," he said, fighting the urge to lean over and kiss her smiling mouth again. *Like one would kiss a sister, he reminded himself.*

"So, where to begin in this cleaning we have to do? I guess I'll go find myself a room and see what shape the beds are in. Care to go test beds with me, Ellis?" she asked with a wily smile.

Ellis tried hard not to picture himself testing beds with Desirea. "I'll go see what shape the master bedroom is in," he said with a calmness he didn't feel. "Come. I'll show you the way to the sleeping chambers."

As she swung her legs off his lap, he could see she was excited about exploring his house, and this thrilled him. She took his arm and he escorted her up the wooden steps, noticing how they needed to be re-stained and how a couple of the boards were loose. Tomorrow, he and Desirea would have to make a list of what needed fixing in each room. He found himself looking forward to her contemporary ideas and thoughts as they made their list.

At the top of the landing, Desirea let go of his arm and began to open doors with a joyful flourish. He laughed. "I'm going to go look in my chambers," he said. "Let me know when you've made your decision."

"I will," she replied before walking into another room. He moved toward the end of the hall to the master suite, crossing over the threshold with a groan. One of the windows had shattered and leaves, sticks, and dead bugs littered the floor. He picked up a large rock, assuming it the culprit for the broken window. Probably some young boys who wanted to hear the sound of breaking glass. Suddenly, Desirea's scream rent the air and he dropped the rock, running out of his room.

CHAPTER NINE

Desirea screamed like a madwoman as she ran into the hall, shaking her head and smacking at the unseen bird. "Get it out!" she yelled, her arms waving frantically as she ran toward Ellis.

"What is it?" he asked, darting to her side and smacking at her head.

"A demented pigeon. He's stuck in my hair. Oh Lord, Ellis. Get it off me! He's tearing my hair out! Ow! Fu…udge!"

"Stop moving!" he shouted, his hands closing in on the bird, which squawked, digging its claws deeper into her scalp and causing her to scream and squirm.

Desirea tried to hold still, but this was impossible when being ripped bald. "Damn it, Ellis! Just grab the frikken thing!" Tears rolled down her cheeks, and then suddenly the bird loosened its grip and flew off down the hall into Ellis's room.

Desirea stood dazed, her hands searching her hair for the damage the damn bird had caused. She held a clump of blond in her hand. "Blasted, stupid bird!" She began to laugh hysterically, thinking of what an idiot she had just looked like in front of her future boyfriend. *Way to impress.*

"I've never seen a bird do that before," said Ellis, seemingly shocked. "You know you really shouldn't be laughing. I can see your scalp." Ellis grasped the sides of her face and tilted her head to assess the damage. He laughed with his own share of mirth, which quickly silenced her.

"Seriously?" she screeched.

"No, I'm only bamming you, Desirea." This time she knew the meaning of the word.

She laughed, smacking his hands away. Calming her laughter, she said, "I told you. The bird was demented." Her hands still trembled from her battle with the creature, and she gave them a shake in an effort to stop them. Ellis noticed, and she suddenly found herself pulled into his warm muscular body. Without hesitation, Desirea willingly melded her front to his.

"Thank you," she said as he rubbed her back, trying to calm her, which wasn't necessary. But it felt so good being in his arms, as if she always belonged there. *He smells awesome, woodsy, musky, and male.* She rested her head on his chest, listening to the steady, calming beat of his heart. She knew she should probably pull back for she was calmer now, but she didn't want to leave his comforting embrace. He'd make the best boyfriend.

"Are you all right?"

She smiled, lifting her head to look into his deep green eyes. She could drown in those pools of green.

"Desirea?" he asked in a whisper.

"Yes?" she murmured back.

He leaned his head toward her and words were no longer necessary as his lips met hers. The kiss was hot. There was no other word to describe it. Her insides seemed to melt, her body quivered, and her hips moved instinctively toward his. His hands roamed her body, skimming over her sides, searing through her clothing as they explored her body and she explored the contours of his. She wanted this man more than she ever wanted anything in her life. Why was this? What was this time period doing to her?

Hesitantly, his tongue met hers and they moaned in unison while they experimented with each other, learning each other. His hands were busy molding her breasts, but the sound of the bird hitting a window stopped Ellis and he stepped back.

"I think the bird is trying to find a way out of your room," Desirea said, feeling suddenly shy. She'd never been moved more by a simple kiss, but then a kiss by Ellis was anything but simple.

"Desirea, I'm sorry. I don't know why I keep kissing you. It's inexcusable."

"It's lust, Ellis. Nothing to be ashamed about," she told him, and she walked off down the hall toward his room, trying like mad to calm her racing heart and her hunger for him. She reached the spacious room overlooking the sea and smiled at the spectacular view. Then she watched the stupid bird fly out a broken window as she took in the sea-scented breeze rushing into the room.

"About this lust," Ellis said, entering the room behind her.

She turned to face him. "Ellis, when two people are attracted to each other like we are, then lust is as natural as breathing. Do not torture yourself for giving into temptation and kissing me." She smiled, and then said saucily, "I'm hard to resist."

"I'm aware of the threat you make to my sanity, but still, there's no excuse for my actions." He seemed appalled by his behavior.

Jeez-Louise, he is such a prude. "Ellis, you are a man, are you not?" She walked by him with a seductive sway of her hips, slowing to drag her finger across his chest as she walked to the door. "Then act like one," she said haughtily, not looking back to see his response. The duke was a man used to being in total control over everyone and everything, she knew that well enough. *It is time for a lady to take some control over this man.* Desirea thought herself a perfect candidate for the job.

She knew he hadn't followed her, but his hard-to-get routine only made the game more challenging and the reward even greater. After all, she had wanted him to make capturing his heart difficult, and seems she had gotten her wish.

With a sigh, she tried the first door next to his. The walls of this spacious room used to be yellow but now merely looked dirty. The walls that weren't stone throughout the entire place would need to be repainted. She moved toward the large bed and pulled off the dustsheet. The bed was beautiful, dark wood with pineapple end posts and a brown leather headboard. The bed was stripped of all its linens, and she opened the dust-covered trunk at the bottom of the bed to find a quilted burgundy coverlet with pillows. Nodding in approval, she stepped to the window and looked out. The view wasn't as great as it was in the master suite, but she could see a small part of the sea and a great deal of an overgrown statue garden. *Cool.*

She walked inside the closet and was happy with the shelving and hooks. The closet was quite large and more than enough room for her clothes. Finding another door, she opened it to find a blue tiled bathing chamber, complete with copper tub and washstand. There was even some plumbing going to the tub, and the water closet housing the toilet was made to remove the waste from the house, which was certainly better than doing her business in a chamber pot. This room was hundreds of steps above the attic room she'd been assigned before.

Like the rest of the house, however, everything was coated with dust. A few of the tiles had fallen from one of the walls in the bathroom and the broken pieces lay scattered on the floor. Stepping out of the area, she walked back into the room and opened the last door.

She found herself standing in Ellis's room and laughed. "Well, looky here. Our rooms are connected."

"Probably because that room is intended for my wife." He pulled the linen off his bed, exposing a dark square wooden headboard. The wood was weathered enough to look like it was salvaged from a Viking ship.

"That's silly. Why wouldn't you share the same room with your wife?"

"That's not how it's done, Desirea," he said in a lilting voice, seemingly finding amusement as he enlightened her.

"As I said, silly. I, for one, would want the heat of my husband to keep me warm and make me feel safe at night."

"Do you not feel safe when you sleep?" he asked, his gaze meeting hers.

Marvin's attack slipped into her mind. She had tried so hard to push away the terror she felt when he tried to rape her, but when it was dark and she was alone in her bed, it was sometimes difficult. She hated Marvin for making her feel unsafe. Although once she realized she had crossed into another century, those fears had diminished. She looked up to find Ellis waiting for her answer. "Uh, no, or at least, *sometimes* I feel safe. I certainly feel safer in your time period than I ever did in mine."

"You are safe with me, Desirea. This I promise you."

"And I thank you, Ellis." She smiled.

"About that," he said.

"About what?" she asked, frowning at his lecturing tone.

"About you calling me Ellis."

"Oh for heaven sakes, not this again."

"Miss Leighton," he said, and she huffed in irritation. "We are to be working together in this house and living in close proximity, and I have neighbors to consider. Neighbors I have known my entire life who will feel obligated to visit here once they learn I'm in residence."

"No, I will not be your maid again." She crossed her arms over her chest, adamant about this. He already thought her beneath him. Her servant status had to go.

He laughed. "Somehow I knew you were going to say that. Fine. Not a maid. Then, what?"

"How about a visiting cousin or something?" she suggested hopefully.

"I don't have any," he pointed out.

"And I assume these guests will know your sister?"

He laughed. "For longer than they've known me."

"Could I be an interior decorator?"

"Hmm," he said, scratching his chin. "If I understand your meaning correctly, are you any good at it? I mean, my visitors may ask for your expert opinion."

"Ellis, I'm an actress. There's no role I can't play."

"A famous decorator from America?"

"That sounds off," she said.

His brow wrinkled in contemplation. "It does, doesn't it?"

"I could practice my French accent," she said.

He shook his head no. "How's your cooking?"

She laughed hysterically at this. "I can make toast and nothing else, but besides, I don't wish to hide away in the kitchen when you have company."

"Of course you wouldn't," he said caustically, and she smiled.

"How about…" She paused. There was another option, although he would think it crazy, but the thought would not go away. Knowing she'd blush after her boldness, she blurted out, "I could play your lover. I know I'd excel at that role." She didn't think the word girlfriend existed in this time.

Ellis shut his eyes and she watched his body stiffen. The man was physically fighting his desire for her. *It is a battle he will lose.* When he opened his eyes again, she had moved forward and cupped his face with her palm. She loved the feel of his stubble on his cheek. His gaze met hers and he visibly trembled. Desirea tried to hold his steady stare. Knowing his desire for her was as strong as hers was for him caused her to have to fight back a smile.

"I can't marry you, Desirea."

She dropped her hand from his face and leapt away as if burned. *What did he say?* "Whoa, back up the truck. Who said anything about marriage? Kind of rushing things, don't you think?" *Shit, shit, shit*! She was speaking too contemporary. He likely didn't understand a thing she said. But the marriage thing really threw her. Not that he asked to marry her. He had clearly stated that wasn't his intent, which actually irked her. "Ellis, I understand people do things differently here. I mean, I like you, tremensely."

"Translation?" he asked with what she thought was an adorable quirk of his brow.

"Very much," she said, although the word was actually a combination of tremendous and immensely combined. He had her frazzled and freaked out. She was speaking in a way he wouldn't understand. She tried to focus on her words to better formulate her thoughts. "But I'm only twenty years old. I'm far too young to marry."

"Twenty and a half," he said.

"Yes, well, even then."

"Don't you see, Desirea? I can't tell people you're my lover any more than I could tell them you're my bride. First, they'd never believe it."

"Wait one fu… I mean, one cotton picking minute!" *Ugh, that sounds ridiculous.* But she was trying desperately not to swear, which was becoming increasingly difficult since Ellis was thoroughly starting to piss her off. "Why would they not believe I'm your bride?" What a rude statement for him to make.

"Desirea," he moaned as if she should already know this answer. "I can't claim you as my lover because people around here know the Duke of Lancaster would never bring his lover to stay with him at his ducal estate, which would be beyond the pale. I have a reputation of making wise moves, of staying away from scandal and gossip. In short, it is simply something I would not do…ever."

She seethed. He didn't answer her question regarding the marriage thing because whatever he had to say wasn't kind, and she had a feeling it had everything to do with her occupation as an actress and singer. *What a frikken prig!* She turned in a huff and marched back through the door to her room. She held the door in her hand in preparation to slam it after her last words. "I don't give a hog's rump what you tell them. And I'm taking this room!" She slammed the door shut and slunk down on the floor against it, tears welling in her eyes at her hurt feelings. He thought she was unworthy of him, probably because of her speech and her unpolished manners. She had a perfectly acceptable occupation. *Phooey on him. He sucks.*

A soft knock sounded above her head. "Desirea, can I please talk to you?"

"Go away, Ellis. Oh, I'm sorry. I mean, Your Royal Dukeness. Trust me. You don't want to talk to me right now. I'm liable to punch you in the nose and curse like such a madwoman that you'd never want to talk to me again. I can be mean when I'm pushed. So don't push."

"I'm sorry again, Desirea," he said through the door. "I'm not used to arguing with anyone, let alone a woman. As far as the room…"

"Go away, Ellis!" she shouted, and she heard his footsteps as he walked away.

Not five minutes later, Ellis knocked on the main door to her chosen room. "Desirea, are you calmer now? Can we talk?"

Desirea laughed at his soft tone and his persistence. It was adorable, but then most of the things this man did she found adorable.

At her continued silence, he knocked again. "Desirea? I sent the driver for food and he has returned. Would you like something to eat?"

She couldn't stay mad at him. Desirea got up from the floor and walked to the main door. Opening it, she said, "Come in, Ellis."

"Thank you," he said with a childlike smile as he walked into the room and looked around as if he'd never seen it before. "My wife never let me in here," he said, which she found surprising, even sad. He moved to sit on the edge of the bed. "Are you still mad at me?"

"No, Ellis. I know you cannot help the way you are. You were raised to believe yourself above others."

"That's because I am," he said in a no nonsense tone.

She waved a dismissive hand at him. "So you believe."

"No, Desirea. I am." There was no mistaking his adamancy.

"Fine. You're a superior being. Happy?"

"Not when you say it like it's not true."

She sighed, not really knowing how to handle his obstinate nature. She sat on the bed beside him and took his hand. "And just what makes you better than others?" she asked in her most understanding tone and giving his hand a friendly pat, trying not to run her fingers over the contours of his strong, slightly hairy male hand in the manner she truly wished. He'd likely find her gesture very inappropriate if she were to fist one of his fingers.

"My title and bloodline make me who I am. It may not be important to you, but in my time, my ancestry means everything."

"Yes, I know," she said, moving her attention from his hand to his face. "But did you choose to be born a duke?"

He gave her a sidelong look, charming dimples and all. "No."

"So basically you hit the mother lode?"

"The what?"

She huffed, frustrated that he didn't understand. "You're a duke because your parents had a boy and your father happened to be lucky enough to have a title to give you."

"Now that's where you are wrong, Desirea. The Lancaster title was earned by my forefathers. Luck had nothing to do with it."

"But did *you* do anything to earn it?"

He scowled and released her hand. "I am a vocal member of parliament, a patron of the arts, and give to numerous charitable organizations, as have all my ancestors before me. Do you think I don't deserve my title?"

Did she think that? *No, of course not.* But she gave to many charitable organizations as well, but that still didn't make her better than others. "That's not what I'm saying."

"Then what are you saying?"

Yes, Desirea. What are you saying? "Just that you *are* lucky. But you should try not to look down on others not born with the same privilege and prestige." *Or me.*

"We aren't talking about 'others' are we? We are talking about you. You think that I think I'm better than you?"

"Don't you?" She looked up at him. He was standing in front of her now.

"I told you, Desirea. In my time..."

"Oh just stop! In my time, blah, blah, blah... This conversation is going nowhere." She stood. "I'm starving. Let's eat." It was senseless arguing with the man. He'd been brainwashed into thinking himself superior. She could not change a lifetime of thought in a day.

She stood and shook out her skirts, taking the arm he offered her. "A truce?" he asked.

"For now," she said, and he laughed.

They walked into the dining area to find a large lopsided table. It seemed one of the legs was missing a few inches. Ellis stared at the table as if in a quandary about what to do. Desirea let go of his arm and walked out of the room. She went into the book-filled study they had passed, snatched up a couple of leather bound tomes, and returned to the dining room. She went to the short leg. "Ellis, lift this corner of the table," she instructed. He looked at her oddly but stepped toward her to do what she asked. Once he lifted it, she placed a couple of the books under the leg. "All right, put it back down."

The table was now close to level and Desirea smiled. "See? All fixed. Now where's the food?"

"Through that door. In the kitchen," he said, placing his hands on top of the table and giving it a shake. "Who would have thought to use a book for such a purpose?"

Desirea laughed. "Oh, yes. It's like rocket science," she teased, and he stared at her, taking a second to get her joke.

"Like the one they sent to the moon?" he asked.

"Now you're getting it, Ellis." She was thrilled he understood.

Once they were seated and eating some kind of meat pasty, he said, "Tomorrow we need to go to town and find us a chef. I fear you and I will starve to death without one."

"I agree," she said, wiping her mouth with her napkin and frowning at the peeling wallpaper. "So, Ellis. Why did you let your castle get like this?"

"Napoleon's war kept me pretty busy," he said.

"Were you a soldier?"

"No. I'd describe myself as a voice of reason in the House of Lords."

He poured her some tea. It was cold just the way she liked it. "Thank you," she said. "So now, with the war over, you thought to make your castle great again?"

"Something like that," he said.

"What do you mean?" She speared a potato with her fork.

"I..." He looked up, his green gaze meeting hers before he looked down at his plate. He was obviously hesitant to answer this question. "I need to fix the place for my wife and future children."

She suddenly found it difficult to swallow her food. "You mean your future wife?" she croaked.

"Yes. It's become imperative that I find one."

"Why?" she asked, upset by his answer.

"Because I owe it to my title, to my ancestors, and most importantly, to my father. I need an heir."

She was struck stupid by this. She wanted to tell him he didn't have to get married to have a child, but she knew this was not how they did things in the nineteenth century. Marriage? She had always imagined living with a guy for a few years before tying the knot. Getting to know the other person's habits and oddities seemed important when you committed yourself to someone for life. Truthfully, she had never really thought much about marriage. She believed herself too young to think of such things, but now, she thought about it.

Marriage to the Duke of Lancaster did have its possibilities. Perhaps she wasn't too young to contemplate marriage after all. She resolved to do so when she found some alone time. It was too heavy a subject to decide if she was ready for such a step in the next five minutes. "So, basically, you live your life according to your title?"

"As you pointed out, Desirea, I'm one of the blessed. So, yes, I take my title most seriously. Making sure I have an heir to carry on my name is one of the most important tasks I have as a duke."

"That's a lot of pressure for your future wife. What if she can't conceive?" Not that Desirea feared she couldn't have kids, but the thought of having kids without the delivery taking place in a modern hospital, without drugs and emergency equipment, well, it didn't sound at all appealing. What was she thinking? She hadn't even decided she was ready for marriage and now she was contemplating kids! *What the hell is happening to my thought processes?* She seemed to be mentally aging at an alarming rate. A wife and mother at twenty-one? What was she, some backwoods farmer's daughter?

"Then I would have to petition the courts for an annulment and find another." His statement zapped her away from her thoughts.

"What?" Her head snapped up as she looked at him. "That's heartless." Her appetite had suddenly disappeared.

"It's how my world works," he said, taking a bite of ham and chewing it as if his statement wasn't extreme.

"So you would divorce the wife you love if she can't give you an heir?"

"Who said anything about love?" he quipped. "And I said annulment. I'd never consider a scandalous divorce."

She widened her eyes in surprise. "Did you not love your first wife?"

"Not particularly, no. I mean, I liked her well enough. We were friends, of a sort. My future wife will be paid handsomely when she gives birth to my heir. It's in the inheritance papers."

"Oh," she said, falling silent for a few seconds. He made it sound so formal. "But what if you are the one who cannot father a child? Then what?"

"It's never the man's fault, Desirea," he said with a scoff as if her comment was nonsense.

"You live in a world of delusion if you don't realize that some men are incapable of fathering children. Some men have lower sperm counts and erectile dysfunction. Trust me, I know. There are pills you can take for all kinds of things in my time. And modern science has found that men often have trouble fathering kids, with no fault to the lady." *So there!* She felt like saying it aloud but didn't.

"Interesting. Although I'm not worried about my lack of ability to father children. Everything seems to be in fine working order." He laughed as she felt a blush fill her face.

"Yes, well, I just thought you should know. It's good to be educated about such things instead of blaming females for every failing."

"Are you wishing to argue with me?" He placed both his arms on the table beside his plate and leveled his amused gaze on her.

"Uh, no. I don't think so. We see things differently, that's all." She shrugged.

"I know," he said. "It's refreshing."

"Because you're used to everyone agreeing with your every word?" she asked.

"Precisely. Aside from my sister, you're the only female I've met who isn't willing to agree with every word out of my mouth. And trust me when I say I've purposely thrown out some reproachable gibberish for amusement purposes, and no one dared to say a word."

She laughed. "You're impossible."

"Thanks," he said. "So are you." They both laughed.

"It's growing late. We should probably prepare those beds if we are to garner a good night's sleep." He pushed back his chair and stood.

Desirea slid back her chair and stood with a stretch. Traveling to Seaham had really taken its toll, not to mention that trying to get Ellis to see things from a different point of view was challenging unto making her bone tired. "Yes, I'm beat… I mean, I'm exhausted."

Ellis offered her his arm and they went to ready themselves for bed. "Do not be scared of the dark, Desirea. I will be in the next room if you need me."

His vow of protection moved her, and Desirea cuddled to his side as they went up the steps.

CHAPTER TEN

After breakfast, Ellis suggested it would be best if they made lists of what needed fixing. They started with the most pressing issues, like the leaking roof in one of the bedrooms and the broken window in the master, before moving on to the paint and plaster repair.

"I love the coves in the hallways, and the curved wooden doors to all the rooms are charming. Although the handle is loose on this door." Desirea wiggled the wrought iron handle, awkwardly writing it down on her long list with what constituted a pen. She would have thought this experience less than enjoyable, but she found, with Ellis's teasing and stolen glances, the work didn't seem at all like work, her favorite kind of labor.

"Did you write down the wood around the back bedroom window has all but rotted away?"

She scanned her list, loving how they worked so well together. "Yes, it's on here." They had been at it for hours, and as midday approached, Desirea's stomach growled.

"Hungry?" he asked from his stooped position as he checked a loose floorboard in the kitchen, the last room on their list.

"Yes, which is odd because we ate such a huge breakfast." Ellis's driver had returned from town with an enormous breakfast for them.

"Are you not used to enjoying a large morning meal?"

"No. I usually just grab a latte and a piece of fruit on my way to the gym." His head cocked sideways, and so she answered his unspoken question. "A latte is a type of coffee made mostly of milk, while a gym is a place where people go to exercise. They have equipment to help people keep their bodies in shape by working their muscles."

"Ah, a gymnasium," he said.

"You're a very fit man, Ellis. What do you do to stay in such fine shape?"

He shrugged and puffed out his chest, which made her laugh. "I box and fence on occasion."

"Sounds like fun," she said. Moving to a small round table, she noticed how scratched up it was and wrote it down on a list of items that needed to be given away to whatever constituted the Goodwill or the Salvation Army in this time.

"How about we clean ourselves up and head into town? We can find something to eat at Maude's. We need to put some staff in here now that we know which direction to send them."

"All right. I'll go change." She was covered in dust. He nodded and she went off down the hall and then up the stairs to her room. After washing up in the bathroom, she rifled through the closet, finally deciding on her pink walking dress etched with white lace. It had taken her a good hour to put her clothes away last night, but it had helped take her mind off the man in the next room, if only briefly. She donned her clothing and pinched her cheeks for color, wishing for some lipstick and eyeliner, and then left the room. She found Ellis in the hall. His hair was damp and combed away from his face. He wore black pants tucked into black boots and a white shirt with a deep teal waistcoat. *He looks scrumptious as usual.* He was in the process of putting on his black topcoat.

"Ready?" he asked, holding out his arm.

"I think so," she said, and they descended the stairs. She was nervous though. After all, she was going to the city of Seaham with the Duke of Lancaster. He was sure to be recognized. How would he introduce her? As his well-dressed maid? She wanted to ask but didn't. For his sake, he had better not classify her as part of his staff in front of anyone. She'd had just about enough of that.

When the vehicle entered the city, Desirea fought the urge to stick her head out the window to better see the stone buildings lining the street. Kids played in the road with a stick and a ball, running back and forth and laughing, and anyone who noticed the vehicle, stopped to stare. Some even hollered a greeting to the popular and obviously missed duke.

It was an overcast day, but it was warm and dry for the moment and so they decided to walk along the storefronts. Desirea looked in all the shop windows along the way, stopping when she saw a cobbler making shoes inside one of the stores.

Ellis stopped beside her. "They make shoes where you are from?" he asked teasingly.

"Yes," she said. "But in factories, and certainly not like that." She watched the man mold the leather around some metal contraption.

"Come," he said, leading her to the corner and pushing open the door into a quaint little eatery. Her stomach growled again at the smell of cooked meat. Ellis found them a table in the corner. The restaurant was completely empty. A tall woman with dark hair came out from the back, where Desirea assumed the kitchen was located. The woman's smile widened upon seeing the duke.

"Your Grace, how wonderful it is to see you. You've been away far too long," she admonished with a grin.

"Indeed I have, Maude. It is good to be back. How are things? How are your children?"

"Everyone is well, Your Grace. They will be happy you asked of them. They miss playing ball with you. You just missed the Everly sisters and their cousin Lady Faring. I'm sure those three would have fallen all over themselves if they saw you."

Desirea saw Ellis grimace at such a thought and Maude laughed. "But I see you have brought a pretty young lady with you," Maude said, looking around Ellis and winking at her.

Desirea got to her feet and moved forward, silently waiting for Ellis to do his gentlemanly duty and introduce her. When he turned back to look at her, Desirea smiled at him sweetly. When he continued to remain silent, she fought back a groan and moved closer with her smile still in place. It seemed Ellis wasn't good at making up stories.

"Hello," said Desirea. "I am Miss Leighton, a dear friend of the Duke of Lancaster's sister."

"A friend of Lady Darlene's? How nice it is to meet you, Miss Leighton," said Maude with an even bigger smile. Ellis merely looked at Desirea in open-mouthed astonishment. "I've heard your sister is expecting her second child." Maude turned to look at the duke, who thankfully had closed his mouth by this point.

"She recently gave birth to a girl, and both mother and child are doing well," he said, and Maude asked him to congratulate Darlene for her before taking their order. Ellis's statement made Desirea realize he had not shared this wonderful news with her, which saddened her, but she smiled and then walked back to their table to sit.

When Ellis reclaimed his seat, Desirea asked, "Why didn't you tell me you were an uncle again?"

"Why didn't you tell me you knew my sister," he teased.

"Well, you seemed struck stupid by Maude's question. I thought to swoop in and save you."

"I'm impressed."

"Why didn't you tell me about the new baby?" she asked again.

"Are you miffed?" he questioned.

"Yes, I guess I am. I thought we were getting closer, and yet you didn't share this news with me."

He shrugged and laughed. "I didn't think you'd care either way, but now that I know you do, I'll be sure to keep you apprised every time my sister gives birth."

"Yes, please do," she teased, and they both chuckled. "So who are these ladies who fall all over themselves for you?"

"Ladies who wish to see me as their husband. It's the same everywhere I go."

"Yes, I know exactly what you mean," she said, trying to remind him that she too had been much sought after. "They won't be visiting you, will they?"

Maude brought out two steaming Sheppard's pies and sat them on the table before disappearing into the kitchen again. Desirea had dined at enough Irish restaurants to recognize her meal. This had not always been the case since her arrival, and she was not one who liked to try different things.

Ellis laughed as if he thought of something really funny, but he didn't share his thoughts with her. "Oh, without a doubt. We'll be hard-pressed to keep those three women away."

Her head came up from her plate as she eyed him. "Are you joking?" She did not want three women flitting around the house, hanging on her man.

"No, I'm not."

"Hmmm," was all she could think to say. It seemed they'd be having company whether she wished it or not. "I think you should tell me more about your sister so that I carry off this ruse. Has she ever been to America? Where could I have met her?"

He smiled. "Plotting?" he asked.

"Someone has too," she said haughtily. "You don't seem to be very quick on your feet."

"Pardon?"

"Oh, nothing. It's merely that you lack the talent to pull off this faux friendship thing I have going with your sister."

"You know what, Desirea?"

"What?" she asked, noting that he was looking at her and had a sweet dimpled smile, his green gaze locked on hers.

"I like you tremensely."

She sat up straighter and smiled back at him. Her heart immediately upped its tempo. "Thank you, Ellis."

"I'd be honored to tell you about my sister," he said digging into the potatoes and cheese layering the top of his handled bowl. "I can even envision the two of you as close friends. I know Darlene would find you a hoot."

She didn't know if she liked being thought of as a "hoot," but she didn't take offense for she was sure he meant it as a compliment. He began to tell her about some of the times he and Darlene had fought in their youth, moving on to tell her about the despair they suffered at their parents' deaths, finishing with Darlene's great love affair with the Scotsman she married and the birth of their two girls.

"Are you done eating?" he asked, and she looked down at her half eaten meal.

"Yes. Your sister sounds like a wonderful person. Perhaps I can meet her someday."

"Perhaps," was all he said, and she felt a sliver of disappointment.

"Well, let's go. Mrs. Bogilvy usually keeps a list of people in the area looking for work. Her shop is down the way. It's the local mail office. Shall we go find ourselves a cook?"

"Yes," said Desirea, standing from her seat and taking his arm. She waved goodbye to Maude while the duke gave the woman a royal nod, and they headed for the corner mail shop. The people on the walkway stopped to bow slightly and greet his grace as they passed. It was like he was the king or something, thought Desirea. He got far more attention when out in public than she ever had. She didn't envy him in the least.

They entered the quiet interior of the post office, and Ellis approached the short gray-haired woman behind the wooden counter. Behind the woman was a floor-to-ceiling shelf segmented into square niches like open mailboxes. The woman immediately smiled, nodded her head, and turned to fish a letter out of one of the boxes. "This letter arrived for you, Your Grace. I was going to have Harry bring it to you first thing, but seeing as you've brightened my day with your visit, I have the honor of giving it to you myself."

The woman was fairly gushing, and Desirea hid her smile.

"At first, I thought it wrongly addressed, but I assume you must be Miss Leighton," the woman said as she turned her attention to Desirea.

"The letter is for me?" Desirea was very surprised.

"If you are Miss Leighton, then yes, dear, it is yours," the woman said with a kind smile, and Ellis passed Desirea the letter. She stared at her name on the front of the paper and then put it in her pocket for later. It had to be from London Burton for she knew no one else in this century. It was likely an invitation to her friend's wedding. *Desirea couldn't help but smile. Perhaps my dreams can come true like London's.*

Ellis watched her, nodding at her smile as if to say, "Oh, good. Everything's fine." He turned his attention back to Mrs. Bogilvy. "We have come looking to re-staff Castle Lancaster. It is my hope there's at least one decent chef on your list."

"There's not one on my list, Your Grace, but my nephew, Philip, has recently finished his training with a French master. I've sampled many of his dishes, and they are divine."

"Wonderful. Please send him. I also have need of masons, painters, upholsterers, gardeners, stable hands, a housekeeper, a butler, and some…" He paused to smile at Desirea, before saying, "Maids. Including one for Miss Leighton, who's a dear, dear friend of Darlene's and awaiting my sister's visit."

Desirea looked at him then. Did he say his sister was coming to visit?

Mrs. Bogilvy beamed with happiness. "This is so wonderful, Your Grace, restoring Lancaster Castle to its former glory. I will round up the very best for your household. I'll send my nephew over right away so you can enjoy your evening meal."

"Splendid, Mrs. Bogilvy. I'll see you paid handsomely for your troubles."

"You're always most generous, Your Grace."

Desirea felt a bit dazed as they walked out of the mail shop. "So that's it? You're not going to interview anyone or look at references?"

"I have you in the house, Desirea. I'm sure you will inform me if one of them is not up to snuff." He assisted her into the vehicle.

"So, what? I'm like an overseer?"

"For the moment, you are the lady of the house."

She liked the sound of that, her servant status dropped in favor of a title that suited her better. She was now a friend of the family who met Darlene years ago at a party and had kept up with her through letters ever since. "Is your sister really coming to visit?"

"I daresay, she will." He laughed. "Eventually."

The carriage ambled toward Lancaster Castle and Desirea decided to ask the one question she still couldn't figure out. She broke the comfortable silence. "Ellis, I still don't understand why you let the castle fall apart. I mean, you seem to have the money to hire people to look after it for you."

"True," he said.

"Then, why did you neglect it?"

"This upsets you?" he asked. "Why?"

She shrugged, not really having an answer. "It just seems a shame."

"Because it is a shame actually. My one and only shame. I think that is why I did it. Does that make any sense?"

She thought about his answer for a moment. "Um, no. Not really."

"I married my wife at twenty. She was seventeen. One year later, she died, and her death was the only thing I ever heard when my name was mentioned. No one ever spoke about how my words in Parliament may have been enlightening or even helpful. All anyone wanted to talk about was the poor duke and his grief, how everyone, aside from my sister was taken from me. Even when the war was in full swing, people still talked about my loss. It was frustrating. Not that I wasn't upset when my wife died. I merely wanted people to stop talking about it."

"So you decided to give them something else to talk about?" The Bonnie Raitt song popped in her head. Musical references often popped into her head after hearing a sentence or even a single word, which was probably why music was one of her passions.

"Yes. I let the castle fall into ruin, and the plan promptly backfired. People began to gossip about how my grief had led me to give up on the things I care for, like the ducal estate. For awhile I let it go, and then my sister's letter came; and I realized, whether I wish it or not, it's time for me to beget an heir, which means I must find another wife." He ran his hand over his face as if the very thought of marriage was bothersome in the extreme. This was likely because his outlook on marriage was completely warped, thought Desirea. *He acted like he would marry a baby-maker and nothing more.*

"When you love the person you marry, marriage can be wonderful."

"Says the girl who doesn't wish to marry," he scoffed.

"I never said that," she said, offended. "I only said that I'm too young to consider marriage at this point in my life."

"Well, when you are ready, I warn you that it's not a simple task, but that is especially the case for a duke."

"Because people like you for what you are instead of who you are?" She understood these feelings very well. She had just spoken the main reason she came to dislike being a celebrity.

He studied her for a moment and she heated at his stare. She wanted to melt into him, but he continued to hold her at a distance. "You know how that feels." It wasn't a question, but more of an acknowledgment.

"I do," she said, thinking of all her failed relationships and how every one of those so-called boyfriends only liked her for her fame. They always wanted to go out for the evening, to be seen and photographed. None wished to spend an evening chilling in front of the TV with her. She didn't believe it even entered their tiny little brains. She tended to date the kind of men in the category of "looks good, carries heavy things."

"I guess it doesn't really matter. I'm not getting any younger," he said.

"None of us are," said Desirea, not appreciating his blasé attitude toward marriage in the least. "You've never been in love before?" she asked. Neither had she really, but she had at least felt the stirrings of love before. She felt those stirrings now, with him.

"No, I haven't, nor are they linked together in my time."

"Now, that I find hard to believe, Your Grace. Love, after all, is said to be the universal language."

"Perhaps, but since I've never felt love, I wouldn't know."

"What are you looking for in a wife?" she asked, although she already knew she most likely wouldn't fit the bill. After all, she was an actress and didn't have wide, childbearing hips.

"The usual, I suppose. A lady of quality, free of scandal, and of impeccable birth. These three things are most important. And it would be nice if she was still young and impressionable, with the ability to charm her audience, while becoming a leading hostess in our circles, since society is impressed by such things. A duke is expected to have the best entertainments, and thus, if only on occasion, she must reign supreme in this arena. Of course, it goes without saying that I need a woman who's devoted to her duties as a duke's wife."

"You mean a woman dedicated to seeing you receive your heir?" Desirea said goodbye to being an impressionable youth many years ago, but she knew she would excel at the rest of the things on his list. Entertainment, after all, was her forte. Of course, he scorned the very occupation responsible for her reaching her ultimate potential, but her talents made her who she was. *Could he not see he described me almost perfectly?*

"Now, why did you make that sound, like you might spout smoke out of your ears at any moment?"

She shrugged. There was no getting through to this man. They both sat back silently as the vehicle pulled down the drive and finally came to a stop. Pleading a headache, Desirea disappeared to her room.

While there, she contemplated the path her heart was telling her to take. Was she fooling herself into believing she could make Ellis overcome all his beliefs and fall in love with her? Would he have the courage to withstand society's censure if it meant they could be together? Could she make her dreams reality? Could she marry him and give him the heir he needed? Did she want to? Was she ready for marriage? And children?

The questions that flew at her brought on a panic attack, and she threw open the window for some needed air. She was surprised to hear the sound of giggling females nearby. She looked out to find two lovely brunette ladies trying to walk through the tall weeds at the back of the statue garden while calling for a dog named Wags, at least she assumed it a dog's name. The ladies were lovely, slim, elegantly dressed and coiffed, and both had a fair amount of cleavage showing. It wasn't hard to deduce that she was looking at the Everly sisters, the Earl of Rollingsworth's daughters, and according to Ellis, his closest neighbors.

She jumped at the knock on her bedroom door. "Yes," she said, and it opened to reveal Ellis.

"I thought to warn you the Everly sisters have arrived."

"Yes. I saw them out the window. I think they lost their dog."

He laughed. "Yes, so they will claim, but they always act as if one of their father's wolfhounds broke free."

"Oh." This news didn't sit well with Desirea. The ladies were here for no other reason than to pay homage to the great Duke of Lancaster, how irritating.

"It may be best if you stay in your room. They're bound to ask you many questions, and without a chaperone staying in the house, our situation is most improper."

"I need a chaperone to stay with you?" she asked, not realizing how strict the code of conduct was in this time. This meant having her here was risky for him, and she couldn't help but smile at the thought that he had brought her to his estate anyway. Of course, now she would have to protect him.

"Yes, and since we don't have one, it's probably best if you stay out of sight. I will tell them that you were not feeling well and are tucked in your room with your lady companion."

"Oh," she said again, not liking this idea. But she also didn't wish to start gossip swirling.

"I'll visit with them and have them gone before you know it," he said. "The house is not exactly ready for guests."

"No, it's not, and I think you should tell them that," she said with a smile.

He smiled back, and with a bow, he turned on his heel and left. Desirea looked about her room and then stood near her door to hear the duke greet the women in the front entry before inviting them inside. She wondered what happened to the house-not-being-ready thing.

Desirea moved closer to the door and opened it a few inches more, straining to hear the voices below.

"Your Grace," one of the ladies gushed with excitement in her voice. "How utterly pleased we are to have you back. I was telling my sister how lucky we were to share a property line with the most sought after duke in the realm. I feel flushed seeing you again after all of these years. I believe you are even more handsome than I remember."

"Then fan yourself," replied another female voice, her tone filled with obvious competitive hostility toward her sister. Ellis invited the ladies into the parlor, and Desirea could hear no more. She wished she could see these two would-be interlopers, but there wasn't a way, unless she left her room, which she was told not to do.

And since when do you do what you're told?

CHAPTER ELEVEN

Contemplating what to do with unwanted guests, Desirea remembered a box of stage props in one of the storage rooms, props Ellis told her his mother had used to entertain her guests, and a brilliant thought struck her. The short brown wig she had found in the box would be absolutely perfect for what she was about to do. She only hoped Ellis could keep his cool and play along. She cleared her voice and practiced a New York accent. "I'm Bella Zucker, Miss Leighton's companion. I wished to inform his grace that Miss Leighton is feeling much recovered and will join you shortly." She smiled at her reflection in the mirror. As long as she wore a bonnet, looked down obediently, and shuffled her feet, no one would notice her face. As Mimi had told her, "Servants were not to be observed, but should be helpful and obscure." Desirea could do that. It would be a quick appearance. She'd duck in and assure these ladies that nothing untoward or scandalous was occurring under the duke's roof, and then she'd duck back out again. Simple enough. Surely, her chaperone's appearance would put the duke's anxieties about this matter to rest.

It took longer than expected to get herself in a drab brown dress and her hair tucked up into the short wig with the bonnet hiding most of her face. Practicing her line again, she marched down the stairs as if they were the entrance to the stage and she was about to give a spectacular performance.

She knocked once on the open door and immediately dropped her gaze to the floor as three heads turned in her direction. "I'm to inform you, Your Grace, Miss Leighton is feeling much improved and will join you shortly." At the last moment, she had realized a woman in a chaperone position would never introduce herself to guests of the duke. Great, now she could only hope Ellis took her cue and new the part she was playing.

"Thank you, Mrs. Hatchett," said Ellis, his voice filled with calm indifference. "Please tell her it's not necessary."

She did not look up to see is face, but he seemed to be handling this quite well. She nearly laughed at the name he chose for her.

"Your Grace," said one of the lady's. "We'd love to meet Darlene's friend. I mean, she traveled from America to visit your sister and so must be a good friend indeed."

"Yes, we should meet her," replied the other.

"Please tell Miss Leighton that we await her presence," Ellis said with obvious reluctance, which probably made the Everly sister even more curious about her.

"Yes, Your Grace." Desirea backed out of the room and then spun on her heel, racing up the stairs. Whipping off the wig, she hurriedly worked on her appearance, wanting to look her absolute best and smiling to find make-up wasn't necessary for this. Jumping into the petticoat, she pulled the teal gown over her head and struggled with the pearl buttons, wishing she had a maid. Once fastened, she adjusted her breasts to their best advantage. She was flushed by the time she finished, but the color looked good on her. Pulling her hair back with a simple white ribbon, she hurried out the door.

Admittedly, she was somewhat nervous. She always had the most difficult time befriending women, most of whom kept company with her for attention and personal gain; and when they witnessed the fawning adoration thrown Desirea's way, they usually disappeared and never came back around. Unfortunately, this couldn't be helped. Even *she* grew *tired* of the attention she garnered. Not that she planned to become good friends with these ladies, since they were after her boyfriend.

Calming her rapidly beating heart, she slowly walked into the parlor as if she were on a runway stage. She heard both sisters suck in a breath at her appearance, and Ellis's eyes widened in what she assumed was admiration. She tried not to smile at their reaction. The deep teal gown was made for her figure. It drew the viewers' eyes to all the right places and offered a tantalizing view of her cleavage. The two Everly sisters looked dowdy in comparison, but then, she knew from experience, first impressions could be everlasting and she wished to put her haughtiest foot forward. It was the only thing puffed up people appreciated.

"Your Grace," she said, curtseying in the appropriate manner.

Ellis seemed to turn to stone at her appearance, but now he got to his feet as protocol dictated and made the introductions. It was as if he only now realized how lovely she was. He even appeared somewhat clumsy as he immediately retained his seat. This thrilled her.

Desirea smiled sweetly at the sisters and then sat herself next to Ellis on the loveseat. She heard the sisters gasp before Ellis jumped up to offer everyone tea. *Is there a proper distance to sit from people? Jeez-Louise, we weren't touching. Well, my dress may have touched his leg, but come on!*

"Ladies, what brings you to Lancaster Castle?" she asked, hoping to deter questions from being asked of her.

"One of our father's hounds escaped and we thought he may have gone this way," said the one named Anne with a tilt to her head as if she couldn't quite figure Desirea out.

"Did you find him?" Desirea asked, purposely being difficult. She saw Ellis smile in amusement at her question.

"No. He probably ran back home by now," replied the one named Lauren.

"Why search for the dog if you know he'll return?" Desirea couldn't help but ask. Both of the pretty ladies stared at her in stunned silence. *Is no one in this century capable of making up a plausible excuse for anything?*

"His Grace tells us you met Darlene years ago at Carlson House," exclaimed Anne.

"Yes. Do you know Darlene well?" Desirea asked, wondering how well these ladies might be able to see through her false tale.

"Oh, no. We were still young when she lived here, but we've met her plenty of times since. Not since she moved to Scotland, of course," said Anne.

"When do you leave for Scotland?" the older of the two, Lauren, asked. It was evident these ladies did not like her rooming with the Duke of Lancaster.

"My sister is coming here," said Ellis, and Desirea smiled at his quick reply.

"Didn't she just give birth?" asked Anne.

"Anne!" scolded Lauren.

Ellis laughed from his place near the fireplace. Obviously he had decided it was safer to stand than shock the sisters further. Desirea suspected his laughter was to try to make Anne feel better after her sister embarrassed her. "It's quite all right, Lady Lauren. Yes, Lady Anne, I have another niece. But my sister does plan to introduce her to me when she's ready enough for travel."

"And Miss Leighton is staying here until your sister recovers and travels all the way here?" Lauren Everly didn't look at all happy about this. In fact, she looked very angry and glared at Desirea.

Not wanting to start anything that would reflect harshly on the duke, Desirea said, "We hope she has a speedy recovery. I'm so very happy for her. We spoke of children often in our letters. I can't wait to meet her daughters."

"I daresay we all look forward to seeing your visit behind us," said Lauren with another glare in Desirea's direction. Unlike her sister Anne, Lauren was a bona fide bitch, Desirea decided. Both were brunettes with bright smiles and deep brown eyes, and they were probably a couple of years younger than Desirea. Both were unwed, but only Lauren was forthright enough to say something so rude.

Desirea's temper flared. She didn't consider herself easily riled, but when she was, all who had witnessed it knew to look out. Desirea got to her feet, ready to give this woman a verbal-lashing she'd never forget, but she found Ellis behind her, gripping her elbow firmly. "Could you ladies excuse us for a moment," he said, leading Desirea from the room. She willingly went with him for she needed a moment to cool down.

When they were in the study with the door firmly closed, she moved out from his hold and spun around to speak to him. "How can you stand to have such detestable women in your home?"

"Lady Anne's not so bad," he said with an amused smile.

"Really?" she said sarcastically. "What is she, all of seventeen?" She waved her hand at him. "Lauren is terrible. She's lucky I didn't jump that table and kick her face in. She definitely has issues."

Ellis laughed.

"Why do you put up with them? Why do you not throw them out the door on their ass…I mean, behinds?"

"Because I'm a duke," he said, straightening from where his back rested against the door.

"Which gives you the authority to throw them out and never have to look at them again," she thought to point out.

"And have them telling people I throw guests from my home? No, Desirea. I will do no such thing. And you will not be kicking anyone in the face."

"And why not?" she asked, wondering why he was moving closer and looking at her in that way that said, "I'm about to kiss you."

"Because you won't have time," he said, his lips hovering over hers.

"And why not?" she whispered, closing her eyes, letting her senses take over.

"Because you're going to have your hands full," he said.

"With the house," she asked breathlessly, her anger forgotten.

"No. With me," he said, and his lips claimed hers in a kiss so all consuming and sweet that her knees nearly buckled beneath her. Heat filled her body and tingles of pleasure and excitement skated across her skin. He pulled back, resting his forehead against hers. "Let's go play nice with our guests and send them on their way," he suggested with a seductive drawl she couldn't refuse. It seemed he was finally ready to admit defeat when it came to their attraction to one another. Desirea couldn't be happier with his decision.

"I'm an actress, and so I suppose I could *pretend* to be nice," she said, knowing there was a reason she always brought up her past occupation. She sought his approval and was bothered he had still not given it.

"By the bye," he said, taking her hand and opening the door. "Your companion part was brilliant. Well played, Desirea."

"Yes, well, her name was to be Bella Zucker, not Mrs. Hatchett. Couldn't you come up with something better?" she teased.

"I apologize. I looked up at the wall of weapons and…" He shrugged.

They both laughed.

"Besides, I was taken by surprise at your appearance. I clearly remember telling you to stay put."

"Yes, I know. And your word's law, blah, blah, blah…"

He laughed and squeezed her to his side. "You look outstanding."

She smiled up at him and snuggled closer.

When they returned to the sitting room, Ellis had an easy time ridding them of the Everly sisters. He claimed he heard their dog outside, and since they wouldn't dare disagree with the duke, they had no other choice but to take their leave.

With them gone, Desirea had hoped Ellis would continue that kiss he had started, but no sooner had the ladies left than there was another knock on the door. This time there were fifteen people on the porch. The new staff had arrived, luggage and all.

After locating the housekeeper and butler in the fray, Desirea began to help make room assignments and to designate chores. This work took well into the evening and Desirea did not see the duke, who had been busy instructing the masons, gardeners, and stable hands, again until dinner. It was one of the busiest days of Desirea's life. She sat at the dining table barely able to keep her head up.

"It's been a long day," he said, taking a bite from the roll in his hand. With his fork, he tore into the roasted duck with orange sauce. The menu had certainly improved with a chef in the house, but duck held no interest for Desirea. She stuck with the rolls and side dishes.

"Exhausting," she agreed.

"Have the servants all been placed where they should?"

"Yes. I think things will start running more smoothly… months from now," she said with a laugh.

"And your letter from Miss London Burton?" he asked. "All is well?"

"Yes, she is to wed. How did you know the letter was from her?" she asked.

"I recognized the Earl of Nankin's crest on the wax seal."

"You're very observant, Ellis," she said, and he smiled.

***

Ellis forked in another bite of duck, watching Desirea push her meat to the side of her plate. She was so lovely that he had a hard time keeping his gaze off her. He thought her brilliant, in her own fabulous way, and if it wasn't for her background, he was sure he'd view her as a potential spouse. But Desirea was a product of her environment, which was nowhere near ordinary in his time period. He was, in fact, amazed he had an actual actress and singer residing in his house un-chaperoned. Remy would love this, the Duke of Lancaster acting completely out of character and shaking the stellar foundation he had built for himself by letting his lust overpower his mind and his strict code of conduct.

Ellis was actually having a hard time believing this charade was happening, indeed that he was allowing it to happen. Desirea smiled at him again, and he felt his entire body warm. She had a hold on him, one he didn't understand. He was drawn to her in a way that was inconceivable, and thus he had no idea what to do about it. Not true, said a small voice in his head. He had an idea. It just wasn't an idea he would have customarily had. She was changing him, he could feel it, and this scared him. He'd always known who he was, a stoic man, but Desirea had his mind wandering into impossible dreams. She had him thinking of nothing but her, of what he could do with her, what it would feel like to have her wiggling in ecstasy beneath him. She had him wondering what it would even feel like to have her love if he gave up the fight with his sanity and allowed himself to take exactly what he wanted.

"You're staring at me like that again," she said in a teasing manner.

He gave her a crooked smile, glad she wasn't a mind reader. "Like what?"

"Like I'm dessert," she said sweetly, turning his insides into a heated inferno. He clenched his fists beneath the table.

"Sorry," he said, bringing his napkin to his lips before returning it to his lap.

"Well, don't be. I like it," she said with an impudent laugh.

They sat at one end of the table and so it was simple to close the distance between them. As he leaned forward to kiss her, she pushed their plates out of the way, coming out of her seat to place her lips upon his. Before he knew it, she was straddling his lap in the chair and he was lost in the feelings of sensation, lost in Desirea. Her body undulated against him as he skimmed his hands up her sides, molding her body, feeling every sensual curve that made up her amazing figure. Never had he felt such urgent lust; it shook him to the core. He wanted to lay her back upon the table, lift her skirts, and rut like a crazed man.

His tongue met hers and they both moaned in unison. He felt air on his chest as she undid his cravat and pulled his shirt over his head to reveal his body. Her eyes widened in the most complimentary manner before she ran her hands over his muscles, leaning down to place kisses upon his chest. He cupped her round breasts in his hands, running his thumb over the puckered peaks begging for his attention. Her head fell back and he pulled her breasts out of the top of her dress while he ran soft kisses down her neck, which made her squirm even more on top of his ever growing erection. He inhaled deeply, taking in her heady scent.

"Take me to your bed, Ellis," she instructed in a breathy voice.

"Desirea, you know I'd like nothing more, but I cannot commit myself to you. I have responsibilities, a duty." He choked out his words because she began to move her hips in a rocking motion on top of him.

"Has anyone ever told you, you think too much?" she whispered in his ear, her teeth gently nibbling the side of his neck. *Good heavens, Desirea will be the death of me.*

"I've heard it mentioned," he said to her breasts, not able to resist taking one of the peaks into his mouth, making her writhe all the more, in turn torturing himself as his cock pulsated to be freed from its confines.

"Would it help if I told you the only thing I wish for you to commit at the moment is your body to mine? I'm not asking for promises or marriage, Ellis. I'm only asking that you share yourself with me."

He hissed at her words, wanting nothing more than to lose himself in Desirea, even if temporarily. "This is what you want? You won't come to regret our union? You won't make demands and promises of me that I can't keep?"

"I only demand that you give me pleasure," she purred, her fingers fumbling with the buttons on his trousers.

When she freed him and wrapped a tight fist around his cock, all reason fled. He wanted Desirea.

He was going to have her.

Right here.

Right now.

Before his mind tried to convince him that this was folly, he stood and she slid off his body. He kicked his pants down to his feet, sat her perfect ass on the table, nudged her legs apart, and threw up her skirts. *Oh, dear heavens, she doesn't wear drawers!* And her mons were visible, something *he* hadn't seen in quite a while. "You're…" He didn't know what to say. He'd never seen such a thing.

"Hairless," she said with a smile. "Yes, I know. I hate being hairy, and so I shave it. Not easy to do with those blades you people call razors. I nicked myself far too many times."

"You remove your hair?" He ran his hand over her soft petals, astonished and so unbelievably filled with need that he moved his head down. He had to taste her, this woman who shocked him with her candor. He had to have her, to claim her, to have this once in a lifetime original.

***

"Oohh," she said as his tongue tantalized her most intimate parts. "So my lack of hair doesn't bother you," she said with a husky laugh before allowing the sensations of being Ellis's dessert pull her into a maelstrom of lust she hadn't experienced in all of her years.

"I'm enthralled," he said as he gently bit her thigh and continued his onslaught of pleasure.

"Do you still think we should stop?" The question was only half in jest, only half teasing. She didn't want him having regrets either. His tongue darted inside her and she moaned.

"Never," he said, and Desirea gave herself over to her passions. Freeing her mind from further concern, she marveled at the orgasm of a lifetime. She fell apart under Ellis's skills, and when he positioned himself above her, she reached for him like a lifeline, needing desperately to feel him inside her, loving her, caring for her, claiming a piece of her.

She scooted herself to the edge of the table, bunching her skirts up in one hand as she watched him slide inside her. Her gaze went up to meet his. He was watching her. She smiled. His hips began a slow steady movement, but soon she was grasping the table and moving herself against him, undulating, needing, feeling, and loving every blissful moment. She splintered into a million pieces as another orgasm washed over her, and she watched Ellis plunge one last time inside of her before removing himself and spilling his seed on her thigh. At the feel of his warm fluids, she widened her eyes in surprise. Then she sighed in relief at the sight. She was not ready to be a mother. Not that his method was foolproof, but it was certainly better than no method at all.

He stepped back, cleaned her thigh with his handkerchief, and then gently pulled her skirts back down as he assisted her off the table.

"Good thing the leg held up," she said, surprised the table hadn't collapsed beneath them due to all the rocking.

Ellis said nothing. He kept fixing his clothes, buttoning everything. "Are you okay?" she asked.

"I've never done that before," he said with evident shock in his voice, as if they had committed some dastardly deed. *Damn! The man seems to have regrets.*

She gave a small awkward laugh. "Come now, Ellis. There's no such thing as a born again virgin."

He laughed and Desirea dispelled the breath she was holding. "I'm not virginal by any means," he said. "Nevertheless, I've never had sex on the dining table, nor have I ever had sex with a lady like you. And I certainly never imagined doing so under my own roof."

What did he mean: "a lady like you?" She hoped he wasn't referring to her career. She decided to protect her feelings and not ask for further explanation. "Yes, well, we can do a sex tour of the house if you wish. Perhaps we can initiate every room with our passions." She smiled as he yanked her into his embrace.

"Now that sounds like an offer I can't refuse."

"So you aren't disappointed that we finally caved into our need?" She looked up at his handsome face.

"Assuredly, I am not. It was by far the best sex I've ever had."

Thrilled by his words, she smiled. "Then you and I shall have great fun, Ellis, because you haven't seen anything yet." She pulled his head down and kissed him for all she was worth. Her heart wanted to sing with the joy she felt at being in his arms and being his woman.

"We should retire to our rooms," he whispered.

"Separately?" she asked, disappointed he was calling an end to their wonderful evening.

"Perish the thought, Desirea. You did choose the room connected with mine, and seems a shame if we don't make use of the door."

"You make *me* sound shameless," she said.

He kissed the end of her nose. "I think your shamelessness is what I like best about you," he teased, and she laughed as they retired to their rooms.

Moments later, Desirea was blissfully naked and exploring Ellis taut, muscled chest with her mouth as Ellis worshiped her body with his again. *Life in the nineteenth century is awesome.*

CHAPTER TWELVE

Three glorious weeks later the castle was coming along nicely. Desirea loved watching the transformation, which made walking around buckets, ladders, and drop clothes tolerable. She was now busy picking out fabric for the master's chamber and Ellis's future wife's chamber. Seated in the study near the window for light, she was looking through fabric swatches the upholsterer provided when she heard voices through the open window. She looked out to find Ellis walking with a pretty lady who had thick brunette curls dancing about her angelic face. They were walking in the statue garden, laughing. The lady was holding on to his arm with both hands. *Who is she?*

Desirea sat frozen, listening to their laughter and noticing how close their heads came together as they spoke. She couldn't make out their words no matter how close she got to the window. Should she introduce herself? Would she be intruding? They laughed again and her insides clenched.

Because Ellis saved her from the alleyway, she tended to think of him as hers, silly perhaps but unavoidable. The fact that he was sharing her bed also gave her the feeling of possessiveness toward him. Since her father's death, Ellis was the only man who had tried to care for her and see to her wellbeing. He was her rock during a time of uncertainty and radical change, even if he wasn't, perhaps, aware of this. He kept her fear of facing a new world at bay with his presence.

The Duke of Lancaster was a wonderful man, and it was hard not to fall in love with him, but she didn't like to think about how dependent she had become upon him. She felt a pull toward him on a metaphysical level, if that was even possible. *Oh my God, I'm starting to sound frikken crazy.*

And she was going to lose him. She knew this. She had none of the requisites Ellis required in a wife. She wasn't a member of the aristocracy. She wasn't the least bit obedient.

She couldn't dance the waltz, or ride a horse, or speak a bunch of different languages. But she could entertain, and throw lavish parties the likes this Regency world has never seen. She could blow high society away with her mastery. And yet Ellis seemed oblivious of this fact. *Ugh, I have it bad!*

Sure, she had Ellis's attention, but she didn't think she had his heart. She couldn't forget that he was on a mission to marry some perfect aristocratic lady and impregnate her at lightning speed.

The last few weeks, she had fallen completely for Ellis. He was so caring and sweet every time he took her in his arms, as if she were some rare treasure and he its keeper. He read Shakespeare to her while she acted out her scenes, laughed and applauded, seemingly entertained by her talent. He even fed her tidbits of food at dinner, encouraging her to try new things. They often talked at length about his time period and hers, and at night, their passion was beyond anything she ever experienced. She never wanted to leave him. She wanted to be his, even if she had to marry him to make that happen.

In this time period, she'd be considered old and on the shelf by the age of twenty-three, which was laughable. But she reminded herself that she was no longer in the twenty-first century and needed to get with the times, to conform, at least somewhat, if she wanted to be happy.

Another tinkling of laughter had her on her feet and out the door. It would be rude if she didn't greet their guest. After all, Ellis had made her the lady of the house.

But as she drew closer to the laughing couple, she felt awkward interrupting the happy scene, especially when she saw the reason for their laughter: two little girls trying to catch the fish in the center fountain with their hands, the fronts of the dresses wet from their efforts. She was going to turn around but Ellis looked her way with a smile and the lady next to him turned.

"Hello," the pretty brunette said, and she stood as Desirea approached.

"Hello," said Desirea.

Ellis introduced her to Lady Amelia Faring and her two young half sisters, Penelope and Anna, his neighbors. Lady Amelia was Ellis's age, he told her, and they grew up together. They seemed quite close and Desirea tried not to let their obvious friendship annoy her. Aside from her beauty and poise, which made her a threat in Desirea's mind, Lady Amelia was being kind. She complimented Desirea's dress and even commented on the pretty blueness of her eyes. She then shared a few stories about her and Darlene, telling her how she loved to visit with Darlene just so she'd get a chance to see Ellis. Apparently, there wasn't a lady in the vicinity who didn't have a crush on the duke, some even going so far as claiming a friendship with his sister. Did the two of them not see anything wrong with that? It certainly sounded unfair to Darlene.

"I thought to come by today and invite you to a cricket match on our west lawn this Friday. All the neighbors are invited. You are welcome to join us too, Miss Leighton. We'd be happy to have you."

"We wouldn't miss it," said the duke, answering for Desirea, but she didn't mind since she loved being with him. Although Desirea could have sworn Amelia thought the duke's response for them both odd, if her expression of surprise was anything to go by.

"When did you say your sister was expected to visit?" Amelia asked him, and Desirea had the feeling that Amelia's sentiments echoed Miss Lauren's when it came to her rooming with the duke.

"I didn't," the duke said with a shrug. "I suppose she'll arrive when she's ready."

"And Miss Leighton is residing here until then?" As expected, Lady Amelia didn't sound happy with this arrangement.

"Yes, Amelia," Ellis replied in an appeasing manner. "Along with her chaperone, Mrs. Hatchett, and a dozen other servants. Why?"

"Oh, no reason." Lady Amelia turned three shades of red.

Desirea's eyes widened when Ellis picked up Amelia's gloved hand in his and brought it to his lips, placing a kiss upon her knuckles. "And here I thought you were expressing some kind of jealousy toward me. I'm hurt to find it untrue."

What the hell did he say? The man was blatantly flirting with Lady Amelia. And in front of her, no less. Desirea smiled stiffly when Amelia looked toward her with a full blush. "Your Grace," said Desirea. "Can I have a moment? I want to ask you a question about the upholstery for the dining chairs." *And beat the crap out of you while I'm at it.*

"Oh," Lady Amelia said as if she just figured out something important. "You're helping the duke fix up the castle for his future bride. How sweet you are, Miss Leighton. It is a chore you will relieve of his wife, and a monumental one that no new bride would wish to take upon herself given the state of things here. I know if I was his duchess," she said, turning and batting her eyes at Ellis, who smiled in return, "I would be forever thankful for the work you've accomplished."

Desirea was unsure why this would be the case, since in her time young married couples often had much fixing up to do in their first home. "I find the work effortless as well as rewarding. Good day, Lady Amelia," Desirea said, before walking back into the house.

"Excuse me. I won't be but a moment," Desirea heard Ellis say behind her. Her temper heated even further. *The asshole isn't even sending Amelia home. Calm yourself, Desirea. You can yell, but try not to swear. Ah, shit! Why is not cursing so difficult?* It was a bad habit, one she was set on breaking.

She could hear him behind her as she continued to make her way into the study. He closed the door after he entered. Desirea walked across the room to close the window. She might be able to hold back her swearing, but she couldn't chance holding back her volume at the same time. "What the hell was that, Ellis?" she demanded, spinning around to glare at him. She decided *hell* and *damn* wouldn't be considered swear words. After all, a girl did need to have some leeway.

"What was what?" he asked, all smooth innocence as if he did nothing wrong.

"Trying to charm the knickers off of Lady Amelia, that shit?" *Okay, shit isn't a swear word either.*

"I'm only being nice to a lady I've known my entire life, a lady of proper breeding and decorum who has a strong sense of familial duty and understands hereditary obligations."

Is he frikken kidding with this shit? He is courting the damn neighbor before my very eyes. Oh, ow! That hurt. She swallowed back her hurt feelings, refusing to shed a tear in his presence. *I know he is going to have to marry someone else, but come on!* "You wish to make Lady Amelia your bride?"

"Don't look so hurt, Desirea. You know my plans for the future. You know what I must do and why. I have familial obligations. A duty." He threw his hands up as if frustrated by her behavior. "I thought you understood this. Have I not mentioned my obligations repeatedly? You are aware the future security of my title is my immediate concern. My top priority, if you will. You do understand this?"

"You never mentioned wanting to marry your neighbor," she huffed, crossing her arms over her chest. He looked at her in adorable confusion. "Just saying," she said sarcastically. They had grown so close over the weeks, the best of friends who laughed and even conspired to send the Everly sisters on their way almost daily; and they were lovers at night, sharing their hopes and dreams for the future. A future she envisioned with them together as a couple, although she knew the future he envisioned only included her as a friend, "his closest confidant" he had called her. She would not be his hidden secret from his wife. She was no man's mistress.

His interest in marrying his neighbor told her exactly how much he cared for her, which evidently was not one iota. He made it all too clear that a future was not going to be possible for them, and obviously, no matter the amount of time she spent with him, loving him, talking with him, she was never going to change his mind.

He may not see her as his social inferior any longer, but he knew society would. She was not born of the aristocracy. *Hell, I am not even of this time period.* Ellis feared scandal, but even more so, he felt his family duties more important than his own happiness. He had made a promise to his dying father, and she wouldn't ask him to go back on his word. It meant too much to him.

Strangely, as much as that realization hurt, she actually admired his honor and sense of duty. The feeling of having her heart severely battered told her that she had put far too much feeling into this relationship; whereas his feelings had been feigned. Unfortunately, she realized, she was delusional enough to believe she alone could make him happy, duped herself into believing in the dream of happily-ever-after, and now she would suffer for it.

She suddenly longed for a friend. Really, she wanted the impossible, because she longed to talk to her father. She wanted her dad to reassure her that everything was going to be okay, even in the nineteenth century. She blinked back tears. Ellis was no longer representing a safe haven for her. He was destroying her. Taking a deep breath, she pasted on her I-could-care-less smile, benign but effective. "Your Grace, I have found my time here must come to an end. I thank you for your generosity and kindness."

"What do you mean, your time here? Are you returning to your time period now?"

She blinked back tears, not because she couldn't return to the future but because he didn't sound like he cared either way. "I'm afraid I must leave right away."

"But what will I tell my neighbors when you disappear before my sister's arrival? Couldn't you postpone your trip for a few months? I'm sure Darlene will pay a visit by then." Of course he was concerned what others would think. "I had thought to take you to the theater to see *your* play."

The tears burned her eyes again, but she wouldn't let them fall. She turned her back to him as a few unwillingly slipped down her cheeks. She would have loved seeing the Shakespeare montage with him. Wiping at the tears, she turned to face him. "I'm afraid you'll have to take your future wife," she said, and walked out the door before he could utter another word.

What a complete idiot I was to trust in my feelings for him. She had thought she could make him see that social standing didn't matter, to make him not care about the society he so wished to please, to make him see love conquered all.

But she failed. Her heart ached terribly.

Although her bedroom window overlooked the statue garden, she could not see the bench where they sat from the angle of her room. She knew Ellis returned to Lady Amelia because she could still hear them laughing. An hour later, she was packed, and she looked out the window again when she heard childlike squealing to find Ellis chasing Amelia's two younger sisters around the statuary. It seemed he liked children. She would have thought him too stuffy to picture him playing with these girls, but then he didn't let many people see this side of him often. Amelia was dear to him, of this Desirea was certain. Ellis and Amelia would likely marry and have a dozen children for him to chase around this spectacular castle. This vision caused more tears to slide down her face.

A couple of weeks ago, the garden was so weed-choked that their running wouldn't have been possible. The house, as well as the yard and stables, had radically improved in a relatively short amount of time. They now had horses in the barn and flowers in the pots, and… Desirea was going to miss the place. Unfortunately, she knew she'd miss the man even more. "Goodbye, my duke," she whispered, choking on a sob.

How had she let this happen? She had taken one look at Ellis in that alleyway and had practically thrown herself at him. The time they shared together was precious. She wouldn't have traded it for anything, but all she wanted right this minute was to go home. She wished to return to her Malibu home, where everything was normal, at least normal to her. She closed her eyes to listen, pretending the sea crashing upon the shore in the distance was the Pacific Ocean, trying to picture crowds of people swarming the beach and basking in the sun. She imagined busy sidewalks choked with roller-bladers, tattoo-covered men, and food stands; but all she heard was the sound of Ellis and Amelia's soft voices and the waves faded.

She huffed in irritation, turned away from the scene, and slammed the window shut. She had one more favor to ask of Ellis. Since her mind was focused on her broken heart, she hadn't realized how difficult leaving would be until she had finished her angry packing. Unfortunately, her car wasn't parked right outside. She thought to visit London Burton. According to her friend's last letter, she was to be married next week.

Desirea wasn't sure when it happened, but she realized she was no longer as selfish as she once used to be, probably because she let herself fall in love with someone she couldn't have, self-sacrifice at its finest. And to prove this point to herself, she decided to be an adult and do the right thing in this situation. Unlike the old Desirea Leighton, she had decided to leave Ellis to fulfill his life as he was likely predestined to do. She had no right to alter his life's course. After all, she wasn't even supposed to be here.

And as London's friend, she would not miss the big event that was her wedding. She wondered how London felt about changing the Earl of Nankin's destiny? Surely Lord Nankin would have married another if not for their arrival in this time period. This was all so confusing. Why was she here? Would she ever know?

She needed to speak to London. Hopefully her friend could tell her how she found the strength to move forward in a land so foreign. Desirea decided that Amelia couldn't have timed her visit more perfectly, since it was time to for Desirea to go anyway. She had a wedding to attend.

She closed the trunk at her feet. She'd return the trunk to Ellis when she found permanent lodgings. She was going to have to ask him for use of a carriage though. Surely if she wrote London a letter asking for a ride to her wedding, she'd be more than happy to send a vehicle to pick her up. Then she wouldn't have to ask the duke for anything. Her friend had already written that she'd be happy to have her stay with them, although London had no idea how touched Desirea was by the invitation. Yes, her days of relying on the duke were coming to a quick end. Admittedly, this scared her to her core, but she was used to being on her own. *I'll be fine. Fear is understandable. This world is a different place than mine.*

Desirea took a few deep breaths. She was about to give the performance of her life and act as if leaving didn't matter. She was going to pretend her heart wasn't broken into a million pieces.

Walking to the desk, she pulled out some paper and jotted a note to London Burton, accepting her invitation and asking her to send a vehicle. She dropped her letter outside the door, knowing the new housekeeper would see it posted. Then, in her simmering anger, she snatched another piece of paper and began to jot down curse words that she normally would use and substituted them with words more appropriate in an effort to rid her mind of her current frustrations. Instead of saying "shit," as in, *Ellis is a piece of shit,* she could use "garbage." And instead of saying, *Ellis is an asshole,* she could say he's an *insufferable toad of a man who broke her heart and deserves to live out his days cleaning privies!*

No, that didn't feel invigorating at all. It wasn't harsh enough. She threw down the pen at the sound of Amelia's laughter filling the atmosphere again through the closed window. *Whore.*

"Bloody stinking bastard!" There, that sounded totally British and fitting. Squeezing back the tears filling her eyes, she closed the window shutters. Unpacking her nightgown from the trunk, she decided to crawl into bed before the sun set. Once in bed, she pulled the blanket over her head and tried to wish away her hurt feelings. She planned to vanquish all her feelings for the duke by morning.

)()()(

Ellis sat on the side of his bed, confused. He knew he hurt Desirea's feelings, which was ridiculous, considering he told her not to expect anything more from him. But perhaps that was his fault. Women had a tendency to become overly emotional and to expect more, usually much more. But Desirea knew that, no matter how he felt toward her, they could not wed, ever. Of course, women tended to have softer hearts, easily penetrable and easily hurt, which is why he always kept the women in his life at a distance. But he had erred mightily with Desirea. He had let her in, shared his life with her, confided in her in a way he had never felt able with anyone else. He had shared his past grief and his thoughts of the future, which revolved around restoring the castle to its former glory. And she had told him wondrous stories of her life, how she became famous, of the movies, plays, and concerts she starred in. She shared with him her numb feelings of her mother's desertion and what it was like being raised by her father, whom she loved deeply and still missed.

She shared the story about her friend London's visit to his home. She was awed by what she proclaimed "the most romantic gesture she'd ever seen," the earl throwing Miss Burton over his shoulder and carrying her out of his house. Desirea said she felt tears as she witnessed Devonhurst's love for London.

Ellis had told Desirea how happy he was to have her with him because, in truth, he had never felt so wonderful in his life. In essence, he loved her, and now she was leaving. He told himself her leaving was for the best because there wasn't a future for them for she wasn't, on paper, who he needed her to be, no matter how perfect she was for him in every other way. She was a match for him in so many ways, but none of the ways that mattered. He knew he jumped to the wrong conclusion earlier when he thought she meant she was returning to the twenty-first century. He later remembered she had said that wasn't possible, which meant she was probably returning to the village. She was leaving him. It would be much easier if she were returning to her own time. Knowing she was only in London would make it a thousand times harder to forget her.

He scoffed, knowing forgetting her would never happen. It was strange, but he had never really felt this kind of sadness. He'd felt grief aplenty, but not this hopelessness toward the future, which he imagined quite bleak without Desirea.

Desirea hadn't come down to dinner, nor was she waiting in his room as had become her nightly habit. He had found pleasure the likes he had never known with Desirea. A sense of comfort and understanding consumed them whenever desire took control. She had loved him, cared for him, and teased him in a way that had him fighting for breath at the thought of her leaving.

He was very grateful she was still here. He took that as a positive sign. Perhaps her temper had cooled and she decided to stay with him until he wed. A little time together was better than no time at all.

But then he couldn't see Desirea doing anything of the sort. She was a stubborn, feisty woman filled with independence and determination. Just look at how quickly she transformed the castle. *And you.* She had him wishing for things he would have never thought he wanted. *Like the gumption to marry whomever I damn well feel like and to hell with everyone else's thoughts on my choice.*

One thing was certain. Desirea was not the type to play subordinate to anyone. He couldn't even compliment a neighbor without Desirea getting her dander up. *Blast my stupid wishful thinking!* Pure selfishness made him think their relationship would remain unchanged until he wed. Her absence told him exactly how serious matters had become.

He stood and walked to the door separating their rooms. He was about to knock, but decided not to, assuming she'd refuse him entrance. Instead, he turned the knob and walked in. He could see the lump on the bed where she laid buried beneath the covers. The room was dark except for the shafts of moonlight coming in between the shutter slates. He moved to sit on the edge of the bed. They had so many in-depth conversations over the weeks that it was strange to feel himself at a loss for words now. "Desirea?"

"Go away," she said from beneath the blankets.

"I thought you might want to talk." Didn't women love droning on about their feelings? He tried to pull the blanket away from her face.

"I don't," she said, gripping the blanket to her, not allowing him to even look at her in the moonlight, which he suddenly found himself desperate to do. He was so unbelievably drawn to her that he was now questioning how he was going to survive without her. He needed her in a way that defied reason. She had him actually wishing he wasn't a duke. He felt like he was under a spell, like Desirea put some futuristic love drug in his morning tea every day. He wished he was free to make her his wife, wished that he could allow himself to wed because of his bothersome feelings of… *Bloody hell. I am in love. It is definitely time to say goodbye.*

Knowing this was the right decision for his title. He strengthened his resolve to put her out of his life as duty demanded. "Then I will be the first to say goodbye." Her head came out from beneath the blankets at his words and he fought the urge to kiss her. "I have found our time together to be the best part of my life," he said honestly, feeling the sting of tears. "You were my gift, Desirea. I shall never forget you."

"I won't forget you either," she said with a trembling smile. He saw tears pool in her eyes, which served to make this even harder. His own misted up again.

"We've had a splendid time together. I wish you every happiness. Is there anything I can do for you? Do you need a place to stay in the city? Or money?" Ellis's heart thudded as his mind protested: *Don't let her go, you dolt. It will be the worst mistake you ever make.* While his conscience hollered, *You are the Duke of Lancaster. You promised your father. You are honor bound to do what's right by your family.* It was the hardest internal debate he'd ever had with himself, which only told him how much this woman really meant to him, told him how close he was to throwing everything he worked for away for his feelings.

"Uh, no. I'll be fine," she said resolutely, as if no longer upset. "Don't worry about me. I'm a survivor."

"You're a strong determined woman from the twenty-first century, and so I guess I should have no worries."

"I do have one favor to ask," she said.

"Yes?" He hoped it would be a request he could fulfill.

"I need to stay here for a few more days. Are you okay with that?"

"Of course," he said, thinking he was in no way "okay" with that. Her mere appearance had him at sixes and nines. He felt like a lust-filled beast in her presence. When she was in the room, his body seemed to gravitate in her direction. It couldn't be helped. He was most comfortable when she was near. He truly doubted he could ever get enough of Desirea.

"Thank you," she said. "I'm very tired now, Ellis."

"Sorry, I'll go. Uh, goodnight, then." He stood from the bed, feeling a weight settle into his chest. He knew what they had once shared was over, and he ached from the loss.

"Goodnight," she said, pulling the blanket back over her head.

With a heavy sigh, Ellis went back to his room, dropped his robe, and crawled into bed. He missed her already and she wasn't even gone. The worst part was that he knew he'd probably see her again. She would likely show up at some party he was obligated to attend, and he'd have to watch her laugh and flirt with all her admirers from across the room. It would be intolerable. He'd never be able to touch her intimately, laugh with her secretly, listen to her voice, or just look at her for long periods of time.

There was nothing he liked more than watching Desirea in action. She demanded nothing but the best from those around her, and the improvements already witnessed at the castle were proof of her tenacity. He couldn't help admiring her. She was an utter joy to be with and he would miss her dreadfully.

He did not like this feeling of sadness engulfing him. He needed to put her out of his mind and concentrate on doing right by his title and his ancestors. Lady Amelia Faring seemed the right direction for him. They were already friends, of a sort, even if they weren't as close as he and Desirea. Surely, their friendship would develop over time. It was funny, but a few months ago, friendship was something he wouldn't have even considered a possibility with his future spouse. Desirea had changed his way of thinking in many ways. Through her, he realized how splendid intelligent conversation could truly be with a witty woman. At least he still had a few more days to enjoy her company, and surely that would be enough time to drown himself in her attentions. He smiled at the thought and then immediately frowned. Would she be as distant with him as she was this evening? He prayed not.

***

He should have known hurt feelings wouldn't keep his Desirea down. She appeared at breakfast, bright-eyed and smiling. She brought sunshine into the room, and she looked so irresistible, Ellis nearly groaned as her lovely scent filled the air.

"Good morning, Your Grace," she said formally as he stood and pulled out a chair for her. He motioned to a footman to make her a plate and then signaled the man out of the room.

"You look very fetching, Desirea."

"Thanks," she said, not looking at him. She was far too busy concentrating on the food on her plate. She was being aloof, he realized. *Aw, hell. That is probably best for both of our sakes.* But he had hoped to enjoy their last days together.

"What is your plan for the day?" he asked. Usually she would have already told him this information by now.

"You're looking at it," she said, forking some eggs into her mouth.

"You plan to eat eggs all day?" he teased, frowning when she didn't even crack a smile.

"No. I plan to enjoy my last week here as a spoiled guest. I'm usually impossibly catered to, and it seems fitting I find the real me again."

"So you are preparing to take London by storm?" he asked. It was killing him not knowing her plans.

"Although you may wish me far away, Ellis. I'm afraid London is where I..."

"Your Grace, Lady Faring and the Everly sisters are here. I have placed them in the parlor," the butler announced from the doorway.

"Very good, Temple. I'll be there shortly." The duke nodded, trying not to show his irritation at unexpected visitors, and then he turned his attention back to Desirea. "I don't wish you far away." *Only far enough away to gather my feelings back under control so I can fulfill my responsibilities. Surely she understands this.*

She slid back her chair to stand. "I have some things to do, and so I'll leave you to your fans."

"I would like your company," he said, offering his hand to her.

Her face scrunched in what looked like disgust as she glared at his hand as if it had dog waste on it. "I'll pass, thanks." She fled the room before he could protest. But he knew it was again likely for the best. He felt awkward paying close attention to Amelia with Desirea in the room. If he was going to do what he knew he should, he needed to concentrate on Amelia, but not now. He'd have plenty of time to court her further once Desirea left. His plans could wait one week.

He wondered how his life would have been if he had married Amelia years ago. They'd probably have filled the castle with heirs by now. But he had found his first wife, Evelyn more to his liking. Evelyn was the daughter of a duke and well-placed in society. She was also meek and obedient. Unassuming, is how he found her, but Evelyn's prudish nature toward sex made him not want to have any. In fact, his wife hadn't shown much interest in him, other than the money he gave her. She never refused her wifely duty and she did bed him, but she didn't enjoy the taking. Evelyn had been the wrong choice for him, which wasn't a mistake he wished to make again.

But Amelia knew Ellis, well perhaps not the man he had become but surely the youthful boy he used to be. He couldn't expect her to understand him like Desirea seemed to because he really hadn't spent time with her in many years, but she was pretty and appeared kind and would certainly understand the importance of her role as a duke's wife far better than Desirea ever could. Desirea, being from another time, couldn't possibly understand the inner workings of the aristocracy or how to portray herself as one of them, which would be necessary for his wife.

Nonsense! He needed to stop imaging Desirea as his wife. It wasn't going to happen, and so it didn't matter.

But his thoughts turned that direction anyway, for something told him his new bride would never be able to compare with Desirea in the bedroom, a thought that didn't sit well with him. How would Amelia measure up to Desirea?

Her beauty couldn't hold a candle to Desirea's, but he wasn't planning to marry her for her looks. He scolded himself as soon as he had the thought. *Best not to compare the two for I am sure to find Amelia lacking in every way, which simply will not do.*

CHAPTER THIRTEEN

Ellis walked into the parlor to find three ladies awaiting him with obvious enthusiasm, their wide smiles proof. "Hello, ladies. How nice of you to call on me." He held back saying, *again.* "I see you have tea. Can I get you anything else?" he asked, taking a seat on a chair across from the sofa where the Everly sisters sat, while Amelia sat in the chair next to his.

"Where's Miss Desirea?" asked Anne, the youngest of the Everly sisters.

"She's around somewhere, probably overhauling another room. She's been very instrumental in turning this place around," he said proudly.

"The two of you have grown close?" asked Amelia, and Ellis realized he needed to put forth a more stoic expression when he spoke of Desirea.

"We have become friends." He brought his leg up to rest on his opposite knee.

"Have you spoken with your sister as to her arrival date?" Lauren Everly reached for her teacup in an effort of nonchalance, but he heard the scorn in her voice. Little did she know that he would never marry a spiteful woman like herself.

"No, I haven't. I assume it's still too soon for her to travel or she'd be here." He decided a change of topic was necessary. "So, tell me, Lady Amelia, how are your sisters faring?"

"They are well, Your Grace. They wanted to come with me."

"You could have brought them," he said. "It's nice to see children running about the place." He heard Lauren snort.

"Are you well, Lady Lauren?" he asked, purposely calling attention to her rudeness.

"Yes, I'm fine. I merely find it amusing that you'd ask Amelia to bring her younger sisters. Children can be such a bother."

"Not all people find them so," replied Ellis, who genuinely always liked children. He admired their exuberant smiles and carefree ways. He wished Lauren would find a more useful way to fill her mouth. Perhaps he should insist she eat if only to shut her up. He wasn't conversing with her anyway. He'd been addressing Amelia. He was surprised and a bit disappointed that Amelia didn't defend her half sisters. After all, he had led the conversation purposely in the direction of children to garner Amelia's thoughts on family. "Do you find your sisters a bother, Lady Amelia?" He found he had to ask after Lauren's implication.

"I'm afraid I do, Your Grace. They follow me like little ducklings. It's beyond tedious, especially when my stepmother insists I take them everywhere I go."

He was taken aback by her answer. "But you escaped from them today?" he asked, not liking the feelings Amelia had toward her half sisters. Ellis cherished his sister. The time they spent together was important to him. But then Darlene was the only family he had left in the world. Her happiness meant much to him.

"Indeed I did, Your Grace, but I had to use trickery to do so," she brazenly admitted.

"Tell him what you did," Lauren encouraged with great enthusiasm, as if she thought Ellis would not approve of Amelia's answer. In truth, as much as he wanted to ask what Amelia did to escape her sisters, he did not wish to give Lauren the satisfaction.

Amelia was glaring at Lauren, her hands clenched into tight fists.

"Lady Amelia," he said, "walk with me in the garden." He stood, offering her his arm, which told the Everly sisters whom he favored in the room. Besides, the Everly sisters were not yet twenty, while Amelia was a perfect twenty-four and thus far more suited for him.

Amelia stood with a smile, passing a gloating look to the Everly sisters, which Ellis chose to ignore. She took his arm as he led them out the doors and into the statue garden. He headed toward the bench they sat on during her visits. No matter how hard he tried, Lauren's snappish comment would not leave his head. He had to ask. "So how *did* you trick your sisters into remaining home?"

"I'd rather not say, Your Grace. The castle looks wonderful. What will Miss Leighton do when the renovations are finished? I think it looks complete."

Ellis was silent for a moment. She had not only changed the subject but was beginning to sound like Lauren in regard to Desirea. He did not like it. *Very well. If she wants to avoid my questions, I can play the same game.* "Your cricket match is tomorrow. Is the house and yard set up for the games?"

"Yes, and I've partnered us together. I hope you don't mind."

She is a controlling little lady. "Actually, Lady Amelia, I believe I should be partnered with Miss Leighton. After all, she doesn't know anyone in this area."

Amelia laughed, but he noted that it wasn't genuine. "Your Grace, how will Miss Leighton fly if you clip her wings? You do wish her to meet other people, I assume. You can't keep her all to yourself, or is there more to the story regarding the two of you?"

Damn, I am beginning not to like Amelia. Her tone was condescending and her manner off-putting. How did he not see this before?

He and Desirea had done a wonderful job of preventing scandal from occurring, or at least, Desirea went out of her way to make appearances as her own chaperone in the effort to see his name unblemished. He admired her for her concern and fortitude. He wondered where Desirea was right this moment.

He decided that he was done talking to Amelia. There was no thrill running through his blood, which is what he felt whenever Desirea was in the vicinity. He needed to rid himself of Amelia and the other two ladies so he could seek out the one woman who didn't talk petty nonsense to him.

"She's a friend of Darlene's, but I'm happy to call her my friend as well."

"I see," said Amelia with a rough edge in her voice. His information seemed to anger her. *Impudent chit. Does she not realize to whom she is speaking?* He closed his eyes as Desirea's words filled his head and he realized he was no better than Lady Amelia Faring. He was only better placed. But he was certainly nicer than Amelia was. Tomorrow he'd send a message with their regrets. He and Desirea would not be attending the lawn games at the Faring residence.

"I think it is wonderful the two of you have grown closer," she said, and he looked down at her, trying to gage her sincerity. She seemed in earnest and he thought perhaps he had been judging her too harshly, but it was hard not to when she made such irritating comments and kept company with the oldest Everly sister. And she had tricked her way out of spending time with her sisters, which didn't seem very sisterly.

Ellis now decided to attend the lawn games tomorrow, if only to judge Amelia's behavior; but if he could convince Desirea to go, which he thought he could, he would insist she be his partner. He told himself that Desirea would need a familiar face in the crowd. She would need him. At least he hoped she would. He knew his thinking was addled for she didn't belong to him, but his feelings on the matter couldn't be helped.

Desirea only had a week left in his household, and he wanted her to experience some countryside amusements before she returned to the city where parties and gaiety abound. Lawn games were a huge attraction for the people of this time, and he had promised to show her his era. Archery and cricket may not be as exciting as the future games Desirea described, but he planned to show her how people of his age entertained themselves.

"It's been lovely visiting with you, Lady Amelia." He stood. "I look forward to tomorrow."

Seeing as he was dismissing her, she had no choice but to stand and take his arm. He led her back toward the glass French doors off the back of the room, where they found the Everly sisters bent over with their ears against the main door, which opened to the foyer. Clearly they were eavesdropping on someone's conversation. He cleared his throat, and they spun around to look at him, their cheeks turning a ruddy shade of red at being caught.

"Oh, Your Grace." Lauren was the first to speak. "We did not hear you return."

"So I assumed," he said.

"Yes, well, we really should be going," said Amelia, letting go of his arm and taking one of Lauren's and one of Anne's before they all uttered "good day" and fled as quickly as they could.

Ellis followed them out of the room, looking for whomever they could have been listening to. He spotted two of the maids further down the hall, near the coat closet. Once the front door closed, he made his way toward them. "I'd like a word," he said, upon his approach.

The maids curtsied and then remained before him with heads down and hands clasped in front of them. "What were you discussing five minutes ago?"

"We were…" The shorter of the two started to speak and was elbowed by the other. "We were contemplating the sturdiness of this table," she said, walking a few feet away to the only table, which was more than sturdy.

Ellis had no patience for nonsense. Untrustworthy staff could lead to scandals of renowned proportions. "Listen," he said, smiling at his Desirea-like tone. "I'm your employer. I wish to know exactly what you were saying because my neighbors overheard you. Do I need to explain to you that matters in my household must remain in *my* household? I believe this was explained thoroughly before you began work here. I am a duke, and thus people tend to scrutinize anything that goes on in this house. This scrutiny is often brought on by gossip. This means that I only hire staff I can trust, people who are loyal to me." He crossed his arms over his chest and glared at them. "Now what were you discussing?"

"We're terribly sorry, Your Grace. We had no idea anyone could hear us," said the taller one with big brown eyes.

"It's my fault, Your Grace," the other interrupted. "I was so shocked. I mean, I've never seen anyone…" The maid's face filled with a blush, which now had him really wondering what in the hell was going on. Whatever it was, the maid looked reluctant to speak of it. "I promise I will never speak of it again."

"I second that promise, Your Grace," said the other maid. "We are most loyal and respect your privacy."

"I'm afraid I still do not understand the situation, though I appreciate your regrets, and accept your apologies."

"It's Miss Leighton, Your Grace. She is acting most peculiar." The maid looked at the floor again.

What has Desirea done this time? He already witnessed her intentional use of slang from her time whenever one of his employees wasn't doing a thorough job, which was often because Desirea held them to very high standards. He had found her ability to leave the staff bewildered amusing, but Desirea usually didn't send them to blushing. Perhaps it would be best if he found Desirea and put an end to whatever this was. "In the future, please keep the gossip to a minimum, and always remember the walls have ears when you work for a duke."

"Yes, Your Grace. Again, we are terribly sorry."

"Very sorry," said the other.

With a nod, he dismissed them and went in search for Desirea. He entered her room to find the bed made and her dress for the day set out upon it with appropriate undergarments. He checked the bathing room and the closet, but she wasn't there. He was about to call out for her when a breeze caught the curtain and it billowed toward him through the open French door, which led to a small balcony and steps leading into the grassy stretch of heather on the far side of the statue garden. He moved to the door and the curtain tried to fall back into place. It settled around his back as he stared transfixed at the sight before him.

Amongst the heather, upon a large linen lay Desirea, bared-assed for all the world to see. The visual was enough to cause his heart to race and his blood to pump faster through his veins. His cock's response was instantaneous. *What the hell is she doing lying naked in my yard?*

Without further thought, his feet led him in the direction his body wanted to go. Not able to help himself, he dropped his coat on the stone steps, which was quickly followed by his cravat. He reached her as he pulled his shirt over his head, and tossed it amongst the flowers surrounding them. "What are you doing?" he asked, sliding his body down beside her. His hands trailed down her back and over her perfectly round derriere, hot from the sun.

"I'm sunbathing. My tan has all but disappeared," she said in a lazy manner.

"Explain, please," he said, continuing to explore the curves of her glorious naked figure, warm and golden from the sun's rays. Never had he imagined making love in the heather, but now the thought would not leave his mind. He pushed his cock against her and she rolled over with a smile.

"In the twenty-first century, some people like to sunbath. It's relaxing, and it turns the skin a nice bronze color if done correctly."

"Ladies strive to stay out of the sun in this age," he said before taking a pert nipple into his mouth. He saw Desirea clench the linen in her hands. "But I'm thinking you have the right of it."

"I've noticed the pale faces," said Desirea, arching her back. "You got rid of your fans rather quickly."

He leaned over her, ignoring the comment. "People sunbathe naked together in your time?"

She laughed. "Only on beaches that permit nudity, but for the most part, we wear bathing suits. I usually wore a bikini, which was like this." He watched as she traced a finger along her body, showing him how such a garment hid the private areas of a person.

"It doesn't appear to be a large garment," he commented. "Am I to assume all of this remains exposed?" He brought his head down and began placing kisses on her stomach.

"Yes," she said shakily, his manipulations working. He didn't know if she'd let him back into her bed, or let him have her in the heather, as the case happened to be. He was thankful she wasn't pushing him away. He couldn't seem to get enough of her.

"I think I would like your time," he teased, nibbling her neck.

She smacked at him playfully and he latched on to her nipple again.

"On second thought, Desirea, I would not want any man viewing so much of your lovely body."

Settling himself between her legs, he smiled down at her, looking into her lovely blue eyes, wishing he could look in them for a lifetime but knowing it wasn't possible. She brought her mouth to his and he slid his cock slowly inside her, reeling from the sensation, trembling from being with her, the woman he loved but couldn't have.

***

Desirea writhed beneath him, loving the feel of his body on top of hers as he claimed her, making her feel sensations she never imagined possible. She felt the tenderness and wonder that she had felt every time they made love, a feeling of oneness as if they were really two halves of a whole. She had never felt this way toward any man. She knew Ellis was possessive toward her. She saw it in his every glance and heard it in his tone of voice. The thrill of being in love with him had her climaxing almost instantly. Sex was so much better with the man you love, and sex between her and Ellis was mind-blowing. She placed her legs upon his shoulders and Ellis grunted in pure male satisfaction at her move.

It was only a few moments later when they both exploded in ecstasy. Desirea looked at the sky in wonder as tremors raked her frame, and then Ellis's mouth came down to meet hers. Making love outside was absolutely invigorating. Then the significance of what they did struck her and her heart filled with even more love for this man. Ellis had stepped out of his comfort zone for her. He had made love to her out in the open, where anyone could have seen them. Well perhaps not anyone, since it was somewhat isolated here, but he had neighbors and servants. Surely he had considered his actions and the consequences that could have ensued and hadn't cared, obviously, or he wouldn't be lying naked next to her now. He had said he was so smitten by her that he wasn't thinking clearly, and she understood what he meant by that comment now. So, although her heart expanded with love for his actions, she loved him too much not to protect him. "I'm sorry, Ellis." She put her arms through her robe and then stood to wrap it around her waist.

"Sorry?" he said, sitting up to look at her. "For what are you sorry? I just had one of the best moments of my life, Desirea. There's no reason to be sorry."

"Yes, I know, but look around you, Ellis. Someone could have seen us."

"Actually, someone did see you, love: the maids, who were overheard by the Everly sisters as they spoke about their shock at seeing you…sunbathe naked."

"The maids saw me?" She had thought herself quite secluded in her spot, unless one was looking from the balcony of her room, which is what obviously happened.

"Yes, one of them did." He stood to pull on his pants.

"And the Everly sisters overheard this exchange between these shocked maids?"

"Yes, I believe so. At least, they were trying desperately to hear. They had their ears to the door."

Desirea began to laugh hysterically at this news. She was sure the Everly sisters were shocked by such an image as her nudity. Tears came to her eyes at the thought of their expressions upon hearing this news.

Ellis joined her merriment. "Their faces were unbelievable when I walked in with Lady Amelia. They nearly jumped out of their skin when I cleared my throat."

Her laughter died. "Where were you and Lady Amelia coming from?" She cursed herself as soon as the jealous words left her mouth. His relationship with Lady Amelia was no concern of hers. At least it wasn't supposed to be. *Damn my frikken feelings!*

"The other side of the statue garden," he said, scooping up his shirt and not looking at her, which was just as well, she thought, since she felt the sting of tears.

"And how are all of your lovely neighbors today?" she asked, trying to be pleasant after what they shared. She didn't want to ruin their last days together with her jealousy.

"Conniving as always, but such is the way of women, I suppose." He pulled his shirt over his head.

Wisely, Desirea turned on her heel and fled back up the steps and into her room. She closed and locked the door so Ellis couldn't enter. *How dare he generalize about women in such a manner!* She huffed and threw herself on her bed, right on top of today's clothes.

But he let his guard down and did something he normally would never do, make love to you outside, the voice in her head reminded her. *He loves you,* said the same voice, and she knew it was true, which was the worst part of this entire situation.

Who was she kidding? They had both let their guard down. Desirea had certainly never made love outside. Where was *her* sense of propriety? It seemed all Ellis had to do was smile at her and she melted. She hadn't cared who saw them, because all she saw was him. She had tunnel vision whenever he was near and she believed he suffered from the same madness.

She closed her eyes, trying to find some inner peace, when a knock made her jump. Ellis stood on her balcony, fully clothed, his posture stiff. Unfortunately, the sheer curtain did not hide her from view.

"What are you doing, Desirea? Let me in. I want to talk to you," he cajoled. "You know I wasn't including you with my comment. You're not like other women…"

She threw open the door and glared at him with her hands on her hips. "Did you say I'm not like other women? How many times do you wish to insult me?"

He gave her a look that said he thought she was mad. "I meant that in the most complimentary way," he said, coming into the room and moving to pull her into a hug, which she backed out of with a shove.

"Explain," she said, throwing the same word at him that he usually did her.

"How about we discuss how wonderful you are over lunch? I find our blissful exertion has left me hungry."

"And you plan to sing my attributes over the afternoon meal?" she asked, feeling mollified.

"Perhaps not sing, but I'll shout if you'd like." He smiled, and she took his arm. She was quite hungry too, and she truly did not wish to fight with him.

Once seated with a cold pasta dish and some mini sandwiches in front of them, Desirea smiled at him. "You may begin to sing, or rather, shout my praises now."

To her surprised delight, Ellis began to recite all the things he liked about her. "For one, you are the prettiest woman I have ever seen. But aside from your beauty, I admire you for your intelligence, your grace, your wittiness, and your ability to laugh at life, while making the best of everything that comes your way. I cherish every conversation we have had. I admire your talent, and I find you completely delightful, even when you're cursing at me. And the excitement and satisfaction I find in your arms surpasses everything I've ever imagined. In you, I have found a true friend and a splendid lover. Thank you for coming into my life, Desirea."

"Wow! I'm truly flattered, Your Grace." His words made her feel giddy with love. "I'm willing to admit that your words make me want to crawl across this table and have my way with you again, Ellis."

"Might I suggest you be mindful of the bad table leg when you do so." He moved his chair back and motioned her forward. "I'm waiting."

With a laugh and the pull of Ellis' desire as he watched her heatedly from across the table, she hoisted herself on the tabletop and moved toward him, her focused stare telling him exactly what she wanted to do with him.

CHAPTER FOURTEEN

Later that night, after a game of chess, which Desirea won thanks to her father's lessons, they sat on the sofa with her legs kicked up on his lap.

"I want you to go to Amelia Faring's country party with me tomorrow."

She couldn't help but blink rapidly at him. *Is he out of his ever-loving mind? Why the hell would I want to watch him court his future wife?* He did not seem to understand how torturous this would be for her. "I don't think so, Ellis."

"What if I told you that I will be your partner? I will be most attentive to you and only you, Desirea. Please allow me the opportunity to show you the entertainments to be had in the country before you return to the city. We have less than a week, so let's make it unforgettable."

He was convincing, and she really wanted to enjoy their last moments together. "And you won't throw any of your charm Amelia's way?"

"No. I will direct all my charms only at you." He gave her a smile and waggled his brow.

"All right then. I'll go. But only if you promise to behave. Save your wife hunting for when I'm gone."

"Agreed."

"I'm sure to make a fool out of myself playing this cricket game."

"I'll teach you. It's easy."

"Well, I should warn you, I'm very competitive."

"Yes, so your recent win at chess has proven." He gave her legs a gentle push and they fell off his lap to the floor. He stood to take her hand.

"What?" she asked, coming to her feet.

"Let's go practice cricket."

She laughed. "It's dark, Ellis, or haven't you noticed?"

"Oh, I've noticed, because when it's dark I think of you joining me in my bed. Come," he said, pulling her toward the door. "I have an idea."

It took the servants a full twenty minutes, but eventually Desirea stood on the freshly scythed lawn on the east side of the house with hundreds of candles and candelabras set up in a large oval. Shadows were everywhere, but the candles and the full moon provided enough light necessary for the late night lesson. Desirea realized that most women may have opted out of the practice, but she wasn't kidding when she said she didn't like to lose.

The game wasn't difficult to understand. She took practice swings with the oblong bat as Ellis pitched to her. She'd always been good at batting cages, and so she had no difficulties. Ellis appeared astounded by what he considered her "natural ability." As he continued to explain the intricacies of the game, she paced out the length of the pitch and experimented with how fast she could run back and forth.

Ellis laughed as she ran. "You don't like to do anything in half measures, do you, Desirea."

"Anyone can be average, Ellis. I happen to strive to be better. The other ladies play as well, do they not?"

"Yes, of course," he said.

"Then I plan to be able to beat them…and some of the men too."

He held his sides, laughing hysterically.

She came to a stop and wiped the sweat from her brow. "Woo, that's quite a workout."

She was surprised when he grabbed her and hugged her tight, but she hugged him in return. This had been so much fun. She couldn't even remember the last time she played a sport. How sad was that? She was only twenty… *Well, and a half.*

"I'll call the staff to put out the flames and collect the candles." He began to turn away, but she didn't release him. "What?" he asked, in a manner she would have used and she laughed.

"Nothing. I like looking at you in the candlelight. You are smoking hot, Ellis. I know you think ladies flock to you because of your title, but I must tell you, I think you're completely wrong about their motives."

He smiled and then picked her up in his arms and carried her through the French doors of the parlor and up the steps. He deposited her in the middle of his big bed and then disappeared back down the hall, to tell the servants to gather all the hodgepodge of lighting they had scattered in the yard, she assumed. Sighing in contentment, she stared at the ceiling above her head, wishing she could remain in this spot forever.

"The inferno we created outside shall be extinguished," Ellis said, reentering the room, locking the door and pulling off his neck cloth.

"I guess that leaves the two of us to extinguish the inferno in here." She couldn't take her gaze off him as he continued to undress, baring his chest and his sculpted abs. He stalked toward her, his gaze full of sensual promise and hidden pleasures. She squirmed in anticipation. She fumbled with the ties on the front of her dress, nearly screaming in frustration at the fastenings.

He was fully naked now. His cock stood out to greet her as he slid his torso over her. Turning to lay beside her, he moved her hands away from her bodice and ripped the strings free of the dress with a quick yank.

"Wow, how did you learn to do that?"

He laughed. "First time."

"I'm impressed." She kissed his chin.

"So am I." He chuckled, and then he began to kiss down the side of her neck toward her chest. His kisses seemed to brand her as he moved them down her arm, then back over her chest. He slowly and torturously showed her how much he adored her. She felt as if she were floating on a cloud and being showered with the one thing that gave her life, Ellis's kisses.

***

Ellis slowly moved his cock into her wet sheath. He leaned down to inhale her sweet scent as he inched further into the rightness he felt with Desirea. She undulated beneath him, moving her hips in unison with his, biting her lower lip as she stared at him with passion and love, and he knew she loved him for he could feel it in their sexual explorations. It felt as if they both were trying to build something everlasting, to create a memory that would never fade, regardless how much time elapsed. It was obvious they both feared fate wouldn't allow them to come together again.

When they finally lay depleted in each other's arms, Desirea snuggled into the warmth of his side and fell fast asleep.

***

Come morning, Desirea was very surprised to find herself still cocooned next to Ellis. As was his habit, he usually carried her to her room to avoid any type of servant gossip, but for him not to move her spelled trouble. His sudden lack of concern toward scandal worried her. She did not want him to come to regret their relationship, or come to hate her if people began to criticize their association.

Because she cared for him deeply, she did the only thing she could think to do. She slid out of bed, trying not to disturb Ellis, and then made her way barefoot to the door connecting their rooms. Taking one last look at Ellis, she hurried back to her room, closing the door gently behind her. She then disturbed her bedding to make it looked slept in. She was still naked when she turned from her bed to see the main door opening after a single knock. Her assigned maid walked in.

"Good morning, Miss. I was going to open your drapes."

"Thank you, Mura, but I'm up now anyway." Desirea grabbed her robe on the hook near the closet and put it on, belting it around her waist. *That was a close call. Five minutes later and the jig would have been up. Well, it wasn't five minutes later, and so catastrophe averted. For now.*

"Has his lordship risen?" she asked, complimenting herself for sounding like a nineteenth century lady.

"I don't believe so, Miss. Breakfast will be served in an hour," said the maid before she walked into Desirea's closet and returned with a light blue walking dress.

"What are you doing?" asked Desirea, watching as the maid laid the dress across a chair.

"I'm picking out your clothes so you can dress, Miss. You did wish to eat, did you not?"

"Yes, of course, I just..." She tended to favor picking out her own outfit for the day, but she saw no reason to upset her new maid, who appeared to be taking her duties quite seriously. "The blue dress is fine."

"If you'd prefer something else?"

"No. Like you, I'm going through an adjustment period, that's all." And the adjustments she had to make were huge, she thought.

"I think we'll pull your hair back with some of your lovely tresses curled to frame your face. All right, let's get started." Mura pulled a white chemise from the drawer, along with stockings and the "drawers" that constituted underwear. Little did her maid know that the underwear were so cumbersome that Desirea refused to wear them. She didn't wish to tell Mura this, however; the twenty-something year-old woman would probably have a heart attack if she were to admit to such wickedness. *Going commando in the nineteenth century, what fun.*

After dressing and then going behind the white wooden divider to rid herself of the detested drawstring drawers, she sat on her stool in front of the vanity while Mura worked on her up-do.

"I think I hear his lordship stirring," said Mura.

"Yes," replied Desirea. She had heard him as well. Last night was so wonderful she felt extraordinary this morning.

"I assume you'll be attending the Marquis of Thornbrook's gathering this afternoon? Lady Amelia Faring has invited most of the countryside."

"Yes, I'm going, but I can't say I'm thrilled about it." She shrugged. She hadn't thought beyond breakfast and had completely forgotten about the country party.

"Good heavens. Why ever not, Miss? It's sure to be a grand time."

"Do you know Lady Amelia? I mean, did you grow up around here?"

"I do know her. I've spent my entire life in Seaham."

Mura placed the extra hairpins in the bowl on the vanity and stepped back. Desirea smiled at her fashionable hairstyle and thanked Mura. "It looks lovely. Now tell me more about Amelia." She turned on her stool to face Mura instead of speaking to her through the mirror.

"I am a servant, Miss. I cannot speak ill of my betters."

Desirea had learned to respect the importance of having a job in this time period, and she didn't want this maid thinking she risked losing hers. She stood and took Mura's hand, leading the confused maid to the side of her bed, indicating for her to sit. Keeping hold of her hand, Desirea sat beside her, ready to charm the answers she needed from her maid.

"I am not asking you to speak ill of anyone, Mura. I can tell you are a wonderfully loyal maid by looking at you. You work hard, and you probably, sometimes, don't feel appreciated. But I want you to know that I appreciate you, Mura. I wish to be as knowledgeable about this area and its people as you are, but I know such a thing isn't possible. This is why I need your expertise. You are a woman, and as such, you are likely a keen observer and have astute listening skills." Desirea shrugged as if all women had these talents, and Mura smiled in agreement. "For most women, it's a gift. And I have a feeling you have this gift."

"In this you may be right, Miss. I do see and hear things that people often think I don't," Mura replied with excitement at learning about a skill she didn't realize she had.

Desirea smiled. "See, I could tell that about you. It's in your eyes. You have pretty brown eyes."

"Thank you, Miss. You are too kind."

Desirea remained silent hoping Mura would now speak. She didn't have long to wait. She liked Mura. It was too bad she was leaving soon. Perhaps they could have been friends.

"I feel I should tell you that she isn't the sweet tempered young lady she portrays," Mura admitted.

"Yes, I noticed that too," said Desirea, wondering why Ellis didn't see through Amelia's act. "Do go on. What did she do to show her vicious side?"

"Well, from what I hear, her father has introduced her to many handsome, titled gentlemen, but none have found favor with her. The Laird of Camster, that's Lady Darlene's husband, was in this area to meet the fair Amelia. Of course the Scotsman took one look at sweet Darlene and declined his introduction with Lady Faring. I've heard the young lady threw a tantrum the likes her household had never seen."

"Why? If she never met him, why did she care if he chose another?"

"Jealousy, I am told. She didn't want Darlene to have him since he had initially been chosen for her."

"Huh. So she wishes pretty badly to marry?"

Mura tilted her head to the side and looked at Desirea as if she were crazy.

"Oh right," said Desirea, rolling her eyes. "Every young lady wants to marry here. I keep forgetting."

"Pardon, Miss? I'm afraid I don't understand."

"Oh, it's nothing. What did Amelia do after her temper tantrum?"

"I can't recall she did much after that. Men still visit her house and they still leave faster on the way out. She has a tendency to frighten them off. It's such a shame, seeing as she is quite pretty and could do well with a bit of ladylike restraint. Men do not wish to have their future wife locking their children in closets."

Desirea was busy wondering why Ellis did not see this side of Amelia when Mura's last words brought her head up. "What?"

Mura whispered, as if they could suddenly be overheard. "I have heard she locks her sisters in closets so she can escape her house without them following her. One day she left them there for three hours. I heard the Marquis of Thornbrook punished his oldest daughter for this by locking her in her room for a week. According to my friend who works in the Thornbrook household, Lady Faring now has her maid release her sisters once she is a safe distance away. It seems the only lesson the young mistress learned from her father's punishment was to be more discrete in her misbehavior."

Desirea threw herself backwards on her bed. *Holy shit! This girl is meaner than I thought.* She couldn't allow Ellis to marry such a monster. What if Amelia locked up Ellis's children? What kind of person would lock a child in a closet, regardless of the reasons? *The bitch is crazy.* "Wow! I'll tell you, Mura, I thought the girl conniving, but her ruthlessness has me stunned. Why would the duke not know about any of this?"

"The duke has been gone from this area for many years, Miss. Besides, the Thornbrook household keeps things quite hushed. That's why it's important you don't tell anyone what I've told you."

"Trust me, Mura, your name will not be mentioned in regard to Amelia."

"I appreciate that, Miss. I really do."

Desirea nodded and continued to pace the room, trying to come up with a reason she could not attend the country party at the Thornbrooks today. *Perhaps I could twist an ankle or come down with some ailment?*

"Can I ask you something?" Mura stood and began to fluff Desirea's pillows.

"Yes, of course," said Desirea.

"You care for his lordship?"

It wasn't much of a question but Desirea replied, "Yes, yes, I do." *Only too much.*

"And you are asking me these questions because you believe his lordship has taken an interest in Miss Faring?"

"Yes, he has, which makes me really not want to go to this event."

"I admit that I am new to this household, Miss, but I do know love when I see it, and I agree that Lord Lancaster is in love, with you."

Her words made Desirea feel warm and gushy inside. "That might be true. Nevertheless, his lordship does not view me as a viable candidate for the position of his wife."

"Nonsense, Miss. He adores you."

"Yes, Mura, he does." Desirea fell silent.

"You have to go today if only to keep his lordship away from such a woman as Lady Amelia."

"Yes, Mura, I do," said Desirea. With a quick thanks, she went down to breakfast. Perhaps she was sent here to prevent the Duke of Lancaster from making the worst mistake of his life, she thought. After all, there had to be some purpose to her being sent here, and this was as good a possibility as any other she could come up with.

***

Ellis sat at the breakfast table waiting for Desirea. A stream of light from a nearby window gleamed off the table's wooden surface. The buffet table behind him was full of silver-domed covered breakfast fare. The aroma of bacon filled the room.

His heart sped up when he heard Desirea telling the housekeeper to make sure the rug in the main parlor was removed and cleaned outside. She sailed into the room with a bright smile, and his heart leapt with love for her. How he wished he could awaken to her smile every day. "Good morning, Desirea. Your hair is stunning."

Desirea smiled and took the seat he pulled out for her. "Mura has a magical touch. I know the gemmed hairpins are a bit much for daytime wear, but Mura will only have time to do a touch up before we leave."

He retook his seat and, with a nod, indicated that the nearby servant was to make them plates, which he did efficiently and then placed them on the table. With a wave of his hand, Ellis dismissed him and the man left the room. "I'm glad you are joining me. I daresay you will amaze the countryside with your skill on the cricket field."

"Thanks to your lesson, I'm sure to do well."

"You have a natural ability, but I'm willing to take all the credit." He smiled, and she laughed, which made him feel wonderful.

They ate in companionable silence for a while before she asked, "Ellis, how well do you know Amelia Faring?"

He looked at her sideways with a fork full of kippers paused before his lips, then set his fork back on his plate, kippers forgotten. He did not like the sound of warning in her voice, as if she were more knowledgeable regarding *his* neighbors than he was. He still had not forgotten her I-know-more-than-you comment. "Better than you know her," he replied.

She crossed her arms and placed them on the table, leaning toward him. "Are you sure about that?" Her left brow raised and she cocked her head sideways.

"Positive."

"And you find Amelia fun to be around? You enjoy her company?"

Was she worried he'd embarrass her by fawning over Amelia today? He took her hand. He did not want to wreck this time they had with talk of Amelia or his future. For now, he wanted, no needed, to live for this moment and this moment alone. "I thought you understood that I would court no one until you and I are over."

"Over," she said in such a sad voice that he came to his feet, feeling uncomfortable by the feelings swamping him. She knew what he had to do, and discussing it would not rid him of his obligations. Such talk only saddened her further and he had no desire to do that. "I need to check on the new mare. I'm off to the stables." Without another bite of food, he left. His appetite had waned the moment he'd seen the hurt in her eyes. The impossibility of their situation was killing him.

CHAPTER FIFTEEN

Desirea sat in the quiet of her room staring out the window overlooking the side of the statue garden. Two male gardeners were digging out dead bushes, which were to be hauled away and burned. Clouds formed, turning the sky gray. Of course, Desirea was praying for rain, but with her luck, she thought, it wouldn't come. She could smell the lilacs from the arrangement on her nightstand. She'd always loved the scent of lilacs, which reminded her of spring and Easter dinner with her dad. A tear slid down her cheek. How she wished she had her dad's guidance and reassurance right now.

Her heart felt heavy in her chest. The word "over" rumbled around in her brain, haunting her. She didn't want them to be over. More tears fell down her cheeks, and she wiped them away in frustration. She'd do whatever was necessary to make sure Ellis saw Amelia for what she was; but then she'd leave, and when she left, she'd be leaving behind her heart.

Mura's knock at her door found her strengthening her resolve to oust Amelia. She didn't imagine this task difficult. After her earlier conversation with Mura, it was clear many men saw through Amelia's cool façade. Surely, after spending a day in Amelia's company, Ellis would realize what an evil person she was too.

And why would you believe such a thing? The man seems oblivious to Amelia's vicious streak.

She stood and let Mura in so she could get ready for the country party she did not want to attend.

***

Mura was about to pull the daydress over her head when the first fat drops began to fall. Desirea jumped off her stool in her jubilation. *Yes! It's raining.* She fought the urge to sing loudly

BJ Thomas's *Raindrops Keep Falling on my Head.* She settled herself, trying to put on a frown. "Looks like the party will be canceled."

"You don't fool me, Miss. I know you were hoping for such a thing. I'm glad for you," said Mura. "Do you still want me to put you in this dress?"

"No, I think my wrap will be good. I want to be comfortable. I think I'll watch the rain for a while. Thanks, Mura." Desirea slipped her robe over her white chemise, and Mura left the room, shaking her head as if watching the rain was so out of the realm of normal thinking.

At a knock, she turned to find Ellis standing in her doorway. He entered, closing the door behind him, and she smiled as images of them doing the bump and grind on her bed popped into her head. "Are you disappointed the festivities have been canceled?"

"Not if it means I have you all to myself while you are dressed in your nightclothes." He moved forward.

"Will you do me a favor?" She moved toward a comfy oversized chair and gave it a pat.

"Yes."

"Will you move this piece of furniture onto my balcony?"

His brow creased in confusion. "You are aware it's raining?" He looked outside at the storm and then back to her. "Don't tell me you sunbathe naked in the rain too? Or wait, do tell me that." He moved closer and pulled her into his arms. She laughed at his playful manner.

"No, that would be silly. There's no sun. I like to sit and watch the rain. It comforts me. I know that might sound weird, but I used to sit on my dad's lap when I was little and we would watch the rain for hours. I always felt refreshed by the experience, and I could really use the rain's comfort right now." She blinked away tears. She did not wish to burden him with her fears for the future, but she was scared, and she needed the rain.

He asked no further questions but threw open the French doors and hauled the loveseat outside. He shut one of the doors and backed the seat further away from the balusters so the cushions wouldn't become wet in the downpour.

She snatched the comforter off her bed.

"Now what?" he asked with a serious smile. She noted that he was truly trying to help her and likely sensed her sincere need for peace, which only made her love him more. But the icing on the cake was when he approached her and scooped her up in his strong arms. She snuggled into his chest and he carried her to the chair and sat, keeping her comfortably on his lap. She curled herself against him, laying her head on his shoulder while she stared out at the rain coming from the sky. The rain shushed the atmosphere, so all she heard was its soothing sound and Ellis's heartbeat. She sighed in contentment, watching the rain paint the railing with its drops. Ellis placed his head on top of hers, and she felt his body give into relaxation.

They stayed that way for a full hour. Desirea had nearly fallen asleep. The rain slowed and was nearly gone when she sat up. She stretched her arms over her head, feeling spectacular after her rest. Ellis's gaze focused on her exposed cleavage. She leaned into him and caught his lips with hers, kissing him with all the love she had.

A knock stopped them from further exploration.

"Ignore it," she said. She had a feeling the party was back on, since the rain was leaving.

"I can't. What if something's wrong?"

"Such as?" She was purposely being stubborn. She did not want to leave the comfort and security of his lap.

"It could be a house fire or…"

"Or one of your axes fell off the wall. Or, I know, Mrs. Hatchett, my fake chaperone, has gone missing." They both had a good laugh at that. She scrambled out of the blanket and got to her feet, tossing the comforter on his lap before adjusting her robe. Facing the inevitable, she crossed her room and went to the door to take the note from the butler, then returned to the balcony. "Here," she said handing him the piece of paper. "But I say we don't open it."

"You really don't want to go to the Thornbrook's?"

No, she didn't, but if they didn't go, how would she know if Ellis figured out Amelia's cruel streak. She had to go, if merely to make sure he took off his blinders regarding this woman. "What does it say?"

It's from the Marquis of Thornbrook. He claims the fields are too wet to play cricket, but he says that Lady Amelia has saved the day by hosting an impromptu play and other entertainments."

"A play, huh? Which one? Did she cast herself as the lead? I'm sure she'd excel as a villain."

"Shall I write back and express your interest in a role."

"Not unless it's the lead," she said under her breath, but he heard her and laughed as he got to his feet.

"Come, we will go."

"Yes," she said grudgingly. "Let's go."

"You know," he said, stopping as they entered her room. "You may enjoy yourself."

She thought about that for a moment and then smiled. She realized she could outclass and verbally manipulate Lady Amelia Faring without an ounce of difficulty. "You know, on second thought, this may be a hoot." She used one of his words, and he smiled before he kissed her.

"I'll meet you downstairs at half past the hour. I'll send in Mura."

"Thanks," she said, grabbing the iridescent plum dress she adored from her closet. It was far more elegant than the daydress she was going to wear to the cricket match earlier. She knew the plum color would look awesome with her blond hair. She made a mental note to thank her friend London "for all the kickass clothes." She had a feeling her friend had made a special shopping trip on her behalf.

***

They pulled down a tree-lined drive and waited behind a line of carriage traffic. Ellis's eyes seemed to be glued to her from the moment she met him in the foyer, and he had even stuttered when he complimented her attire earlier. She noted that she had finally completely enraptured him with her beauty, which pleased her immensely. She smiled at him and then gulped as she looked out the window. Seether's song *Rise Above This* filled her head. She would get through this afternoon, she told herself, and Ellis would realize he was barking up the wrong tree with Lady Amelia. And by the beginning of next week, Desirea would be on her way to London's wedding. At least she had a future destination and a place to stay. This comforted her in a way. She tried not to dwell on the fact that she wouldn't be taking her boyfriend with her. She was sure her heart would be calling out for him every day.

"Wow. It looks like a big turnout."

"Yes, it's sure to be a crush. People often suffer from ennui after a long stint in the country and crave entertainment of any sort."

"So it seems." She peered out the window at ladies being assisted out of their vehicles, at men with hats and canes in hand waiting to escort their women. It was like watching a Jane Austin movie, but in real life. *It is a total trip.* "Let's do this thing," she said, and Ellis laughed.

A good fifteen minutes later, they finally entered the house and were now standing in the receiving line to greet Lord Thornbrook and his family. She noticed Amelia's two half sisters were not in the line, apparently not included in the adult festivities. Amelia, unfortunately, was. Her face lit up with a bright smile when she saw Ellis. Her brown hair was pulled up in a knot on top of her head in a pretty fashion, and the diamonds hanging from her ears had Desirea missing her own posh ornaments. Amelia's dress was canary yellow, which Desirea thought made her look sickeningly innocent. She watched Amelia greet a man standing in front of her but noted that her brown-eyed gaze never left Ellis's fit form. Desirea's stomach twisted into a knot. *Back off, she-wolf. This one is mine.*

Desirea pasted on a smile and gave an appropriate greeting to the gray haired marquis and his very young, very pretty wife. The marchioness could not have been thirty. If Desirea were in Amelia's shoes, she'd be disgusted with her father for taking such a young wife. *Yuck.*

If I was in Amelia' shoes? What am I thinking? She shouldn't be sympathizing with her adversary.

"Your Grace," Amelia crooned. She turned to address the group of ladies behind her. "I have dibs on the duke's time this afternoon, ladies."

Desirea's black satin-gloved hands tightened around Ellis's arm. She wanted to kick the crap out of this girl. *Just who does this bitch think she is to call dibs on my escort?* Desirea stepped forward and laughed. "How silly of you ladies to place *dibs* on the duke," she scolded as if they had offended him. "Clearly his lordship will divide his attention as he likes." She leaned into Ellis at this point, and he smiled down at her with such adoration that she blushed. He was making her job to show Amelia and the other women that he was hers far too easy.

"Miss Leighton, shall we search out refreshments?" he asked with a superior tone.

"Yes," she said. They walked away from the women, conscious of their whispering remarks, which were likely harsh.

They found a refreshment table set up against a set of glass doors. The potted ferns placed at each end of the table were decorated with white daisies. Ellis gave her a glass of champagne punch, and she sipped it as she turned to look around the place. The dome-like ceiling had a sky scene with angels flying above their heads. Thick white molding drew her eyes to the artwork above, and she noticed a black piano in one corner with a harp. Chairs were set up in rows in front of a raised wooden platform, obviously the stage for this afternoon's performance.

When the receiving line broke up, Lord Thornbrook stepped onto the platform. The crowd took notice and began to hush.

"Lords, ladies, and gentlemen, thank you all for coming to our home today. We are terribly sorry a cricket match will not be possible. It seems Mother Nature had other plans." He laughed as if he said something funny and a few people followed suit. "My lovely daughter has worked very hard to come up with some alternatives to entertain this rambunctious crowd." He laughed again and then called Amelia to the platform. With a walk that Desirea thought would do a runway model proud, Amelia moved forward, kissed her dad dutifully on the cheek, and then turned to the guests.

"Mrs. Wainscradle's mother has taken ill and she had to return home. Since we are going to present the story of Aladdin, I need someone to play the princess's maid. Which one of you ladies would like to show these gentlemen your fine acting talents?"

Ellis leaned to whisper to Desirea. "Do you want me to obtain you the part?"

"I can get it myself," she said, stepping forward.

"I would be happy to play the part, Lady Amelia," she said so sweetly that she wanted to gag.

"Oh, Miss Leighton," exclaimed Amelia. "How kind you are, but I'm afraid I'm looking for someone more seasoned. You, Miss Maryweather. You shall play the part," Amelia announced to the young blond shaking her head in confusion. Desirea turned back from looking at Miss Maryweather to find

Amelia had left the platform. *The rude, bitch.* Taking a deep, calming breath, Desirea turned to find Ellis right behind her.

"Did you see that?" she asked. Desirea wasn't used to being treated without fawning respect.

"I'm afraid that wasn't well done on Amelia's part."

"Really, Ellis? Not well done? You think?" she said sarcastically. "She's a… Well, I can't even say what she is because I'd turn your ears red."

He laughed. "Don't let Amelia bother you."

"I'm afraid that's easier said than done. I assume she is to play the part of Aladdin's pet monkey?"

"Pet monkey?" He laughed. "He doesn't have such a thing."

"No?" She shrugged. "Well he does in the Disney version of the story, and I think that part would be perfect for her."

He laughed even harder and took her arm. "Come, let's obtain another refreshment and find our seats. I'll let you critique everyone's performance on the way home."

"I would have done so without you letting me, but thanks." She hugged his side and he cleared his throat, placing her at a more respectful distance from his body, which irritated her to no end.

Once seated, he asked, "You know the story of Aladdin?"

"Yes. It's one of my favorite Disney movies."

"One of those plays done on that big screen you described."

"Yes." She nodded.

He leaned over and whispered, "How cool."

She laughed as the audience hushed and the play began. Desirea knew the story well enough to know they started at the magic cave. She could picture the part in the movie where the sand cat opened its large jaws and roared, "Who disturbs my slumber." She loved that part. Just as she expected, the part of Princess Badroulbadour was played by none other than Amelia, and she absolutely stunk, though Desirea was less-than-surprised. "She has no stage presence whatsoever," Desirea said to Ellis.

"Critique later," he returned quietly, looking around to see if someone may have overheard her.

"Just saying," snapped Desirea.

Ten minutes later, she said, "I really don't understand what you see in her."

"Miss Leighton, hush," scolded Ellis.

Desirea crossed her arms over her chest and continued watching the novice spectacle before her. She could not hold back her sigh when Amelia overacted completely by throwing herself into Aladdin's arms, nearly knocking the man to the floor. When they bowed, the crowd slowly rose to their feet to applaud.

As the man playing Aladdin walked off the platform, Amelia addressed the crowd. "Please take a moment to refresh your beverages and help yourself to some goodies from the food tables. For the latter part of the afternoon, I thought we would allow some of the talented people in this room to entertain us. I know for a fact that Lady Rivers would love to sing. Come forward," Amelia instructed the lady, and the crowd parted, allowing Lady Rivers through. A man dressed in a long black tailcoat took a seat at the piano and music filled the room.

Instinctively Desirea began to sway. Oh, how she missed music. She had not heard a single note, other than her own voice, since she arrived in this century. The sound moved her. She closed her eyes, letting Lady Rivers' mediocre voice lift her spirits and buoy her soul. When the song ended, Desirea wanted to cry. *More, more,* she cheered in her head. She had never in her life gone so many days without music. It wasn't natural. Her iPod had practically been a part of her attire.

"You enjoyed Lady Rivers' singing?" Ellis stood at her elbow watching her. They had left their seats before the singing began to refill their glasses, and they now stood to the side of the chairs near the wall. A few glass doors in the room were open to circulate air around the room, and Desirea could smell the damp earth and fresh rain mingling with cologne and perfume. Desirea preferred the scent of the outdoors. Perfumes and colognes tended to give her a headache. As always, however, Ellis smelled wonderful, spicy and exotic.

"I adore music. I always have. Even as a child I'd stick my ear right against the stereo speaker." His brow quirked, and she said, "Where the sound comes out. I like my music really loud." Motley Crue's *Some Like It Loud* popped into her head. She smiled at the memories the song evoked. Her dad had loved eighties rock, and so she had come to love it too. She spent many hours in her trailer with her headphones blaring in her ears, listening to some sweet tune. *Fun times.* Although she sang pop and opera, she tended to prefer rock music when it came to her listening pleasure.

"Would you like to sing?" he asked.

Her heart raced. Oh, how she would love to sing. "No, I don't think so," she said instead. She was fine just listening as long as she was with Ellis.

"Oh but you must," said a female voice behind her, a voice Desirea recognized all too well.

"Lady Amelia," Desirea greeted her as she turned. *The chick was obviously listening to our conversation.* Desirea looked over at Ellis, who smiled his adorable smile at Amelia. *Come on, Ellis. Wake the frik up!*

"You really should sing, Miss Leighton. I feel terrible that you couldn't be in the play." Amelia grinned at her, but it was so phony Desirea almost laughed.

Desirea did want to sing, but she knew if she said so Amelia would deny her the chance. Obviously, Amelia thought she had refused because she wasn't any good. *Now that really is funny. Perhaps it is time to show this century my talents, especially Lady Amelia Faring.*

"Oh, I couldn't possibly, Lady Amelia. It's been quite a while since I sang in front of people." This was true, aside from Ellis. She sang for him quite often.

She looked at him now and saw his smile widen. He was aware of the game she was playing. Ellis was an intelligent and perceptive man. She needed to remember that. He could be working her over for all she knew and she was not yet wise to it. But if he was playing the love game, she didn't recognize his methods.

"Oh, nonsense. I insist." Amelia reached out and took her arm.

Desirea cast a gloating smile to Ellis and allowed herself to be ushered forward through the crowd. As she walked, songs filtered through her head while she thought of a great song to showcase her voice. She wanted to choose something that wasn't too modern. Picking one of her songs from the future didn't seem right for this. She wanted to wow them with her talent, not have them puzzled by linguistics. She smiled when she thought of a love song, satisfied with the ancient choice she made. She whispered to the pianist and he nodded. Of course Donizetti was an old composer. Even better, she decided to sing it in Italian, since she knew it would impress.

"Hello, ladies and gentlemen. I'm going to sing the Italian composer Gaetano Donizetti's *Amiamo. Let's Love.*" She gave a nod to the pianist, took one last look at Ellis, filled her lungs with air, and belted out the melody in her best soprano. The music engulfed her, and then it seemed to radiate through her body as she sang the high notes, giving it her best.

The feeling she had on the platform was euphoria, and so very familiar that she ached. Rounding out the chorus again, she felt a tear slide down her cheek as her voice finished the last note, which was followed by awed silence. She curtsied, and a roar went through the room, several chairs hit the floor as people jumped up to applaud loudly. Even some hoots and compliments sailed through the air.

Amelia came forward with a bright smile and then whispered in Desirea's ear, "You are nothing but a schemer who has caught the fancy of the duke, but I assure you, Miss

Leighton, it's all an illusion." With a huff, Amelia turned and disappeared into the crowd, which was still on their feet and applauding.

Ellis approached the platform with a wide smile. "Well done, my sweet."

She stepped off the dais and took his arm. She saw Amelia give her another nasty look before she marched off.

Ellis laughed. "I do believe Lady Amelia was hoping you wouldn't fare so well."

"You think?" she teased.

"Come, let's go home."

"Really?" she asked, thrilled by the thought of leaving this house.

"If we don't leave now, I fear I won't have another opportunity to speak with you," he said, nodding in the direction of all the people waiting to compliment her on her singing.

The real reason she was there prevented her from leaving. "I think we need to go spend some more time with Lady Amelia." That was the task before her, after all.

"I see what you're doing, Desirea."

"Do you?"

"Indeed, and it's not necessary."

She wanted to stomp her feet or, better yet, stomp on his. "I care for you, Ellis. I'm sorry if that's some kind of crime. But I will feel better about leaving next week if I know what kind of person you plan to set up house with."

"Vivacious."

"Don't mock me. I'm serious, Ellis. Amelia worries me." He took her arm and steered her through the guests. A few gentlemen tried to stop them, but Ellis wasn't stopping. "People are going to wonder if you are crazy," she warned him. "Where are you taking me?"

"Let them wonder." Now he was definitely talking crazy. He hated gossip of any kind, and yet he was sure to stir some up with his behavior.

"And as I told you before," he informed her in the same no nonsense voice. "We are going home."

"What about your precious Amelia?" she huffed, but in a whisper.

"She's far from precious, as you and I both know. Now would you like to stand here and argue or would you like to enjoy the few days left to us by allowing me to take you home so I may have the pleasure of ripping off your clothes."

That caught her by surprise, but then her singing did tend to put him in a randy mood. "That sounds like a very nice beginning, Your Grace."

He winked as they retrieved their coats with many of the other departing guests. The rain had decided to make another appearance, and many guests wanted to return home before the roads became too muddy.

Amelia was standing in the foyer as they were saying their goodbyes.

"Your Grace, do not tell me you are leaving." Amelia's voice carried through the entire crowd.

"I'm afraid so, Lady Amelia. Miss Leighton's lovely performance has tuckered her out."

"Well then, she should go, naturally," she said, waving a dismissive hand at Desirea. "You, however, must stay. I absolutely insist." She pursed her lips into a pout, causing Desirea to fight off a laugh.

Amelia moved closer to Ellis and crossed her arms over her chest as if challenging the duke with her stubborn refusal to allow him to leave. "I will not take no for an answer." She grabbed Ellis's arm. Desirea wondered if the girl was demented and watched the exchange in amazement, trying not to snicker. The look on Ellis's face was priceless, as if Amelia were some gruesome parasite.

Ah, today's mission accomplished.

"Unhand me," he said coolly.

Amelia was obviously a clueless woman, since she still refused to release the duke. Desirea could see Ellis's features tighten with anger as he glared at Amelia.

"Your Grace," Amelia said quietly.

Perhaps Amelia was gaining control of herself, Desirea thought. *I could have sworn the chick was about to lose it.* Most of the guests continued on their way after Amelia lowered her voice, not paying further attention to their conversation, but Desirea could hear them quite clearly.

"Don't you think you and I need time together to, um, discuss things?" asked Amelia. "You know, the things that are going to happen between us. Our future."

"There's no future for us, Lady Faring." Ellis yanked his arm away and Amelia jumped back as if slapped.

"Fine," she screamed, and everyone who remained in the foyer turned around to witness Amelia's meltdown. "I will *not* accept your proposal," she hollered. "You are a bumpkin. Duke, bah! You are nothing but a..."

"Amelia Lucinda Monteray Faring, you apologize to His Grace for your deplorable temper," Amelia's father bellowed. Lord Thornbrook, who had stepped into the foyer at that very moment, looked to be on the verge of losing his temper as well.

"I will not," shouted Amelia with fists clenched and her face red with temper. The girl was like a powder keg ready to blow.

"Then I will," replied the marquis, bustling around a few clusters of people to approach Ellis. The poor man was clearly horrified by his daughter's display. "On behalf of my family, Your Grace, I sincerely apologize for Amelia's behavior. I don't know where she gets it." The man shook his head, clearly at a loss about what to do with Amelia's explosive temperament. "I've tried everything."

"I accept your apology, my lord. Emotions are hard to contain for some," replied Ellis with a nod of understanding.

The marquis shook Ellis's hand.

"I can't believe this," screeched Amelia. "You are siding with him, and against me, your own flesh and blood." Amelia looked around at all the guests, their attention fixed on this spectacle. "What are all you stupid people looking at? The party's over. Go home." Amelia went to stomp away, but then she turned back and pointed at Desirea. "You are never welcome in my home again."

When Amelia left, the marquis issued another round of apologies to his guests and they left. Ellis assisted Desirea into the vehicle, an umbrella held by his footman towering above their heads. Minutes later, they were on their way.

"Now that was an interesting turn of events," he said. The rain pelted off the vehicle's roof, and with the windows' curtains pulled closed, the coach turned into a very cozy setting for two people in love.

"Yikes, is all I can think to say," she teased.

"Agreed."

"And did you find Amelia's behavior enlightening?" she asked, lifting her brow.

He laughed. "Yes. Amelia Faring is as mad as a March hare."

"Just as long as you finally get the picture."

"I'm seeing very clearly right now, Desirea."

She didn't know if that was a good thing or a bad thing, but when he indicated that she should climb onto his lap, she didn't hesitate. She adored being near him.

"She caused quite a scene back there," she said, settling herself on his lap. "I'm sure your neighbors will have a field day with that one."

"A field day?" he murmured.

"You know, have fun with it, talk about it, probably print it in the papers."

"Ah," he said, but she got the impression he wasn't really listening. He was far too busy concentrating on placing these perfect kisses on her neck.

CHAPTER SIXTEEN

His carriage wasn't conducive for comfortable sex, but it was definitely perfect for the fast and furious lovemaking he and Desirea shared. This woman took his breath away. He could feel the power of their love, the power of their connection.

A connection he was going to break. The very thought nearly buckled him over in agony. He scolded himself for his selfish thoughts. He was honor bound to marry well. *Why oh why couldn't Desirea be from the titled or at least the landed gentry? Or even from this time period?* She had saved him from folly today by insisting they go to the party. Desirea had known Amelia Faring was not right for him. *Desirea is right for me. Damn it to hell!*

How he wished he could speak to his father. If his father had been alive to meet Desirea, then perhaps…

He knew he was fooling himself. His father would not have accepted Desirea. The thought hurt. How could he not grant his deceased father his last wish? What kind of son did that make him for even considering such a crazy idea as marriage to the woman he loved? As a duke, he was well aware that love played no part in his future marriage. After all, he'd been down this road before.

He replayed Amelia's scandalous scene in his head, cringing at the gossip it would cause. Of course, there had been plenty of witnesses to vouch for his exemplary behavior. He had done nothing to bring on such heated vehemence in the woman. *What is wrong with Lady Faring?* He couldn't help but wonder.

He looked down at Desirea huddled against his chest. She had shined like a bright star this afternoon. From the moment they entered the Thornbrook's, all of the men in the room turned to give Desirea their full appreciation. Men, himself included, couldn't seem to stop staring at her beautiful curves and astonishing magnificence. And then she had taken the stage and reached into her audience's heart with her singing. Ellis actually heard a man behind him sigh with joy when she finished. That's when he knew it was time to go. His time with Desirea was limited, which made it precious, and he didn't wish to share the time they had left with others. He was surprised they left without a line of men following them, but then Amelia's outrage had taken over the foyer and distracted the men in the room long enough for him to usher Desirea away from their appreciative glances.

Perhaps he was being selfish by not sharing Desirea with others, he admonished himself. Surely he could have allowed her to converse with other men, but he didn't want to. And that was the rub. Soon he'd not be able to guide her away from the male wolves in society, and although Desirea thought of herself as a woman of the world, she was not of his time period and thus couldn't understand how ruthless some men of his time could become when they find a woman they want. In London, she'd suffer through endless rounds of trickery as men tried to convince her to go off with them in secluded alcoves or darkly lit gardens. He was worried about her, worried what would become of her once she left him, worried about who would watch over her and keep her safe.

"Desirea," he said, his heart beating rapidly. Sweat broke out on his brow as his worry for her increased.

"Yes, Ellis?" she said in a singsong voice with her chin still nestled on his shoulder. They had dressed after their lovemaking, but his jacket was unbuttoned.

"I've told you what I need in a wife. What about you? I mean, when you deem yourself old enough to wed, what do you want in a husband?"

"The most important aspect would be love, followed by trust and friendship. I didn't have many friends and I never found love where I'm from, and so I hope to do so here." She lifted her head and smiled up at him. He realized she already had his heart and love. "Aside from those major things, I want my husband to be well off. I've slept in an attic as a maid, and I didn't care for it." She smirked and said, "So money is a must." She frowned as if she didn't like the way her words sounded, which was silly since the women in his time often *only* married for money and position.

"You see, I plan to throw extravagant parties. I've always been a bit of a party girl. I also want to put on my own plays, which I will perform in." She got a faraway dreamy expression on her face. "My parties will be talked about with awe, and this takes money. I'm used to posh... I mean, I am used to a luxury filled lifestyle, and I'm afraid I've grown accustomed to being spoiled. I understand how blessed this makes me, but truthfully, I'm used to being a leader of the pack. I have no qualms about my rise in high society."

She shrugged. "Perhaps my time in the sun is over. Who's to say. I certainly can't go back to the stage, nor do I wish to. I guess I want a man I can imagine sharing the rest of my life with. That is the kind of man for me."

"I know you can't return to your time, and I'm sorry for my earlier blunder in this regard." He wanted to correct his wrong assumption. "So you are off to London to find this man?"

"Not really," she said. He knew marriage was not something she seemed to contemplate let alone worry over. He envied that.

"At what age do women in your time marry?" He couldn't help but be curious. She was nearly twenty-one and seemed to have no dire need for a spouse. He couldn't help finding that odd.

She sat up and smiled at his interest in her era. They both loved explaining the intricacies of their centuries. "It's kind of a loaded question because people marry at so many different ages. I guess most women marry around twenty-five, but many wait until thirty."

Ellis ran his fingers through his hair in surprise. "Thirty? Amazing. Why so long?"

She shrugged. "Some people want to finish their education, but truthfully, I probably wouldn't have even thought about settling into marriage until I was at least twenty-five. Getting married any younger seems folly. Although I'm sure many couples who marry young make it work, it's just not as encouraged as it is here, and the rate of divorce is high in my time."

"But you have discussed your ideas of marriage with me," he pointed out.

"Well, of course, Ellis, because you asked. I never really thought about marriage until I showed up in your century. I'm beginning to feel like an old hag in this era."

He laughed and pulled her into a hug. "Perish the thought." The vehicle stopped in front of the house moments later.

***

Desirea entered her room, pulled off her gloves, and threw them on the bed. She was sitting on her vanity stool in front of the mirror starting the process of hairpin removal when Mura entered.

Her maid hurried to her side, swept Desirea's hands away, and began to let down her hair. "So how'd it go, Miss?"

"Not well, or should I say, far better than expected."

"Lady Amelia made a spectacle of herself, then?" asked Mura.

"You could say that. She threw quite a little temper tantrum when the duke announced our departure."

"I heard about it," said Mura.

"Really?" Desirea's head snapped up in surprise. "I'm amazed by the speed that gossip travels without phones and the internet."

"Pardon, Miss?" Mura's face scrunched in complete confusion.

"Oh nothing. I'm surprised you heard so quickly."

"Yes, Miss. Me too. That maid, Miss Pollyann, is a fountain of gossip."

"Just as long as she's not badmouthing the duke," said Desirea, wondering if she needed to have a talk with this gossipy maid.

"Oh, no, Miss. Not that I've heard, that is. She seems to do her job well enough."

"Good," said Desirea. She had far more important things than a maid's tendency to talk on her agenda, like getting the duke to admit he loves her and wishes to marry her. She didn't know what she'd do if he allowed her to leave in three days. Yes, she had a place to go, but she didn't wish to go anywhere without him. This did not seem at all like the strong, independent, and fearless woman she used to be. This thought did not sit well with her.

***

"He's going to marry her," said Amelia Faring, red faced, fists clenched, and her teeth bared.

Her most trusted maid and confidant, Pollyann, stood nearby with a bottle of spirits and an empty glass. "How do you know this?" She lifted the spirits and Amelia nodded for her to pour her a libation.

"I just know." Amelia took the glass, drank down its contents, and handed it back.

Pollyann had been around since Amelia was a child, and since they were of the same age, they had grown up together but at opposite ends of the social ladder. Although Pollyann knew her place, she was also the only person who questioned Amelia about her behavior and the things she seemed to know, but should not be any more privy to than the next person. In fact, as close as the two of them were, Amelia trusted no one with her secret, including Pollyann. She feared, if anyone ever learned of her curse, she'd be locked away forever.

"You just know. Bah! Milady, that is all you ever say. As if that explains how you know things other people don't."

"Well, I'm afraid I can't explain it further, but you are missing my entire point. The Duke of Lancaster is going to marry Darlene's mousy friend. This cannot happen! Are you understanding this?"

"Yes, I understand. You wish to wed the Duke of Lancaster."

"No, Pollyann. I *must* marry him. It's for his own wellbeing. Besides, I long to leave this house. I can't abide living under this roof forever. I need a life of my own. My mother would have wanted me married by now, and if she were alive, I'm quite sure she would have made it happen." Amelia often wondered about the mother she couldn't remember. Had she been cursed like Amelia? Did she pass the curse to her only child?

"See? I was right. You believe they are in love," said Amelia.

Pollyann's face turned white as it often did when Amelia plucked thoughts from her head. "How do you do that? Can you hear my thoughts?"

"Don't be silly, Pollyann. No one can do such a thing. I'm merely reading the look on your face and drawing my own conclusions, but I see I'm right. You think they are in love?" she asked, even though she had already heard Pollyann's answer.

How she wished she couldn't hear the girl's thoughts, or anyone's thoughts for that matter. What was this curse? Why did she have it? Would it ever go away? Perhaps at times it had its uses, but more often than not, she only heard all the rotten things people thought about her. Lately she was having a harder time containing her rage at others. Cursed with the ability to hear mean, even evil thoughts people had about her was not a blessing. She had clearly heard Miss Desirea Leighton wish to do her bodily harm the moment she had grasped the Duke of Lancaster's arm today. Miss Leighton's thoughts were enough to ignite Amelia's temper. After all, Miss Leighton had imagined smacking Amelia's head into the foyer wall in front of the assembled guests. The lady had to be deranged to think such vicious thoughts. No, she couldn't, as a good neighbor and long time friend, allow the duke to marry someone of Miss Leighton's nature.

"She's not right for him," she told her maid.

"And he's the man you want to spend the rest of your life with?" asked Pollyann.

Amelia thought about that. In truth, she didn't want a husband at all. Many men had been paraded before her, and their thoughts had been unbearable. She screamed many men right out of the house, which only isolated her further from her father. She had no doubt that the Earl of Thornbrook thought her mad. Of course, she heard her father's thoughts too, and he was really worried about her, not that she blamed him. She was worried about herself too.

She didn't know if she could ever be close to anyone, and this saddened her; but the Duke of Lancaster was her friend and he had never thought ill of her. Even in the foyer when she had all but begged him to stay and then lost her temper, his thought had not been malicious. He was merely curious for he didn't understand why she was acting the way she had. Could he be the one person she could explain it too? She really doubted such a person existed and assumed her life was meant to be spent in solitude. She was starting to hate people, and this scared her most of all.

"I need you to return to your job at Lancaster Castle and gather any information you can. Come see me as soon as you learn something."

"You really think Miss Leighton is a harmful person?"

"Yes, Pollyann. I think she is a very mean, malicious person with a mind bent on savagery."

"Oh my," Pollyann exclaimed before she hurried out of the room.

Amelia crossed her room and looked out her window toward Lancaster Castle. It was too far away to see, but she knew it was out there in the distance. Truly, Lancaster Castle would probably be the best place for her. The people in Seaham already found her odd, and her father would only be a short ride away. But could she marry anyone? Even a man as fine as the Duke of Lancaster? She somehow couldn't picture it. Nevertheless, she would not allow him to come to harm. Surely anyone who carried thoughts like Miss Leighton's would cause him harm. Yes, she would prevent such a travesty, and perhaps she would have to marry him to do so.

Saving the duke through marriage was the right thing to do, but of course, when she refused to have his children, he'd be angry. She assumed when that time came, she would have to tell him about her curse and how she had no wish to curse any child of hers in such a way.

She could hear her half sisters thoughts from beyond the door. The girls were afraid to knock and intrude on her privacy. She smiled with relief, knowing neither of them had been cursed with her affliction. This was why she assumed she inherited the curse from her deceased mother. She loved her half sisters, even if they were often a bother. Of course, some people in Seaham would say differently, since Amelia had found it necessary to lock them in a closet on occasion. But then, if people were privy to the devious plans the two young girls were plotting each of these times, perhaps they'd understand what triggered her to act in such a way. Locking them up had been necessary for her sisters' safety.

"Come in," she said. Her sisters flew into the room like two tiny tornadoes, nearly knocking her over onto her bed. She hugged them close, feeling vulnerable. She knew her father would be paying her a visit any minute now.

"What happened, Amelia? Why is father yelling? What did you do this time?" asked Rosalyn, her cherub little cheeks rosy.

"Father's enraged about what happened. What happened?" asked Sarah.

"I'm afraid I lost my temper with one of the guests. I acted deplorably and father has every right to be enraged, Sarah. I blundered badly this time." She really hadn't wanted to lose her temper.

"It's all right," they said in unison. She hugged them again, holding them close and taking in theirs scents, reading their thoughts of sympathy for her.

A throat clearing at the open doorway had her lifting her head from nestling with theirs. The Earl of Thornbrook stood in the door looking exhausted, his anger depleted and his hope for her future gone. She knew his faith in her was disappearing. Her sisters scampered around Father and out of the room. Amelia felt the sting of tears in her eyes. Her father was so disappointed and lost about how he should proceed with her.

"I'm sor…"

"Do not apologize again, Amelia Lucinda Monteray Faring. You have done it this time. You have insulted the Duke of Lancaster. Good heavens, child. What were you thinking?" He entered and closed the door.

"I assume you believe I *wasn't* thinking."

"You dare to try and rationalize such behavior?" He crossed his arms over his chest and then let them fall with a sigh. Her father loved her. At least she had no doubts of his feelings. But he didn't know what to do with her.

"No, I can't rationalize it," she admitted. She would not burden her father by telling him about her curse. She had thought to do so numerous times, but she failed when she saw his thoughts and imagined how he would react. She knew well enough that people tended to think their thoughts private, and she did not want to be viewed any more harshly than she already was, especially by her father.

"I had thought, with his return to Lancaster Castle, the two of you could explore the friendship you once shared as children. I had thought him a match for you, young lady, and you have ruined it."

"I know you believe so, Father, and I'm sorry. Will it make you feel better if I tell you I plan to marry the Duke of Lancaster?"

Her father didn't believe such a thing possible, she could read that clearly, but he sat on her bed next to her. "Actually, that would thrill me to no end. However, I think that ship has sailed for calmer waters, my dear."

"Perhaps," she admitted. "But I haven't given up hope, and I don't want you to either. He may be the right man for me."

Her father was now praying to God to make this so. She could hear his pleas. "I wish you every happiness." He kissed her head. "Please try to stay close to home for awhile, at least until the gossip dies down."

"Yes, Father," she said, feeling terrible that she had embarrassed him yet again. She sat calmly in place as he came to his feet, kissed her once more, and then left the room, closing the door behind him. He felt helpless, and she felt like a failure as a daughter for his feeling this way. She let her tears fall from her water-filled eyes. "Blast this curse," she whispered. Why couldn't she have been normal.

CHAPTER SEVENTEEN

The last three days at Lancaster Castle were absolutely beyond the best days Desirea had ever had. Even so, today she was leaving and this thoroughly depressed her. She was walking in the back garden this cloudy morning, taking time to smell the newly planted roses before she left. She was wearing a lavender traveling dress with an ivory pelisse and ivory cuffs.

"Your vehicle is ready, Desirea," said Ellis, coming up behind her. "I really wish you'd allow me to escort you to the city."

"I told you that I don't like drawn out goodbyes, Ellis." She kept her back to him, fighting back tears. The long trek back to London would allow her plenty of time to let her grief flow freely, and she hoped to be all cried out by the time she reached London. Allure's song *All Cried Out* filled her head for a scant second.

"Yes, I know. So what are you doing in the rose garden?"

"Saying goodbye," she said, and she leaned over to smell the wonderful fragrance of a fuchsia rose in full bloom. "I've already said goodbye to my room, and of course, your bed." She turned and smiled at him.

He laughed, but it didn't reach his eyes. She didn't understand why he was so sad when he could easily stop her from leaving with a few simple words, or even one word: stay.

"I hate that you are leaving."

Yes, well, this she knew. "It's for the best," she said, not believing such nonsense for a second. He was the one who kept saying that line, and so she threw it back at him. Unfortunately, he nodded in acquiescence. *What was the saying? If you let something go and it comes back, it's yours; and if it doesn't return, it was never yours to begin with. Something like that.* Perhaps Ellis would come back to her, but more than likely he'd go off and get married and that would be that.

He looked contemplative as he stood near the rose arbor, his one hand running through his hair and his face taut, like he didn't know what to do. He was dressed in black trousers with a white lawn shirt. His glorious blond hair was slicked back from his face, showcasing his well-defined cheekbones, which accentuated his mesmerizing green eyes with their long lashes. "What is it you seek in the city?" he asked.

It's not as if he didn't realize she wished to stay with him. He knew this. He knew everything about her because she had shared herself with him in a way she had never done with anyone else. "Why do I need to be seeking something?" she asked.

"Because most women go to the city…"

She turned fully toward him now, and he stopped speaking before the glare that she sent him. "I thought we decided I'm not at all like most women, Ellis. I'm going to the city to find a sense of self, not marriage." She added the last because she assumed that's what had him worried. She didn't even understand why it mattered to him since he planned to marry as soon as possible himself.

"But who will watch over you? Who will steer you away from the bounders and cads? Lord Nankin will be a newly married man and hardly in a position to keep watch over you. Who will be looking out for your wellbeing when he's off honeymooning?"

"Now that's funny, Ellis. Please tell me you aren't insinuating that I will not survive in your time without a male figure in my life."

He looked uncomfortable and she could detect a hint of a blush filling his tan face. "I was saying nothing of the sort, or at least I didn't mean to imply a lack of competence on your part. I'm worried about you, Desirea. Surely you can understand my concern."

She took his hand and smiled. "I do. Thank you for caring." It really meant the world to her. "Nevertheless, I plan to prove to you, and hoity-toity society, if necessary, that I can fit in here." Most importantly, she needed to prove this to herself. She needed to rebuild her confidence and independence. To make it in this new world without Ellis, she had to be strong.

"Of course you fit in here. Don't even say such things. Look at what you've done to the castle. The Thornbrook's afternoon party was a smashing success because of you. I'm amazed by your accomplishments. I know you will take society by storm."

"That's the plan," she said with a smile, trying to lighten the mood. Originally, her plan had been to capture the heart of this duke, but then everything didn't always work out according to plan.

"Miss Leighton's luggage has been loaded and secured, Your Grace," a fancy dressed liveryman with a mop of brown curls on his head announced from the doorway of the kitchen.

"Thank you, Smith." The servant left and Ellis snatched up her hand. "I hate this," he said, pulling her into his warm and familiar embrace.

"Me too," she said quietly into the folds of his coat, trying to hold herself together until this part was over. They began a slow walk to the front of the house, through the garden, around the side of the house where they had made love in the heather, and back to the front where the vehicle her friend London Burton, soon to be the Countess of Nankin, had sent stood at the ready, her luggage stowed on top and two footmen as well as a driver in attendance.

"It looks like this is it." She turned out of his arms, but not until she inhaled his scent one last time. "I will miss you more than words can say. Take care of yourself."

"I will. Please take care of yourself, too. And remember," he said, taking hold of her chin and tilting her head up to look in her eyes. "If you need anything, anything at all, please contact me."

"I told you I would. Sheez, you'd think I was going to be a walking disaster or something. Have some faith. I'll be fine,

Ellis. No worries." Of course *Don't Worry, Be Happy* by Bobby McFerrin popped into her head. She really missed music. Unfortunately, she'd miss Ellis even more. Once she left him, she just knew she'd never be happy again.

She moved toward her vehicle, swatted away a bee, and then stepped up onto the pulled out metal step. She had hoped he'd grab her arm and pull her back, but he didn't, and so she climbed inside. She bit the inside of her cheek as she gave him a small smile. The pain of her cheek kept her from thinking of the stabbing pain in her heart. "Well, bye," she said as he closed the door, and she felt the vehicle shift as the driver climbed into his place. A couple of drawn out minutes later, her carriage lurched forward and she waved to Ellis one last time.

They didn't even make it down the drive before her grief overwhelmed her and she put her head in her hands and sobbed. She continued to sob and curse until she had nothing left. She pounded on the roof and the vehicle came to a stop. Not able to help herself, Desirea threw open the door and vomited on the long grass below. When she was done retching, she lifted her head to find Mura standing beside her. She was dressed in her light gray uniform with its ivory lace collar and matching gray gloves.

"Where'd you come from?" Desirea couldn't have been more surprised to see her maid. She lifted her head and used one of the handkerchiefs stacked next to her on the seat, which were soaked from her tears and nearly toppling to the floor. She knew she had to look a hot mess by this point.

"I was riding in the tiger's perch, Miss. I wanted to give you some time to yourself. I know leaving the duke was not easy for you. The duke told me that I work for you, and so here I am. Besides, I like you."

"Well, you aren't riding in the tiger's perch," said Desirea, appalled her poor maid had sat outside. She backed up away from the door and invited Mura inside, shoving her dirty hankies in a side pocket of the door to allow the woman a seat. Mura climbed inside with a bright smile and Desirea gave the roof a knock to signal the driver to continue.

"Are you all right, Miss?" Mura asked with concern.

Desirea was sure her eyes were red and puffy. She was also quite sure Mura had been able to hear her sobs of agony. "Not really, but I'm no longer nauseous, which is good." Her body still trembled and she still felt like sobbing, but she tried not to for Mura's sake.

"So where are we heading?" her maid asked with good cheer.

"We are going to stay with my friend, Miss London Miranda Burton. She goes by Miranda now, since her first name is London and it seemed to cause too much confusion. She's marrying the Earl of Nankin next weekend. So, soon she'll be the Countess of Nankin. I simply cannot miss the big event."

"I've never left Seaham. This trip is sure to be an adventure for me."

"For me too," said Desirea, her mind filling with doubts that she could pull this off and get people to like her without her celebrity and without Ellis by her side.

"Were you not in London before coming to Seaham?" asked Mura, her brow wrinkled in confusion.

"I was, but I really didn't see much of the city." She decided it best not to tell Mura about her stint as a maid in the duke's London residence. She was sure her maid would understand that Desirea did what was necessary to keep a roof over her head and food in her mouth, but she thought it might belittle Mura's occupation and that she would not do.

"Is the Earl of Nankin's house grand?"

"I'm not sure," said Desirea. "They have room for us, so it must be big enough. And Lord Nankin is somewhat snobbish in demeanor. I assume he has reason to be."

"Snobbish?" Mura was wearing that confused look Ellis had when she hit on a word they had yet to learn.

"Uh, high in the instep. He has a superiority complex, like most of the titled men here seem to carry."

"They don't have titles in America."

"Not hereditary ones, no." Of course there were titles and labels galore in the 21st century.

Desirea did not want to talk about the differences between this century's England and the US of her own era. The differences were vast, but mostly she had no intention of telling more people of her true origin. They'd all consider her a nut job and lock her up. Or she'd screw up their lives somehow by telling them things she shouldn't, which had only occurred to her recently as a possible downside to sharing how she got here. She changed the subject to something she could really use Mura's help with. "Have you ever been in love, Mura?"

"Yes, Miss. At least, I believe I was once, but I was only fifteen at the time."

"So what happened?"

"His family moved away and I never saw or heard from him again."

"Oh," she said for lack of something better to say. She immediately wondered if she would ever hear from Ellis again. "How did you cope with the loss?"

"Have you never suffered loss?" asked Mura, her head cocked to the side.

"I have, when loved ones passed or just up and left. But I've never shared my heart with a man and walked away with it crushed. I've never allowed myself to become this vulnerable."

"I believe to experience true love one most open themselves up to heartache," replied Mura.

"Yes, but how do you get over it? How do you forget about the man you love?"

"Oh, I never forgot Johnathon, Miss. But I had to accept that, if he really loved me, he would have sent for me once he was established. He never did. As years went by the feelings faded until I began to wonder if I really felt what I thought I felt." Mura shrugged. "When an influential and powerful man agrees to take your entire family into his service, Miss, one does not refuse. It was an honor bestowed upon Johnathon's family."

"Why? Was his family large?" Desirea asked, remembering her friend London had said the Lord of Nankin had three brothers and four sisters. Since London and Desirea didn't have siblings, she was sure her friend was going through quite an adjustment. Desirea didn't know how she'd handle a house full of people, but she hoped that more people would mean less time to dwell on Ellis.

"There were twelve of them in all."

"Huh," said Desirea. The J. Geils Band's *Love Stinks* came to mind. Desirea kept up a constant stream of conversation with Mura for a full hour before they both finally fell silent and into their own thoughts. Desirea leaned her head against the side of the vehicle and starred off at the sunset over the treetops. It was beautiful. A sunset was one more thing she'd never share with Ellis again. Silent tears streamed down her cheeks, soaking her lap. Mura handed her another hankie without comment and returned her gaze out the opposite window.

***

Four days later, when they were three hours from the city, Mura tossed a hankie at Desirea and huffed. "Now, Miss," she said as the vehicle shifted over a wooden bridge, rocking them in their seats.

"Now what?" asked Desirea, blowing her sore nose.

"It's now time to turn off the waterworks. We will be entering the city limits soon. Do you plan to arrive at your friend's doorstep as if you are in deep mourning? Should we purchase you some black bombazine so you can fool the soon-to-be Countess of Nankin about your grieving state?"

That got a chuckle out of Desirea, which she knew was Mura's intent. Her maid was a gem. "No, you're right. I'm being ridiculous."

"One would think four solid days of tears would be plenty," exclaimed Mura.

"Yes, I know. I'm sorry I'm being unbearable. I can do this. I can get over Ellis."

"Of course you can, Miss. You need to put him far from your mind. The city is said to be filled with bachelors, and perhaps it's time to get to know someone new. This crying period is wearing on both of us. You claim to be strong. I need you to act…strong."

Yes, act. I can do that. If Mura only knew what a superb actress Desirea could truly be. But her maid was right. She was letting her feelings get the best of her, allowing Ellis's rejection to destroy her. No more. Perhaps he wouldn't come for her, and if that was the case, then so be it. She would overcome. Creed's song *Overcome* entered her mind and then a slew of vicious swear words flew through her thoughts, but she didn't dare repeat them out loud. Ellis was all the bad things she called him in her head and then some. What a sniveling coward, kowtowing to high society's dictates. If that sounded harsh, she really didn't care. She was done being compassionate and understanding.

"You're right, Mura." Desirea wiped away the last of her itchy tears from her face and sat up straighter on the cushioned seat. "Today I will see my friend again. I have missed her." Not to mention she had a thousand and one questions for London. She was really glad the wedding was still four days away, which would allow her time to talk with London. "I plan to not allow Ellis in my thoughts. I'm here to celebrate my friend's new beginning."

"That's the spirit, Miss. I know you can do it."

"Thanks, Mura." Her maid believed in her, which she found more comforting than she would have imagined.

"You're welcome." Mura smiled and Desirea gave her a small laugh. They were friends. She marveled that she now had more friends in this bygone time than she'd ever had in her whole life. She was thankful to Ellis for sending her maid, but she refused to think of him further than that.

Three hours later, they drove through the city streets, both with their heads out the same window. "It's just as my mum described," said Mura, awe lacing her voice.

"I'm afraid I don't remember much of it." Aside from the filthy condom-filled alley and her short visit at the Back Room Gentlemen's Club, Desirea hadn't spent much time outside Ellis's home on Parker Street. When they had left the city for Seaham, Ellis had closed the curtains, not opening them until they were on some empty country road. At the time, Desirea had thought he'd closed the curtains in the vehicle to allow them privacy, but she now realized it was because he didn't wish to be seen with her. There she went again, thinking about Ellis. *Ugh!*

They turned down another lane and they heard the driver yell out Mayfair. Her friend lived in this part of the city and so Desirea knew they were getting close. She ducked her head back inside and sat back, pulling Mura in with her. "All right, how do I look?"

"Well, your eyes are no longer red and puffy, and your face no longer has those red splotches with that terrible red ring around your mouth."

Desirea's eyes widened.

"I'm bamming you, Miss. You are as beautiful as always."

"Then my face didn't really look like you described?" asked Desirea.

"Oh, no, it did," said Mura. They both laughed.

***

Two days after Desirea's departure from his home, Ellis's life took a dive into the muck. No one in his household seemed to know how to proceed without Desirea telling them what needed to be done. It was like, once she left, she took his staff's competence with her, leaving him surrounded by a bunch of bumbling fools.

Earlier, his housekeeper had disturbed his bout of depression when she entered the private sanctuary of his study, upset because the cook was out of a special kind of mushroom. Like Ellis could solve the mushroom problem. He was a bachelor. He was used to eating out at his club every night. He was not used to menus needing his approval. Desirea had seen to this task. It had been three years since he left the castle, and now he remembered why. *The damn place is bloody lonely.*

To make matters worse, he saw Desirea everywhere he looked. Not literally, he wasn't crazy, as of yet, but he could envision her…everywhere. He heard her as well. When he was about to shake out his umbrella in the foyer, her voice filled his head. He remembered how appalled she was when he had scattered raindrops all over the newly done area after one of their walks in the rain. He'd likely never see rain again and not think of Desirea. Or hear music. Or listen to a Shakespearean play. He wondered how her idea for the production at the theater was progressing. The opening night was less than three weeks away. He had wanted to take Desirea to see the play and had even imagined her entering on his arm. Admittedly, he even looked forward to her critique, which she would feel compelled to share.

He could not seem to escape her because he couldn't shut off his thoughts. He could envision her in his bed after lovemaking when they lay listless and spent. He could envision the times they sat together in the great room, talking for hours about their centuries and the differences. How would he ever forget their walks in the garden or the mindless chatter they shared concerning his new tenants and servants as they ate their meals together, all the while watching the castle come back to life. How could he ever forget the extraordinary sex they shared on that same table.

Memories swamped him. He remembered every moment. Like when she hit her head on the cupboard in the kitchen and laughed uproariously, the time the bird tangled itself in her hair and she came down the hall swinging her arms like a madcap.

Her angelic voice captivated him. Her soft kissable lips held him enthralled. She had the body of a goddess and a dry wit that amused him every second. Why had he not foreseen how miserably hard every single moment without her would be?

Of course he knew her leaving would hurt. He loved her. There was no sense in denying it, and yet, he had let her go. He had all but driven her away. He had thought her departure was for the best, but the best for whom? His deceased sire? Wouldn't his father want to see him happy? Was it Ellis's fault his happiness lay with Desirea? His aching sorrow clawed at him.

He would have helped any woman who found herself lost in that disgusting alley, but it hadn't been just any woman he found. It had been Desirea. Another thought haunted him. Since Desirea did not seem to know why she was sent to his time, was it possible she was sent for him?

He knew such logic sounded grossly inaccurate, because then he'd have to assume that God sent Desirea to him. And why him? Did he think himself so superior as to be a man smiled upon by the Divinity? What if he really was throwing away a gift from God. He had no desire to upset the will of the Almighty. Moreover, he completely agreed with his Maker that this woman was a gift.

He stood and walked to the door to holler to his butler. "See that my bags and vehicle are loaded. I'm off to the city," he announced, and the butler actually smiled. Yes, he thought, his country staff liked Desirea, too.

He walked into the great room, looking at the wall of medieval weapons. Pushing a heavy wooden chair toward the stoned wall, he stepped up on top of the chair and pulled down the hatchet with a smile. His decision to go after Desirea was the best one he had made in a long time.

***

"And then she left. She packed up her trunks, and with her maid riding on the back, I watched her drive out of sight."

"Pollyann, this is the best news ever," said Amelia. An inner glow of peace and harmony filled her when she realized she wouldn't have to wed the Duke of Lancaster. She really didn't know if she was ready for such a drastic step. In recent years, she hadn't spent enough time with Ellis to know if she could put up with his male thoughts. Amelia stopped her good cheer when she noticed Pollyann's face was not lit up in victory.

"There's more?" asked Amelia.

"Unfortunately, I was told the duke left today."

"What!" shrieked Amelia. "Is he going after her?"

Pollyann nodded and Amelia screamed. She then went and pulled open her dresser drawer.

"What are you doing, milady?"

"I'm packing. Here, you do it." She backed out of the way. "I need to go tell my father I'm returning to the city."

"Do you think he'll allow you to do so, milady? London is a four day drive, and I don't think your stepmother and half sisters like the city much."

"Neither do I," said Amelia. In fact, Amelia hated the city. There were far too many people with far too many thoughts going through their heads, which nearly drove her crazy. It was difficult to concentrate on anything when a hundred peoples' thoughts were echoing in her mind. But she'd go because she owed it to her friend Ellis, the one man who had never had a mean thought toward her.

And her father would allow it because she'd take a mass of servants and stay with her aunt. Surely her father would allow her to visit his sister.

It was beginning to look like her marriage to Ellis had become a possibility again. This news didn't thrill her, but she would save Ellis from that vicious woman, Desirea Leighton. The lady's thoughts were ugly. Ellis deserved better. He'd already suffered great loss in his life, and Amelia knew this because she had spent many hours at his bedside when he lay injured from the carriage wreck that claimed his parents' lives. She liked him, and truthfully, there were very few people she liked in this world.

CHAPTER EIGHTEEN

Desirea looked up at the whitewashed Palladian mansion where London lived and smiled. Obviously, her friend picked a winner in the money department. No wonder Lord Nankin was such a snob about his title. He felt entitled, and now she knew why. His abode was most impressive. Desirea stood on the porch and knocked on the massive wooden door before her.

"Perhaps I should enter from the back, Miss," said Mura.

"Nonsense, Mura. You are playing the role of chaperone as well, are you not?"

"Well, yes, Miss. I guess I am."

Desirea noticed Mura seemed to puff up with pride at her new title. Desirea smiled. She turned back toward the door when she heard it open. After the appropriate introductions, Mura was sent off to their assigned rooms and Desirea was escorted into a sitting room.

The spacious room had two light paneled walls, the other walls painted a deep rose. A cozy fire was ablaze in a thick white marble fireplace, the stone shot through with dark crystal veins. It was probably Italian marble, Desirea realized. The fire cast warmth and light upon the thick upholstered leather chairs and the long sofa that faced the hearth.

At the sound of hurried steps behind her, she turned to find London standing in the doorway, breathless from her speedy dash. Her friend was dressed in a very sharp ensemble, a taupe satin dress with a square neckline and brown lace at the bottom of the sleeves and around her breasts, flattering the A-line design. She looked exactly like a nineteenth century lady should look, which Desirea thought funny considering that, when she first met London, she was wearing blue jeans and a green satin shirt with rhinestone buttons. And of course her hair was down at that first meeting and not done up in the latest nineteenth-century mode as it was now.

"I heard you were here," she said, sailing into the room and shutting the door for their privacy. She pulled Desirea into a tight hug and Desirea hugged her back. Hugging London made her think of home, and for a moment, she didn't wish to release her.

"Oh my gosh, I can't believe you're finally here," exclaimed London as she held her at arm's length to look at her. "I knew that dress would be lovely on you. I'm so glad you decided to stay with us. I already love having you here."

Desirea allowed London to lead her to the sofa and they both sat. Her friend seemed really glad to see her. Desirea wasn't completely accustomed to having a real friend, but London seemed to genuinely care for her and want to spend time with her. She had always longed for a BFF to share her thoughts, dreams, and fears. "Thank you so much for all the awesome clothes."

"You're welcome. So how was your trip?"

"My trip was…" She thought about her endless tears. "Sad," she said honestly.

"How so?" asked London. "Would you care for some tea?"

"Yes, please."

London got up and ordered the tea, then hurried back to sit down. "Now why was your trip sad? I thought you were having an awesome time in the country, at least that's what you said in your last letter."

"I totally was, until I stupidly allowed myself to fall in love." Desirea suddenly remembered her friend's wedding was four days away and backtracked. "I mean love is wonderful. I, however, chose someone hereditarily unavailable, or at least that's how he sees it. You see, I'm too far beneath a duke. I'm afraid my fame and the fact that my father was a big movie producer doesn't pull any weight here."

London smiled at Desirea's sarcastic tone. "No, I guess it wouldn't. Truthfully, Desirea, I have so much to tell you that I don't know where to begin. I'm sure you have loads of questions. I think, in an hour or two, we will both be feeling much better about our positions here."

"Dude, if you've come up with an explanation for the how or why of us being in this time, then I'd really love to hear it."

"And you shall, but first I should order some food. This is going to be a shut-in. No one can hear what we discuss."

"If your smile is anything to go by, then I'm really glad I'm here. I could use a good pep talk."

It took a good ten minutes before the ladies sat with ham sandwiches and iced tea. "First," said London. "I want to begin with what happened when I left you last time."

"You mean when Declan physically carried you from the duke's house?" Desirea smirked.

"Yes, that's the time," London said with one of those smiles ladies get when they think about their lover.

"Before I came to you, I spent a few hours in Newgate prison."

"You what?" Desirea shook her head. "Holy shit! Why did you not tell me this then? And why the hell did they arrest you?" Desirea was angry her friend had suffered in such a way. She was sure the prisons were far worse now than their modern counterparts.

"I was set up and then used by the British government to catch a traitor. This traitor-sicko then attacked Declan and me when we left you that day. He abducted me."

"Oh, dear God," said Desirea.

"He took me to this small cottage where his mother was dying in the other room, from illness and not from anything he had done. Let it suffice to say that I escaped the nut bag when he took me to the Back Room to meet Declan for a trade: me for this man's gold he claimed my fiancé stole."

"So what happened?" Desirea couldn't believe her friend had gone through so much and she felt bad that she hadn't been there to help her.

"Well, I tricked the bad guy by getting him into the hidden closet. I never expected the time-portal to open, but it did."

"And he was sucked down the secret corridor?" Desirea shivered, thinking of their terrible ordeal with that tunnel.

"Yes, and hopefully sent to the Ice Ages. But I was nearly sucked into it as well, and I would have been if Declan hadn't saved me in time."

Desirea noticed London's hands were shaking from the retelling of her story, and she pulled her into a hug. "That must have been terrifying. It sounds like it should be in a horror movie. Thank God you're all right"

"I was lucky."

"And now you are in love and getting married." Desirea tried to bring up something happier.

"Yes, and I have much to tell you about that as well." London gave her hand a pat. "Where to begin…" Her fingers tapped on the sofa's arm as she thought.

"The beginning is often a logical place," said Desirea, impatient to hear the words of wisdom her friend had to share regarding love and marriage.

"All right, then. I came to London, England in an attempt to rid myself of the grief that was taking over my life. I lost my son in a car accident and that caused me to lose myself."

"Oh, my God. I'm so sorry. How terrible." Her friend's stories seemed to be going from terrible to tragic.

"Yes, it was." London was silent for a moment, probably thinking of her son, Desirea assumed, and then she continued. "I loved London when I arrived, so many new faces and sights and nothing to bring back memories of my tragic loss. I loved the Back Room Tavern as well, and so I went there nearly every day. Some days I'd talk to the locals, but other days I would read the documents that Conner, the owner, had under the glass of the bar or framed and hung around the room."

"Did any of these documents talk about time travel or the secret corridor?"

London laughed. "I wish, but no. The ones under the bar top were marriage documents of the four original owners of the Back Room Gentlemen's Club. Declan Devinn, the Earl of Nankin, and my future husband, was one of them."

"This is it, isn't it? This is where you tell me how we have forever altered history and the people we have come in contact with are doomed."

"Calm yourself, Desirea. This is where I tell you about the proof I have that you and I belong here."

"Say what?"

"What." London's smile widened as Desirea took in all she said.

"You mean we are supposed to be here? Tell me. I need the proof, because if what you say is really true... Well, it will make me extremely happy. Changing someone's destiny is not something I take lightly."

"Okay, here's my proof. I have what you may call a photographic memory. I remember things I've read or even merely glanced at in print. So I recognized my name." Desirea said nothing. "Did you hear me?" asked London with obvious excitement. "My name was on the marriage document dated in 1817. Miranda Burton was written in *my* handwriting, Desirea."

"Wow." Desirea sat back against the cushion. "I mean, I never dreamed. This is so unreal. How do you know I belong here and not only you?" Desirea prayed her friend was not about to tell her that she goes on to marry one of those irritating men she met upon their arrival.

"Because, if you'll recall, I wasn't even going to get into the closet."

"True," said Desirea, remembering how she yanked London on top of her. "You were being stubborn."

London laughed, and then Desirea laughed too. Then they both laughed until tears ran down their faces. Eventually

Desirea sucked in a breath. "I can't believe I'm supposed to be here. How cool. I do like it here."

"And you love the Duke of Lancaster?"

"I do."

"Then he is likely who you are meant to be with, Desirea. Do you feel a special humming vibration when you're near him? Do you feel like at times you can finish his thoughts or that you know his true feelings without him having to say the words?"

"Yes, yes, and yes. I feel we are MFEO."

"Which means?" asked London.

"Made for each other. Do you feel that way with Declan?"

"Yep," said London. "It's fate."

Desirea pulled London into another hug. "Thanks. This was the best news ever."

"I thought it might be."

This news could not have been more welcome. Desirea now felt empowered to go after Ellis. The man couldn't refuse their union if fate decreed it. She'd stay through London's wedding, and then it was back to Seaham to make a stubborn duke change his mind. Taylor Swift's song *You Belong With Me* filled her head like an anthem.

"Hey, I didn't want to ask and jinx it, but where are all of Declan's siblings?"

It took ten more minutes of conversation for her to learn everyone's whereabouts. "Sheez. I don't know how you remember all that."

"I can't wait for you to meet them," said London. "They will all be here for the evening meal, along with Amorita's fiancé, Lord Hastings, a most delightful man."

"Wow. How do you do that?"

"Do what?" asked London.

"Sound so much like them?" asked Desirea, knowing it was necessary for her to learn this trick.

"In this household there is always someone talking, and so I have been trying to stick with words they often use when describing things. It helps me blend in."

"I'll bet. I don't think I've ever strung the words 'delightful' and 'man' in the same sentence." They both laughed.

***

Ellis sat behind his oak desk feeling victorious that he had made it back to London in time to attend the Earl of Nankin's wedding. He thought of Desirea the entire journey back to the city, further cementing his decision with every mile he traveled closer to her. He planned to marry Desirea Leighton.

Society knew nothing of Desirea's background and all would think he simply married an American. Perhaps they'd frown upon a duke making a foreigner his duchess, but he no longer cared. His deceased father, and society, would have to wrap their heads around the fact that he, a duke of this realm, was marrying for love.

He poured himself a celebratory libation and then kicked his feet up on his desk, rocking back in his chair. The knock at the door had him putting his feet back to the ground and sitting forward. "Yes, what is it?"

"Sorry to disturb you, Your Grace. There is a Lady Margery Cummings and a Lady Amelia Faring, calling."

"Thanks, Temple. Show them to the parlor," Ellis instructed. No one on his staff, including Mimi, had asked after Desirea, but he knew they wondered. They'd have one hell of a surprise when he brought Desirea home as his bride. But then his staff was clever enough to realize Desirea had never fit in with them in the first place. He knew they were loyal enough to keep Desirea's beginnings, what they knew of them, quiet.

He stood, trying not to overreact to the fact that Amelia Faring had arrived in town, clearly riding in on his dust. She even brought along her very nosey and interfering aunt. *How pleasant.*

Forcing himself to be calm, kind, and understanding, he walked out of his study and down the hall to the parlor. He fervently hoped Amelia wasn't here to throw a tantrum.

He pushed open the double doors. "Lady Cummings and Lady Faring. What a pleasure to see you both." He couldn't help but wonder at Amelia's intentions. She rarely left the countryside, at least that's what he'd been told.

"Before you start thinking I followed you to town, Ellis, you should know my aunt asked me to join her to take in some of London's social whirl."

"Ah," he said carefully. "Would either of you lovely ladies care for a beverage?" He felt better knowing Amelia hadn't followed him, and he already forgave her for the scene she caused at her home. She seemed to be under some kind of pressure. He had sensed it in her since they were kids. He wished there was a way he could help her, but truthfully, he didn't know what bothered her.

"So shopping and parties," he said, after ordering up some refreshments. "No weddings?"

"No, Your Grace, we were not invited to the Earl of Nankin's nuptials, and for that I am gladdened." Lady Cummings looked down her nose as if to say the earl's wedding was beneath her, though she herself was once married to an earl, but then her brother was the Marquis of Thornbrook and so she felt herself of higher rank.

Ellis knew he didn't want to know the answer, but he found himself asking, "Why are you gladdened? I thought all women loved a good wedding."

"Oh you poor, poor, man. Have you heard nothing of Lord Nankin's bride? Let us say that she is not up to snuff."

Lady Cummings was acting like a cold-hearted prig, something Ellis knew much about, since he had once teetered on that brink himself. But Desirea had changed all of that. He now looked upon people as people, not as a representative of their status. He now actually found himself wondering if the boy working in his stables had ever felt love or if the maid who used to work in the hall but disappeared this past week really ran off to get married. He truly had never pondered love, and he had never cared about other people's love and happiness as he did now. This was due to his love for Desirea.

He looked at Amelia and noticed the reddening of her face. "Are you warm, Amelia? I could have a servant… I mean, I could open the window."

"No, Your Grace. I am fine. I assume you are attending the Earl of Nankin's wedding?"

"Yes."

"Aunt, wouldn't it be bad form if a man were to propose to his love at another couple's wedding celebration?" Amelia asked her aunt.

Ellis shook his head, slightly confused by such an odd question. *Now how the hell did she know I was planning…*

Lady Cummings looked surprised by the question, but she paused as if to give it serious consideration. "I believe that would be beyond the pale, my dear. Why do you ask?"

"Merely wondering," said Amelia with a nonchalant air.

Ellis couldn't help but stare at Amelia for a few silent seconds. It was strange, but he could swear Amelia had read his thoughts. The idea was absurd, but then so was time travel and Desirea was proof *that* existed.

"Amelia, can you hear me?" he asked in his head.

Her face didn't so much as twitch. She sat serenely with her teacup and saucer in hand and a pleasant smile on her face. He had to be losing his mind. Of course, she couldn't hear his thoughts. Perhaps his consuming love for Desirea was taking over his common sense.

After a few more pleasantries about the weather and some upcoming soirées, Amelia put down her teacup. "Thank you for the refreshment and conversation, Your Grace. We won't take up any more of your time. I only wished to say hello and apologize for my outburst. I'm afraid I can't help myself at times."

"Apology accepted," said Ellis. He wished no ill will upon Amelia. As a matter of fact, he wished her happiness and love.

"I'm sure we are bound to run into each other in the coming months," she said as she rose to her feet.

"You are always welcome to visit," he said, meaning it. There weren't that many people he had known as long as he had Amelia.

"You know I will," she said with a sly smile, which he chose not to analyze, and the ladies departed.

CHAPTER NINETEEN

Dressed in a mauve ensemble with a white fur pelisse, Desirea made her way up the dozen steps of Saint George's Church to find a seat for her friend's wedding. The church was located in the middle of the influential neighborhood of Mayfair. The structure, with six huge columns, which looked to be five feet in diameter and at least thirty feet high, and a clock tower with a weathervane on the very top on the building, reminded Desirea of one of America's government buildings.

She followed the other guests into the church, excited to see what it looked like from the inside. She loved churches, loved the feeling of being closer to God whenever she visited one. She hadn't been a regular church-goer most of her young life, but she went often after she lost her father.

The doors were open and Desirea walked inside, her gaze traveling around the place in one sweep as she tried to take in the full effect. The ceiling above her was an arched cove, sectioned into squares with woodwork. The ground beneath her feet was gray stone, the pews oak with high backs. There were three galleries above and a heavy canopy over the pulpit. To the left of the altar was another place for people to do readings.

The upper wall above the altar held a Venetian window. The window had a sectioned top and stunning stained glass. She learned something about the scene it depicted when she overheard the well-dressed couple next to her. The man said it represented the Tree of Jesse and the figures were Kings who were earthly ancestors of God. There were two other stained glass windows, but she was ushered toward the pews by the crowd behind her and so had no time to examine them.

She saw a hand waving at her and looked up to see the smiling face of Lord Nankin's younger sister, Nadine. Desirea excused herself as she maneuvered around a few people and then approached the young woman. "Quite a turnout," she said.

"It's sure to be a crush. Society has always taken a keen interest in my brothers, especially my oldest, since he's the earl." Nadine moved further into the pew. "Come and sit with the family. This is where you belong."

Desirea smiled at that, and with a nod, she stepped into the pew aisle and sat. "Thank you." The only people aware of London and Desirea's true origins were Declan, Ellis, and Lord Gabriel Insley. Both women felt that the fewer people who knew the truth the better.

When the last of the guests found their seats, music filled the church and Desirea's smile was instantaneous. She looked up at the Last Supper depicted on the wall in front of the altar and below the stained glass window. The disciples were reclining on sofas around the table, and it looked like Judas was trying to sneak out of the scene.

"That was painted by William Kent," said Nadine, obviously noticing Desirea's study of the painting.

"It's very good."

"Look. Here she comes. Oh, she's beautiful." They both turned to look behind them.

"Yes, and happy," said Desirea. Everyone got to their feet to watch the couple walk down the aisle together. Desirea wasn't sure if that was how it was done here or if London had changed the wedding program so she wasn't walking down the aisle alone, but it didn't matter. *They look totally hot together. A perfect match.* London's dress was a stunning white satin and glittering with crystals from the v-neck to the long sleeves and train. Declan looked like he was floating on cloud nine as he walked proudly with his bride. He chose to wear formal black.

Desirea tried to concentrate on the ceremony, but it was difficult keeping Ellis from her mind at a moment like this. Like London and Declan, the love she and Ellis shared was strong and all encompassing, bigger than the both of them. Why couldn't Ellis see this?

The robed minister droned on with his bible in hand, but Desirea couldn't concentrate on his words.

Why didn't Ellis come for her? Her mind ventured back to the perfect weeks she spent with him in the country. She thought of all the times they had made each other laugh, how Ellis always pulled her playfully onto the couch and the wonderful praise he gave her when she sang. She thought of the huge smile on his face as he'd clap vigorously after one of her impromptu plays. She even thought of Ellis, her hero, saving her from a darkening alleyway, which had been scary as hell and filled with disgusting condoms, not to mention it was next to a brothel.

When the music began again, the bride and groom kissed. Cheers and hollers filled the church and people began to shuffle out toward the doors. The reception would take place back at the Devinn home in Mayfair, and so they didn't have far to go.

***

At the reception, Desirea finally found London in the garden when she was not surrounded by twenty people. "Dude, you should really stop staring at him like that," Desirea teased.

"I can't seem to help myself," London admitted happily. It was good to see her friend so in love. She only hoped she could convince her soul mate that they were meant to be. But since Ellis wasn't here, that wouldn't be possible, for now.

"Who's that redhead giving it to Lord Insley?" Desirea asked. "Don't tell me she's the one who came out of the time corridor?"

They both looked over at the disgusted face of Gabriel Worthing and laughed.

"It is," said London. "Miss Bennett from the sixteenth century."

"Wow," said Desirea.

"My wife claims she's Gabriel's intended," said Lord Nankin, coming up behind them to wrap his arms around his wife. "But I have serious doubts as to that possibility," replied Declan, taking London's hand in his and bringing it to his lips for a kiss.

"I know it's your wedding," said Desirea. "But please spare us all the PDA." She couldn't stop herself from calling them out in a teasing manner. She was envious. London was so lucky to be able to express her love for Declan publicly while Desirea had to try to kill her feelings for Ellis. What felt like a lightning bolt of longing speared through her chest.

"The what?" asked London.

"Public display of affection," said Desirea with a laugh. She used her best acting skills to portray happiness and hide the fact that she was stuck in a state of mind-numbing sadness. Declan seemed to find her comment funny and took a moment to give London a kiss.

"OMG," said Desirea.

London smiled, saying, "Kissing is a lot of fun. You should try it with your duke." Desirea never told London how far things had gone with Ellis, but her friend knew full well they had far surpassed kissing.

"Kissing? Huh, I never thought of that," replied Desirea, causing London to laugh.

They all continued to watch Gabriel, who had just finished smacking his hand into his forehead.

"All couples argue on occasion," London told them as if this was new knowledge.

In Desirea's opinion, a love-match between Gabriel and Miss Bennett looked highly unlikely. They were talking quietly enough, but they were clearly having a huge dispute over something.

When they thought the argument was finished, Miss Bennett hoisted a large crystal punch bowl from the table and the three of them watched, along with just about everyone else in attendance, as the young lady stretched up as high as she could, since Gabriel was a large man, before she dumped the punch over Lord Insley's head. To say Gabriel's face reddened in the matter of thirty seconds would be an understatement. The man was furious.

"Perhaps it's time to intervene," Declan suggested, but he didn't make a move to do so.

London and Desirea stifled their laughter behind their hands. Gabriel looked fit to be tied.

"Intervening at this point might be best," London said, tears of laughter in her eyes.

Gabriel certainly had more than he could handle with Phoebe Bennett. The English lady was a force to be reckoned with.

Declan went to make his way to Gabriel, but he must have changed his mind as he turned back to sweep London into his arms for another kiss. This one lasted much longer. Cheers and applause broke out among the guests as they witnessed love in all its glory.

When Desirea groaned a teasing complaint, London smiled. With a wink, Desirea turned to make her way toward the rest of the Devinn family clan. She nodded at a few people as she traversed around the statues in the garden. When she reached the fountain, someone grabbed her arm.

"Desirea," said the voice, and she knew in an instant Ellis had come. Her heart immediately began to pound faster and butterflies pooled in her stomach. She turned with a smile, feeling wonderful and amazed that he actually was here. He came for her.

"Is there somewhere we can talk?" he asked in a far too serious tone for this reunion. And he'd yet to smile back at her. *What the hell is his deal? Why come here at all? Please, Lord, don't let him explain, yet again, why we cannot be together.*

"I don't know, Ellis. This house has over sixty rooms. Do you believe it possible that they are all occupied?" She caught a hint of his smile that time. Her heart was still racing because she couldn't seem to read him. She didn't wish to get her hopes up. *But why is he here?*

He grabbed her gloved hand and pulled her toward one of the many back entrances. "Come," he said, ushering her into the house, his body stiff beside her. He was acting strange, but she hurried along with him, very curious by his behavior.

He pulled her around a corner and she hurried to match his steps. He halted in front of a door, knocked, listened, and then opened it, closing it quickly behind them as his eyes scanned the room.

"We're alone, Ellis. I happen to know that not a single person in this family favors this room."

"Really?" He looked about the pale blue walls and shrugged before pulling her to a white couch, which looked uncomfortable with its exposed wooden arms and wood above the cushioned back. She sat forward on the cushion so she wouldn't knock her head against the backing. Ellis remained standing.

"Sit with me," she said.

"No, Desirea, I can't. I…."

"You what?" She was quickly growing impatient and angry. "Can't sit with me? Won't sit with me? Why are you here, Ellis?" He flinched when she yelled, but this was so unbelievably frustrating. He was here and she wanted to throw herself in his arms, and yet he wouldn't even sit with her.

"I'm here to ask you to be my wife," he said, and she immediately understood his behavior. The poor man was nervous. Now she felt terrible for yelling, but it was his fault for not stating his case immediately. He had given her too long to ponder all the bad things he might say. She had never expected this.

"So why did you not just ask right away?"

"Ah, hell, Desirea." He sat down next to her. After about two seconds, he reached over, picked her up, and placed her on his lap. "I've missed this," he whispered in her ear, leaning his head against hers. "I know I've been a fool. I was about to make another mistake and marry according to other people's dictates. I had set my mind to follow through on my promises. It was a matter of loyalty and honor. But then, I thought, where is my loyalty and honor to you, the woman I love? Should I not give the best of what I can be to you?"

She snuggled closer to him. This was exactly what she wanted to hear.

"Now I know you deem yourself too young for marriage, but you are not. You are such a strong woman, Desirea, and wise for your years. Your courage is unmatched in my opinion. You are far braver than I."

"Nonsense, Ellis, but do go on," she said with a smile.

"What I'm trying to say…is that, through you, I have come to realize the importance of love, not only ours, but even other peoples, if you can believe it. I've come to see others in a different light and realize everyone has their own path in life to follow, which more often than not, doesn't revolve around me," he said, giving her a cocky grin. "Like me, they search for a love of their own. I didn't even know I wanted love until I met you, Desirea. I've come to understand the importance of choosing one's life partner beyond any considerations of money, status, and peerage."

"Don't forget babies," she said, and he laughed.

"And babies." He touched his forehead to hers, and then he moved back a few inches to say, "What you were has made you who you are today. I can find no fault in that. You are spectacular. I love you. And although you may not wish to have a wedding now, I want to make our betrothal. Once I share my unbelievably good fortune with my sister, I would like to post the banns. After the third reading, even if you decide the wedding will be months from now, at least I will have everything in order for when you are ready. So I have two questions for you, my love. First…" He lifted her chin with the crook of his finger and she looked up into the bright green of his eyes, as he asked, "Will you marry me?"

She didn't answer at first. She was too busy covering his face in kisses. Tears filled her eyes. The joy she felt could not even compare to a hundred-thousand applauding fans or her albums going platinum. Nothing had ever felt this great. "Yes, Ellis, a thousand times, yes."

He pulled her even tighter and she giggled as she wrestled in his arms to loosen his playful grip.

"Now what's the second question?" she asked, wondering if it was something about where'd they live, country or city, or where they should have the wedding, again country or city. Or maybe his question was about how grotesquely huge a diamond he should buy her. *Oooh, that was a good one.*

"How old do you need to be before we can 'do this thing,' as you would say?" he asked.

She smiled at his use of her phrase. "Seeing as I feel a decade older in this time, and seeing as how I can't seem to keep my hands off you, perhaps it would be best if we just 'do this thing' now."

"Truly?" He gave her a wide smile and she nodded, too choked up to speak after she saw pure joy fill his face.

"I love you, Ellis Pemble, my Duke of Lancaster."

"And I love you, Desirea Leighton, movie star, singer extraordinaire, and my lovely duchess."

"The Duchess of Lancaster, Desirea Leighton Pemble," she said. "Yes, I definitely like the sound of that."

***

Ellis left the *London Times* offices with a spring in his step. He had posted the first of the banns announcing his upcoming nuptials to Desirea and felt on top of the world. His next stop was a visit with Desirea. He was taking her riding in the park. He couldn't wait to show off his lovely fiancée. He wished

Desirea could reside with him, but they had agreed it best she stay put until they were officially wed. Society would not permit them living together, even if Desirea claimed that was how they did things where she was from. This was not the twenty-first century, and so although Desirea viewed some of their traditions and social mores as arcane. Nevertheless, those traditions and mores were still expected to be followed, and they both knew it was wise to act in accordance to the dictates.

He skipped over a few of the Earl of Nankin's steps as he reached the front door. Escorted into a parlor, he didn't have long to wait before Desirea stood at the door looking so lovely and so perfect he felt his heart leap.

"Hello, handsome fiancé," she said and she walked into the room and right into his arms.

Ellis pulled her close, breathing in her scent and wondering how he'd be able to keep his hands off her until they wed.

"I posted the banns today," he announced with a wide smile.

"Did you?" She stepped back to look at him. "And what exactly does that mean?"

"It's customary to have the banns read in the paper for three weeks until you obtain your marriage license and the service can be performed."

"And what purpose does this serve?"

"It gives people an opportunity to object to our union," he said, rubbing the back of her hand.

"Objections? People can object to our marriage? People I don't even know? Do you think that fair, Ellis?"

"Uh, no, I don't, but it's how it's done. Relax, my dear. No one will object."

"And why would you believe such a thing? Even if they don't know my background, I'm afraid my American heritage will be impossible to hide."

"I don't want you to hide who you are, Desirea," he said. And then he added, "Well, not completely."

She laughed and hugged him again. The future he envisioned for them stretched out before them like a paradise of delights waiting to be savored. "No one will oppose our marriage because I won't allow them to do so. Now, I want to take you for a ride in Hyde Park."

"All right. I'll go grab my hat and gloves." She hurried out of the room.

Ellis looked about the parlor as he waited, but all his thoughts were focused on Desirea and how happy they were going to be together. He couldn't wait to show off his pride and joy in the public park. He was tired of closed curtains and enclosed carriages. Today he would drive her around in his fancy two-wheeled curricle for all to see how fortunate he was in finding a bride as lovely and intelligent as Desirea.

She returned a short while later wearing a very pretty rose-colored riding habit lined with white fur on the cuffs and around the matching pelisse. The smile on her face was enough to make him laugh. She appeared as happy as he was that they were finally together, and perhaps nearly as relieved to have the hiding behind them.

***

"This is nice," Desirea said as Ellis maneuvered the vehicle down the driving path to take her along the side of the Serpentine, the water sparkling in the midmorning sun. They nodded and made appropriate remarks to everyone they passed.

"I can't believe we are riding about in public."

He felt guilty about that; he never meant to hide her away. But with the way he felt about her, and considering where he found her, he had thought it best. "I never want you to hide again. I truly never meant…"

"I'm only teasing, Ellis. I know your intent was to keep us safe from gossip. I appreciate it. Although I was tired of constantly being talked about back home, I'm sure news of our marriage will be quite the sensation, considering your prestige."

"Indeed, it may be difficult going for awhile, until someone else does something worth gossiping about, which will likely be only a matter of days. Eventually people will find something else to discuss instead of our nuptials."

"Won't we cause talk today, since I don't have a chaperone?" she asked, wondering if the looks they received were because of the powerful and titled man beside her or because she was unknowingly behaving in what they considered a scandalous manner.

"We are in a public park in broad daylight in an open vehicle, so no. But to put you at ease, I took the liberty of bringing your chaperone with us."

"Say what?" she asked, her head turning back to see if they were followed by a maid or a retinue of servants. He smiled when she turned her gaze to him. "Where'd you hide her?"

"Here," he said, reaching beneath them and opening a drawer under the seat. He pulled out the hatchet with a wide grin.

"Aww, you brought Mrs. Hatchett. How thoughtful." They both fell into laughter.

Ellis pulled down a less traveled lane and moved off the road under a canopy of trees.

"This is cozy and private, Ellis. Just what do you have in mind?" she asked in a husky tone, slowly traveling her gloved fingers down his arm and moving one of her legs along his.

He gave her a sly smile and then shifted to the floor on bended knee.

She giggled at him, nudging him with her leg to teasingly knock him off balance. "Why do I have the feeling you are about to propose to me again?"

"Because I am, but this time I have this." He withdrew the ring from the inner recesses of his coat pocket. "Now, since you already said yes, I won't ask again. However, as the love of my life, I would like for you to accept my mother's ring as a symbol of our love and the strength we have together. I know I have done this before and failed, but I have never loved anyone as I do you; and I promise you, and God, that I will love you, support you, and stand by you no matter what comes."

"So you won't divorce me if I can't have babies?"

"What? No, of course not, darling," he said with a hand to his chest, appalled that she'd believe he could do such a thing. He knew he had told her he would annul his marriage if it did not produce an heir, but that was before *she* had agreed to be his wife. "We are a perfect match, and even if God doesn't see fit to bless us with children, at least He blessed us with each other. The only other woman to wear this ring was my mother." He wanted her to know his deceased wife hadn't worn the band.

"Ellis, the fact that you are giving me your mother's ring means so much to me." Thunder roared in the distance and they both looked up at the sky, which was quickly turning gray.

"Did you bring an umbrella?" she asked, holding out her hand to take the ring. He slid it on her finger and she stared down at the old-fashioned antique scroll band with its six diamonds. "It's beautiful. I'm touched," she said, and tears filled her eyes. Moving to his feet, he sat next to her to pull her into his arms as the thunder continued to rumble around them and the leaves on the trees shook overhead.

"With this ring, I thee wed. With my body, I thee worship, and all my worldly goods, I thee endow. In the name of the Father and of the Son and of the Holy Ghost. Amen."

"Right back at you, Ellis," she said with tears in her eyes. He kissed her then and the clouds opened up to shower them with its blessings. At least they decided to see it this way.

She laughed as he stopped kissing her to struggle with the back hood of the vehicle. "I didn't think it would rain," he said by way of explanation, to which she laughed some more.

CHAPTER TWENTY

As Mura put the finishing touches on her hair, Desirea couldn't seem to hide her happiness, not that it was necessary but she didn't wish to nauseate everyone around her with her I'm-so-happy-to-be-in-love vibe. She had yet to tell Ellis about fate and how they were meant to be. She'd been too busy listening to him declaring his love to interrupt. And then the rain came with a vengeance, sending them to their respective homes to change. But she was to see him again in about an hour. She couldn't seem to settle herself down or stop staring at her vintage wedding band.

Her friend London was off in the country enjoying some alone time with her new hubby, and so Desirea was attending tonight's function with Declan's twin sisters, Lydia and Evadne. Desirea enjoyed their company, but really she just couldn't wait to see Ellis again. They hadn't officially been seen together at a high-society function, but that would all change tonight.

"You are very fidgety, Miss. It's hard to get this hairpin in correctly with you wiggling around. You're excited to see His Grace?"

"Yes, as always," Desirea replied, concentrating harder on sitting still.

"Have you set a date yet?" asked Mura, a hairpin sticking from between her pursed lips.

"No, but I think June sounds like the perfect month, don't you?"

"It doesn't give you much time for planning, Miss, but yes. I think next month sounds splendid."

"Yes, me too." Now she would only have to convince Ellis. She was sure that wouldn't prove the least bit difficult, because the sooner they married the sooner they could share each other's beds, and thoughts, and meals, and… Oh, there were so many wonderful things she was looking forward to. Desirea

Leighton was no longer alone. She had found love. She had found Ellis Pemble, a man hand selected for her by fate itself. *Thank you, God, for sending me into the past.*

***

Desirea stood near a potted palm next to a large fluted column sipping her rum punch. She scanned the faces of the guest attending the party, looking for Ellis, but her peering about only brought her more male attention. Evadne was busy conversing with an older women, who stood leaning on her cane and nodding with a smile as Evadne described her brother's wedding. Lydia had gone off to speak with some friends and had yet to return. The Devinn brothers, at least the ones still in town, had opted out of tonight's festivities, which was just as well since the second oldest, Morgan, tended to flirt nonstop with Desirea. The Devinn family's Aunt Margaret was serving as the girls' chaperone for the evening. She sat with some other matrons conversing while keeping a watchful eye on her nieces.

When Desirea heard someone say, "It's the Duke of Lancaster," her head turned toward the ballroom's entrance.

There he was, dressed in black and looking like the yummiest man on the planet. His green-eyed gaze met hers and her heart picked up its already cantering pace. He smiled and her hands began to sweat as he made his way toward her. She almost laughed. The way people moved out of his way, he looked like Moses parting the Red Sea. She fought the urge to move forward toward him.

"You are by far the loveliest woman in this room," he said by way of greeting, and she nearly melted into a puddle at his feet. When Ellis poured on the charm, it made her breathless. *And I am going to marry this hottie. Unbelievable.* Surely she'd die young from a heart attack if her heart continued to beat this fast around him for years to come.

Lydia returned with a bright smile and her hazel eyes beaming with excitement. She was tickled pink to be at a party, and it was very evident. London had told Desirea it was the twins' first Season, meaning Lydia and Evadne were new to this atmosphere. By contrast, Desirea had been to so many parties, albeit most of them in another century, that they tended to blend together. She noted the differences to parties in the nineteenth century, like there wasn't a DJ playing the top hits but an orchestra playing while people danced a cotillion. When the music ended, she watched as the partners bowed to each other before more dancers took to the floor for a slow waltz. Comparing the supposed scandalous waltz to the bump and grind dancing Desirea was used to witnessing was comical. And instead of bellying up to the bar and waiting in line for a drink as would happen in her century, waiters came around with trays of beverages. Not that she hadn't been to tons of fancy parties with bands and waiters, but the atmosphere was different here in an old-fashioned way. There were certainly no strobe lights or disco balls, but the candlelight set an atmosphere that was totally romantic.

"You look wonderful too, Ellis, but you already know that." Desirea smiled at him and he winked.

"Dance with me," he said, holding out his arm.

"I would, Ellis, but the waltz isn't really my cup of tea."

"And I assume that means you don't waltz?"

"Uh, no, I don't."

"But you can dance?"

"Of course, Ellis. You should see me move."

"I would love to. Come."

"Oh, no. I can't dance like that here. My dancing should probably wait until we are behind closed doors. I'd hate to scandalize all these people with my gyrating hip action."

He leaned toward her ear. "I'm afraid to ask what that exactly is, but you will show it to me soon. Anything that involves your hips has my full attention." She laughed.

He glanced back out at the dance floor with a look of longing. "I didn't realize you were so into dancing," she said, surprised to realize that he really wished to dance.

Lydia and Evadne were now on the dance floor twirling around in their partners' arms. The girls seemed to be having such a great time. "Okay, come on," she said. "Let's dance."

"But you said…"

"Forget what I said. You will lead and I will follow. It can't be that hard. I've learned some unbelievable moves for parts I've played on stage, and so I'm sure I can handle the waltz."

"Well, I did imagine you dancing in my arms this evening." A smile filled his face and lifted her heart to soaring.

She grabbed his arm. "All right. Teach me the waltz, my love."

He pulled her into his side for a hug and then led her to the dance floor amidst the twirling couples. She loved the feel of his hand on her back and his stiff formal stance. She had watched *Dancing with the Stars* a few times and so recognized the proper positioning of his carriage. Although she was nervous of making a cake of herself, she followed his steps and concentrated on the pattern, and before she knew it, she no longer had to look down at her feet. Ellis spun her around another couple and she laughed at their speed. "This is fun, Ellis."

"I thought you'd enjoy it."

Desirea stared up at the man who had captured her heart so completely and let herself go with the music, allowing Ellis to lead the way with his smooth steps. She was having an awesome time.

When the music ended, Ellis led her to a waiter carrying a tray, snatched them a couple of refreshments, and found them a semi-private spot next to the dance floor to rest.

"So you sing like an angel, move like a dream, kiss like a seductress, and make love like a tigress. Dare I say I am the luckiest man alive?"

"Yes, you should say so. Honesty is the best policy after all," she teased. Shania Twain's song *Forever and For Always* filled her mind and she smiled.

"There you are," came a familiar voice, and Desirea turned her head to find herself looking at Amelia Faring. To say she was shocked to see the chick in London would be an understatement. *Just what is this tricky, manipulative woman up to? And the million-dollar question: why is she still sniffing around my boyfriend? She must not have gotten the memo on our upcoming nuptials.* Desirea's body stiffened automatically. She was sick of seeing Amelia, sick of her fawning over her man, and sick of her untimely interruptions in her life. But since she had won this particular tug-of-war, she put a smile on her face and held back the what-the-hell-are-you-doing-here line that she wanted to use.

"I have looked all over this ballroom for you, Ellis." She slapped Ellis on the arm in a playful scolding manner that set Desirea's teeth on edge. *Yes, Ellis is a gorgeous specimen of man, but he is my man, and if this bitch doesn't retract her claws there is going to be hell to pay.*

"And yet here I am in plain sight," he said with a smile as he stood and bowed a greeting to his interfering neighbor.

Crazy-ass psycho neighbor seems a far more fitting description. Desirea grudgingly got to her feet. Miss Faring was beginning to remind her of Marvin. She was entering stalker category.

"Yes, you are. And with Miss Leighton." Amelia's tone turned almost accusatory, which did not help Desirea's growing irritation.

"Fancy seeing you here. I don't believe you mentioned coming to the city," said Desirea, wondering how to get rid of this irritant.

"Last minute planning, I'm afraid. I did stop by His Grace's home. Did he not mention my visit?"

Desirea knew the game she was playing, but no, Ellis had not mentioned Amelia's visit. Amelia was trying to make her jealous, and it was working. If it wasn't for the fact that Ellis had actually slated this loon for a bride, Desirea wouldn't have thought much about her. But then, he had actually considered her, as a marriage prospect.

"I'm afraid your name doesn't come up in our conversations," replied Desirea with a so-take-that tone. *Seriously, if this chick doesn't move her ass out of my sight, I am going to smash her face in.* Desirea could even picture herself grabbing that dainty ass feather out of Amelia's brunette hair and breaking her nose with a very hard fist.

"Your Grace, can I please speak to you for a moment?" Amelia screeched, suddenly looking very alarmed. Her eyes had widened so the whites dominated and she was trembling as if suddenly scared, which didn't make sense at all. It was like she saw a ghost or something.

"Perhaps we should share our news with your neighbor," said Desirea. She wanted this woman to know the duke was taken and off limits.

"Desirea," said Ellis, and Amelia sucked in a breath as Ellis called her by her first name.

Did Amelia believe that, since she knew Ellis as a boy, she somehow knew him better than she? *Stupid girl.*

"Lady Faring appears distressed," said Ellis. "Desirea, return to the Devinn sisters while I have a word with her." She watched Ellis take Amelia's hand and place it on his coat sleeve.

Is he frikken kidding? No. He wasn't. Left with no option, and not willing to cause a scene because she knew how much the duke hated them, she nodded and went to walk off.

Ellis grabbed her hand before she left. "I'll come find you shortly," he said.

"Whatever," she said with a roll of her eyes. She couldn't help being angry. *What did Amelia have to say that was so damn important? And what is with that frightened rabbit routine?* Desirea turned back and watched as Ellis led her nemesis outside. From the window, she could see them standing on the balcony, and she recognized the desperate and pleading look on Amelia face. *What is the chick saying? Likely bad mouthing me, the interfering pain in the ass.*

Desirea had been about to tell Ellis of fate and how they were destined to be together, when loony toony Amelia had to saunter up. She walked over to Lydia, who was standing with a group of men. Desirea silently fumed, not listening to the conversation around her.

***

"All right, Amelia. What is this all about?" asked Ellis. He had not liked the look on Desirea's face when he told her he wished to speak to his old childhood friend, but then he was partly to blame for these two women not liking each other. "Desirea's not happy our evening was interrupted, and neither am I. I have known you a long time, Amelia, which is why I was willing to face Desirea's anger. But our childhood friendship doesn't give you leave to interrupt the evening I had planned for my fiancée."

"You're what? Oh, dear Lord in heaven, say it isn't so."

"Pardon me?" he asked, stunned by her abject response.

"Ellis, please, you must listen to me. That woman is no good for you. She's evil."

Ellis couldn't help his response to such a ludicrous statement. He threw back his head and laughed with mirth. Desirea? Evil? The very notion was ridiculous. But the fact that Amelia felt so strongly about this that she insisted on warning him was a problem. Perhaps Amelia was more intuitive than most and realized Desirea was somehow different compared to everyone else around her.

Wiping the tears of amusement from his eyes, he sighed. "Sorry, I forgot myself." He held out his arm and waited for her to take it before leading her down the steps and out into the privacy of the garden. He didn't want any of Amelia's nonsense overheard.

"It's not nonsense," she said haughtily.

Ellis stopped and stared down at her in shock. "How did you…? Never mind. Listen, Amelia. I appreciate your concern for my welfare, I really do."

"You're marrying me," she said adamantly, interrupting him.

"I'm doing no such thing," he replied, continuing walking and finding them a bench for her to sit. She sat, but her hands twisted on her lap uncontrollably as she looked up at him. He couldn't help but pace in front of her as he tried to find a way to let her down without hurting her feelings.

"She's evil, Ellis. I like you too much to allow you to marry anyone evil. So the deal is, you marry me and she goes away, and then you'll be safe."

"Amelia…"

"No, I'm not finished. I know I'm considered eccentric by some, but I know what I know, and I know this lady is no good for you. You can choose not to believe me, but you can't choose not to marry me."

What the bloody hell is she talking about? He was the one making the decision in his life, not her. "I'm not marrying you, Amelia. I'm marrying Desirea."

Amelia stood now, her hands on her hips and glaring at him. "No. You're marrying me. If you don't marry me, I plan to tell everyone who has ears about Desirea Leighton's history. I will tell them about her career on stage and her life as an actress. I will tell them how she doesn't belong here. I will tell them of her evil intentions."

"What evil intentions?" he yelled, fed up with this game of threats and blackmail.

"I'm not telling you."

"What?" Amelia was behaving like a child. He moved toward her, furious, leveling his gaze on her. "You will tell me exactly what you think you know about my fiancée." He had no idea how Amelia found out about Desirea's stage life or the fact that she was different, but he intended to find out.

"You're right. I will tell you. The moment we say 'I do.'"

He moved to tower over her. "We will never be saying I do."

"Fine, then if you'll excuse me, I have an announcement to make." She went to step around Ellis, but he grabbed her arm.

"The bloody hell you are. If you make even one derogatory remark concerning my fiancée, I will…"

"You'll what, Ellis?" she asked, moving forward to show him she wasn't intimidated by his scare tactics and cursing.

"I'll tell your father about your blackmail scheme." He was quite proud of himself for coming up with that one.

"My father wishes to see me wed, Your Grace. Now that I'm twenty-four and I've scared away all my suitors, do you really believe my father cares any longer how I go about obtaining myself a husband? You are a duke. He'd be thrilled by our match."

She had him there. The Earl of Thornbrook would be thrilled. Ellis sighed, feeling defeated. "Amelia, we are friends and we have been so for a long time. Why are you trying to destroy our friendship?"

"I'm trying to save you, Your Grace. You're merely too blinded by lust to see it."

"It's not lust, Amelia. I love Desirea. You are a good woman, and one day you'll find…"

"I've already found him, Your Grace. You. I guess you'll have to grin and bear it or face the consequences."

"You've the gall to threaten me!" he roared.

"I think this conversation is over." She walked away without a backward glance, and Ellis was left starring at her helplessly, wondering what in the hell he was going to do. He couldn't allow Amelia to lead a verbal assault on Desirea. Lord knew what vicious lies, or even truths, could come forth to destroy Desirea's future standing in society.

He walked back inside the ballroom with a heavy weight in his chest and his hopes for a future crushed.

He heard her laughter from somewhere behind him and turned to find Desirea sandwiched between ten men. *For crying out loud, men were like wolfhounds following a new scent.* He wished for a club to beat them all away.

"Excuse me," she said the moment her beautiful blue eyes met his. With neither of them breaking eye contact, they made their way to each other.

"So how'd it go?" she asked with a scrunched brow of confusion. Obviously she read the look of hopelessness on his face.

"Retrieve your things. I'm taking you home." He held out his arm to lead her away, but she didn't take it.

"Why? What did Amelia say?"

"This has more to do with what she didn't say. At least, not yet. Come, I'll explain on the way home."

"But I thought you wanted to announce our engagement tonight. I mean, you said you weren't going to make a big announcement but whisper in a few ears. Have you done that? Have you whispered in the right peoples' ears?"

"Uh, no, I haven't. Nor do I plan to do so." Tears filled her eyes and she blinked them away, but he felt them just the same.

"You…" She stared up at him, questions likely tumbling through her head, which was fine since he had plenty of questions himself. *Like who the hell did Desirea decide to enlighten about her past?* He was sure she had not shared anything with Amelia, which meant someone had betrayed Desirea's trust. *And how much did Desirea share with this untrustworthy person?* He was mad at her for going against what he said. He had told her, under no uncertain terms should she discuss her past, and yet she clearly hadn't listened.

She had jeopardized their entire future and he was mad as hell about it.

Finally, she must have read his irate mood because she nodded, whispered something to Nadine, and then turned to take his arm. He led her through the crowd without making eye contact with anyone. He wanted out of this place, and he wanted a damn good explanation for why his world was collapsing. He had finally found the courage to take control of his life and lead it in the direction that he desired with the love of his life by his side, and now it appeared his dreams of a life with Desirea would not come to be.

"Smile, Your Grace. People are beginning to stare," she said, and he dutifully showed his teeth.

"I said smile, not snarl," she quipped.

He ignored her. He was so unbelievably furious that he felt like his head was going to explode. He loved this woman, but at the moment he didn't know who he wanted to strangle more, Amelia for her blackmail threats or Desirea for going against their policy of silence concerning her past.

When they were finally ensconced in his vehicle and headed toward Mayfair, Desirea asked, "I assume my chaperone is with us?"

He tried to smile but found he couldn't drum up a speck of amusement under the circumstances. He loved how she always teased. He loved every single thing about this woman. "Yes, Mrs. Hatchett's under the seat."

"Okay. I've waited long enough, Ellis. What did Miss Irritating have to say?"

"Amelia's blackmailing me into marrying her."

CHAPTER TWENTY-ONE

"She's what? Oh, you wait until I get my hands on her," Desirea threatened. Now she was pissed, so pissed, she wanted to scream. "Put your hands over your ears, Ellis," she ordered.

"Pardon?" he asked, confusion written on his face.

"Just do it," she demanded, and when he covered his ears, she let out a string of obscenities so wicked and mean it would have made any nineteenth century person's head spin. But venting her anger always helped, and she didn't remember another time when she was this frustrated.

She finished her rant and told Ellis he could uncover his ears, which he did with a smile. Of course, he had listened to her. "You heard that, didn't you?"

"Hard not to."

His adorable crooked smile made her laugh.

"I'm impressed," he said. "Not only did you use words I have never heard but you used some I've only heard in the back rooms of my men's club. Where did you learn to do that? Do they have a special school to teach cursing in your time?" He was teasing her.

"Yes, I graduated at the top of my class with a doctorate in swearing. I'm quite fluent, as you can perhaps tell."

"I barely notice." He smiled in earnest this time.

"So what are we going to do about this Amelia situation?" she huffed. If this man thought to finagle his way out of marrying her, he was sadly mistaken. She wasn't going to cry again because this nonsense simply wasn't happening.

"First we need to find out how she came by her information."

"What information? I knew that chick was trash-talking me. I should have never let you go with her."

"I'm my own man, Desirea. I go as I please," he said with stiff formality, which made her smile. He had so much to learn about relationships, not that she was an expert but people just thought more about such things in her time.

"I want you to remember you said that, Ellis, when I throw that same line of bullshit back at you. Married couples have to cave to each other at times, Ellis. If I really didn't want you to speak with Amelia, you wouldn't." She shrugged, as if to say, "And that is that."

"And *why* wouldn't I?" he asked as if he really didn't have a clue.

"Because, Ellis, as your wife I could choose not to speak to you or to be mad at you, and I don't think you like arguing any more than I do. Married couples have to have a give-and-take relationship. Compromise, trust, love, and honesty are all essential elements."

"Which we have in abundance," he said, and she couldn't help but smile. "You know, for a lady who claims not to have thought much about marriage, you seem to believe to know exactly how marriage works."

"Yes, well, the magazine articles about relationships in the twenty-first century are endless."

"But you're not in the twenty-first century. Things are done differently in this time."

She couldn't take it anymore. He was skirting the main issue. This conversation was getting them nowhere. "Trust me, Ellis, you don't need to remind me of the differences in our respective eras. Look, what's your deal? Did Amelia's threats change your mind? Are you going to marry me or not?"

"Not."

"Oh my God, Ellis, not this again." Now she wanted to beat him. Where was the man she imagined him to be, a man who was willing to sweep in to love her regardless of circumstances?

"Desirea, I'm sorry, but I'm afraid..."

"Ah, hell, Ellis. You're walking away from me again, aren't you?" Tears filled her eyes as her heart cracked anew. This man was killing her.

"I can see no alternative." She could see in his face that he meant his words. He really thought there was no chance for them.

She put her hands to her face. "I don't believe this. Why? What happened? What did she say?" She tried to hold her sobs in check, tried to focus on her anger. *What a stupid fool I am. But fate...*

"Ellis, listen to me. I know whatever Amelia said has got you frazzled, but I have to tell you something."

"And I have to ask you something, Desirea. I want to know in whom you confided about your past. Who did you tell that you could act on stage? Whomever you told has shared all the scandalous details with Amelia."

Now Desirea was surprised. "And Amelia is threatening to announce my origins and my career to society?"

"If I don't marry her."

"Why that conniving bitch. I can assure you that I have told no one of my past or of my previous career. All anyone knows is that I come from America and have a spectacular voice and I'm good friends with your sister and the new Countess of Nankin."

"She found out about you somehow, Desirea. I sure as hell didn't tell her."

She reached over to pat his leg as her mind settled on her solution. Seemed she needed to pay a visit to the blackmailer and have a little girl talk. "Don't worry, Ellis. I will handle Amelia Faring."

"No, Desirea," he said, alarmed. "You should stay far away from her to avoid further gossip and speculation. Lord knows what havoc she could bring."

"Nonsense, Ellis. I'm not scared of her. And besides, there's no possible way she can know the things she claims to know. Did she come straight out and tell you she knew I was an actress?"

"Yes. She mentioned your career on stage and your life as an actress, used those very words."

"Then perhaps she assumed from my flawless singing performance that I may have those origins?"

"She also mentioned how you don't belong here."

"She still could mean my being an actress or being with you."

"I had thought of that as well, Desirea, but you weren't there. It wasn't what she said so much as how she said it, like she knew all your secrets. She knows you aren't from this time."

"You're being ridiculous, Ellis. She couldn't possibly know such things."

"And I'm telling you she does."

"Fine. Then she does. So what."

"So what? The chit singlehandedly put an end to our nuptials and you say 'so what'?"

"No, Ellis. You are trying to put an end to our nuptials, but I won't allow it."

"You won't allow it? What the hell is going on in this world? Have I fallen off the planet and into the world of mad women? She won't allow it. You won't allow it. Oh thank God, you're home. I'm going to pass on walking you to the door. That is if *you'll* allow it."

Desirea harrumphed at his smartass comments. "You know, I don't think you do sarcasm well," she quipped as she got out of the vehicle.

"Good," he said, like a child of eight. He reached out and closed the door, signaling the driver to jump back into his perch. "You have a glib enough tongue for the both of us."

"We're still getting married, Ellis, because fate has decreed it and so have I," she shouted as his carriage moved into motion. She turned and marched angrily up the steps. The interfering Amelia Faring had much to learn if she thought she could mess with Desirea's life. "Anything unattempted remains impossible," she said aloud, inspirational words of wisdom to strengthen her resolve in giving Amelia the one-two punch. *How dare Ellis give up on us again? This isn't happening.*

***

The next morning Desirea stood with Mura at Lady Margery Cummings front door, waiting for admittance. She took a deep breath, striving for calm. She wanted to be pleasant but unbending when she told Amelia to butt the hell out of her life.

After a solid eight minutes, they were finally permitted to enter. Desirea was sure her extended wait on the porch was intentional. She walked into a modest sitting room with salmon colored walls and cream sofas. The scent of candle wax filled the room for there were at least twenty candles lit and it was early morning. Desirea found so many glowing candles weird at this time of day. Nevertheless, with Mura left sitting on a bench in the hall, she made her way to the sofa to wait for Amelia. She really hoped the girl didn't bring her aunt with her. *Best to handle this situation with a one-on-one.*

She looked up when she noticed someone near the door. Amelia looked lovely, decked out in a pretty morning gown of cranberry with white satin accents, her brunette hair done up with fashionable jeweled clips. She looked like a million bucks, and not at all like one should look like at ten in the morning. Desirea stood for battle in her cornflower blue morning dress. "Good morning, Amelia. It seems we have some things to discuss." *Like how long it will take your nose to heal after I break it.*

"I'm not coming in there with you," exclaimed Amelia, remaining at the door's threshold.

"What do you mean you're not coming in here?" Desirea took a deep breath for calmness. "I don't wish to yell across the room." She began to walk toward Amelia, but the chick immediately took two steps back.

"What are you doing? I'm not going to hurt you." *This girl is crazy. Why the hell is she behaving like she is scared to death of me?*

"I don't trust you," said Amelia, stubbornly remaining in the hall.

"Well, I don't trust you either, so we are even. Now please sit and we can discuss what it is about me that actually bothers you."

The girl moved a couple of tentative steps into the room. "I find everything about you bothersome."

Well, that wasn't very nice. Desirea truly couldn't remember being mean to the lady, at least not overly. So what was her problem? This seemed to be about more than Ellis. "I don't see why. We hardly know each other."

"Thank God for that," Amelia responded.

Desirea frowned and shook her head at her. "You're odd."

"So are you." Amelia crossed her arms over her chest.

Desirea noted that she was a pretty girl with a sprinkle of freckles across her nose and thought that it was too bad they couldn't be friends. She could use a confidant living close by the country estate. But Amelia seemed to have taken an instant dislike of her. Desirea was used to this feeling for women tended not to like her, but still, she didn't like it and this woman seemed to loathe her utterly.

"All right, so you hate me. I get it. I took Ellis from you…"

"I don't want Ellis."

Desirea's eyes widened as she looked at her. "You don't?"

"No," she said. Feeling more confident, Amelia moved further into the room. She perched her bottom on the sofa arm furthest from Desirea. "And I don't want you to have him."

Now that tears it! I really am going to beat this chick's ass.

To her surprise, Amelia leaped up from the sofa and ran to the door. "I'll call my aunt!"

"You'll what? Why? Oh my God, come back here. How many times do you want me to tell you that I'm not going to hurt you?"

Amelia stopped and turned. "You're not going to harm me?"

No, you little chicken shit. "Of course not. What made you think I would?"

"You did. And I don't like to be called names."

"Huh?" Desirea was suddenly confused. This wasn't going at all the way she imagined. She imagined coming in here, telling Amelia how much she loved Ellis, and how she couldn't live her life without him. For some reason, she had thought she could convince Amelia how right she was for Ellis. But this was going all wrong. The lady just admitted that she wasn't interested in marrying Ellis. She just didn't want Desirea to have him.

The girl was literally scared of her. Why? "I don't remember calling you any names," she said, baffled as to why this was even an issue.

"You did. And I heard you. I don't like it. You are a violent woman."

"I have barely moved off the couch. Perhaps you should fetch your aunt. I believe you are in need of medical attention. You seem to have fallen off the deep end." *Perhaps she suffers from some kind of mental illness, or perhaps some physical illness is affecting this lady's brain.*

"I'm not mentally ill, so stop thinking it."

"Holy shit!" Desirea stared at her. "That's it, isn't it? You're a telepath or something? You can see my thoughts?"

"What did you call it?" Amelia looked stunned and pale. Desirea thought the woman might fall to the floor in a moment and so she jumped up and helped her to the couch. "Are you okay… I mean, all right? I'll bet reading minds takes a lot out of you."

"What is the matter with you?" asked Amelia, her brow scrunched in confusion. "You're talking different."

"I'm talking normal, but since I'm from America, you don't recognize some of it."

"What did you call it? My curse has a name? Please, you must tell me."

Everything clicked into place when Desirea looked into Amelia's frightened brown eyes. "It's called mental telepathy, and I believe it's considered a gift, not a curse. It means you can feel or see images of my thoughts."

"Yes, but I do get words sometimes, on occasion even entire sentences." Amelia had numerous questions lurking behind her eyes. Desirea could almost see the wheels spinning in her head. "I always feel a strange warming sensation behind my eyes when it happens. Do you know why?"

"Uh, no, I don't," said Desirea. "Truthfully, I don't know much about mental telepathy other than the fact that some people say they have it. I've unfortunately told you all I know on the subject, which isn't much."

"And how do you know these things? I've tried researching cryptesthesia, but there's not much to explain why I have this or how to make it go away."

Desirea had never even heard of crypt-whatever. "I know these things because a wise woman once told me so." She couldn't tell Amelia that she gained her limited knowledge from the HBO series *True Blood.*

Amelia rang the bell on the side table and then ordered tea from a maid who ducked into the room. *It seems we are about to become friends now.* "You're lying about the wise woman, but that's all right. I understand the need for secrets, and I really wished I didn't know other peoples' deepest and darkest. But your mind is more confusing than most. Your thoughts flash to things I've never seen, but I also see now that you love Ellis. I've come to realize you aren't as dangerous as your mind portrays you, and you *can* seem very dangerous sometimes, by the way. You can marry Ellis. I won't stand in your way."

When the tea was served, the ladies fell silent for a moment.

"I'm sorry if my thoughts scared you," Desirea said the moment they were alone again. Some of her thoughts regarding this woman had been somewhat vicious, she had to admit. "I guess I'm a bit possessive when it comes to the people I love."

Amelia laughed and Desirea felt infinitely better. "Only promise you'll try to refrain from further thoughts of breaking my nose."

"I promise. You wanted to marry Ellis because of my thoughts?"

"Yes," said Amelia. "You always were angry whenever I was around, but I know now that you love him and you were merely jealous."

Desirea could have disagreed, but she knew Amelia had the right of it, plus she could discern the truth from her thoughts. "Yes, I admit I was. You're very pretty."

"Yes, and I am odd."

Desirea stood. "I'm sorry. I have to use the water closet. I'm afraid tea goes right through me. If you could point the way." She hated using the word water closet, but bathroom meant she was going to bathe, and when she said restroom, people tended to think she was going off to take a nap.

Amelia smiled and gave her directions. "You know, Miss Leighton, you're odd too."

"Don't I know it," said Desirea. "We are both… What is the word?" Desirea stood near the door and turned back to hear the answer.

"Eccentric," replied Amelia.

"Yep, that's the word. Everyone has their oddities." Desirea spun around and fled out the door.

CHAPTER TWENTY-TWO

Ellis had a miserably restless night. He had envisioned a life of love and companionship that would never come to be. He tossed, turned, punched his pillow, and cried out at fate for allowing this. He tried not to think evil thoughts about Amelia, but it was impossible. The lady was ruining his life. Who the bloody hell does she think she is, blackmailing me? It would serve her right if he went straight to her father. But he couldn't, and he wouldn't. There was just something about Amelia that wasn't right and never had been. Although she laughed and conversed as if she were like other women, he knew all was not well with her.

Why did all her suitors run out the door after meeting her? Ellis knew firsthand that Amelia was a kind-hearted person, merely misunderstood somehow. Nevertheless, at the moment, he despised her.

Upon morning, he realized that none of this made sense. Amelia was always friendly with him and had never been vindictive. He and Amelia had always been fond of each other, but he knew she didn't love him any more than he loved her. The more he thought about her actions, the more he realized there had to be something else in play. He needed answers and he needed to put a stop to this.

One thing he did decide during the sleepless hours was that, no matter what Amelia said or who she told about Desirea, he was marrying the woman he loved and society be damned. He wasn't going to deny himself or Desirea the happiness they deserved. He dressed with one mission in mind: end Amelia's meddling in his life and bring Desirea home to him where she belonged.

The closer he traveled toward Amelia's aunt's house, the angrier he became. The clarity he felt in the vehicle, enraged him. Amelia thought to keep him from his life's most fervent dream. *Why?*

Even worse, she thought to gossip about Desirea and destroy her chances of fitting into society. Regardless of the pain Amelia's blackmail would cause him, he was furious she'd say or do anything that would hurt Desirea. Lady Amelia Faring would give up this blackmail scheme or she'd find herself explaining her motives to her father. Either way, he no longer cared what happened to Amelia. Ellis was taking back his life.

Ellis jumped out of his vehicle and marched up the steps to Margery Cumming's homestead. Lifting his angry fists, he began to pound. If Amelia thought she could throw a tantrum, wait until she witnessed his anger in action.

***

Amelia sighed as she took a sip of tea. She was relieved she didn't have to save Ellis by marrying him, but she was even happier to hear she was not the only person in the world who could read others' thoughts. Miss Desirea Leighton, whether she realized it or not, had lifted some of the suffocating weight her curse caused her with this enlightening news. Desirea said telepathy was a gift. Perhaps it was time for Amelia to begin treating it as such. She decided that she in fact liked Desirea. They seemed to understand each other, and Miss Leighton didn't judge her for what Amelia had always felt was a deficiency.

She now wished she wouldn't have spoken to Ellis so strongly and held blackmail over his head. What had she been thinking? She hoped the duke would forgive her yet again. First she had to apologize for her temper tantrum, and now this. Although, she was only trying to be a good friend and protect him, he was probably very angry with her.

At the sudden and persistent pounding on the front door, Amelia hurried into the foyer. The door practically shook from the solid banging. Her aunt's butler threw open the door.

The Duke of Lancaster stood red faced with fists clenched and anger flashing from his eyes. Amelia took a deep breath to calm her nerves. "Ellis, please come in." She led him into the sitting room. She knew this conversation wasn't going to be easy.

***

The door opened and Ellis ignored the confused butler to glare at Amelia who stood a few feet further away. She didn't seem surprised by his appearance, but in fact looked somewhat resigned and maybe even embarrassed as her cheeks reddened and she invited him into the sitting room.

He didn't give her time to speak or ask something stupid like if he wanted tea.

"Listen here, young lady. I like you and I've never judged you, but you have gone too far this time. You've crossed the line of friendship and have made yourself my enemy. Before I take action against your threat of blackmail, I want answers and I plan to receive them."

"Yes, I know, Ellis, and I'm…"

"I'm not finished!" She fell silent when he yelled. "I love Desirea Leighton with every part of me. Love *her*, Amelia, not you. Do you even understand what love is? You couldn't possibly, for if you did, you'd never do what you are doing. You are behaving like a selfish woman of low origins on a path of vengeance. And I want to know why. I've been a friend to you. I do not understand your hatred, and I'm here to tell you our friendship is over. You have crossed over the line and I will see you punished. I will…"

"Do no such thing," Desirea said from the doorway, smiling from ear to ear. The look on her face indicated that she had obviously heard Ellis declaring his undying love for her. She looked good enough to eat, but he remained in position near the unlit fireplace that was covered with lit candles.

"Thank God you finally returned," said Amelia. "He

wouldn't even allow me to speak."

Ellis looked at the love of his life's face, and then back to Amelia's secretive grin. Clearly he had missed a great deal this morning. "He's like that sometimes," said Desirea. She walked into the room and over to Ellis to give him a kiss on the cheek. "Good morning, my love. I had a chat with Amelia."

"So it appears."

Desirea smiled at Amelia. "She and I have become friends. Oh, and she no longer wishes to blackmail you or marry you."

"Is that so?"

"Yes, it is, Ellis," Amelia responded. "I'm so terribly sorry for threatening you in such a way. I don't know what came over me. I thought Desirea was cruel, and well, she's not."

"And why would you think her cruel?"

"Oh, that's easy," replied Desirea.

"No, Desirea. I don't think he should know," Amelia shrieked, her face panicked.

"Oh, I'm sorry, Amelia. I will not tell him."

"But I know you want to," said Amelia with a grin.

"True," said Desirea, and then she laughed. "Pointless for me to deny it."

"Yes, it is." Amelia returned her smile and Ellis could tell his future wife was thrilled about something. He didn't know how she did it, but somehow Desirea found a way to make Amelia feel more comfortable in her own skin. Her newfound confidence was written on Lady Faring's pretty face.

"I think you're ability is amazing," said Desirea.

Ellis was completely confused. *What ability?* "The two of you seem to be talking in circles I don't understand. I'd appreciate an explanation. Amelia, we've known each other for years. I have never spoken a negative word about you and I'm not about to start. If you are in some kind of trouble…"

Desirea left Ellis's side and went to sit next to Amelia on the couch. "I know you are scared that Ellis will pass judgment on you, Amelia, but I can assure you he won't. He probably won't even find your gift shocking." He watched Desirea squeeze

Amelia's hand in hers as a gesture of encouragement.

"You don't really believe that?" Amelia asked aghast.

"Trust me. He has a very open mind."

Amelia closed her eyes and Desirea watched her face. "He's still seems angry," she said when she opened her eyes.

Ellis couldn't help staring at them as if they were both deranged. They were certainly acting the part.

"He's angry because he doesn't understand what's going on," Desirea told her.

At this point in his frustration, Ellis stomped over to a chair to throw himself in it. "I'm not angry," he said. "But I'm definitely confused."

"If I tell you something, Ellis, will you promise not to tell anyone?" Amelia asked as if her life depended on his response.

"Will my silence cause anyone harm?" he asked.

"No," Amelia and Desirea both said at once.

"Then I'm listening," he said.

But suddenly Amelia was no longer looking at him. She was too busy staring at Desirea.

"What?" Desirea asked, seemingly as confused as he was by the odd look on Amelia's face.

"I know your secret," Amelia said, the whites of her eyes widening.

"Ellis told you, didn't he?" Desirea asked.

"Yes. He thought it. I knew you were eccentric..." She smiled. "But this is unbelievable. How did it happen? I mean, how did you get here? The twenty-first century? It's hard to fathom."

"All right," said Ellis. "How did she do that? Amelia, can you pluck thoughts from my head?"

***

"Yours and just about everyone else's," Amelia responded with a tired wave of her hand.

"What do you mean, just about?" asked Desirea, her

curiosity piqued. “Have you met people you couldn’t read?”

“Only one,” Amelia told them. “A boy who worked in our stables. He’s moved on since, and I’ve yet to meet another person whose thoughts I couldn’t hear.”

“Your suitors?” Ellis asked, clearly putting together the many pieces that made up Amelia’s gossiped about behavior.

“Their thoughts are beyond repeating, Your Grace. I couldn’t find even one of them to my liking. I’m starting to think I never will.” A tear slid down her cheek and it cut at Desirea’s heart. It had to be difficult hearing the lewd thoughts of men when you were seeking some kind of affection first. Even though Amelia was expectedly virginal, she was extremely pretty and Desirea was sure the men Amelia met had enough sexual images of her to put the woman off men forever.

“Don’t say such things.” Desirea took Amelia’s hand. “I’ve been told you hide out at your dad’s country estate a lot. You know there are loads of men in the world, more in the city than in the country, obviously. So now that you’re in the city, your odds of finding men with better intentions increase.”

“There have been over a hundred men introduced to me through my father,” replied Amelia. “I could hear every single one of them. You should have heard some of them. Ugh! Disgraceful! The greed and selfish motives are enough to make a girl decide against marriage forever.”

“Well, Ellis and I don’t plan to let you drop out of sight. You can’t hide away forever, Amelia. And we won’t let you.”

“We?” said Ellis, who had for the most part remained quiet, likely shocked again, Desirea realized. First time travel and now mind reading. Desirea was sure the poor man was having difficulty wrapping his head around all of it.

“Yes, we.”

“I second Ellis’s thoughts. I don’t see how either of you can help me.”

Desirea scrunched her brow at Ellis, telling him silently to "knock it off with the negative thoughts."

Amelia suddenly laughed. "I was picturing you pulling his hair," she said. "You're most amusing, Desirea. I'm glad we're to be friends."

"Huh," replied Desirea. "I've gotta feeling this being friend's with you thing isn't going to be easy. Is there a way you can try to *not* see my thoughts? Like, shut it off some how?"

Amelia laughed again, harder this time. "Don't I wish!"

Desirea shrugged. "I'll have to try and adjust my thoughts accordingly when you're near."

"But please keep in the amusing parts," Amelia responded. She looked at Ellis. "Do you plan to stay silent?"

"I'm afraid to speak, or even to think for that matter."

Amelia laughed.

"I'm awed by your power, Amelia," said Desirea. "It must be pretty amazing knowing what people are going to say before they say it. I mean, at times. I understand how all the time could become bothersome." They both smiled, thinking of their earlier conversation.

"You mean how I 'wrap my head' around all this?" Amelia plucked the thought from her head. "You know people think I'm mad for locking my sisters in a closet, but they have no knowledge of the mischief I see coming, nor do they realize the girls could be hurt from their plans for exploration. People explain away my tantrums as a brain malfunction. They believe there isn't a man in existence who would marry a demented lady like me, regardless if they think I'm beautiful and a talented pianist. I'm odd is all they know, and no they don't say any of this aloud. Well, some probably do when I'm not present, but their thoughts are always far worse than their words. Often times their thoughts put me in a temper, and unfortunately I react when I should withdraw to my room. Of course, no one even knows what I'm reacting to."

"And why did you get mad at Ellis when we were at your home?"

"Because his thoughts were all focused on you. He couldn't wait to leave. He couldn't wait to kiss you. And do…" Amelia's cheeks turned bright red as she said, "And do other things."

Desirea laughed when she saw a blush fill Ellis's face.

"I was angry that you both found something I will never have. Love. A man would have to be a saint, at least of mind, for me to even like him let alone trust him. There are no such men like that. Ellis, at least, didn't ever think harshly of me. Well, until yesterday, that is."

Desirea smiled at Ellis's kindness to Amelia. "I didn't know you played the piano. Perhaps you could play for me. I love music," said Desirea.

"I've noticed that about you. Just as I've noticed how you change the topic the moment I begin to become upset again. Thank you."

Desirea pulled her into a sideways hug with her arm around her. "Hey, that's what friends are for."

"I'm sorry," said Ellis, coming back from his silent contemplation.

"I know," replied Amelia. "I'm sorry too. I never meant to upset you. I was only doing what I thought was right at the time."

"No, not that. I'm no longer angry, and I understand your motives. But I am sorry I didn't ask you what plagued you years ago, when we were younger. Maybe I could have helped."

"You two are so very kind, but Ellis, you couldn't help me then and I'm afraid neither of you can help me now. I take that back. Having the two of you as friends helps, since I don't have any. And Desirea's having heard of my affliction…"

"Gift," Desirea interrupted.

"All right, gift then. Anyway, it has given me more to ponder. At least I know I'm not alone."

"No, you aren't, and we are here for you too."

"Desirea is right, Amelia. If you need anything…"

"Or if you just want to share some girl-talk," said Desirea. When Amelia's brow rose, she corrected herself. "You know, talk between only us girls."

"I plan to visit you often, Desirea."

"Good," she responded and got to her feet. "We should go, Ellis."

"Yes." He rose. "Please know, Amelia, your secrets are safe with me."

"I trust you explicitly, Your Grace, and I thank you for our many years of friendship." He bowed, took Desirea's arm, and led her out of the house and toward his vehicle, Mura trailing behind them.

"You wish to return to the Devinn household?" He didn't sound like he liked the idea. Desirea wished she had Amelia's gift and could see his thoughts right now.

"No."

"Good, because to be honest, I was unaware he had two brothers staying under the same roof with you, and to tell you the truth, I don't like it."

"I wouldn't expect you to, but it was necessary."

"Of course, and no one realizes that more than I, but I hate it. It's unfair."

"Then take me home with you."

"Desirea, I want to. I really do, but…"

"I only meant for a few hours, Ellis. Relax. Mura's in the tiger's perch, so it's not as if I don't have a chaperone. I agree we have to do all of this right. I want to be the best duchess I can be, and if that means putting on this dog and pony show, then so be it."

"Dog and pony show?" He laughed. Tapping the roof, he ordered the driver to return to his house. Desirea knew her wonderful man would sneak her into his home if necessary, because even with a chaperone, she was not supposed to approach a bachelor's residence in this era. They reached his house to find another vehicle parked out front loaded with luggage and big black trunks.

"What's going on?" she asked, peering out the window.

Ellis's face broke into a huge smile. "It looks as if your long lost friend has come calling. I won't have to sneak you into the house after all."

"What long lost… Oh my God, your sister Darlene is here?"

"So it appears. It also looks as if they'll be staying awhile. Would you mind meeting her right now?"

"Of course not. I can't wait."

"Because she's your long lost friend?" he asked, obviously assuming she was kidding, but she wasn't.

"No, silly, because she's your sister and we can't get married without her."

He scolded the driver when he went to open the door, then reached to hold her face in his hands. "You'll marry me now."

"Yes, now. Right this very minute if you can make it happen."

His lips came down upon hers and she was lost in a maelstrom of desire, longing, and an infinite amount of love. She moved herself onto his lap as he grabbed her hips and slid his tongue into her mouth. He was so warm and his spicy scent filled her senses. She celebrated the fact that this man was all hers. She had broken away from the bonds of her selfishness and had opened herself up for love and friendship. Ellis had made Desirea the woman she always hoped she would be: giving, caring, and infinitely happy.

"So what do you think, Graham? Is this the maid Mimi claimed my brother fell in love with?"

The nearby voice had Desirea whipping her head up quickly. She felt an instant blush fill her face. *How embarrassing*? She's was sitting on the duke's lap in broad daylight, kissing the pants off him while servants milled around them. Of course they were in the vehicle, but the curtains were wide open.

And on top of that, thanks to Mimi, Ellis's sister believed her a maid. "Uh, hello," said Desirea. Ellis appeared to be having some difficulty coming back from their passions.

"Hello," Darlene said, and she gave Desirea a quick smile before focusing her attention on her brother.

***

Ellis looked out the carriage window at the flushed face of his petite brunette sister, who was standing next to her enormous husband, Graham Hamilton, the Laird of Camster.

"Are we intruding on your vehicle at a bad time, brother of mine?"

"Would you go away if I said yes?" Ellis asked in jest as they backed away and he opened the door. He turned back to assist Desirea out of the carriage. He'd been struck mute by his sister's appearance, but he hadn't moved due to the cock stand from which he was suffering, not something a man wished his sister to witness. With his desire finally in check and Desirea on his arm, he made the appropriate introductions, knowing he had further explaining to do since Mimi had decided to fill his relatives in on Desirea's employment in his household. Of course, he knew Mimi would have never shared this information with anyone other than his sister. He was grateful for loyal servants.

Once they were seated in the comfort of his parlor with beverages in hand, Ellis asked after his two nieces. Darlene told him they were sleeping upstairs and would be brought down later for a visit. It seemed his sister had other things she wished to discuss. She looked at Desirea and then back to him again. His brother-in-law was oddly quiet, considering Graham tended to love to give his opinion about everything.

"Does she not have work to do?" his sister asked, and he realized he had to fix this maid mix up now.

"She doesn't work for me, Darlene. I know what Mimi told

you, but Desirea's not a maid at all. She's to be my wife."

"Desirea, is it? And your future wife?" She turned to Desirea. "So you did capture my brother's heart?" Darlene exclaimed excitedly, and she walked across the room to pull Desirea into a hug. "Thank you."

"You weren't this happy about my first marriage," Ellis pointed out. He'd been ready for some kind of objection and was surprised when it did not come. Darlene certainly had plenty to say his first time around.

"You weren't in love the first time."

"Admittedly, I do love Desirea more than I ever imagined possible, but how did you know that?" If his sister said she could read his mind, he really didn't know what he would do.

"Because you never called your first wife by her Christian name, as a matter of fact. Sadly, I don't even remember her name. That's how seldom you used it. Besides, Mimi said love is written all over your face, and I happen to agree with her."

"You're awfully silent, Graham," Ellis commented. "Have you not something to add?"

"I'm happy you've found someone tae share your life with. Congratulations." Graham went over and kissed Desirea on the cheek. "Welcome tae the family. My wife's thrilled tae find herself someone tae conspire with against us males," he teased, and he patted Darlene on her butt, at which the woman merely smiled and smacked away his hand. The Laird of Camster then sauntered back to his place near the mantle where he rested one of his arms.

"That's it?" Ellis was amazed by Graham's lack of commentary.

"Come, let us escape these men," Darlene said to Desirea.

Ellis thought his sister looked wonderful. He missed her and was really glad she and Graham were there.

"Would you like to see the new baby?" Darlene asked as the ladies went to leave.

"I'd love to." Desirea blew Ellis a kiss before she went off with Darlene to visit his nieces. "However did you get your baby weight off so quickly?" Ellis heard Desirea question his sister. "Or is that question too personal?"

Ellis then heard the sound of his sister's laughter. "Oh this is splendid. You're as outspoken as I am. I imagine we're going to be the best of sisters." Then he could no longer hear them.

"How's Darlene health? The baby's delivery went well? No scares?"

"Nae, 'twas a verra long labor, but blessedly without incident. That lass is the strongest, bravest woman I ken."

Ellis could think of another strong and courageous woman.

"A maid? Dare I ask how that came 'bout, brother?"

Ellis laughed and went on to share his story with his brother-in-law. Of course, he omitted the parts about meeting Desirea in an alley, since it would lead to far too much explaining, and there was no way he was going to deal with the time travel issue. Perhaps years down the road, and at that he'd leave the telling up to his wife. Ah, his wife. He couldn't wait to marry Desirea.

"Should I have the horses brought around?" Graham asked.

"For what reason? Do you wish to ride?"

"Nae, I thought you might like tae make a visit with the Archbishop o' Canterbury tae procure you a special wedding license."

Ellis smiled and stood from his seat. "It's like you read my mind."

"Ye gads, that's enough to give me the shivers." They laughed.

CHAPTER TWENTY-THREE

Two weeks later, Desirea Leighton married her duke in a spectacular ceremony with all the pomp and entertainments fitting for the lucky couple. The papers covered every aspect of the grand event, down to the champagne flutes and the fact that the bride insisted raspberries rest in the bottom. Desirea's dress was talked about by one and all. The original creation was spoken of with envy. Of course, there were plenty of ladies in attendance who also envied her capture of the Duke of Lancaster, but that couldn't be helped. *Too bad, so sad for them.*

The wedding night had been out of this world. The sex mind-blowing, and the cuddling after sweet and forever planted in her memory. Desirea had told Ellis about fate and how they were meant to be. Her wonderful husband had responded with, "Yes, I already know this."

Even her new home was perfect, the servants, including Mimi, welcomed her with warmth. One evening, Mimi had hovered in her bedroom doorway as Mura readied Desirea for bed.

"What is it, Mimi?"

"I wanted to say, Your Grace, that I'm happy you've found your proper place in this household. I will enjoy many years working for you." Her words brought tears to Desirea's eyes. Mimi was obviously a sweet lady as long as you weren't working under her.

A week after the wedding, Desirea attended the opening night of the play she had, after a fashion, created. She deemed it spectacular, and seeing it with Ellis filled her with infinite joy.

One month later, Desirea stood in the foyer next to Darlene as she welcomed the crème of society into her home for her first official gathering. She had gone over every minute detail with the staff dozens of times and was confident, poised, and dressed to perfection in a burgundy ensemble with burgundy ribbon woven through her blond hair and diamonds dripping from her ears. She wished to display one of her many wedding gifts from her wonderful and very generous husband while showing Ellis how much she loved him and his gifts. When he presented them she had deemed the earrings "kickass."

Ellis was in the corner talking to London's husband. The two had grown close due to her and London's friendship. Lady Amelia Faring entered the house, and Desirea hurried over to greet her. It had taken days to convince her new friend to attend for Amelia found it overwhelming when so many thoughts were echoing around in her brain, and though Desirea imagined it would be tough, how was her friend going to find a husband if she stayed sheltered in her father's country estate? She felt it necessary to help Amelia however she could. The girl needed her. She planned to recruit London's assistance as well.

"Thank you for coming. I know it wasn't easy," said Desirea as she hugged her.

"Yes, well, I read your mind and I thought it would be best to come on my own accord to forego you dragging me here by my hair," Amelia quipped.

Desirea laughed, knowing Amelia's ability was only good to about twenty-five yards. They had tested distances the previous week. "Come in. I'm sure you know some of the people."

"Your friend London is here?"

"Yes, she's…" Desirea turned but couldn't see her friend.

"She's behind that wall talking to her husband," said Amelia.

"Amazing." Desirea took her arm and linked it through hers. "I want to introduce you."

"Have you told her about me?"

"Of course not, silly. I wouldn't do that. But I had hoped you'd tell her. After all, she and I come from the same place." Desirea knew she wouldn't have been able to hide London's origins from Amelia, since London's thoughts would give her away anyway, and so she had told her how they arrived in this time together. "It's possible she knows more about mental telepathy than I do, but then it's possible she knows even less. I didn't ask her because she'd only ask me why I was wondering such a thing and I prefer not to lie to my friends when it can be avoided. Not that we need to have this conversation today. For now, I only want you to relax and enjoy yourself, to socialize and be seen."

Amelia laughed.

An hour later, Desirea found herself seated on a sofa enjoying some iced tea, Amelia sitting next to her. Amelia was amusing her by going about the room and telling her different people's thoughts.

"What's he thinking?"

"About his dog."

"And him?"

"His debt."

"Him?" She put her elbow into Amelia's side and nodded her head to indicate a man across the room without actually pointing.

"Oh my." Amelia's cheeks turned bright red.

"What is he thinking?"

"He's thinking of Lord Tarnackle and the image, I..." Desirea watched as Amelia visibly shuddered.

"Oh my, do you mean he's imagining the two of them crossing swords?"

It took Amelia a moment to get the reference, and then she laughed uproariously. "You're funny, Desirea. A real wit. I never had this much fun with my affliction."

"I told you it's a gift, and I think it would help you to consider it as such. I can think of countless times I would have loved to have had your ability. Oh look, two of the Devinn brothers have arrived."

The butler announced the latecomers and the gentlemen headed toward them.

"What are they thinking?"

"Well, the one on the left thinks it's a shame you married the duke and…" She didn't get to finish because they now stood before them. She and Amelia stood to greet them.

Morgan and Isaac Devinn were both extremely handsome men, and it was clear by the way Amelia's pupils dilated upon meeting them that her friend agreed with her. Both had sandy colored hair and green eyes, and both were dressed to the nines, considering this was but a afternoon gathering and not an officially formal affair. Desirea was happy they had come, since she'd grown close to them when she stayed at the Earl of Nankin's home.

Morgan gave her a flirtatious smile and asked, "So how's married life, Desi?"

"As boring as it appears, would be my guess," replied Isaac.

Desirea laughed. "It's not boring; it's wonderful. The two of you should follow suit."

Now they both laughed. *Ow!* Desirea looked to see why Amelia was elbowing her in the ribs. "What's your deal?" she asked quietly. The Devinn men had turned to speak to Lord Mayville, who had grabbed Morgan's shoulder as he passed by to gain his attention.

Amelia took Desirea's arm and moved her a few more paces away from the men. "I can't hear him," said Amelia. She looked panic-stricken and she shook Desirea's arm.

"Can't hear who?"

"Lord Isaac," she whispered. Her face scrunched and she stared harder at the back of Isaac's head. "Nothing."

"Huh. Well, that's fabulous, isn't it?"

"Is it? It feels odd and I don't know if I really like it. I mean, what if I can't hear him because he's a dimwit or he's without feeling so he has no thoughts. I tend to rather like knowing what people are thinking when I first meet them so I know to act accordingly, but with him I don't know and that scares me."

"Well, welcome to my reality. It shouldn't scare you though. Jeez, that's how the majority of folks do it."

Amelia gave her a nervous laugh. "Oh no."

"What?" asked Desirea.

"He's looking at me."

Desirea looked up to find Isaac Devinn giving Amelia that I'm-undressing-you-with-my-eyes look. "He's giving you the look, so go over and talk to him."

"You are far madder than I. And if anyone tries to tell you otherwise, I wish for you to correct them. Go over there? Approach a man I don't even know? You're as mad as a March hare. There's no other explanation for your boldness."

"I just introduced you." Desirea laughed hysterically, which caused Isaac to tilt his head questioningly at them, and then she laughed again. He approached, which Desirea knew he would since he assumed they were talking about him, which of course they were. They had been about to retake their seats on the sofa when Ellis approached them as well, arriving with Isaac. "Here, Isaac. Take my place." Desirea nodded her head toward the sofa and smiled triumphantly at her nervous friend when Isaac sat down next to Amelia.

"She can't hear his thoughts." She leaned over to whisper in her husband's ear. "I think we may have found her a beau."

"Wow," Ellis whispered in her ear, and she laughed at his use of one of her favorite words. "Her beau, huh? You're starting to sound more like us every day."

She watched as Ellis then picked up a champagne flute and the metal decorative snuffer to put out candles. He clanged the snuffer on the side of his glass to gain their guests' attention. Desirea wanted to know why he wanted everyone's attention.

"It has been three hours since I have had my wife to myself," he announced.

"What are you doing?" She turned toward him to speak so no one could hear her. He was causing a scene at her first party and she decided she was going to kill him. "Ellis," she warned, and she felt her cheeks turning red as her temper began to rise.

"You see, ladies and gentlemen, I'm afraid I'm admittedly smitten with my wife and I find three hours too long to bear…"

"Ellis," she grabbed his arm, embarrassed now.

"See," he said. "She's anxious to be alone with me too."

"You're causing a spectacle." She heard everyone laughing and saw men nodding in some kind of male understanding, but still, this was embarrassing.

"Yes, I know." He winked, and then to her horror, he scooped her up in his arms and began to march out of the room.

It was then that Desirea realized why he was causing such a scene, and she laughed, her heart exploding with infinite happiness and love. "You are the best, Ellis."

"Yes, well, I thought my arms would be preferable to tossing you over my shoulder. I love you, Desirea. I don't care what others think. You are my beauty, my love, my goddess, my time traveler, my perfect duchess, my wife," he said as he made the way down the hall to their bedroom.

"Don't tell me you've run out of titles for me." She gave him a fake pout and he laughed.

"On the contrary. I've merely begun." He tossed her on the bed and his body came down on top of hers. "My temptress, my fate, my life..." With each compliment, he layered kisses across her chest. She reached for his face and crushed her lips with his.

To find out more about the author, please visit her web page at *www.lahilden.com* and you can also follow LA Hilden on FB, Twitter, Google+ and Tumblr.

Also By Lori Hilden:

A Necessary Heir
(book #1 in Alter Ego Series)

London's Quest
(book #1 in Destiny Series)

Born Reckless
(book #2 in the Alter Ego Series)

Excerpt from 'Born Reckless' by L. A. Hilden (a Regency Historical)

CHAPTER ONE

London, England 1816

Clarissa hadn't been able to get out of the house fast enough, but now her heart beat a swift cadence as she hurried down the stone steps. The cool night air was a welcome relief, instantly stilling the atmosphere swirling around her. From the moment she entered the overcrowded ballroom, she felt all eyes upon her. People couldn't help but take notice of her for her garish apparel. One thing was certain: she couldn't tolerate anymore of the you-poor-girl looks everyone was throwing her way. Escape was not just her desire but completely necessary.

Clarissa Mayfield had claimed she had yet another headache to pardon herself from Lord and Lady Greenleigh's once-a-year soiree. Thankfully, like the soirees of past years, Prinny and his entourage were present, and the Prince Regent's attendance helped to divert some of the undue attention her atrocious attire garnered lately — but not nearly enough of that attention. This was her first official London season, and it was unbearable.

But the officious judgment of London society wasn't what disturbed her most this night. Over the last month, her rising concern for her father had nearly choked her. She was truly starting to believe someone was out to harm the Earl of Loring.

A chill stole up her spine as the eerie sensation of someone watching her made her shiver, the same peculiar awareness she had felt often in the last week. She studied her surroundings with utmost concentration, but aside from the footman tucked away in the manor's alcove above, she appeared to be alone. Finding no one there when she glanced around to reassure herself didn't make the feeling of being watched diminish, however. The hair on the back of her neck still stood on end.

She willed the strange feelings away, deciding instead on a quick escape. Her exit could not have been more flawless, and in spite of her disquiet, she congratulated herself. She now stood on the paving stones in front of the elegant mansion belonging to the Earl of Greenleigh. No one had been so impolite as to leave this early but her, but then no one else was being ridiculed endlessly about their attire or worried sick over their father, she assured herself. Then the sensation someone was watching her grew again, causing her to tremble.

"Humph!" she said, deciding her unsettled feeling was due to the duress she was under, that she must be imagining being watched now after the scrutiny of those inside.

While waiting impatiently for her carriage to be brought around, she busily tapped the ground in agitation with the bright purple slipper on her right foot. She should never have agreed to come, but her mother had burst into a flood of tears at the thought of coming alone. She felt obligated to at least see her mother through the doors and deliver her to her ever growing number of friends, but in truth, the argument that quickly escalated between her parents over her not attending was too much to bear.

She choked back a sob just looking at her flamboyant attire. Her wardrobe dilemma was getting out of hand. Someone had to put a stop to her mother's meddling in her apparel or she'd never find herself a proper husband, and it was imperative she do so. She could no longer tolerate her father's tirades, which included throwing priceless treasures around the house. How she longed to flee such insanity.

She decided she would just have to marry, and quickly, before her mother could do further damage to her social standing. Lately, the scandal sheets were overflowing with snippets about her clothing and questions about how "poor Lady C can handle being so mismanaged by her mother." Moreover, the threat from her father to procure her a spouse was enough to set her into action.

Where is that confounded vehicle? She looked down the drive in both directions, dancing from one foot to the other in her impatience to remove herself from the possibility of being seen. If one more would-be suitor approached her with that lopsided, apologetic smile, she was going to scream, in turn initiating a scandal that would outrage both of her parents far more than her early escape from this gala.

Finally, a sleek black vehicle came barreling around the corner. She jumped back at its approach for fear of being trampled, but the matched pair of high-strung bays came to a quick halt in front of her, the horses snorting when they stopped. One of them pawed the ground restlessly. She glared up at the driver in irritation, and he nodded at her with a gap-toothed grin. "Here I am, my lady."

"And just who are you? Where's my father's driver and equipage?" Her hands instinctively went to her hips even as she realized she looked ridiculous dressed this way, like an eggplant full of indignation.

"Nat's in bed. He says it's his innards are hurtin' him, but he'll be right as rain in no time," the man informed her matter-of-factly.

"And my horse? Those two beasts don't look at all manageable."

"Nothin' Harvey … " He doffed his brown cap at her, and then said, "Nothin' Harvey can't handle. Your horse threw a shoe. He's at the smithy down the road."

Were these inconveniences connected with the threat to her father? Or perhaps I am being utterly ridiculous and my imagination has now taken over rational thought. "I see," she said, waiting for the man to jump down, pull out the steps, and assist her inside. She wished to return home, check on her father, and get out of this blasted dress with the ridiculous turquoise bows.

"So what's the hold up? Am I takin' you home or not?"

Clarissa shook her head in exasperation. Just then, Lady Whitley exited the mansion surrounded by her entourage and began to descend the steps toward her. The sooner Clarissa removed her sorry appearance from public scrutiny the better.

Pretending not to notice their descent behind her, she opened the door, not bothering with the steps, and hauled herself inside by the handle. Calmly, she closed the door, leaned back against the cushioned squabs, and let out the pent up breath she was holding, thankful to be hidden from the sympathetic gazes of those in so-called polite society.

No sooner had she settled back than the carriage flew into action with a quick jolt, sending her head into the side of the vehicle and causing her to stifle a very unladylike curse as her conveyance careened down a busy thoroughfare. She could hear angry shouts from those they rushed past in a blur. It took all her strength to keep herself centered to avoid bodily harm. The carriage, practically on two wheels as it turned down a less traveled lane, didn't slow, the horses maintaining a gallop no matter the terrain.

She wondered what in the blazes was wrong with her driver. Finally able to focus on the passing scenery, she realized the vehicle was heading out of the city, further away from her home. Heavens above! What is the meaning of this?

She pounded on the roof with her fists. "Stop," she shouted. "You're going the wrong way!" Her pleas were ignored. She looked out at the passing fields. Should I jump?

Fear gripped her, and then panic became desperation. What is happening? She knew the driver was still controlling the horses as the vehicle headed at its brisk pace on the well-traversed road north.

Then it dawned on her: I'm being abducted!

The dreaded thought rang through her head, subduing her common sense that tried to tell her the idea was preposterous. Who would abduct her? She had no enemies, no overzealous suitors to her knowledge. For what reason could she possibly be taken? Were the villains she believed to be after her father extracting some kind of sick revenge by using her? Had they been watching her this last week, studying her habits, looking for the perfect opportunity to nab her? The thought filled her with dread, and she shivered and broke out in a cold sweat.

Regardless what treachery was afoot, she could not sit idle as this vehicle hurried to God knew where. She tried to open the door and realized it wouldn't budge. Shaking with rage now as well as fear, she quickly tried the opposite door. It would not budge either. It was as if they were nailed shut.

It dawned on her that she was going to have to go through the window or remain seated until this carriage reached its destination. Realizing it would be best if she slipped out unnoticed, she sat back to plan her getaway. She decided to wait for a more heavily wooded area so she could hide.

As the vehicle continued at its steady clip, Clarissa looked out the window to plan her fall, hoping it would not be to her death. It was still early evening and so fairly light, and she could see a grassy field up ahead beyond a copse of English Oaks.

Snatching off her detested purple-feathered comb that was affixed to the top of her head like a dratted bird, she convinced herself that headfirst was the way to go, for then she might be able to roll upon her landing, which with luck would soften the blow. Then she removed her gloves and tucked them away in a pocket, her reason giving way to cold terrifying fear.

In the end, she decided she could not willingly hang her body headfirst out the window without losing her courage to save herself. So she remained seated, wiggled herself to the edge of her cushioned seat, and placed her slippered feet out the window. She felt the breeze breathing upon her stocking clad legs as she inched further and further out the opening. Suddenly the vehicle made a quick veer to the left, and because she was now barely balanced, she was thrown out the window, but not all the way. She found herself stuck from going further by the layers and layers of petticoats her mother insisted she wear. To her utter horror, the carriage stopped.

There she was, half of her body dangling out the window and clad in only stockings and drawers for all the world to see, while inside the confines of the carriage, fabric and coarse netting floated around her, bits of it bunched in the window about her thighs. She actually sensed a delirious bubble of laughter lodged in her chest at such a ridiculous sight as she must certainly be. She had never felt so discomfited in her life. Then tears of fear leaked from her eyes as she fought off the madness of a chuckle. Although she had always longed for adventure, this was not what she had in mind.

The only part of her body on the cushion was her head, and her neck was beginning to hurt from the strain of holding herself in such an awkward position.

"What is the meaning of this, Harvey? You damn near ran over a dog in your haste. What are you about today?" A deep male voice filled with obvious humor came from beyond the window her body blocked. A shiver ran through her. Acute embarrassment set her face aflame. This was beyond humiliating. Even her ugly attire was better than nothing. She tried to wiggle herself free, but it was to no avail. Saints be praised. Please let this be a nightmare, a product of the fanciful imagination my father believes I possess.

"I brought her to you just as you wished," the driver said.

"You brought her to me? Whatever do you mean? Whose legs are those?" the unknown man asked. "What have you done?"

Clarissa sucked in a breath as two warm hands slid up the length of her calves.

"You wanted to help the lady, so here she is. I thought you'd be pleased."

"Change the horses, Harvey."

Clarissa squirmed, kicking her legs to free the lecher's grasp. He chuckled at her effort. "Get away from me. How dare you! Don't touch me!" she bellowed loudly, something she strived never to do, but fear was taking over her mind. More tears welled in her eyes.

"Now you have me curious, Lady Clarissa Mayfield," the mystery voice said.

Oh, lord, this isn't a case of mistaken identity. That possibility had been one of her fleeting hopes. She didn't want to know what this pig of a man was curious about. She just wanted to be seated and composed when she gave this scoundrel the scolding he deserved.

"You see," he continued, heedless of her struggles for freedom, "as a man with very pernickety tastes, I wonder if the rest of you is as prettily presented as your bottom half."

Clarissa sucked in a sharp gasp at such an inappropriate comment, but she remained silent and shaking.

Finally, the voice moved around her to the opposite window, and she looked up at the face of the man who had dared to take liberties on her person. Surely the blood rushing to her head was making her body react oddly, for a jolt of attraction surged through her with the power of a lightning bolt. This man doesn't look like a villain, more like a golden haired angel sent down from heaven with the ability to pleasure a woman on sight. She had to be suffering some kind of delirium from her unwieldy position, she decided. Besides, he was upside down. But the descending sun surrounded him with a halo of light as he looked down upon her with an amused smile.

His compelling sage green eyes, with their long lashes, locked on hers and she felt near to swooning. His face was finely chiseled with a strong jaw line, aristocratic cheekbones, and a teasing smile that had a smoldering effect on her already overwrought senses. His lips were full, sensual, promising — capable of kissing a woman senseless. Here was a man who made her stomach summersault, a man so roguishly adorable that she lost her ability to speak. Her mouth went completely dry. She wondered if her petticoats were hiding enough of her legs, but she couldn't move enough to check.

He opened the door with surprising ease, his smile still crooked with amusement at her predicament. "Give me your arms."

She didn't move. She just glared at his too-handsome face and wondered why this man, whom she had clearly never met, was doing this to her. His green eyes twinkled back at her in the most charming manner.

"Unless you're comfortable as you are?" he asked casually, climbing into the vehicle to sit in the seat opposite of her. She felt the vehicle shift with his added weight.

His large frame filled the limited space, and the scent of male virility threatened to take her very breath. He was a strong, powerful man with an athletic build and a face any woman would covet. She quickly surmised that any woman in this man's presence was in danger of losing her heart, or worse, her virtue.

He broke into her thoughts. "I must say the view from this side is equally breathtaking."

The handsome villain was paying her a compliment. Clarissa knew that, if it were possible for further blood to fill her face, she'd be blushing, and she would be giving him some coy response as if she were in some elegant salon — if only she were upright. I really need to gain a hold on myself. This man has kidnapped me.

Hardening her resolve not to give into his captivating smile, which was heart-stopping in its splendor, she wordlessly held out her arms to him. His strong, ungloved, masculine hands wrapped around her forearms as he pulled her free and her legs fell into the vehicle with a thud.

Quick as a rabbit, she darted upright into her seat, smacking down layers of silk and petticoats around her. Her limbs tingled as the flow of blood returned to them. With a look of utter loathing born of her sheer embarrassment and the fact she was here against her will, she glared at the green-eyed man who was now studying her. Pulling back her arm, she sent a hard smack into his clean-shaven cheek. "Don't ever lay a hand on me again, you miscreant. I will see you hanged for such an assault on my person," she fumed. Such a punishment was not truly possible, but it felt good just to say it.

Truly, his handsomeness had rattled her more than the blasted kidnapping. He rubbed at the handprint on his face, although his crooked grin remained. Perhaps the man is unbalanced. "Are you the man responsible for this obscene abduction?"

"It was a bit of a misunderstanding with my driver, but I am afraid I must take full responsibility," he said, nodding his head. "Allow me to introduce myself, Lady Clarissa. I am the Marquis of Camden, Grayson Mathers."

"The Marquis of Camden," she screeched. "You can't kidnap me! You're a peer, for pity sake." She put her fingers to her throbbing temples. "Saints be praised! You can't get away with this!" Her entire future crumbled into dust before her eyes.

"On the contrary, my dear," Lord Camden said jovially, giving his stinging cheek another rub. "I believe I already have."

***

The irate woman went to strike him again, but Grayson captured her hand, and with care not to hurt her, he shoved her into her seat. He shook his head, running his fingers through his hair in frustration. The lovely Lady Clarissa looked ready to flay him alive with her prettily manicured nails. Not that he could blame her.

"I demand an explanation for this insanity," she said hotly, her hands curling into tight fists. "Do you even realize what you've done? How dare you sit so calmly across from me when you have single-handedly just ruined my life. I will be forever ruined in the eyes of society. This is a catastrophe. You've made me an outcast."

"I assure you, Lady Clarissa, this is not a 'catastrophe,' as you so delicately term it." This was, in truth, the stupidest thing Harvey had ever done, and it was entirely Grayson's fault for even mentioning a ridiculous idea like abducting Lady Clarissa in front of his driver in the first place. Harvey always went out of his way to please. But abduction? Grayson never thought Harvey would go to such criminal lengths. Of course, this entire abduction plan had been imagined partly in jest by Grayson's friend Lord Rand Fitzroy. Right now, Grayson couldn't help but be pleased as Punch to see the object of his desire sitting in front of him.

Rand had told Grayson this woman could cure his woes. "A romantic adventure," he had called it. "What lady wouldn't enjoy a little romantic adventure," Rand had said when he concocted his imaginary story of kidnapping Lady Clarissa. Romantic, my arse. Lady Clarissa is plum terrified of me. And why wouldn't she be? This entire situation borders on lunacy.

But Grayson could fix this, or rather, he would fix this. This was certainly not the scenario he had envisioned when he saw Harvey storm into the inn yard with a woman's legs dangling out the carriage window. In fact, he had never seen anything so ludicrous and had no idea what those fine legs portended.

Without a word, he stepped back out of the vehicle, rattled off a list of things to his nearby servants and a hired messenger, and then he climbed back inside the vehicle with a smile, fairly confident he had just fixed the problem.

Lady Clarissa continued to stare at him when he sat back down, still obviously seething. But what could he really have expected? The woman had been kidnapped from a party, a party Harvey had known she'd attend and then flee at the first opportunity because Grayson had made it one of his missions in life to learn more about this woman. And, unfortunately, he had shared what he learned with his overzealous driver.

Lady Clarissa was correct about her immediate concern for her virtue, which is why he had taken such immediate measures to ensure such scandal never touched her.

As he played back possible scenarios in his head, he realized his ploy to save her reputation was sound. More than sound, actually — inspired. He decided to trust in his plan to see him to his goal. Perhaps, when she learned the truth of how much he needed her, she'd see his driver's desperate move as endearing, for Harvey had kidnapped her in an effort to help Grayson heal. Surely the man's heart is in the right place and he deserves leniency. Of course, his driver had absolutely nothing to do with Grayson's decision to keep the lady across from him. And he was going to keep her. Now that she was by his side, he wasn't about to let her go. He considered this a bold, courageous undertaking, but also necessary.

But then Grayson was a man used to receiving whatever he wanted, and he wanted Lady Clarissa with a need that far surpassed reason. Nevertheless, he had a feeling his need to be near her had nothing to do with his rampaging lust and everything to do with his tortured soul, and he couldn't prevent himself from hoping she was indeed the answer he sought.

Perhaps she'd be impressed by the cleverness and originality of his plan, or perhaps not. She might view me as unbalanced and homicidal. She was still looking at him as if she wanted to slice him to ribbons. An admirable trait really, when one considers that most women would be blubbering hysterically. But then he knew at first sight that Clarissa Mayfield was not like other women. Like a pretty bird in a gilded cage, she longed for flight.

He needed to be near her.

He almost groaned when he looked at her. She glared at him with an anger so strong even he couldn't help but question his sanity. *By Jove, she is beautiful!*

He watched her intently, almost daring her to look away first, enjoying the blush stealing across her face at his unswerving gaze. He was apt to believe she was attracted to him — *unless I am confusing the trepidation in her eyes for interest.* Although Grayson considered himself to be an unpretentious man, he was well aware of his effect on the opposite sex. Most women found his looks more than passable, and at one time, he was even known to be charming.

But it was more likely she wasn't attracted to him at all, and he was allowing the months he had thought about her to cloud his judgment. On closer inspection, in fact, she appeared ready to do him bodily damage. Her vivid blue eyes were practically shooting fiery sparks of anger. Her posture stiff, she seemed reenergized and poised for battle. Glorious strands of blond hair had escaped her coiffure to float enticingly around her pretty, heart-shaped face.

She broke into his reverie.

"Is there someone I know who owes you money, for I assure you it is not I," she said. "You certainly can't mean to ransom me. I'm not an heiress, for heaven's sake."

Keeping her is likely the stupidest idea I ever had. I really should just escort her back to London, but I don't want to. He really didn't have the time to make a trip to the city anyway. Plus she had written and asked for his help with something, and it made sense to figure out what she needed him for, didn't it?

Her luminous eyes widened when the vehicle lurched into motion and the sound of harnesses and chains rattled around them. Stark terror crossed her lovely features and a stab of empathy for her fear hit him smack in the face. Upsetting her was the last thing Grayson wanted to do. "Please calm yourself," he said, watching as she closed her eyes. His mind flashed to the haunting night two years before and a shiver ran through him as he tried to swallow the never-ending anguish that made up his life.

To ease her fear and erase his torturous memories, he turned his mind to a happier moment, his first glimpse of Clarissa. He remembered this moment keenly, for it had felt like a stab to the heart when he noticed her. His pulse had raced erratically and he had momentarily forgotten to breathe.

"The first time I saw you, Lady Clarissa Mayfield, you were at the Childress wedding, or Waterford, as it was called at the time."

She opened her eyes, which he took as a signal to continue. "I thought you gloriously appealing, even dressed in the horrendous purple gown your mother must have insisted you wear." He noticed her fists still clenched tightly. She was unmoved by his compliment. So he continued more poetically, spilling the truth of how he saw her. "You were stunning, your corn-silk blond hair pulled up so perfectly into an artistic coiffure, revealing the lines of your elegant neck." A neck he had wanted to layer kisses upon. "Your dress rested slightly off your perfectly shaped shoulders." He took a moment to remember how creamy white and smooth her skin looked and how he wanted to run his fingers along the dress's square neckline, dipping them beneath the garment to gently brush across her lovely breasts. He recalled the desire he had felt that night, for in fact, he felt it now and it hadn't diminished in the least.

She still appeared unmoved by his words. He held back asking if it had suddenly grown hotter in the vehicle and instead leaned his head over to cool his face in the slight breeze. The change of position didn't help his desire one iota because her neck and collarbone were visible even now.

He wondered if he should tell her that it wasn't her beauty that snared his attentions but her spirit that held him so entranced. Perhaps she'd be charmed, or at least, less angry, if he told her other things he admired about her. He smiled just thinking about the animated scene he had watched between Clarissa and her friend Lady Abigail.

The manner in which she arrived to him today had come as a shock, but he had imagined his next meeting with the lovely lady across from him, though his imagination had not included her lower half displayed from a moving vehicle. Thankfully, no one but he and Harvey had witnessed what was surely a demoralizing moment for her. He refused to bring up the incident so as to avoid causing her further embarrassment and anger. The man he once was wouldn't have hesitated to bring up the humor of the situation, however, and even as melancholy as he was now, he had found great amusement at the sight.

He admired her courage and her sheer force of will to escape, and he was glad she didn't injure more than her pride in the process. If anything, his interest in knowing her increased ten-fold with her sudden appearance. He was very much going to help her, though whether she still wanted his help was another question completely. She was glaring at him most vehemently.

"I demand you return me to my home immediately." She looked out at the passing fields, likely trying to decipher the direction they were heading.

His accolades for her beauty didn't seem to diminish her anger a bit. He followed suit, now gazing out the window too, where he noticed some sheep in a far off pasture. She didn't seem to recognize the scenery, but then, much of England's countryside of rolling hills and wide-open grasslands looked the same, he reminded himself. A cool breeze came in through the window and swirled with the air inside the carriage. He inhaled the sweet womanly scent of Clarissa. Heavenly.

"I'm afraid I can't do that, my dear. See, I'm in the middle of a very important investigation and I haven't the time to make a trip to the city," he informed her. "Nevertheless, since my old school chum, Jackson, insisted I come to your aid … " He threw out his arms with a flourish, trying to make light of Harvey's lawbreaking blunder. "Well, here we are. The Marquis of Childress wouldn't have contacted me unless he believed I could truly help you. I am forever willing to help a damsel in distress." He hoped to quell some of her fear and to assure her he had no intention to harm her. After all, she had contacted him first.

"You, sir, are the one causing my current distress." Her fingers went to her temples. "How dare you insinuate that you had me kidnapped in order to help me. The entire idea is preposterous. You have compounded my problems, not aided them. Oh, saints be praised. God save women from well-intentioned men."

Yes, she is a strong, capable woman. She also has a quick wit. At least she wasn't holding on to the look of terror he had seen in her eyes when the vehicle lurched into motion. "I did not orchestrate your abduction. As I said, it was a misunderstanding. Nevertheless, I'm happy to find you here."

She actually pointed one of her dainty fingers at him as she demanded, "You have this vehicle turned about at once!"

"No." He knew he should have been ready for her attack, but he wasn't, and again, his cheek felt the sting of her hand. When she raised her hand to repeat the assault, he grabbed at both her wrists and yanked her bodily across him.

"Let me go, you despoiler of women!" His lascivious thoughts wouldn't allow him to object to her comment. She squirmed relentlessly against him, and he wrapped one of his legs over her to still her movements. She was literally panting in his arms from anger. Her scent filled his head, the smell of wildflowers and woman. Intoxicating, to be sure. His mouth grew parched and his body tensed as certain parts of his anatomy sprang to life in the forced embrace. Lust for this woman coursed through his blood, making him hot and edgy. *I have been thinking of her too often over the last few months.* "If I release you, will you promise not to strike me again?" he asked, needing her to say yes, needing her to be a safer distance from him.

"Wonderful! Now you're playing the victim?" she replied acerbically, twisting again for freedom. He released her, pushing her gently back to her side of the vehicle.

"I'm never the victim, my dear." He closed his eyes as nightmarish visions filled his head. *At least, I will never allow myself to be one again.* Pulling himself away from the past, he looked at her. "As I told you … " He took an exasperated breath before continuing. "I have a couple of things to see to before I begin your project … "

"I contacted you over a month ago. And I'll have you know that my concerns are not frivolous and should not be looked upon as some infantile project."

"Yes. Of course. I meant no insult. I assume time to be an issue of importance, as it often is in these situations. Thus, I plan to look at this predicament we find ourselves in as beneficial. We will now be able to save time and expedite matters. It's actually a blessing you were brought to me."

Besides, I could no longer put off seeing you. Somehow, Harvey sensed my desperation for this woman.

As of late, Grayson had found it difficult to focus on the investigation concerning his family when visions of Lady Clarissa continued to float through his mind.

"You're mad. It's the only reasonable explanation for this. I can assure you, I don't need help from a lunatic."

He gave a mock chuckle and ran his fingers through his hair in complete irritation. Why were women so difficult? She needed help and here he was. One would think that simple enough and the lady would simply explain her dilemma. Instead, this beauty thought it more productive to slander him, to heap unfounded insults upon him. True, she had been kidnapped, but that didn't mean they shouldn't discuss the assignment she wanted him for. He was covering their tracks the best way he could and her abduction was no longer of import. But like every female, she was insisting upon some kind of rationalization for his behavior, as if he could explain his not returning her to where she belonged as something besides lunacy.

He decided to err on the side of caution and was vague with his explanation. The last thing he wanted was his family's business to be fodder for the gossip mill. No one could know about his family's past, including the lady across from him. At the moment, she'd most likely dish up a whole heap of scandal if only to give him his just desserts.

"You have a brother, Clarissa?"

She sucked in a breath at his use of her Christian name, or perhaps it was the fact that he knew she had a brother. He couldn't say which. He smiled at her surprise. What did it matter? She already thought him unhinged.

"Would you do whatever it took to help him if ever he needed you?"

"Within reason," she said with a huff. "I want him to be happy and safe."

Her answer pleased him. It showed her willingness to help a loved one, while it also showed her intelligence as sufficient not to become involved with something she couldn't handle. She was waiting for further explanation, and he paused, not sure how much of himself he was willing to share. "I feel the same way about my younger brother Reggie."

She rolled his eyes. Apparently, the kidnapping had painted him in a very dark light. Perhaps her view of him would change when they reached their first stop. "My brother Reginald and his twin daughters are the only family I have left in this world. It's important to me they are kept happy and safe. I will do whatever is necessary to see to this end."

"Including kidnapping me?" Her tone practically dripped venom.

The woman's mind appeared to be stuck on her abduction. He was becoming annoyed explaining things to her. He was beginning to believe she hadn't heard a word he said through the rage she was obviously now indulging for it should have passed by now. With exasperation, he answered, "Precisely. I'm glad you understand." He hoped she'd remain quiet until they reached their destination … such was not the case.

"I, in no way, understand, sir," she said haughtily.

"It's Lord Camden."

"You have in no way earned my respect, so I shall call you what I wish. It's my reputation that is now in tatters! You, sir, are an uncaring fiend to have wrecked my chances for a future. I shall see you repaid in kind."

Formidable wench. He found her threat amusing albeit frustrating.

"You and I are going to be spending some time together. If you wish it to be difficult … " He shrugged. "So be it. But no matter what, Lady Clarissa." He leaned intently forward. "I am going to help you."

"Let me see if I understand this correctly," she said in such a superior tone his teeth gnashed together. "You are refusing to return me to London, thus ruining my reputation and my chances of procuring a proper husband. And you claim to be doing so because of some obligation you feel to an old school chum who asked for your help on my behalf?" Her voice turned shrill and he winced.

"Not to mention, you sent letters to me asking for my help," he said challengingly. "But need I remind you that I have other matters to see to first."

"Yes, of course — your pressing matters. How dare I forget?"

She was seemingly irritated he was bringing her along. Perhaps he was wrong in being concerned about a time constraint. He was about to apologize over the fact that he obviously thought her matter of some importance for Lord Childress to have contacted him, but she continued in that unnerving tone of voice that indicated she believed he had not an ounce of intelligence in his head. "So then why keep me here? Why don't you finish these other investigations and then come to my aid?"

He was tempted to tell her the truth, but common sense, and the intelligence she thought he lacked, wouldn't allow him. He needed to concentrate on his family's current crisis. He'd do whatever was necessary to prevent his brother from having to hear more heartbreaking news. Losing his wife had been the final blow for Reggie. His brother had been through enough.

If only he had arrived at the marquis' wedding before Lady Clarissa was saying her farewells. He would have been able to gain a proper introduction. He had wanted to begin a courtship and set off to London to do so, but the moment he walked into his townhouse on Park Lane he was bombarded with messages from his estate manager insisting he return to his residence in Sussex immediately. The matter was said to be urgent and of utmost importance. Since Victoria's death and his brother's abandonment, he hadn't returned to that particular residence.

Thus, his visit to see Clarissa was postponed until his return to London, and with all the investigating he had to do in the country, he hadn't had the opportunity to return to the city. When he went through the rest of his correspondences on his ride back to Sussex, he came upon the Marquis of Childress letter asking that he lend assistance to Lady Clarissa Mayfield. He also received numerous letters from the lovely young lady sitting across from him, pleas to speak with him. He had marveled at the coincidences but tended to think of their meeting as fated. He had no idea how she would arrive in his life, however.

Circumstances, his own need to know her, and Harvey, had led him down this path, but also too much brandy — and he certainly couldn't leave Lord Fitzroy out of this. His longtime friend acted as if this imagined plan was foolproof. Now he looked like a fool. The lady was looking at him with blatant hostility, and so he finally answered her. "The matters I must take care of are pressing and private, but I want you to know that I plan to assist you as well. Jackson's letter indicated a need for immediate help. I assumed from his ominous letter and the messages from you that the matter was of great importance?"

"As is my reputation," she pointed out.

He smiled at her ire. There were so many things he wanted to know about this intriguing woman, but he held back his questions. First, he'd solve her problem, and then he'd try to better understand this undeniable yearning he had to be near her. "I promise you that your reputation will not be tarnished by this ... " She started to interrupt, but he stopped her by raising his hand. "And I always keep my promises. Now, instead of worrying about your reputation, why don't you tell me what brought you to me."

She glared at him, and he smiled at his bit of humor. They hit a rut in the road and she had to grab the leather handle to steady herself. He reached out to assist her, but she hurriedly moved back in her seat.

"Sorry about that, my lord," hollered Harvey.

"Why do you need my help, Clarissa?"

"I don't," she said, making a show of adjusting her bright amethyst skirts with turquoise bows, indeed the ugliest dress he had ever seen. Her mother was clearly partial to purple.

"You don't need my help?" He quirked a brow with his query. The woman is being typically stubborn. "My lady, I'm sorry for the manner in which you were brought to me. Harvey often lacks finesse and common sense. I'm especially sorry you were frightened in the process. However, I am going to help you."

She wouldn't meet his eyes, but she said, "I find I no longer have a need for your services. So if you could direct the vehicle to the next town, I will find my own transportation back to the city."

He sighed, running a hand over his face in irritation. It is my fault she was scared to death. He grabbed her hands. She tried to yank them back, but he wouldn't give in. "Look at me, Clarissa." Slowly her bright blue eyes fixed on his. He hoped she could see into his battered soul, see how much he wanted to help her. "Please let me help you."

Grayson had a reputation for solving problems others couldn't. He began making inquiries for friends and acquaintances who needed help with problems to do with suitors or debtors or threats made against their person out of sheer boredom five years ago. He had never considered it a profession, but more of a hobby, which often proved most entertaining in his bachelor's existence. After the tragedy with his brother's wife two years ago, he no longer bothered lending such aid to others, however, not until Lady Clarissa Mayfield had stepped into the picture asking for his help.

A tear slid down her cheek and she swiped it away with the hand she wiggled free from his grasp. After agonizing minutes of silence, she finally nodded her head in acquiescence. "I do need help."

"Then I'm the man for the job. Is a pesky suitor giving you trouble? Do you want me to rid your mother of credit so she can't dress you in such outlandish fashions? Just tell me the problem and I promise to facilitate a solution."

Lightning Source UK Ltd.
Milton Keynes UK
UKHW040604191118
332582UK00001B/16/P

9 780982 989760